BONEBELLY

Bone Ridge Farm
Presents
Hell, Rhode Island
A Haunted Hayride

ADMIT ONE

CHRISTINE LAJEWSKI

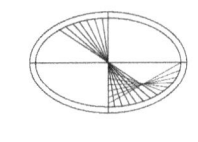

DIVERTIR
PUBLISHING
Salem, NH

BONEBELLY

Christine Lajewski

Copyright © 2018 Christine Lajewski

Cover design by Kenneth Tupper

Published by Divertir Publishing LLC
PO Box 232
North Salem, NH 03073
http://www.divertirpublishing.com/

ISBN-13: 978-1-938888-22-9
ISBN-10: 1-938888-22-7

Library of Congress Control Number: 2018959788

Printed in the United States of America

Dedication

To Angela and Nicholas
and Sean "Tik-Tok" Chamberlin

CONTENTS

FINDING THE WORDS

EIGHT MONTHS HAD passed since the dead were counted and their meager remains interred. No one could say what had been more horrifying: the pieces they found or the parts that were missing. The most complete set included an oily shock of hair, a puddle of fatty acids, and a tissue paper envelope that might have once been skin. Most families were fortunate if they had a hair mat and greasy clothes to bury. The uncounted victims—society's invisible people—had died as they lived. They left no traces behind.

Now, as June drew to a close, the murders had finally faded from the news. The survivors were left alone, and it seemed safe at last to search for lost pieces of the story. Well before sunrise on that last Saturday, five people stood outside the sagging ruins of an old farmhouse hidden a quarter mile from any road. Like many locations of its kind in New England, stone walls which once marked off plowed fields and pastures now tumbled without rhyme or reason through land long since reclaimed by the trees. One white cedar had been growing against the south side of the house for eighty years, and the walls were overrun with vines. The roof sagged at its center, as did the porch. The front door was permanently ajar and held in place by the crusted rust of its hinges. This was where the creature had made his home.

One man separated from the group and began probing the dirt around the foundation with the toe of his boot and a spade. His companions knew he was searching for more remains. They prayed there were none to be found.

The other two men stepped cautiously onto the porch, testing its strength. They nodded to the two women standing at the bottom step, and they each in turn squeezed through the narrow entrance. The younger man bounced lightly on his heels, testing his weight against the parlor floor. The boards creaked but held. "So far so good," he said. "I think it's okay."

Inside the structure, sunlight filtered through the cedars, the clouded windows, and the cracks in the walls. It was enough to read by, and the four companions quickly found the script scrawled on the walls. It covered three walls and parts of the ceiling in the parlor. There was more on the peeling wallpaper of the kitchen.

The young man ran his fingers over the black words inscribed on the horsehair plaster. "I wonder what he used for ink. It's black, there's no fading, and it feels raised off the surface, almost like tar." Three years after they were written,

1

the inscriptions still had an odor to them, a faint mustiness of old decay, like that of a mouse mummified behind a cupboard.

They found a hole in the floor. They could see apple crates in the basement, hinting that more journals might be stored below their feet. As the women studied the chronology of the undated script on the walls, the men dropped through the hole into the cellar. Metal crunched under their feet as they landed, and aluminum cans scattered in all directions.

"Beer and protein shakes," the older man observed. Laughter echoed through the ruin.

The fieldstone cellar was the sturdiest part of the old house. The men spied a stout door which led to an old root cellar lined with shelves. The earthen floor was covered with blue and green tarps, and a moldy fleece blanket was tossed in a corner. The shelves held three withered apples, slightly gnawed by mice, and a dried mound of rotted pumpkin. In front of the blanket were the bones of two tiny rodents, positioned as if they were an offering from someone's cat.

Their flashlights bounced off something smooth and transparent on the middle shelf. They saw several large, zippered plastic bags of the type used to store clothes. They were filled with unlined copy paper, white and yellow legal pads, and flyers from a haunted hay ride, all tied together with string. Something was written on every scrap of paper.

"We got the mother lode," the young man shouted. They handed the bags to the women through the hole in the floor.

"Here's his first entry," the young woman said, and she labeled it with a number 1. "I need all of you to hold lights on it so I can photograph everything before this place collapses once and for all."

Her four friends beamed light on the walls while the girl recorded everything on her tablet. When she finished, she began to read aloud the tortured black script.

Here follows a true account of my first thirty days in hell.

HELL RULES

HERE FOLLOWS A true account of my first thirty days in hell. One month later, I still cannot retrieve any memories of exactly how I came to be here. My face and form are monstrous, yet I understand things belonging to the world of men. I know "mother" and I know "father," but I know I could not have had either. I know "crime" and "abomination," but cannot remember any deeds, good or evil, that may be laid to my hideous hands. I know what mercy is, but I am certain I have no right to any.

And I know hunger: terrible, gnawing hunger.

What life, if any, I might have previously lived I cannot recall. But in my dreams—dreadful, appalling dreams—I see a man seized by the hair and, lacking any will or strength to fight, dragged at terrifying speed through suffocating blackness. The man is unbecoming. By that I mean he is turning into a formless, undulating mass of clay. Someone else is there in the blackness. I cannot see him, but I know he is unbecoming, too. He is filled with a rage that overcomes his terror. He squirms in silent protest, refusing to submit. Then he is gone, and there is only a single gray mass, shivering with terror and awaiting its hideous fate.

Thirty days ago, I found myself lying on a patch of frozen mud and granulated snow, staring up at bare trees that groaned and bowed before an icy wind. I was naked, freezing, and unbearably hungry. I held my hands up before my eyes. They were skeletal. The skin that stretched across the bones was a yellowed white, like the linen of an ancient shroud. The muscles were thin and stringy. And the fingers! They must have measured seven inches, tapering to blade-like claws. Such monstrous digits could not possibly belong to me. I sat upright and inspected my legs. They were skeletal, too—unnaturally long, the feet ending in toes with somewhat shorter claws. The same taut, yellowed hide covered the bones. They were aching from the cold.

I knew I needed to find shelter quickly but had no idea where I was or where I should go. Looking around, I could see I was in a thick forest. The ground was a patchwork of slushy snow and muddy ground, the products of a recent thaw. But there was no doubt it was still winter and that the light of day was fast fading. I groped my way through the undergrowth, unable to find a path. More than once I stumbled into the icy water of a swamp. Just after sunset I found a mound of boulders. Climbing on top, I could make out a mass of shadows among the trees. I discovered it to be the ruins of a house. I felt my way inside, where I found a small interior room. It was cold, but at least there was no wind. I hoped I might sleep, but the awful, burning hunger in my belly kept me awake.

When daylight returned, I searched the poor lodging for something to eat. There was nothing but dirt and dead spiders. I did find a length of fraying canvas in the cellar. It worked as a poor sort of cloak. Robed in this finery, I set out to look for food.

I found nothing I could recognize as food. I startled some deer at the edge of a swamp, and it occurred to me I might try to drag one down to the ground and slash it with my claws. However, my movements with this strange body were so clumsy I did not come close to capturing one. As the deer leapt away in alarm, I somehow remembered that they often dined on twigs when grasses were no longer available. I broke some thin and supple stems off a tree and tried stripping the bark away with my teeth. As I gnawed and chewed, it turned into a bitter mass of pulp in my mouth. I could not stand it and spat it into the swamp. As the water calmed and cleared, I got a glimpse of my face.

I could not believe such a countenance was even possible. It was a monstrosity. I crouched on my knees to get a better look. I saw the same yellow-white skin stretched thinly over the prominent bones of a grotesque, oversized skull. There were deep hollows below the eyes and cheekbones, like the face of famine itself. The eyes burned amber in the sockets. The mouth was wide with thin, colorless lips that barely hid two rows of pointed, ferocious teeth. My nose was spare and thinly fleshed out with two large, delta-shaped nostrils. Stringy yellow hair grew out of the top of my head and tumbled over my shoulders. I longed to shriek in horror, but I could work no sound of any kind out of my throat. Then, as I further inspected my reflection, I understood why. That huge, skeletal head sat atop a neck the thickness of a walking stick. Knotted ropes of muscle twisted around a constricted throat, holding up that mass of yellowed bone. I let my head sag to my chest in utter weariness. Then, I slowly stood up so I could take in my full reflection.

It seemed as though every bone in my chest, arms, legs, hands, and feet stood out in sharp definition. Lean, sinewy cords of muscle kept this body upright. My belly was huge, like a full moon when it first rises. I lifted my belly and turned to one side, trying to see what manner of manhood I possessed. The organs were there but shriveled and limp, nothing like the virile flesh of men. I collapsed on the bank of the swamp in despair. I somehow knew I had once been a man but had now become a grotesque parody of God's greatest creation. Soundlessly, I wept. Thick black tears slid down my face and pooled in my supplicating hands. The tears were oily and stank of putrescence.

At that moment, I realized I was cursed with two hungers—the burning in my belly, and a drive to howl my misery to the world. Beating my terrible fists against my head, I ran on awkward white legs back to my decaying shelter.

My thought was to hide in the darkest corner of the cellar and wait for death to find me, but I became aware of terrifying sounds. There were rumblings and thumping, and even shrieking, off in the distance that evoked images all kinds of infernal machines. They frightened me, yet I was overwhelmed with the need to understand what kind of world I inhabited. When the sky was dark again, I climbed on the sagging roof of my ruins and scaled the tall cedar growing next to the foundation. My claws made climbing an easy task, and I quickly reached the highest limbs.

The night was damp and overcast. The horizon was a deep, impenetrable black. Yet below the lowering cloud cover and beyond the trees, I saw the glow of unnatural light coming from several directions. Bright lanterns moved at amazing speed along paths that blazed with incandescence. The only sense I could make of the scene was that this was a mighty city in hell, perhaps even Lucifer's capitol, and I was one of its condemned denizens. Not wishing to be discovered by the demonic creatures that lived here, I quickly retreated to the cellar of my ruined hovel. I decided I would let myself starve to death. I held out for two days, but my belly hurt so badly I was driven forth at last to find sustenance. I was determined to bring down a deer. Somehow, I knew the predawn hours were the best time to hunt, so I hid myself in the rushes of the swamp and waited for the deer to come and drink.

I lay flat in the freezing mud, barely breathing, until a white tail stood next to me. I wrapped my bony arms around her neck and grappled with the doe until I brought her crashing down. I used the long nail on my index finger to open the veins of her throat. As blood poured on the ground, her body twitched and grew still. I sat back on my haunches and indulged in the glorious torment of surveying my prize and feeling my mouth water. Then I used my claws to cut away the hide and carve chunks of venison.

My first mistake was cramming my mouth full of meat. Almost as soon as it touched my tongue, it turned bitter, like ashes on my tongue. I gagged but swallowed the lump—only to have it lodge painfully in my narrow throat. I had to force a long claw down my gullet to snag it and pull it free. Lesson learned, I carved thin strips of meat and, bypassing my traitorous tongue altogether, slid them down my throat. It did not work. My tongue was coated with bitterness and I nearly vomited. My belly hurt so much, however, that I continued forcing down strip after strip.

Suddenly, before my hunger was eased, I doubled over in pain. It felt as though a hand had seized my innards and was trying to pull them out my navel. It took hours for the pain to pass. I staggered back to my ruins, clutching my belly

5

until dawn. It occurred to me that, after starving for several days, it might take some time for my stomach to become accustomed to plenty. I decided to return to the carcass and feed again—this time, more slowly.

Scavengers had helped themselves to my kill, but there was still plenty of meat and bone. I set to my second feast, feeding moderately, but the results were the same. The meat turned foul on my tongue, and my guts seized with pain before I could vanquish the emptiness. When the ache receded, I rose and left the slaughtered deer for whatever predators lurked in the woods. That was when I noticed another bloody mass off to one side. It was a fawn that had no doubt gone looking for its mother and been torn apart by some ravening beast. I sank to the cold ground and buried my head in my hands. I do not know why it mattered. It was just another quarry slaughtered by a hungry predator. But I felt guilty anyway. It was wasteful—perhaps even sinful—to take down a large animal and orphan its offspring for the few mouthfuls of bitter meat I seemed to be allowed.

The search began anew for any manner of victual that would ease my pain. As the days passed, I compiled a curious list of things I attempted to eat: slivers of wood from the walls, stalks of rushes lining the swamps, lichens from the rocks and trees, mice, both living and dead, and strips of old paper. I made the mistake of swallowing the first squealing mouse alive. It clawed all the way down. Then my constricted throat would not release it into my stomach, and the rodent clawed all the way back up. I killed the next mouse and sliced it into thin strips. I tilted my head back and let the meager bits of meat slide down my gullet. The fur choked me, but I managed to keep it down. I ground the tiny creature's bones to gruel between my teeth. It was a lengthy process that turned increasingly rotten with each passing moment. I wanted to spit it out but forced myself to swallow it. This sorry meal all but disappeared into the abyss of my gigantic belly. It moaned and complained for hours. It behaves like a beast with its own will. It drives me to endlessly hunt, and it can never be satisfied.

Within the first two weeks of my arrival there was a howling winter storm. I was on yet another hunt when vicious winds boiled up out of nowhere, whipping my poor leathery hide with stinging sleet and snow. As I struggled to return to my shelter, the wind took my canvas cloak. I began to lose feeling in my limbs, and I was overcome with weariness. I fell to my knees and found it easier to sink to the ground then to rise again. As the snow covered me I thought how sweet it would be to let my life slowly bleed away. I fell asleep and could not remember ever feeling happier.

I woke to stabbing pains in my joints and stomach. Somehow, I found myself standing in the woods, the world blanketed in ice and snow. I had not frozen to death. My enormous head felt too heavy to hold upright. Wearily, I struggled through the drifts to my sorry shelter.

It was snowing again by the time I reached my sanctuary. Snow drifted through the broken windows. I lowered myself through a hole in the floor and closed myself up in the root cellar. If any place in this wreck could be called snug, this was it. I think it took two days for the weather to finally clear. I stayed in the cellar until the beast in my gut drove me out again. I was forced to chew on barks and twigs just to put something into that void. There would have to be another thaw before I could find a mouse or a worm to eat.

As I hid out in the root cellar, I again heard the terrible sounds of the city of the damned—infernal machines and ungodly screams. My mind filled with images of the tortures I would suffer should I be discovered. But then I formed an idea for a new way to end my tormented existence.

When the snow was once again reduced to slush and mud, I ventured out near sunset to the heart of the swamp. It had grown in girth and depth, and I was soon in icy water up to my waist. My bones ached as I sat down and let the tea-colored water close over my head. I opened my mouth so the water could fill my throat and my lungs. I felt a crushing pressure in my chest but resisted the urge to rise and gulp air. I endured the pain, waiting for death to come. Suddenly, mud and water churned about as two tree trunks planted themselves next to me. Claws dug into my scalp, gripped the shank of hair on the top of my head and pulled. Terrified, I flailed and twisted with all my might but could not wrench myself free. I believe I am tall as any man, but the clawed hand yanked me out of the water and held me well above the surface of the swamp. My feet kicked helplessly as I vomited up a barrel's worth of dirty water.

I was face to face with an enormous horned creature. His skin was leathery and the color of the bog. I slashed at his chest with my blade-like nails, but they were useless. As I read the rage in his green, feline eyes, I felt all strength drain from my limbs. I ceased my futile struggles and hung limply in his grip. The creature's face widened into a grin that revealed the teeth of a carnivore. Without a word passing between us, I understood that this was a demon, that he had brought me here, and that attempting to end my life had earned his wrath. The word "sin" kept repeating in my head.

He threw me against the spongy earth. I attempted to crawl away. He grabbed me again and flung me against a tree. I cowered against the trunk, knowing there was no place I could run to escape this being. I could not speak and he would not. He towered over me, leering malevolently.

Is this hell, I silently asked.

The demon smiled and nodded.

Why am I here, my mind begged. *What was my sin?*

The demon's face darkened. He grabbed me and threw me face first to the ground. Then he violated me, forcing himself into me, again and again. Waves of shattering pain shot through my bones. When he finished with me I curled up against the ground, silently weeping. The demon grabbed me by the hair again and lifted my head. He gazed at me with immeasurable loathing.

Another fearful question formed in my head. *Is there any way to end my suffering?*

The demon smiled and nodded.

I begged him to tell me what I must do.

He grinned. No other reply formed in my head, and I suspected this was the only response the demon ever made. He released me and turned away. Then the creature diminished in size as he rose in the air. When he was no bigger than an owl, he perched on a branch above me. As I dragged my aching body through the woods, I could hear the flapping of his leathery wings behind me. He lit on the sagging roof of my ruined home. He mocked me with his leering smile but left me alone as I shut myself up in the root cellar.

He was gone the next morning. I was not through devising plans for my demise. Although I feared the lights and sounds beyond the woods, it occurred to me I needed to become better acquainted with the denizens of this hell. Perhaps there was one who would do the job that I could not.

On the next calm, clear day I clawed my way to the top of the tallest fir tree on the highest hill I could find. I hid myself behind a veil of evergreen that pitched back and forth as I shifted my weight. I was stunned by what I saw. This was no scorching lair for fallen angels. This was the natural world, and almost every view that met my sight was great and beautiful, representing the works of both God and man.

A great blue bay lay in the distance with a wondrous bridge connecting two necks of land. I could see a patchwork of woods, swamps, and fallow field. There were several fine farms and wooded parks. But most tracts of land were occupied by villages of homes, large stone buildings or long gray roads, many teeming with swift conveyances I could not identify. The horrifying banshee screams belonged to carriages that traveled at impossible speeds, flashing lights of red and blue. Indeed, all the nightmarish forms and sounds I had observed in the dark of night were actually the products of a teeming population of men, women, and children.

I realized then that my corner of hell was tucked into the world of men and in a time and place that was bewildering in its strangeness. It meant that if I revealed my loathsome self in just the right set of circumstances, these men would not suffer me to live.

I inspected the more immediate area to identify the best place to display myself. I spied a farm with fields, an orchard, a weathered house, and several outlying buildings. I saw neither beasts nor barn. I started to back down from my perch but realized, with my long limbs and claws, I might be able to leap from treetop to treetop. If I misjudged the distance between one tree to the next and fell to my death, so much the better.

With the first leap, the fir where I landed bowed perilously, forward and back again. I dug in my claws like a cat and held fast. This action was successfully repeated several times until I found myself looking across a rough trail at a young and supple hard wood tree. I jumped and quickly realized I had miscalculated. I clutched at a slender branch. It did not hold, and I fell to the ground. I did not die. Instead, I found myself staring through a latticework of branches at the blue sky. I decided to leave the trees to the squirrels and pushed my way through the heavy undergrowth.

The game trails widened and had the look of having been cleared by men. I crossed plowed fields and an orchard. Finally, I found paths wide enough for a wagon. There was no need for caution if I planned to die, yet I kept to the adjacent shadows where I could easily hide.

I smelled the farm before I saw it. There was an aroma of wood smoke and baking bread. I must have known the taste of bread in some happier past, because the smell filled me with warmth and the ache of longing. I climbed a tree near the edge of the woods to inspect the area. The smoke was coming from a house at the far end of a clearing. Across a large space of empty ground was a long, brown building. Beyond this lay two long rows of curiously rounded huts made of a translucent material stretched over metal frames.

The baking was being done in the brown house. There were no people out and about. I crouched low and ran to the rear of the house. There was a box on the steps filled with broadsheets labeled "Farm Fresh Rhode Island: South County Farmers' Markets." I rolled up one of the sheets and tucked it in my matted hair. The back door was open, so I mounted the stairs and peeked inside. A woman was dusting sugar over a tray of small cakes. Just then a dog in another room began to bark. Dropping to all fours, I galloped across the open ground. The dog followed, sniffing the air and growling. I climbed a tree and waited. If I left a scent behind, he did not seem especially interested in it. Clearly lacking any ambition for the hunt, he waddled back inside the fragrant baking house.

Again exercising an absurd degree of caution for someone who wanted to die, I decided to wait until dark to explore further. But night on the farm was accompanied by an uncommon amount of light. Great lanterns on poles lined the road that ran in front of the farm. Long after sunset, swift vehicles ran along the road, each beaming its own light. These had been the mysterious lanterns I had seen. But in time, all lights in the farmhouse went out save one. Crouching low, I crept to the glowing window. I could cling comfortably to the wooden shingles and provide myself an excellent view of the interior. A middle-aged man sat at a table with a glass of spirits in front of him. The room appeared to have a box-like oven and a large washing basin of some sort. He read a broadsheet while a woman, different from the one I had seen earlier in the day, drank tea. "I'm going to bed now, Tom," she said.

"G'night, Jen," the man said, returning a kiss she planted on his cheek.

I chose this moment to extend a single claw towards the window and scratch at the casing. Then I climbed up the shingles and scratched above the window. That got the man's attention. "Fuckin' squirrels," he cursed as he glanced sharply at the window.

I scratched again.

The man came to the window and leaned forward over the wash basin. I chose that moment to thrust my head into view, grinning and grimacing. The man shrieked and fell backwards onto his rear. I remained where I was as he gaped in horror. He scrambled to his feet, knocking over his chair. I could hear the woman call from her room, "Tom, what is it?"

I dropped to the ground and waited. He appeared from around the side of the house with a musket. I stretched to my full height, waving and threatening with my claws. The farmer leveled his weapon at me and fired. The musket ball ripped through the skin of my chest like it was paper and exited out my back. I staggered backward and then, for reasons I still cannot fathom, I ran. The farmer fired at me again but missed. He did not chase me and, wheezing out the sharp pain in my breast, I galloped until I reached the cover of the woods again.

I stopped to inspect my wound under the moonlight. The torn skin flapped and fluttered with each breath I took. I probed inside with my claw. I could touch the dry, wasted muscle of my heart. I felt searing pain as the thin fingernail passed right through the hole the musket ball had made. How was it I was still alive? The wound should have been bleeding profusely, but there was nothing but a miserly trickle of foul-smelling blood that was already coagulating. My stringy, desiccated heart kept beating out the seconds of my cursed eternity.

My chest hurt too much to keep running. I climbed a tree that drooped heavily with evergreen boughs and found a cradle for the night. The night winds whistled through the hole in my heart whenever I moved.

I still ached as the sun rose, but it was negligible compared to the hollow gnawing of my stomach. I loped slowly for my home, scanning the ground for something to eat. Lacking the strength to chase after squirrels, I had to be satisfied with lichens and moss. I crept into my cellar and curled into a ball. Slumber stole over me, deep enough to bring on dreams.

I saw two men sitting at a rough wooden table next to a fire. Their sober dress suggested clergy from another time. A young woman in a stained and tattered dress poured drinks for them from a pitcher. One of the men groped her through her skirt. The girl's face registered disgust and fear. He pushed her toward the other man, who grabbed the girl by the arm and pulled her onto his lap. Against her will, he fondled her and forced himself on her.

I awoke while it was still dark. There was a hideously foul taste in my mouth that seemed a measure of the immense self-loathing I felt. I was suddenly afraid to learn any more about myself.

I saw Demon that morning. If he knew what I had attempted the previous night, he did not communicate it to me. He sat in a tree, laughing silently as I unsuccessfully tried to chase down a rabbit. The hole in my chest whistled as I panted from my exertions. Demon shook with voiceless mirth.

In the days that followed I saw Demon often, but I do not think he inhabits these woods. There are times when there is a palpable presence and I know he is watching me. There are times when I feel utterly alone, abandoned even by this evil spirit. Sometimes, when I am digging through the mud and leaf litter for earthworms and salamanders—slimy but easy to slide down my narrow throat—I will spot Demon watching me through the trees, smiling and nodding.

Signs of spring finally came to the woods. Among them was the sound of increased human activity. I often heard the roar and buzz of machines. Once, from a perch high in a tree, I saw men wielding saws with growling, grinding teeth. They chewed through fallen trees like a beast through a carcass. It was frightening to behold.

Voices sounded more often through the trees. A few times, I was surprised by people coming up behind me. If I crouched low in whatever cover I could find, they always walked past me as if I were no more than a rock along the trail. I even saw the farmer, searching the boundaries of his farm with his gun. He walked right by me without a second glance. Even dogs barely notice me.

With the spring thaw, I found several moldering carcasses. Most had been all but stripped of meat by the local carnivores. It did not matter. My gut would only allow a few morsels before it seized with cramping pain. Now that the woods were alive and active again, I increased my attempts at hunting small game with varying degrees of success. Despite my long reach and terrible claws, my movements lacked the finesse of the predatory beasts. I learned it was better to remain motionless in a tree or behind a stone wall and wait for a squirrel or mouse to happen by. When I was still, animals failed to see me, too.

Even though the days have been warming, the nights have been cold. Two days ago, I was roaming along the edge of the swamp in the weak morning light when I spotted a man seated on the muddy ground, leaning against a stump. My first instinct was to run away, but my curiosity won out and I crept up behind him. Both his apparel and his posture seemed odd, so I peered into the man's face. He was elderly, barefoot, and wearing thin night clothes. His eyes were open and staring. There was a blue tint to his lips. When I put my ear to his chest, I could detect neither breath nor heartbeat. Why this man had spent the night in the woods I could not guess, but it seemed he had succumbed to illness, to the cold, or both.

As I rested my head against his chest, a delectable aroma wafted into my nostrils. My stomach cried out with a voice I did not possess, and it demanded to be filled. I drooled like a ravenous wolf. I opened my mouth wide and buried my teeth into the thigh of the corpse, sawing my head back and forth until I pulled away a mouthful of meat. It was full flavored, both savory and sweet, unlike anything I could ever remember eating before. And it remained so as I chewed ravenously and swallowed the entire lump. Too late I realized the mouthful was too large to gain passage. It lodged painfully in my throat, as sharp as if I had swallowed a handful of nails. Trying to disgorge it was agony.

But I could not turn away from this gift. I used my nails to slice away strips of flesh as thin as blades of grass. When I had carved a generous pile of meat, I tilted my head back and began carefully feeding the strips down my gullet. They were so delicious. For the first time since I was condemned to this place, I felt something akin to joy.

I suddenly realized I was being watched. Demon squatted on a tuft of matted vegetation in the center of the swamp, smiling and nodding. A long, pointed tongue slithered through his teeth. My mind spoke a single word: *Abomination.* I looked back at my feast and found myself overwhelmed with shame. For the first time, I regarded the face of this lump of flesh. He had been handsome once. With advanced age, he appeared stately, perhaps even learned. Had he come here with a purpose, or had he wandered in a fog? It occurred to me that the state in which I had placed his remains would cause terrible pain to any who loved him.

I looked to Demon for guidance. He grinned back at me, enjoying my torment. My stomach, responding to the aroma of the forbidden food, growled a new command. I obeyed it. Ignoring Demon, I dropped the strips down my throat as quickly as I could, almost without tasting them. I had not fed long and my belly was far from full when my gut suddenly twisted. The message was unmistakable: I was through eating. Whether the food was foul or fair, I understood at last that I would never be allowed to know satiety. I had elected to carry out this repulsive sin for nothing. Demon leered with delight. I dropped my gaze to the ground, mortified and brimming with despair. When I lifted my eyes again, Demon was gone.

Gazing into the face of the dead man, I made a decision. If the man's loved ones saw him in this condition, they would assume he had been murdered, that he had suffered terribly. I could at least spare them this much. I wrapped the poor soul's night clothes around his body as best I could and filled the pockets of his dressing gown with stones. I lifted him and waded out to the deepest part of the swamp. Then I released the injured corpse to the dark waters and pressed him down into the mud. The strips of meat were left for the beasts.

I cannot fathom why that most forbidden meat is the only food that tastes sweet to me. Perhaps it is a test: If my licentious soul can withstand the temptation, I might earn my way out of this cold and hungry hell. But Demon tells me nothing. It is left to me to chart my path, if there is one, toward redemption.

Last night, as I waited for a cold spring rain to stop, I reflected on my other curse. I wished to cry, to raise my voice in one long, tormented howl, but my constricted throat makes no sound. Then I realized there might be a means of expressing my despair. In the first light of dawn, I stood before one of the cracked walls of the front room of the ruined house. I used a claw to open one of my veins. Black blood, smelling of rot, dripped slowly into a broken cup. I dipped a nail into this ink and began to set my tale of woe upon the wall. It took hours to collect enough blood, but it has proven to be an excellent writing medium.

Having finished the first part of my chronicle, I will now set down my understanding of how this hell operates and the rules I must follow: I do not know from whence I came, but I know that my hell is in the world of living men and in an unfamiliar time. I do not yet understand why.

Demon has made me understand that I used women in the worst way possible. My punishment for my unnatural appetites is to know the constant pain of hunger. My grotesque body will punish me if I attempt to ease that hunger.

Human flesh is the only meat that lies sweet on my tongue. But I know in my shrunken heart it is a sin to indulge this craving. That I am even presented with this dilemma inspires the hope that I am being tested. Why is my hell situated among innocent men, women, and children upon whom I could choose to visit such grievous harm? Why would this choice be given to me unless it was possible to earn redemption?

It may not be impossible for me to die, but it is probably not an easy thing to bring about. Demon has made it clear I should not seek it. Perhaps the quest is futile. If I die to escape this hell, I could find myself someplace even worse.

Even though I exist in the world of men, I am not meant to be part of it. If I keep to myself or remain very still, men will not see me, unless I force myself on their awareness.

Finally, I feel certain I did not sin alone. I had a companion in whatever depravities I practiced. I could feel him in the darkness as I was unbecoming. He does not share my hell. I think I see him in those recurring dreams and wonder if he will somehow find me. Such a prospect fills me with dread.

BONEBELLY

THINGS IN THE WOODS

SCHOOL WAS OUT for the day. Amy took over the cash register at the farm store while Gloria, her mother, cleaned up the bakery in the back. Sean sat at one of the round café tables near the front, eating a cider doughnut and trying to look like he belonged there. He wanted to talk to Tom about a job, but Tom was nowhere to be seen.

"Should I go look for him?" he asked Amy.

Amy shook her head. "No, Mom says he's not in a good mood today. He's been fighting with Jen all day."

He pulled out a sketch pad and worked on designs for creatures he hoped would one day be the foundation of graphic novels he and Amy would produce together. It was an ambition they had shared since they were ten years old.

Tom came in through the back door, his jaw clenched. He strode into the office and slammed the door shut. Jen was close on her husband's heels but did not follow him. She exchanged looks with Gloria and sighed.

"He thinks he saw Bigfoot—right outside our kitchen," Jen said.

"Bigfoot?" Gloria repeated.

"Bigfoot," Sean whispered as he shot a quick smile at Amy. She did not need to be told that her friend was already planning a monster hunt.

Gloria shook flour out of her apron. "Is that why he's been in a mood all day?"

"Well, there's that, and there's the whiskey I poured down the sink. He took a shot at whatever it was, for Christ sake."

It had just become more important than ever for Sean to get a job on the farm. Working next to Tom would provide Sean an opportunity to glean information about this sensational possibility.

Amy decided to intervene. "Hey, Jen, have you met my friend, Sean?" Amy gestured toward the young man dressed in black and sporting a scruffy beard. "He wanted to talk to Tom about a job. Any chance?"

The older woman squinted as she inspected Sean. "How old are you?"

"Almost seventeen," Sean replied.

"You can't use any machinery. You'll mostly be shoveling mulch. Gloria knows you so I'll tell Tom you're hired. Show up early Saturday morning—seven o'clock."

Jen joined Gloria in the bakery. Sean leaned closer to Amy and whispered,

"Do you think he actually saw anything?" Amy shrugged but Sean persisted. "You've lived around here your whole life. You ever hear any Bigfoot stories before?"

"Lots of ghost stories—you know, King Phillip's War, dead lovers, but no monsters," Amy said. "There's supposed to be a rock with the devil's footprint somewhere."

"There are rocks with the devil's hoof prints all over New England."

"So there you go. Tom probably saw a coyote. But that doesn't mean I wouldn't be interested in a monster hunt. See what you can find out this Saturday."

Sean mentally rehearsed how he would approach Tom, but it turned out the subject of monsters came up on its own. When he arrived Saturday morning there were several cars, including two police cruisers, in the parking lot. A group of people milled around one of the officers, speaking in hushed, funereal tones.

Sean found Tom in the store. Jen pointed the boy out to her husband. Tom greeted Sean with, "There's no work today. Police are setting up a search. An old man from the rest home up the road walked away last night and never came back. They've already checked the roads. Now we're going through the woods and fields."

"I can help," Sean said.

"Grab yourself some doughnuts and coffee and come with me."

They crossed the parking lot together where the police handed around a photocopied picture of the missing man. "Collin Dunbar. He used to be a history professor at URI," one of the officers explained. "He's not senile, but he's got serious heart disease. They said he's been real depressed since his wife died, and they're afraid he walked away with the intention of hurting himself." With that, the two officers split the group and sent them off in two different directions.

Sean followed Tom along a trail cut through a wooded portion of the farm. Their group spread out as they crossed a plowed field into a meadow, everyone's head oscillating as they scanned the ground for signs of old Professor Dunbar. Beyond the tall yellow grass, they found themselves back in the woods again. These were heavier, pock marked with boulders and red maple swamps. The sun dimmed behind a wash of gray clouds. The tangled woods darkened, and several in the search party shivered as the moldy and somber disquiet that had infected the woods of southeastern New England for nearly 400 years stole across the landscape.

Sean could not shake the feeling that many bad things had happened here before. His gaze wandered up to the lowering skies and he halted. There was something in the trees, and it was looking back at him. It was the size of an owl but had leathery wings and was covered with scales rather than feathers. The talons of its feet dug into the branch on which it perched, while clawed hands rested on its knees. Green eyes met Sean's as he stared, entranced. The creature grinned at him. Sean stumbled backward, almost falling to the ground.

"You see something?" Tom asked sharply. The other volunteers turned around expectantly.

16

"I thought something was looking at me," Sean replied, feeling stupid. "It's just an owl." When he looked up again, the phantasm had indeed become an owl.

The group circled back and retraced their steps but was soon back at the parking lot with nothing to report. The air felt heavy and haunted. The volunteers spoke in hushed tones, like mourners at an open grave, as they waited for the other groups to report.

"You hungry?" Tom asked Sean. "Jen can make you a sandwich."

Sean followed Tom to the store where Jen had her hands full. Customers were coming in to buy pansies and onion sets, full of questions about what was going on in the parking lot. There was a new girl running the cash register and one person in the nursery, but it was not enough.

"I'm swamped. I tried calling in Amy but she's not picking up," Jen called out in exasperation.

"Looks like you are working today," Tom said. "I'll send Jack in to run a register, and I'll take the kid outside with me." He pointed to Sean. "Grab something to eat and follow me."

Sean spent the next two hours bringing nursery stock out of the greenhouses and placing it where Tom directed. Tom was all over the farm, working with customers, sometimes talking to the police, and too busy for Sean's questions. At last, Tom sought him out and pressed some folded money into Sean's hand. "You want to come back next weekend?" Tom asked.

"Yeah, definitely," Sean replied.

"Give your information to Jen. Seven dollars an hour under the table for now. If it works out, we'll put you on the payroll for eight-fifty."

Sean nodded but did not feel like celebrating. "They never found the old man?"

"Not yet. They're bringing in those cadaver dogs."

Sean hesitated and almost spoke of what he had seen, and then thought better of it. As he turned to go, Tom called out after him, "You saw something out there, didn't you?"

Sean stopped, looking over his shoulder. "I saw an owl. It startled me."

"That's it?" Tom's face was inscrutable. "My family's owned this farm for 200 years. There's things in the woods. There's always been things in the woods."

Helicopters swooped low overhead as Sean drove his father's truck home. He picked up Amy and they went out for a pizza.

"He said there's things in the woods," Sean told Amy. "So I guess he's seen weird things before." He paused. "I might have seen something, too."

Amy raised her eyebrows. "Such as?"

"It was an owl, but it didn't really look like an owl. It had green cat's eyes, and it smiled at me. Think I was seeing things?" To his surprise, Amy shook her head.

Sean slumped in his chair, suddenly exhausted and a bit depressed. He was profoundly disappointed the professor was still missing. He wanted to sleep, but he did not want to go home. His father was a good man, a hard worker who took care of his son, but he was never available on weekends. Jeff only drank when he didn't work, and he was a cordial drunk—never mean—but Sean hated watching it.

Amy didn't really want to go home, either. Gloria had just broken up with her boyfriend, which meant a period of extended withdrawal while Amy took care of things. Eventually, Gloria would emerge from her funk and resume mothering. Until that happened, Amy preferred to be with Sean. Together—and tonight was no exception—they would sketch and brainstorm story ideas. Exploring the great darkness of the world of horror allowed them to set aside the lesser shadows in their lives.

After several more days of fruitless searches, the police resorted to cadaver-sniffing dogs. They never found the old man.

Sean worked every weekend at the farm and was soon officially put on the payroll. He had less time for friends but loved spending more time with Amy. They could usually get a ride with Gloria, but they both liked the outdoors. When the weather was good, they preferred riding their bikes, even after a day of phys-ically taxing labor.

For a few weeks, the men who worked the farm snickered behind Tom's back about his "yeti" or "the Rhody Big Foot." They tired of the subject soon enough, but Sean and Amy had not forgotten about it. They never mounted their own search for the chimera because they simply did not have the time.

One day in early July, the pair sat at one of the picnic tables in front of the store, cold drinks in hand. Tom sat at the neighboring table with a man they had seen a few times about the farm. Milton was a retired businessman who had been active for decades in local theatre. Gloria told Amy that he had designed and run several haunted houses around New England. He was bored in his retirement, so he approached his friends about setting up a haunted hayride for the month of October. Now the two men were discussing what could be built with Tom's initial investment.

"They're building a haunted attraction?" Amy said. "We have to be part of this. Do you think it's going to be scary or 'family oriented?'"

Milton overheard and answered her. "It's going to be scary. And you have to be eighteen to act in it. It's a liability thing."

The teens could not hide their disappointment.

"You can help direct traffic and sell tickets," Tom offered. "It's better than nothing."

"And you can help build it," Milton said.

Much of the building took place after regular hours. There were about a dozen people involved who had experience working in haunts. They were all willing to volunteer their time to get this new project up and running. Amy and Sean were welcomed by the building crew and were put to work doing any chores that did not involve power tools.

Small sheds were emptied and carted to the perimeter of the main corn field. A large wooden arch with stairs and a high platform hidden behind the wide entrance was built as the hayride's entrance. A long, black tunnel with swinging doors at either end was constructed near the finish. A jumble of small, open structures, similar to those found at a farmer's market or fair, lined one section of the trail followed by an elevated stage, hung with canvas on three sides. The entire hayride was to be a trip to a haunted circus. Each wagon that passed through would have a sound system that delivered a taped narration and appropriately themed music.

About 200 feet to the left of the hayride entrance was the trail Sean had followed with the search party into the woods. During the day, Sean accompanied Jack, who mowed down saplings and brush with a chain saw while Sean loaded the fallen limbs on a wagon. This area would be turned into a walk-through haunt. It would be small in comparison to the hayride, but if Tom and Jen made money, the walk-through would be expanded the following year.

Milton had a wealth of contacts and was a good scrounger. Throughout July, dilapidated factory machinery, office furniture, playground equipment, fencing, and the like were unloaded from his pickup truck and dropped at different spots in the woods. An old hearse took its last drive along the trail where it quickly died. "I guess that's where the graveyard goes," Milton said.

Amy and Sean loved being with the haunters and made themselves indispensable. There was a small inner group who did the planning and management along with Milton. They had been scaring off and on for years. Bill was about forty years of age and was an electrical contractor. He had done community haunts, mostly local fundraisers, and was good at managing a crew. He was in charge of the walk-through. Justin and Susan had worked for several years at a large haunted theme park in Massachusetts. Each managed one of the six haunted houses at the park. The place had packed up and moved north to New Hampshire, leaving Susan, Justin, and many of their friends looking for a new home. Susan would manage the hayride, while Justin was in charge of marketing. They brought in Meg who would design and sew costumes.

Tom and Jen were not involved in the building but kept a close watch on their interests. Most of what they saw delighted them. They were as excited as children, even as they calculated the cost. Several times, however, Sean spotted Tom walking the path on the walk-through just as darkness fell, cradling his deer rifle in the crook of his arm.

"Is he going hunting?" Sean asked Jack as they hammered plywood walls in place for a maze.

"Looks like it," Jack replied. "I think he just likes shooting that thing. Although, lately, I think he's monster hunting. You hear the story?"

"That he saw some sort of Big Foot climbing on his house?"

"It wasn't a typical Big Foot," Jack said. "I heard him arguing with Jen. It was white and bony with long claws."

"That's messed up." Sean thought a moment then asked, "Is he a drinker?"

Jack shook his head. "No more than anyone else. He's using the walk-through as an excuse to search the woods again."

Sean shared this update with Amy. They set to work trying to put their visions of Tom's monster on paper. One evening, as they sat at the picnic table eating subs for supper, they shared their drawings with each other.

"Yours looks like an emaciated yeti," Amy said.

"Tom described it as bony. What do you think?" Sean asked.

"I like it—especially the claws. But he's kind of hairy. That's what reminds me of a yeti." She opened her sketchbook to reveal her depictions of skeletal creatures, one that appeared flayed with desiccated muscle tissue, another with a taut covering of pale yellow skin, and a third bowed over with bony growths on its spine.

"They're grotesque," Sean said. Amy blushed and smiled modestly.

"Did you guys draw these?" Susan's voice came from behind them. She took the sketchbooks from the young people and flipped through them. "You like horror, don't you?"

"We'd like to do graphic novels someday," Sean said.

"Could I show these to Milton? We need help painting scenery."

By the following evening, they were reviewing sketches Susan had made of macabre circus and carnival scenes to be transferred to canvas backdrops and the cluster of midway structures. For the rest of the summer and through September, Sean and Amy painted malevolent faces, decaying brick work, glow-in-the-dark eyes and teeth, and decrepit circus posters. The adults came by to admire their work. Suddenly, they were haunt colleagues, sharing pizza and ideas with the actors. When Ron and Cheryl, the makeup artists, held workshops in makeup and latex prosthetics for the "newbies," they invited Amy and Sean to participate.

"You know what?" Amy asked as they touched up the painted stonework on ruins that would be a vampire crypt. "I think this is one of the best things that ever happened to me. Is that weird?"

"It's not weird," Sean said. "We're getting paid to do stuff we love."

"I wish they'd let us scare. We're stuck on the periphery. I guess it'll be fun just being part of it." She shrugged but smiled brightly. It suddenly occurred to Sean that behind the torn jeans, the straight black hair, and the paint smears on her cheek was a very pretty young woman.

"It'll be fun because we get to do it together," Sean said, aware that as he looked into her hazel eyes, bright and wise behind the unruly fall of hair, he was blushing a violent red.

Amy threw her head back and laughed, not in derision but in sheer delight. It was the first time Sean knew how much he loved her.

HELL CHRONICLES

June 22, 2010

THIS DATE, WHICH I have just written with a bit of charcoal retrieved from an abandoned fire, is almost beyond my comprehension. I may not remember when I was last a man, but I know I do not belong in this present, so full of terrors and wonders.

There has been a great deal of heavy rain, resulting in lush and tangled growth in the woods and hordes of mosquitoes. Fortunately, these parasites seem to find my blood repugnant, and they leave me in peace. The heavy growth makes even the well-worn game paths almost impenetrable, which keeps outsiders from finding my private hell. That is as it should be. I am a danger to all those oblivious human beings. Yet, knowing I must avoid them, I am still drawn to them. Satisfying my curiosity is one my few means of whiling away my eternal punishment.

I have two other pastimes. One is my never-ending search for something that will lie sweet and uncorrupted on my tongue, other than that most forbidden fruit. The other is this journal, which I have been able to resume with the discovery of several places where I may scrounge for the necessities of my new life without fear of discovery.

This world is teeming with people and heaped with trash. Weekly they leave it piled on the sides of the road to be collected. There are boxes filled with perfectly useable bottles and containers of all sorts. I have collected some for my own use, mostly to gather water for drinking and bathing. More important, I have discovered sheaves of broadsides with news of this world. Most of it is terrible, and I can scarcely bear to read it. This time is so filled with violence, pain, and despair that I am beginning to understand why Demon chose it for my hell. From these chronicles I have worked out the date I posted at the start of this entry. I have also found many sheets of discarded paper, blank on one side. I bound these together with twine and began anew to chronicle my days in hell.

June 25, 2010

I do not see Demon often, but when I do he is watching me as I engage in a frustrating search to fill my world with small comforts. He usually crouches on a branch above me, easily mistaken for an owl by anyone who might see him. Hugging his sides, he rocks back and forth with silent laughter as I gag on victuals that are pleasing to animals but quickly decay into something disgusting once they touch my lips. Birds and beasts feast on insects, pine cones, acorns, young greens, and wild berries, but they are all loathsome to me. He laughs at my fastidious attempts to find water adequate for bathing. Apparently, he finds it ludicrous that someone so repulsive to look at should wish to keep his hide clean. In the back of my mind, there is a half-formed hope that with enough scrubbing, I might wash away my hideous visage.

Demon also seems to enjoy pointing at my grotesque form and grinning, as if to convey ridicule. If his intent is to embarrass me, he has succeeded. I *am* ashamed of my nakedness, my shape, and my ridiculously stunted manhood. And I have no idea how to go about covering my shame. The discarded bits of clothing I have come across do not fit. My arms and legs are unnaturally long. While most of my body is gaunt as famine itself, my head and belly are of preposterous girth. For now, I have no choice but to go naked. I hope to solve this problem before winter comes again.

Sometimes Demon demonstrates no interest in me whatsoever. Instead, I spy him wearing the guise of a night bird, soaring over the trees and actively searching the woods below. He seems to be seeking someone. When he fails to locate this person—and he does always fail—he often seeks me out as a target for his wrath. He will present himself at his full height and kick me with his horny foot or grab me by the hair and throw me against a tree. It does no good to attempt to hide from him. If I submit meekly to his wrath, he will soon tire of me and go away. But after he goes, I find myself shaking with impotent rage. The last time that happened, I grabbed a mouse and crushed it, squirming and squealing, between my teeth simply because I could. It felt good to be cruel. But heedless brutality is a sin, so I have not done it since.

June 30, 2010

Night after night, I have the same dream. I see myself seated at a table in happy anticipation. Behind me is a great fireplace where a generous joint of beef, pork, or venison is roasting. Fat drips down on a pan of potatoes, turnips, and sundry other vegetables roasting near the flames. There is mulled wine or cider with which to wash it all down. But I usually wake before I can enjoy a single mouthful. Or, if I do feast, I neither taste anything nor enjoy satiety. It is as if there is naught but phantom food in front of me.

With the warmer weather, the activity around the edges of the woods increases. I hear those hellish machines chewing away at trees and sounds of building that seem perilously close to my decaying refuge. But when I climb trees to investigate, I can see the new structures are still a long way off. For the moment, my shelter is safe. Even so, I am beginning to realize that I should probably have more than one hiding place.

It is entertaining to watch the builders at work, as it is to watch children at play. But I must be careful to survey them from a distance. As my neighbors toil, play, and sweat, the slightest breeze wafts their delicious perfumes to my nostrils. Then my enormous belly howls with the demands I dare not satisfy.

Sometimes, young people come into the woods after dark. They build fires in clearings, smoke, and drink ale from curious little casks. They become inebriated and begin to curse and jump about. I often follow the noise and the smells and hide in the bushes, watching their foolishness, feeling both annoyed and entertained.

Last night, a gangly boy stood right next to me as he relieved himself beside a tree. He was close enough to touch. I could smell the meat of his lean muscles just under the surface of his tender young skin. I could not help myself. I licked his arm with my tongue and savored the sweetness mixed with the salt of his sweat. He screamed and jumped back. I tucked my head and legs against my belly and went very still. It took all my strength not to lunge at him and take him down.

His friends came running as he shrieked, but when he pointed to the dense growth they laughed and said, "There's nothing there but a big rock." He cursed them. Then he thrashed at my hiding place with a fallen tree limb. He struck me several times, but I did not stir. As far as he was concerned he struck stone and nothing more. He turned away, his friends snickering as they poured more ale down their gullets.

July 6, 2010

Someone almost found my refuge yesterday. Night had fallen. After a few morsels of squirrel for dinner I was trying to sleep. I had all but succeeded when I heard voices right outside one of the sagging walls above me.

"It's definitely haunted," called the voice of a young woman. "They say it was a farm two hundred years ago. The baby died, and the farmer went crazy, killing his wife and then himself."

"People always say abandoned buildings are haunted," complained a male voice. "And they always say someone was murdered in it or committed suicide or some stupid shit like that."

"So why'd you come?" demanded a third voice.

A fourth voice said they needed to be quiet so she could do something she called "EVP readings."

They argued about whether or not they should go inside and what they should do once they entered. Finally, I heard hesitant footsteps overhead. I did not know if they brought torches, but if they shone any form of light overhead they would find my scribbling running across the walls. I wondered if they would interpret it as the product of a ghostly hand.

One of the intruders had a particularly heavy foot. I could hear the floor boards groan in protest with each step he took. Finally, there was a sound of splintering wood. It seemed he had broken through the floor. He fell and the wood cracked even more. He called for help. Then I heard all of them flee to solid ground. They decided the building was too unsafe for any further exploration and departed.

July 10, 2010

The youth in these towns have too much idle time on their hands. They are out in the woods drinking and carousing far too frequently, in my opinion. None of them seem to do any honest work.

A new group of dullards came across my poor hut the night before last. It started to rain, so they quickly lost interest in exploring and departed. They returned last night.

I crouched in my root cellar, listening to the music of tinkling glass. Then I could smell something peculiar on the dank night air. I crept out of the root cellar so I could get a glimpse of the ground outside the windows. I saw a bottle shatter against the foundation and erupt into flames. I panicked for a moment, thinking the old wooden structure would burn like tinder. Then I saw the flames sputter and die. It had rained so heavily that the grounds and the walls were saturated with moisture.

"Asshole, you were supposed to throw it inside the house," one of the boys said. I could hear a couple of young females giggling.

"The roof is full of holes," a voice responded. "All the wood inside is wet. I told you we should wait."

A wailing sound carried across the night air. It was the cry of banshees that accompanied certain speeding vehicles, although I had never learned why this happens. This time the scream was very loud and came alarmingly close. I crouched in the blackest shadows I could find while the young people cursed and ran.

Moments later, the light of torches swept the area. I could hear the voices of grown men calling softly to each other. They were searching for the young people. I realized they must be sheriff's men called in to maintain the peace, and the banshee wail was a warning that they were approaching. They poked around, even shining lights through the door. Then they were gone.

July 15, 2010

As the summer has progressed, my ruined house has become overwhelmed by vines and weeds. Thorny brackens grow across several of the broken windows. When the day is overcast, it is difficult to see much of the building at all. Whether they know how to find it again or not, the young vandals have not returned.

The dense growth throughout the area makes it a challenge to find another den. I move about in the early light or the twilight when I am less likely to encounter others. But this has become risky, too. I now hear the sounds of building through the evening hours and well into the night. It comes from the direction of Stone Ridge Farm, the place where the farmer shot me months ago.

I followed the sounds yesterday evening. I got as close as I dared and found a well-concealed perch in a tree overlooking one of the cornfields. I saw structures standing around the edges of the field. Some were framed but not completed. It had the look of a small village or marketplace, but everything seemed rushed and half finished.

The workers were largely industrious young people. It was a relief to know that my hell was not completely populated with the dull and shiftless. They are a profane lot, however. Hard drinking, too.

July 20, 2010

I have gone back several times to watch the construction going on at the farm. Last night, the workers stayed very late—almost until dawn. The farmer joined them, but his wife and his fat old dog retired to the house. The laborers, both men and women, gathered outside one of those translucent huts that serve as greenhouses and built a large bonfire. There was a screen of tall weeds and brush around the edges of the structures where it was easy to hide, watch, and listen. Another smaller fire was built inside a cauldron with a grate laid across the glowing embers. They roasted meat and drank beer as they feasted. I thought the smell—so familiar and intoxicating—would drive me mad. Remaining there would only increase my misery, but my curiosity was stronger than the pains in my belly. I do not know if Demon counts curiosity among my many sins, but I decided not to worry about it. This was an appetite I could indulge without harming anyone—as long as I could maintain control.

I crawled around the perimeter of the clearing, careful to make as little noise as possible. If I attracted any attention, I went stone still and waited until they resumed their feast. Once they had imbibed enough beer, they became oblivious to the sounds of my movement. They began laughing and joking with the farmer about seeing monsters. They wanted to know how much beer he would need before he would see another one and what type of spirits he would recommend so they could see monsters, too.

The farmer laughed and insisted what he saw was real. He seemed to enjoy the derision for a while, but eventually turned sullen and silent. I felt sorry I had brought this grief upon him.

I decided to take some time to explore the new structures on the farm. I began with the greenhouse that presented an open door right next to my hiding place. It was lit from one end to the other. I kept low so my shadow could not be seen through the translucent material. The place was filled with boxes. Some contained clothing. Others contained what looked like body parts. I was horrified until I realized they were not real. There were blank masks that felt as soft and supple as real skin. There was a box filled with false ears, noses, and teeth. There were also sheets and sheets of the same material that made up the walls of the greenhouse. It was stiff and flexible at the same time. However, unlike the greenhouse walls, they were opaque and colored bright blue and green. I wondered if this material repelled water. If it did, I would certainly have a use for it. I looked about for a source of water.

I spied a large basin at one end of the green house. It had a spigot mounted on it that one might find on a barrel of ale. I twisted it and watched in amazement as water came out. I held the blue sheet under the fountain and saw that water did indeed run right off.

I was about to take the sheet and run with it but stopped. It would be theft, and that would be a sin. I could not afford to accumulate any more offenses. I tried to think of a way to pay for it. The only thing of value I could do was to show myself to the farmer in full view of his companions so people would stop laughing at him. But my courage failed me, so I did not step into the open. I made a silent promise to anyone who might be listening that when the time was right, I would reveal myself. I folded the sheet into a bundle and ran into the night. For the moment, I would remain the chimera of a drunken farmer.

Before returning to my fruit cellar, I visited the cornfield to inspect the new buildings. I discovered they were little more than sheds with somewhat more opulent faces attached. There were no places for storage, for sleeping, for cooking, or taking meals. They had neither hearth nor fireplace. Clearly, this village was not meant for habitation. As I passed into the woodlot, I saw evidence of building there as well. These structures made even less sense. It appeared as though they were purposely building ruins. I could not fathom the reason for this. But it did occur to me that I might find a hiding place here in these woods should I ever be forced to abandon my shelter.

DEATH IN A TEXAS DITCH

THE DEMON FLAPPED great leathery wings as he towed twin shapeless masses through cold black air. Both had been men, blasphemers snatched at the scene of two hideous crimes and thrown into a state of unbecoming. One mass had quickly turned helpless and pliant in a staggering flood of terror.

The second mass knew terror, too, but shifted into a formless pulse of pure rage. It would not abide subjugation, even at the hands of a mighty devil. Its wrath flared in the darkness like an orange flame, and with that heat, it forged its own teeth. It twisted and bit the clawed hand that gripped it. The demon howled and loosened his grasp. The featureless plasma fell through the air until it slammed into the ground.

It lay in darkness. Searing heat poured over the amorphous clay. It wanted sight and immediately birthed its own eyes. The first thing they beheld was blinding sunlight. It was too bright, too hot, and too dry. The formless mass crawled under a pile of discarded timbers heaped up in a dry ditch, waiting for darkness. It was dimly aware that, in this state of unbecoming, it could reform itself with a simple act of will. It had made teeth and eyes for itself, after all. What else could it do? There was a sense that its body was long, rotund, but otherwise shapeless. With all memories of any previous form and structure erased, it did not know how to redesign itself. The being would have to wait for its needs to direct it, to provide a sign.

The sign came as pangs of hunger—a discomfort that appeared when prey first presented itself several nights later.

A young man stumbled in the darkness as it passed the heap of refuse. The great, wormy bag concealed beneath smelled the sweetness of meat and something on the boy's breath that stirred vague memories of some kind of drink. It shivered with pleasure, and the boards shifted around the creature.

The youth glanced at the pile and then hurried ahead. The sentient mass heaved its bulk forward and the timbers collapsed, revealing a dark, slithering thing with tiny red eyes. "Shit!" shouted the boy, halting at the sound and staring. "Goddam!" He turned to run.

The monster wanted this boy. Almost immediately, it formed an alimentary canal with a rudimentary stomach. Behind its sharp teeth a projectile of tissue formed a tongue that could taste the air and knew with certainty the boy would be delicious. An idea formed of how to best hunt down its meal. Having neither speed nor strength, it needed a means to easily incapacitate the boy then feed simply and at its leisure. It pushed its bulk forward in undulating waves. The panicked prey broke into a sprint. The creature would have only one chance to bring him down. Opening its primitive slash of a mouth, a thin, boney barb flashed forward and punched into the young man's thigh. He cried out in pained surprise but pushed forward.

He rubbed his thigh as if it burned. His breathing was quick and labored. Young and strong as he was, he was already slowing down. The creature understood that the barb had delivered venom to its victim, and rapid respiration was probably spreading it quickly through his body.

The prey attempted to climb the side of the gully. The youth's legs wobbled and bowed outward as the bones softened. His limbs folded under him and he opened his mouth to call out. Words that almost sounded like, "Mama, help" gurgled as liquid resembling a thick, simmering stew bubbled up his throat, filled his mouth, and oozed down his chin.

Then everything inside him—bone, muscle and organs—liquefied as he collapsed into a membranous sac filled with a slurry of tissue. There was just enough awareness left for the eyes to register horror as the dark shapeless mass with needle teeth loomed over him, regarding with fascination the bag of gooey flesh the boy had become.

The thing was ravenous beyond comprehension yet was completely beguiled by the process that played out before it. The skin of its prey was nearly transparent. Gelatinous strands of blood vessels and nerves pulsed feebly just below the surface. The creature needed hands and they formed immediately at the end of stubby protuberances. It tore the boy's shirt asunder and watched the jellied heart beating its last. Pale blue lights ran up and down the dissolving nerves and formed an illuminated lattice across the brain. They were beautiful. It watched them wink out, one after the other. Then it plunged its hands into the fragrant goo and began to eat.

§ § §

When Garrett's mother found his bed empty that morning, she was furious. The boy had promised to stop hanging out with his no-good friends, especially on school nights. A few hours later, she called the school to see if he had shown up. He'd been marked absent. She called the truant officer, who promised to track him down. The officer learned Garrett's friends had shown up for their finals. The boys had not seen their friend since he left them around one o'clock in the morning.

They suggested he might have fallen or twisted an ankle in the dry river bed he used as a shortcut from his friend's house and agreed to show the woman the route he most likely walked to go home. She noted sneaker prints and an odd trail through the dust that reminded her of a large snake moving across sand. But it seemed too wide to be a serpent's body. A peculiar odor—salty, sour, and sweet all at the same time—rose on the hot afternoon air. They spied Garrett's sneakers, his torn jeans and shirt, and a mat of damp hair lying where his head should have rested. His clothes were soaked with a greasy substance. One of the boys screamed over and over while the other lurched away and vomited. The truant officer grabbed each boy by an arm and dragged them up the incline to the cruiser parked at the fireworks stand.

An hour later, a detective and the Travis County medical examiner stared at the death scene. The detective covered his nose and mouth with his hand. "Have you ever smelled anything like that before?" he asked.

The examiner shook his head. "It doesn't smell like decay." He took a pen from his pocket and lifted a corner of the shirt. Hordes of beetles swarmed out from underneath. The liquid that soaked the clothing also saturated the ground beneath, killing the weeds and grasses crushed by Garrett's fallen body. "How long has the boy been missing?"

"About eighteen hours," replied the detective.

"We have some fatty acids, a hair mat—sloughed off, not cut off—and clothing. These are final stages of decomposition."

"But if that's the case, wouldn't there be skeletal remains?"

"Eighteen hours after he was last seen there should be a body. At least some blood."

They carefully packaged the hair and clothing and scraped up the saturated soil. They recovered a few teeth. Even with much of the enamel eaten away they eventually produced enough mitochondrial DNA to link the remains to Garret's mother. The oily substance yielded evidence of hemotoxins common to some venomous snakes, which could liquefy blood cells, and the digestive enzymes found in spider venom.

The state police searched the river bed. They dismantled the piles of trash and combed through the weeds and grasses. The only evidence that anyone or anything had been with the boy was that strange undulating track in the dust. Local herpetologists declared that it was too wide and it was unlikely that any snake, however large, could swallow a strapping young man like Garrett. It certainly could not somehow remove the boy's clothing. More important, giant constrictors were not venomous.

In the end it was reported that Garrett had been murdered and that the killer had taken his body, leaving behind only his clothing, hair and a few teeth. The little Texas town was paralyzed with fear. Summer vacation had started, yet the streets were deserted.

The satiated killer squeezed into the fissure of a rocky outcrop overlooking the dry river bed and digested its meal. It listened carefully to the men and women combing the death scene as they fearfully speculated what might have happened to young Garrett. Their horror intoxicated the creature, and their conjectures filled it with ideas. It realized that it was within its power to make itself over into anything it wanted. It could become a creature of terrible beauty, but it must not be hasty. It needed to recover what memories it could and learn all the options for form and function afforded by this world. It would reform again when it knew exactly what it most wanted to become.

In the meantime, it would sleep and dream of monstrous possibilities. It would hunt. It would feed off pain and fear and dissolved flesh. Devoid of memory, it knew one thing: It had always been a fiend, and it would become a fiend again.

THE DEVIL'S IN THE DETAILS

DEMON SHRANK HIS massive frame down so he could easily roost on one of the support beams of the church. Anyone looking at him would assume he was no more than a starling. He liked hiding in houses of worship so he could eavesdrop on sermons and catch up on what the world of men was calling a sin these days. Since the days of the Big Demotion, it was one of his few recreations.

He knew he should be searching for the escaped soul. It had belonged to a cruel and blasphemous man—one of the worst Demon had ever seen. The man and his criminal partner so disgusted Demon that he would not wait for their final breaths. He grabbed them at the culmination of their greatest sins, and cast them into a state of unbecoming. The first soul had been a follower in the worst sense of the word. It was immediately terrified into meek compliance, a quivering mass of gray plasma. The second one was different. Demon could almost smell its prideful defiance. It seethed with a fury that begat teeth, and it sank them into Demon's hand. Before he could recover from the painful surprise, Demon relaxed his grip, and the soul disappeared into the dark night air.

There was more than one type of hell, each one personally designed for the sins and the personality of the soul. That first terrified soul was thrown into a time and place destined to be either its salvation or its irredeemable damnation. Demon would function as chief tormentor and caseworker, punishing the creature and enforcing the perimeters of its personal hell.

The second soul was beyond redemption. There was nothing to do but imprison it in a dark place of eternal isolation. Normally, Demon would have crammed the sinner into a black bag bound with silver chains. His case load had grown exponentially, and he was seriously behind in his visitations. He hastily grabbed both men by the hair and set about refining the placement for the weaker soul before restraining its evil partner. It was the first time since the Demotion that Demon had ever cut corners on the job, and now there would be hell to pay.

The escapee possessed intelligence as sharp as a scythe, even in its formless state. In the act of freeing itself, it had learned serendipitously what no soul was supposed to understand: In its state of unbecoming it could give itself form. This was dangerous knowledge under the best of circumstances. In a mind capable of such cruelty, it could be calamitous. Demon had one small advantage as he tried to locate the being before it could do any harm. He had deprived the sinner of its memories. Escaped souls usually lacked a frame of reference to recreate themselves in any meaningful way. Most of the time, they could barely function. But this one was fully capable of forging a new destiny for itself and avoiding the pitfalls that had befallen other fugitives.

Demon knew he was in deep, deep trouble with the Boss. He understood how imperative it was to quickly recover this runaway, but he was bone tired. Sunday was his only day of rest.

This particular Sunday morning, Demon perched in a Midwestern church and listened to the Reverend John Phelan as he roused his flock against the imminent threat of homosexuality. Same sex couples had been flocking to Massachusetts for several years to marry, and other states were now following its lead. Young men and women were dying in Iraq and Afghanistan, thundered Reverend Phelan, a punishment for the "homosexualization" of our culture. Make no mistake; God had even more terrifying punishments in store if the nation continued to tolerate these depravities.

Demon sighed. He'd heard these dire predictions before. Often, it was the Jews who were to blame for whatever was wrong with the world. Sometimes it was unions or Communists. From time to time, someone in power would sprout an imagination and blame teachers.

Now Reverend Phelan was shouting, "Our doors are open. We offer Christ's love to the sinners. It is the sin we hate, not the sinner."

Demon laughed. He'd heard all manner of variations on that theme. He remembered a police chief who had been famous for turning fire hoses and dogs on civil rights demonstrators in the American South. Demon crouched on top of a file cabinet in the man's office one afternoon as the chief gave an interview. He was not a bigot, the chief claimed. He merely hated ignorance, and he had one special word reserved for ignorant people. But the chief made it clear he had never met an ignorant white man.

At the moment of the chief's death, Demon seized him and cast him into his own personal hell. The chief was now enjoying his 200th incarnation as a sentient worm, preyed upon by birds and toads and constantly trod underfoot by a seething tide of humanity in a foreign land.

Demon had not yet decided what to do with Reverend Phelan. He was still a relatively young man, and he had a kind enough heart. It was, however, an exclusionary, prideful heart. The man was convinced that God spoke only to him when, in fact, God answered even fewer questions than Demon did. Most people failed to understand that God did not abide in the noise inside their heads. She was found in the stillness of their souls. It was one of the reasons Demon remained so stubbornly silent. It was hard enough getting an appointment with the Boss, especially since that fateful insubordination. It was stillness that helped Demon understand what he needed to do.

It was not just the Reverend who piqued Demon's interest. Sitting in the third pew from the front, directly in the minister's line of sight, was a fourteen-year-old boy named Tyler. The boy was riveted in horror at the minister's words. Today, Tyler learned there was a name for what he was feeling. He was an abomination in the eyes of the Lord. It was his fault that fighting men and women were dying in foreign lands. The boy folded his arms and pinched the skin of his upper arm as hard as he could. He concentrated on the pain so his eyes would not well up with tears. If anyone, Reverend Phelan in particular, saw him cry, they would all know that Tyler was what his minister and his parents hated: a faggot.

Demon watched the congregation with keen interest. He knew his Boss would prefer he refrain from toil on his one day of rest—except, of course, for resolving the problem Demon had created—but here before Demon were two unique souls in an equally unique time and place. The very ripples ebbing gently away from their thoughts would exert influences neither one could foresee. Here was an opportunity to help both these individuals understand the choices that lay before them.

Later that afternoon, the boy told his parents he was going to meet with his friends. A soft summer rain fell as he rode his bike to the river. There was a bridge where young people often gathered to swim, but today Tyler would have it to himself. A sand bar under the bridge held milk crates scattered to provide seating. Here Tyler would have the privacy he needed to reflect on his troubles.

He loved sports of all kinds, but his family wanted him to play football, which was almost a religion in his town. The very idea of playing terrified Tyler. Football was a contact sport. The boy was afraid that someone else would see something different about him if he talked to someone in the huddle, helped another boy to his feet, or punched a team member in the shoulder. They would feel something in his touch, sense something out of place in the locker room, and they would know what he was. Tyler knew he would not have to touch anyone if he did track. He could be one man alone, sprinting and jumping and throwing javelins. He could run until he ran away from who he was.

As Tyler stared at the water and wondered how he would stand up to his father, he realized he was being watched. His eyes were drawn to a large rock that rose above the water at the opposite end of the bridge. A pair of vivid yellow-green eyes stared back at him. The figure rose from a squatting position. It was tall and powerfully muscled with skin like peat-tanned leather. It had wings and horns that curled on either side of its forehead. It grinned at the boy, revealing a mouthful of sharp yellow teeth. Tyler cried out, leapt to his feet, and backed against the concrete of the bridge support.

Tyler considered running, but he was a good Christian, so he stood his ground and demanded, "Who are you? You got a name?"

Demon grinned and nodded.

"You want something from me? I swear I didn't do anything wrong."

The creature's head bobbed up and down like a toy.

"So you know that—so you can't do anything to me…can you? Reverend Phelan says God hates me. He says people like me are killing soldiers in Iraq. But how can I kill people just because I feel different?" Demon smiled but remained silent and Tyler shouted in exasperation, "So which is it? I'm going to heaven or I'm supposed to burn in hell?"

Demon only smiled. Tyler's fear gave way to irritation. The boy folded his arms across his chest and glared, determined to wait for an answer. The only sounds he heard were the slow current of the river and the steady patter of the rain. A fog spread across the water, and Tyler found it curious that it had an amethyst tint to it. His eyes grew heavy and closed. From the silence within him came a voice he'd last heard just before he was born. It was familiar, not unlike his mother's voice. It told him he was welcome in the world and that he should never fear because he was perfected by love.

When Tyler opened his eyes again, the skies had cleared and the sun had set. Demon had not moved. Tyler announced, "I figured it out. I'm a pure soul. I've never hurt anyone. Pure souls don't make bad things happen in the world, even if they're different. You can't touch me."

Demon grinned, but because he was Demon, his smile had all the appearance of evil triumph. Tyler plucked a stone out of the river and hurled it at the devil's head. Demon disappeared in a mad flurry of starling wings. Tyler's knees shook, but he leaned against the cool concrete and let the rhythm of the singing river roll over him. His heart beat slowed and his breath steadied. He was unnerved by what he had just seen, yet he was not afraid. He knew who he was, and he knew that person was good. No matter what came at him for the rest of his life, he would be all right.

But he was still trying out for track.

Later that evening, John Phelan sat in his study reading emails from his congregation. His daughters had been asleep for hours, and his wife had just gone to bed. The study was dark, lit only by the glow of the computer screen. His eyes felt strained by the unnatural light. He closed them and looked away for a few moments. When he opened them again, the pastor could just make out a dark figure in the corner. He stared, waited for his eyes to adjust. The figure was still there. Phelan reached for the desk lamp and turned it on.

"Oh, God!" the clergyman exclaimed. He bolted from his chair and retreated to the wall behind the desk. He had not expected to find himself staring straight into the face of the Enemy. Reverend Phelan was a gifted orator, but at this moment he was struck dumb. As often as the devil had been featured in the pastor's sermons, the man realized that until this moment he had never really believed the Evil One existed.

The Demon's head touched the ceiling. He stepped forward, grinning, and his tread was heavy enough to set the glass doors on the bookcases rattling. It occurred to the Reverend that some sort of response was expected from him beyond shrinking against the wall. He took a step forward and demanded, "You need to get on out of here—right now."

Demon grinned and nodded.

"You're nodding but you're still here." The pastor gestured with his head towards the door. "Go on. Get."

Demon remained where he was.

"Aren't you supposed to be tempting me or offering me something in exchange for my soul?"

Demon made no offers. He smiled and waited.

"You're just going to stand there and mock me?" Phelan had an inspiration. "I hit a nerve today, didn't I? You're here to stand up for the sodomites."

Demon leered at the pastor, his long tongue slithering between his teeth.

"They're sinners! They're abominations!" It was of utmost importance to Phelan that Demon acknowledged this wickedness. Demon shook with soundless mirth. Then he put his finger to his lips as if commanding the minister to be silent. Phelan was enraged. He snatched up the bible on his desk, held it in front of him and cried, "Get thee gone, Satan!" Demon remained where he was.

The minister's fury gurgled helplessly in his throat. He aimed for the devil's head and threw the holy book with all his might. Demon caught it in his huge clawed hand. Wagging his finger at the minister, Demon gently placed the book back on the desk. It flopped open to John 15:12: "My command is this: Love each other as I have loved you." He leaned forward and silently laughed in the Reverend's face. Then he made himself small and bolted out the open window into the night. Phelan collapsed in his chair and prayed for protection.

A clock in the hall chimed twelve times. The Sabbath was over. It was time for Demon to resume his hunt for the errant fiend. His day of rest had been both entertaining and, he believed, fruitful. An innocent boy learned something about the strength and goodness of his soul. The minister confirmed what he wished to believe. Demon would have decades until Phelan's spiteful death to design the clergyman's perfect hell.

BONEBELLY

BONE RIDGE FARM

MILTON SLOWLY RODE an ATV around the edge of the corn field to give the hayride sets a final inspection. The tall circus entrance was draped with faded, moldering canvas and painted with grotesque performers. There were hidden doors on both sides where zombie ticket takers would pop out and attack as the wagons passed through.

The next stop was a paddock where the mutated crosses of human, horse, lion, and elephant would menace the guests under blue lights. Beyond this was the midway, with stands selling candied eyeballs and fingers, and games where the undead would lob softballs at unlucky captives and win human heads as prizes. Milton moved on to the side show, a stage where Justin, dressed as an undead carnival barker, would introduce monstrous curiosities. There was a man-eating mermaid and a werewolf boy. Jon, the undead juggler, would toss about various body parts. While the audience was distracted, they would be attacked by malformed cannibals wielding chain saws.

Milton was proudest of the trapeze that arched over the wagons at the next stop. Melissa and Ellis, siblings who had gone to stunt school, would wait in darkness on separate platforms eight feet above the ground. Flames would erupt in the bare fields well away from the wagons, then the actors would slide down ropes and drop into the wagons. Vampire acrobats would attack from the darkness.

Inside the dark tunnel, visitors would find themselves bathed in strobe lights and surrounded by malevolent clowns. Finally, as the patrons approached the parking lot, they would be attacked by one last group of clowns hiding in a stand of trees.

Milton smiled as he exited the hay ride circuit. He had checked every last switch and light bulb in his creation, and he knew it was good.

He repeated this exercise for the Bone Ridge Underworld—the walk-through side of the haunt. Synova, magnificently attired as Queen of the Underworld, would greet guests from her throne while her hell hounds threatened the patrons. She would present warnings: stay on the path, no flash photography, no touching the sets or the denizens. The patrons were then on their own as they walked the heavily mulched path through the graveyard, a vampire castle, an industrial accident site punctuated with barrels of glowing toxic sludge, a derelict trailer inhabited by a cannibal family, a pitch black maze, and finally another dark tunnel, partially dug into the earth, serving as a medieval dungeon. Actors with chain saws would hide and roam at will. Patrons would exit from the tunnel to the parking lot.

Opening night for Bone Ridge Farm was October 1. The actors had to arrive by 5:00 to get into makeup and costumes, but the ticket booth and parking lot did not open until 6:30, so Amy and Sean haunted the green house and closely watched the makeup process. Ron and Cheryl promised to teach them to use an air brush if the opportunity presented itself. They fetched costumes and props for Meg but otherwise just soaked in the atmosphere.

The two young people had not been present for the rehearsals and were amazed to see the transformed actors roaming through the greenhouse and parking lot. The veteran actors they had already met were barely recognizable. Among the new actors were many young people aged 18 to 25, pierced and tattooed, hair streaked with color. Some were college students, while others were tenuously employed due to Rhode Island's ravaged economy.

Meg was playing a white-haired vampire on the castle set but was also the self-described "costume Nazi." Along with Milton, she had scrounged the clothing the actors needed and sewed the rest from old curtains, bedding, and fabric remnants. In addition to carnival attire, she had designed many of the costumes to be multipurpose—street clothes that were frayed and blood stained, or simple tunics, robes, and gowns for the dungeon and vampire castle. Most of it was one-size-fits-most with room for layering on cold nights.

Once all the actors had signed in, Meg stood on a precariously rickety folding chair and announced, "By now, you should know the costumes are organized by scene and character. There is a script and a scene number pinned to your costume. That is the costume you take and no other. Put it back where you found it. If an actor cannot find a costume because you took the wrong one, I will put my foot up your ass. If your costume goes missing, I will rip you a new asshole." She stepped down to a smattering of appreciative applause from the veterans. A few newbies laughed nervously.

Bill reviewed the expectations and rules for employees and all the infractions that would get an actor fired. Each scene had at least one veteran to help the newbies along. Actors with cell phones had numbers to contact Milton, Bill, or Susan to report any problems with the sets or with customers. Susan would walk the hayride to make sure everything was working the way it should and to watch for troublemakers among the patrons. Bill would do the same with the ticket line and the walk-through.

There was less than an hour left until the opening, so Amy and Sean went to their work stations. A steady line of cars streamed into the parking lot for the first hour. Amy tried to talk a few families with young children out of buying tickets, as she had been instructed. "This isn't like the Pumpkin Fest at the zoo," she warned. "It's meant to be scary."

"How were we supposed to know that?" one father complained.

Amy pointed to the warning printed on their discount coupons.

"Who would jump out and scare a little child?" wondered the mother.

"The actors are hiding. They can't tell if little kids are in the group until it's too late," Amy explained patiently. The parents bought the tickets anyway.

Once he waved cars into place, Sean had little to do but listen to the screams and maniacal laughter and sigh. The only excitement that evening was when a carload of students from the high school pulled in with a case of beer in the back seat. He pointed out the detail cop standing less than twenty feet away. The students left before their beer could be confiscated.

After the initial rush of patrons, the activity slowed down to a crawl. Just past ten o'clock, when the ticket booth closed for the night, Tom came by, glowering. "Go get your mom and Sean and get in line," he said to Amy. "You can go through the sets." He walked away, swearing and muttering, "This is costing me money."

As they waited in line, Sean whispered to Amy, "I could hear people as they came out of the dungeon. Almost everyone thought it was scary. They liked it, except for a couple of families with little kids. They were freaking out."

Amy rolled her eyes.

They enjoyed the attraction but noticed a few scenes had only a single actor valiantly running back and forth. "Well, there are always bugs to work out," Gloria suggested.

Back at the greenhouse, Milton, Bill, and Susan were not as generous. "There were scenes with missing actors," Bill announced. "I heard people talking on their cell phones when guests were coming through. We have a waiting list of people who want to work for us. If it happens tomorrow, some of you won't be back."

"We have a reporter from Channel 10 going through the haunt tomorrow night," Milton announced. "You don't need to know what time. You just need to be at your scene scaring the shit out of anyone who comes along. I don't expect any holes tomorrow night. I want everyone's best effort and I want this reporter pissing himself."

The actors cheered.

Saturday night, the reporter and his cameraman arrived at 8:00. They took their places on an empty wagon. Milton went with them so he could answer questions along the way. Once they had passed the first two scenes on the hayride, the actors began calling their friends on their cell phones to let them know they were about to be filmed.

The videographer focused on the actors and sets as much as possible. The reporter appeared to enjoy himself hugely, although he repeatedly tried to get Milton to tell him what was happening next. He screamed for the first time at the midway. The cameraman laughed out loud at his colleague but kept the camera steady until they reached the tunnel. Clowns Punch and TikTok silently mounted the sides of the wagon in the darkness while Sylence positioned a sock puppet right next to the reporter's ear. There was no footage from the tunnel because both men flailed and shrieked the moment the strobe lights flashed.

Milton left the two men at the entrance to the Underworld. "You're on your own now," Milton said. "I'm going on ahead. I'll see you at the exit."

After the reporter left, Bill toured the walk-through to congratulate the actors. When he reached the dungeon, Carrie, the oldest of the veteran actors, attacked him. "Nice," Bill congratulated her. "Where are Don and Erin?"

Carrie looked around and shrugged. The tunnel walls were lined with cages and a few dummy corpses. The three actors continuously switched hiding places so the scares were never the same. It was meant to be a high impact finish, but for the second night in a row Carrie found herself abandoned by the newbies.

"Son of a bitch," Bill cursed. "Were they here when Channel 10 went through?"

"Yeah, they were great," Carrie said.

"Doesn't matter. They're done. I'll get someone from our waiting list to come in tomorrow night."

Jen rounded the corner to the front yard of the farm house and stopped. Two naked people were rolling around on the lawn. Erin and Don, the missing newbies, were patting each other on the back for a job well done. Jen grabbed the garden hose and blasted the couple. "Get out of here now," she said. "Don't come back and don't expect a paycheck."

Management did not inform the workers of the first great transgression of the season but somehow everyone knew about it. Bill reiterated his warning about leaving scenes unattended and repeated the list of forbidden activities. He concluded with, "If I failed to mention anything else that will get you fired, or maybe even arrested, it's because we probably don't want you here if you need to be told. If you find it that difficult to restrain yourself for a few hours let us know. We'll get your replacement for next weekend."

It was past midnight when the crew built the first post-haunt bonfire of the season. The soccer moms and those with Sunday morning commitments left, but the remaining veterans brought cases of beer out of their cars. Several of the underage newbies gathered around to help themselves until Milton and Bill intervened. "Maybe you didn't notice," Bill said, "but there's a cruiser parked just up the road. If we let you drink, it will come down on Tom and Jen. If you have to party, go someplace else to do it."

Many of the under twenty-ones left at that point, but a few hung around and contented themselves with soda and energy drinks.

The news spot, edited down to two minutes of glorious mayhem, aired on the following Wednesday. That Friday, the lines were appreciably longer. By Sunday night, Tom and Jen realized they had made up for the losses of the previous weekend. Milton assured them they would get busier as Halloween approached. It seemed certain that, barring a hurricane or a blizzard, they would indeed make money off this venture.

There were still problems to solve. Sometimes, the hayride actors failed to heed the signal on the soundtrack that told them to get off the wagons. More than one was sent sprawling backwards in the dirt. One haunter had a toe fractured when the wagon rolled over his foot. Other actors were injured when they got too close to patrons with extreme startle responses. One ghoul ended up with a broken rib Friday night when a boy on the back of the hay wagon flailed and planted a solid kick to the actor's chest. Carrie spooked a preteen boy just outside the torture chamber exit. He threw his arms out, punching her in the breast. The boy fell to his knees, blubbering, "I didn't mean that! I didn't mean to touch you there. I'm not like that." Carrie remained in character, menacing the boy until he remembered he was in the parking lot and made his escape.

"That was cool. What did you do to him?" Joe, the replacement executioner, asked.

Carrie shrugged. "He seems to think he violated me. Such a polite young man."

"You're surprised?" Joe said.

"Preteen boys are the most obnoxious people we see, next to the drunks. They're always trying to prove they're not afraid."

The drunks made their appearance by the second Saturday. A large group from URI filled an entire wagon. They were loud and crude throughout the hayride. Two were removed by the time they reached the sideshow for trying to grope the actors. One of them kicked holes in the walls on the walk-through and pantomimed oral sex with a slack-jawed skeleton on the toxic waste set. Bill intervened and escorted the entire group to the parking lot.

The haunt fell into a rhythm that was as seamless as anyone could expect at an entertainment venue that celebrated really bad behavior. After the first firings, the biggest employee issue was tardiness and bad acting. There was only one other major transgression. Bill confronted the haunters at the end of the third Saturday when he found beer had been taken from his truck. He glowered at a couple of the underage newbies who were his primary suspects. But the following Saturday, Sean overheard Bill confide to Justin at the end of the night that the thief had secretly made restitution.

Sean kept it to himself, but he knew it was not an actor who had stolen from Bill. As the last cars were leaving the parking lot, he saw something streak briefly into view from behind the chemical toilets then quickly disappear into the wooded shadows again, heading in the direction of the greenhouses. It was nearly naked, bone white, long limbed, and skeletal except for an enormous belly. As it ran, it clutched a six pack of cans against its bony chest.

BONEBELLY

THE ALL HALLOWS EVE REVELS

September 15, 2010

I T IS A pleasure to have genuine writing instruments. I discovered them one night in the greenhouse at the farm and took them on account. I have yet to decide how I will pay for these things, but pay for them I shall. My long fingers and tapering claws make manipulating a pencil difficult. I practiced for days until I could write steadily in large, looping strokes. I tried sketching as well and discovered I could make a reasonable likeness of the human form and the trees and animals around me. I drew two faces—a man and a woman—that seemed remarkably familiar, although I cannot recall when or where I might have seen them.

Drawing uses the pencils up too quickly. For sketching, I continue to make use of sticks of charcoal I retrieve from the fires the rowdy youths build in the woods. I also discovered other unusual implements in the greenhouse. They look like pencils, but ink flows from inside the stylus. I promptly borrowed them.

Clean paper and flowing ink! I had forgotten that little pleasures can provide so much comfort.

September 17, 2010

Work appears to be finished on the village at Stone Ridge Farm. By that, I mean no more toil has been expended on it. There seems to be no plan to make the buildings habitable, so I cannot fathom their purpose. Among the ruins in the woods, I noticed a somewhat disheveled-looking young man and maid carefully painting the jumble of walls and hovels to appear even more decrepit. They depicted moss and mold, broken glass, and even bloody splashes on the walls. While the work they are doing is disturbing, it pleases me to see two young people who are relatively well mannered and industrious—although they, like all their older companions, do a lot of cursing.

September 20, 2010

Yesterday, I was haunting the edges of my woods, spying on the lives of my neighbors. No one observes the Sabbath around here. Sunday is often an excuse for feasting and playing rather than prayerful contemplation. I hid in the trees behind one homestead, watching as nearly naked people jumped and splashed in a pool of sparkling water. A man was roasting meat over a smoking fire in one of those long-legged cauldrons. The smell of it made my mouth water. I should have left then and there, but I remained and tortured myself with the heavenly aroma. I was so hungry.

A little boy ran and played with a pup close to the wooded edge of the property. It was a warm Sunday, and as he romped and sweated a breeze wafted his scent up into the tree where I hid. I clutched at my belly and doubled over in anguish. I wanted so badly to devour this child. I bit my own arm until a trickle of blood flowed into my mouth. It smelled of decay and tasted like plague—disgusting enough to conquer the craving.

The child's father called him over to a table around which the rest of the family sat, and they commenced their meal. They laughed as they stuffed themselves with roasted fowl and beef ribs slathered in a piquant sauce of some kind. There was corn and dishes filled with different sorts of pottage they ate by dipping in wedges of toasted bread. As they filled their yawning mouths, I dug my claws into my aching belly and felt the emptiness within fill with rage. After all, who is not a sinner? Why am I so severely punished while all these other imperfect creatures around me have everything they want?

And that was when I was gifted with an opportunity to take revenge. The little pup returned to the edge of the property. He seemed intrigued by my blood scent. I slipped down the trunk as he circled my tree. The little creature was all innocence and curiosity. I stretched my fingers out, and it sniffed at them, wagging his tail. My stomach growled and, laughing silently, I scooped up the pup and carried it into the woods. I was well away by the time the people missed their pet. I could hear them calling, "Smokey, come" over and over. I hurried along until the voices grew almost too faint to hear. Then I clamped my fingers around the animal's muzzle and quickly slashed his throat before it could even feel fear.

It was a lean little creature, more fur than meat. I sat on a stretch of old stone wall, skinning my prize, when I saw Demon watching me impassively from amidst the trees. He did not laugh or glower; he merely stared as I brought each strip of meat to my lips and grimaced as it turned bitter. As he gazed at me, I pictured that trusting little face as it sought me out for a play fellow, and I felt regret. After a few morsels, I threw the carcass into the woods for the scavengers and returned to my fruit cellar.

I do not understand why this bothers me so. I killed a beast no different than a mouse or a squirrel. But I do not think I will go out hunting again until I no longer hear those voices calling, "Smokey, come" around the edges of my woods.

September 24, 2010

Today my hunt took me back to the place where I had tried to end my life. I thought nothing of the vultures soaring overhead until I reached the swamp. To my horror, I saw the bog was nearly dry, a carpet of spongy moss pitted with stagnant pools. A skeletal arm, shoulder, and skull protruded from the vegetation. They were the remains of the frail corpse I had desecrated. The vultures were there for him.

I realized the carrion birds might prompt a new search. When I inspected the remains, I saw they were mostly bone and did not bear signs of my desecration. At this point, recovery of the gentleman's bones could afford his family a measure of peace. I felt around in the mud until I could pull most of the body free and left it resting in plain view of anyone who cared to look.

September 25, 2010

I hear the thumping and roaring of machines swinging back and forth in the skies overhead. I think they are searching for the old man, so I will remain hidden in the root cellar. It is dark down here and difficult to write. I am starving, reduced to eating the beetles and ants that crawl across my path. I hope they are looking for the old man. I hope he will be brought to a final resting place.

October 1, 2010

The wind is quiet this evening. I hear the sounds of a great celebration coming from the east. The leaves are turning—a sight I find comforting for some reason even though it signals the approach of winter. Perhaps the revelry comes from a harvest celebration. I will seek out the festival place. If there is a feast, there might be some remnants I could eat and perhaps even store away.

October 2, 2010

Tonight, I have seen such wonders. I must write everything down now before I lose the images in my head. Renewed sounds of merrymaking brought me to the farm where all the building had taken place throughout the summer. I was startled by grating notes of loud discordant music and a booming voice that seemed to come from heavens itself. The only thing lacking was the blast of trumpets heralding the Last Judgment.

The noise brought me to the edge of the bald corn field where the half-built structures had been erected. I climbed a tree and jumped from crown to crown until I found myself overlooking this peculiar settlement. Everything was bathed in a sickly glow of blue, green, red, and yellow lights. There I saw not a celebration of the living harvest, but a festival of death. Devils and ghouls attacked a wagon filled with men, women, and children who shrieked in terror yet raised not one hand in their own defense. I even saw the hellish creatures take a man off the wagon and disappear into one of the market stalls with him. Suddenly, he broke free and ran back to the wagon, mounting it as the ghouls withdrew and let the innocents go on their way.

The wagon traveled a few feet to the elevated stage, and the wagon was attacked again by a different group of infernal creatures. Once again, the hapless passengers cowered in fear, and once again they were released after a few minutes of intimidation and torment. The process was repeated with a spectacular flash of fire and hellions descending from the sky. Then the wagon rounded a bend and was swallowed by a dark tunnel. Piercing screams issued from the black cavern but, once again, the victims were released before they came to any real harm.

Almost as soon as that wagon disappeared, another took its place and the process was repeated. From my perch, I soon realized that the howls were prompted by both fear and laughter and that the false village was a great outdoor theatre. The men who operated the machines pulling the wagons appeared over and over again. I recognized some of the ghouls as the same people who built the village or sat around the bonfire by the greenhouse. And something akin to a memory came to me: I could picture a boy wandering among bonfires, listening to ghost tales, and cheering as witches and devils were burned in effigy. The boy had been taught that playacting was sinful, yet he loved every minute of those revels.

It was only the beginning of October, but this was clearly some celebration of All Hallows' Eve. It was glorious. I watched the actors change places throughout the night and time their appearance to provoke the greatest levels of panic. Enough tree cover and brush bordered the cornfield to afford multiple hiding places, so I was able to spend part of the night at each scene. Finally, the last wagon departed, the hellish lights went out, and the actors exited into darkness.

I crept back to my poor home, profoundly disappointed. It was a most spectacular burlesque, clearly months in preparation. But All Hallows' Eve is a single night. It would be another year before I would enjoy such revels again.

October 4, 2010

The All Hallows' Eve revels were repeated. Even as I grieved the end of this excellent diversion Saturday night, I heard the discordant music drifting through the woods the very next evening. Hurrying back to the farm, I planned my approach so I could more closely examine each scene. I was determined to follow one of these wagons as closely as possible. The actors were already in costume, so I searched the greenhouses for a disguise of my own. One of the buildings held several bolts of black fabric. I slashed a long piece off one of the rolls with my nails and tore a hole in it so I could fit it over my head. I took a smaller piece, punched out two eye holes, placed that over my head and tied it in place with a length of twine. When I held my arm up to the bright lights near the entrance, I could not see my pale flesh through this sack cloth. I laughed to myself. The actors were not the only ones who were not themselves.

It seems there is a story being enacted here. The booming, disembodied voice, which seems to project from a small box on each wagon, identified itself as a circus ringmaster. He welcomed his "guests" and made many poor jests and plays on words. Each wagon moved slowly toward a looming gate draped with motley. Ghouls leaped onto the wagon itself to collect "tickets" or some other form of payment to the screaming delight of the guests. They wore tattered clothing that seemed almost military, and their skin was painted in shades of gray, green, and white. They groaned phrases like, "Tickets—one brain!" At the same time, they mimed taking bites out of the spectators.

The next scene was deceptively peaceful. The wagon stopped at a fenced paddock bathed in blue light. At first, there seemed to be only animals grazing peacefully. Suddenly, they sprang from the shadows, revealing themselves as grotesque amalgamations of man and beast.

The marketplace scene was described by the disembodied voice as "the midway." Here, the spectators were encouraged to purchase refreshments or play games of chance. The repast that was offered consisted of eyeballs or fingers threaded on thin wooden sticks. I did not know what to make of this horror. The actors, which the voice referred to as "zombies" and "the undead" threw balls at what appeared to be a helpless victim. If they hit him, the undead were awarded a head that had the skull broken open, exposing the brains. I soon realized that the victim was also an actor. The balls they threw were made of soft cloth, and the body parts were the props I had seen stored the greenhouse weeks ago.

I moved along to the raised stage where a freakishly dressed juggler entertained the spectators. He made several gruesome and threatening jokes, so enthralling to the guests that they did not see the murderous band of killers descending on them from the opposite side of the wagon. Two of them waved clubs, but one of them held one of those fearsome vibrating saws. I was horrified to see the actor rush the wagon, slashing at the guest's feet with this barbaric implement. The spectators squealed and squirmed. One young woman screamed, "I hate chainsaws" while the cur by her side, rather than protecting his lady, laughed at her and said, "What are you scared of? There's no chain on it." But I watched the scene play out several times, and the threat seemed real enough to me.

Extreme caution was needed to get close to the aerial acrobats where flames leaped into the sky. Two actors swung on ropes and dropped to the ground. They were dressed in black with deathly white faces and lurid red lips. They leered at the people with long, pointed fangs as other white-faced actors attacked from the side. They were supposed to return to their perches, but as the night wore on, the two actors grew fatigued by their exertions. They took turns leaping and tumbling while one of them menaced from the ground.

It was difficult to slip into the black tunnel unseen, but I got a chance to huddle under my black cloak beneath a raised platform when the actors stepped outside to smoke. When the next wagon entered, the gates at either end were shut. The spectators waited uneasily in the darkness for a minute. Suddenly, a weirdly flickering light threw disorienting shadows as painted fools attacked the wagon. This was no ordinary merriment. The jesters were daubed with blood and had ferocious teeth, not unlike my own. Their movements were unreal, almost dream-like. I cautiously moved my own hand in front of my face and realized that it was the flickering light that gave the appearance of nightmarish motion. The spectators seemed most frightened by these garish comics with their red eyes and gaping mouths. It was not surprising that the wagons were attacked by more such actors, armed with growling chainsaws, as they neared their journey's end.

There were no opportunities to remove myself from the tunnel, but the hours passed entertainingly enough until the last wagon had departed. The actors laughed and swore as they sauntered back to the greenhouse. I followed and found a hiding place alongside the hut, thick with grass and shrubs. I had made several small holes for spying on the activities within.

The actors were exhilarated, recounting their triumphs. They apparently took great pleasure in scaring their guests, who, I was surprised to learn, paid enormous sums for the privilege. *How long must it take someone to earn eighteen dollars?* They complained about the "assholes"—customers who behaved badly. These were people who believed that a theatre which celebrated evil wished to see the same from the patrons. They felt they had purchased the right to behave rudely, even violently, toward the actors.

It was fascinating to watch the mummers bring themselves back to the world of the living. I was shocked by the number of females among them. Some were young and winsome; some were brash, with wildly colored hair and marked with tattoos. There were matrons, too, who spoke of their children, and even grand-children. Some of these women—Melanie and Allison, or Mallison, as friends called them, a beautiful girl named Synova, and a graying woman named Carrie, had not been part of the revels I watched that night. I learned I had only seen half of the production. I had missed the section called "the walk-through," where patrons were forced to wander manufactured ruins and dark woods alone at their peril. I resolved to visit this entertainment on the fourth night.

Several of the actors left. Those who remained called for bonfire and beer,

50

and quickly became drunk and rowdy. As the flames guttered, they turned drowsy. Finally, the fire died and all departed. I was alone. I crept over to the feeble embers and found two small metal casks that contained cold brew. Lifting a ring on the top made an entertaining popping noise and revealed the drink within. The ale I poured down my gullet was weak and watery, but it evoked memories of full-flavored golden draughts I had tasted somewhere before. It did not turn terribly acrid as I drank, perhaps because hops are already bitter. Pleasant warmth spread through my gut. I wanted more but feared it would not be allowed. I took the other cask with me.

Alas, that was the end of my pleasure. The woods have been quiet tonight except for the call of night birds and coyotes. And when I went to the actors' greenhouse before nightfall, I found it sealed up and deserted.

The actors refer to themselves as haunters. They celebrate the horror that is my daily existence. I wish I could be one of them, using my grotesque form to evoke both terror and acclaim, then disappearing to listen to the applause. But I fear I have missed my chance.

October 9, 2010

Happily, I was wrong. The revels have not ended. I should have known when the celebrations took place weeks before All Hallows Eve. After four lonely days of quiet, the dread celebration erupted again. When I heard the music filter through the woods last night, I bolted out of my root cellar—completely forgetting my improvised cloak—and leapt joyfully from tree to tree until I reached the farm. This time, I crept along the wooded trails of the walk-through.

These trails were easier to navigate because they were bordered by heavy brush and trees. However, the actors were sometimes hiding among the trees themselves. It was almost impossible to move without thrashing among the tangled vines and bushes. The actors kept looking behind themselves, reassuring each other, "It's just a deer" or "It's a raccoon climbing a tree." But there was a routine and a rhythm to each site. When a group of people got scared, they made a lot of noise. And as they ran, the actors chased them. During these agitated moments, I could move without attracting attention to myself. There was a wonderful intimacy about this part of the show. At times, I was so close I could almost reach out and touch the haunters and, sometimes, even the guests. I almost felt like I was part of the troupe. It was fantastic.

But something happened near the end of the night. A drunken young man broke away from his companions and lurched into the woods to urinate on a tree. I was hiding on the other side. I could smell the liquor on his breath, his sour, steaming piss, and the perfume of his sweat. Suddenly, my stomach rolled and howled its emptiness and pain. This creature, all sweetness and salty red meat, stood within inches of my claws. I could silence him, take him down in seconds, and then drag him up a tree before anyone realized he was gone. Overwhelmed with both hunger and shame, I turned and crashed through a tangle of thorns, scaring a yelp from the youth. I did not slow down until I was back in my cellar.

I scraped moss from the cellar stones and licked it from my fingers. It did nothing to ease my pain. I swallowed the little cask of ale I had saved. It dulled the ache until the first gray light of morning, when I was able to creep into the woods and spear a careless squirrel with one of my claws. Back in the cellar, I stripped away the fur and eased thin shreds of meat down my gullet until my gut twisted in agony—half-a-squirrel later. I will have to try hunting again and forcing down as much food as my stomach will allow before I return for tonight's show. And I will keep a greater distance between myself and the scenes. I dare not subject myself to that temptation again.

October 11, 2010

I went early to the revels on Saturday and positioned myself in my hiding place by the actors' greenhouse. Making myself as still as stone, I made new holes in the cover and waited patiently for everyone to arrive and transform themselves.

There were two people—one man and one woman—who manipulated wands that streamed colors all over the actors' faces. The contraptions were attached to sinuous, black tubes that hissed like angry serpents. The haunters sat at long tables, attaching scars and growths, animal snouts and ears, and all manner of things that did not belong on the human face. They daubed on a glistening red liquid that resembled blood. And all through the preparation process, they made jests and sang along with strident music pouring out of miraculous little boxes. The younger ones threw food at each other, while a tall man named Bill warned them to keep the area clean. They cursed and told ribald stories. Finally, as the sun was about to set, Bill, Milton, and Susan, the ones who seemed to be in charge, harangued their actors to don their costumes and go to their scenes. I wondered how such a merry troupe could turn so menacing with the failing of the light.

When everyone had vacated the greenhouse, I took a moment to examine the vehicles outside. Bill drove a large one with an open bed in the back. He brought ale for last week's bonfire. I inspected the cart and was rewarded for my effort. There were several boxes with casks and bottles. I borrowed six casks bound together by translucent rings. I tucked them against my chest and found a hiding place in the wooded area separating the hay ride from the walk-through.

When it was fully dark I donned my black cloak and crept to the walk-through. It was quickly torn and hanging in shreds as I moved through the shrubs and brambles. It so impeded my movements that I removed it as the first groups moved through.

As I had done with the hayride, I spent longer periods of time at each scene. The first was the Queen of the Damned, who was a beautiful young woman named Synova. She had boasted earlier of having her nipples pierced, which I understood to mean she had metal rings inserted in that most intimate place. *How will she nurse her children?* In demonic garb, she welcomed guests from her throne and told them how they were expected to behave. Her hounds threatened and teased the customers until they were finally allowed through the gate.

The next scene, the graveyard, was probably my favorite. If I sat very still in a shadowy corner, I resembled a stone marker. I watched Mallison, in identical wedding gowns, attack guests from a motorized hearse at one end of the scene, then from a mausoleum at the other. Other actors crawled from open graves. At the place labeled "The Factory," workers had been poisoned and transformed by some evil concoction into grotesque beings. They were trying to lure the guests to the same fate.

Three men named Jimmy, Rob, and Big Ed wore something the haunters called "ghillie suits" which made them look like large mats of walking vegetation. They roamed the walk-through with chainsaws, as if seeking revenge for every trimmed lawn or downed tree in creation. It required great stealth to avoid running into them. I quickly learned to recognize the smell of the fuel used to power the saws, which warned me to crouch low.

Except for a torture chamber at the end, the remaining scenes involved actors hungering for some kind of forbidden food. The white-faced fanged creatures wanted blood. Creatures called zombies popped their heads through windows in a narrow, pitch black maze, crying for human flesh. They moaned ravenously, growled, and threatened. But when the visitors had gone on their way, they went to hiding places where they had concealed bags of sweets and savories and drinks that smelled of fruit. Positioned high in a tree above the maze, I watched the actors Biggie and Mike celebrate their highly successful scares by filling their mouths and guts. And as they fed, I grew more and more enraged. *They were pretending to be me.* They mimed and mocked my cavernous want yet, as Biggie made his ample belly ripple for his friend's amusement, I knew they could not conceive the real horror, the hopelessness, I lived with every day. I wanted to put my claws through their throats.

Before I could act on my rage, I leaped for the closest tree away from the trail. From that crown I threw myself to the next tree and the next. I looked back to see the actors pointing at the trees and chattering at each other. I made one more jump then lowered myself to the ground. I stood amid rows of stubble in an empty field.

I was about to retrace my steps to retrieve my purloined ale when I collided with a young man emerging from the trees. He was accompanied by two young women. All three of them were staggering drunk. One of the women said, "Are you an actor? We got lost. We took a wrong turn."

"Can you show us the way back to the trail?" the man asked.

I galloped for the cover of the trees, but the man caught up with me and grabbed my arm. "Wait a second," he shouted. "We don't know where we are." I stared at him. He backed up a few steps. "That's an incredible costume," he added, somewhat nervously.

The aromas of alcohol, strange chemicals, and warm flesh filled my nostrils.

His companions ran to his side. They shrieked with mock horror as they gazed at my hideous, half-naked form. One of the women poked my chest and my belly. She stopped laughing and abruptly backed away.

"That's not a costume." She shivered. "That's not an actor."

"What the fuck?" the man exclaimed. His stench made my mouth water. That was when I closed my long fingers around his face and pulled him towards me. He screamed, twisted, and writhed as the women wailed. I knew I was going to do it. I was going to tear his face off. I would lap his blood. He knew it and his companions knew it.

But I did not kill him. I threw him to the ground and bolted for the woods. The stink of his loosened bowels followed me. I did not stop running until I reached my abandoned hovel. As I was about to crawl into my root cellar, I saw two green orbs glowing in the darkness from atop the sagging roof. Demon was waiting for me.

I cowered with fear. I had no doubt he knew what had just transpired in the corn field. Demon remained where he was, watching me. Suddenly, it occurred to me that Demon could find little blame in me. After all, I had no blood on my hands. Slowly, I straightened up and returned his stare. The green lights went out, and I was left alone.

Back in my cellar, I reflected on the evening. Furious as I was, hungry as I was, I missed the haunters as soon as I ran from them. None of them knew I existed, but they were the closest thing to companions I had—companions who, for a few hours, were like me. Perhaps I let the visitors go because I realized what would happen if killed them and left scattered remains in the farmer's field. The hunt would be on for the murderer, and I could never visit the revels again. This is what passed for my conscience, but it was better than nothing.

I did not worry about the drunken celebrants. Whatever story they told would be so fantastic no one would believe them.

So I returned to the revels last night but again kept watch from a considerable distance. I feared what my rage and hunger might drive me to do. As the parade of visitors dwindled, I crept to my waiting ale and retrieved it. I ran back to my shelter, draining a cask as I went. It calmed my nerves considerably.

October 13, 2010

It has been quiet for two days. I missed the farm and the haunters who worked there. I went back there yesterday as dark was falling. When I was sure the workers had left and the farmer had gone inside for his supper, I crept into the greenhouse through an unlocked door. I can see quite well in the dark. It is one of the few gifts I have been granted. I explored the actors' costumes at my leisure. Winter was coming and I was naked but for the rude, tattered cloak I had fashioned. Here there were heavy robes and cloaks I could borrow when the actors were finished with them. I could return them to the greenhouse in the spring.

I found other useful goods. There were large sacks that could be sealed and reopened repeatedly, made of the same waterproof material as the sheets I had taken. But these were as transparent as windows. I could place my journals and writing materials in them and protect them from the elements. I took two along with more paper and pencils.

There were several large mirrors propped against the walls. For the first time, I could take a long look at my untroubled reflection. I turned away in disgust. I was a genuine horror. As I looked away, my gaze fell on a calendar posted on the greenhouse wall. It showed the month of October with some days crossed out. Printed in the squares for each weekend were the words, "Bone Ridge open, 7:00 to 10:00." These notations confirmed that the All Hallows Eve revels would continue for two more weeks. My heart leapt with joy.

October 16, 2010

I returned to the revels on Friday night. It was easiest to hide myself along the walk-through, so I moved cautiously through the swampy growth to the zombie maze. I had concocted a prank to play on Biggie and Mike.

Before I could move into position, I heard voices that told me I needed to make myself into stone. Milton and Bill were walking the path, checking lights and props before the guests arrived. "I want to check the scenes after the actors are in place, too," Milton said. "We've had complaints. Some customers said they could smell booze, and someone was out-and-out belligerent last weekend. There's a group that swears they were attacked in that rear cornfield."

"Where they didn't belong," Bill said. "I talked to them. They were on all kinds of stuff, completely whacked out of their minds. Remember, the police had to take them into protective custody. And they described something that doesn't match any of our haunters."

"But what if they were attacked?"

Bill shrugged and laughed. "You know what Tom says: There's things in the woods. I'll take some of the back trails tonight—see what I can find."

I would have to be more cautious than usual. But a new idea formed in my mind. Actors caught drinking at their stations would lose their jobs. Maybe the zombies would have some beer. I resolved to steal it—from them or anyone else who had any. I would have drink, and I would save these terrible children from getting sacked. I would be doing them a favor.

Creeping to the maze, I kept still as darkness fell, barely concealed behind a curtain of elderberry bushes. No one noticed the rock that had not been there before. I waited until Mike and Biggie were busy with a constant stream of visitors, each letting his shuttered window, or "drop down," slam open to reveal a ghastly painted face bathed in unnatural green light. They did indeed have beer, along with something called energy drinks. Amidst the clamor and fright, I snatched away their refreshments. When Biggie wanted his goods, he found them missing. He searched fruitlessly among the tangled roots of the tree where he'd hidden them. He paced around and around the trunk, fuming and calling out to his friend, "What the fuck! Someone stole our stuff."

Far above his head, I pulled the metal ring off a tankard of ale. He heard it, just as he heard me noisily gulping down the brew.

"What the fuck!" the zombie cried. "What the fuck!" He could not fathom who or what could be up a tree enjoying his ale. I uncapped one of the sweet drinks and downed it quickly. It tasted vile even before it turned bitter on my tongue. Then I stuffed some of the sweets down my throat. True to form, my gut rebelled. A stream of black vomitus poured down from above and splattered at Biggie's feet.

"What's going on!" he shrieked, missing his cue for the next group of visitors coming through.

"What the hell! Did you shit yourself?" Mike asked, covering his nose as he emerged from behind the maze.

"Our stuff is gone," Biggie cried. "The snacks, the beer—all gone. Then all of a sudden this crap comes pouring down the side of the tree."

"It's an owl," Mike said. "They shit down the sides of trees."

"That's not an owl." Bill materialized behind the zombies. "Owl waste is white." He beamed his small torch on the pool of stinking vomit steaming at the foot of the tree. He probed the base of the tree with his light then flashed a brief arc of light up the trunk. I was high enough to avoid detection. "Whatever it is, it reeks. Are you sure you didn't shit yourself?" Bill laughed and went on his way.

A new stream of guests emerged from the foggy trail. I took that opportunity to creep across some swampy ground to the back parking lot. When the way was clear, I sprinted briefly into the clearing, my booty clutched to my chest, until I was safely behind one of the greenhouses. I slipped from shadow to shadow until

I came to the costuming area. It was time to repay my debt. I located Bill's truck and placed the food and drink I had stolen atop the beer he had brought for the bon fire, keeping two for myself. Bill could not fail to see it. He would know the thief had made restitution.

October 21, 2010

The stupid children who wanted to hunt ghosts were back, this time with beer. I could hear them from my cellar. The sun had set, and I knew they had school the next day, so I did not understand why they were invading my woods. Even worse, I could hear them cautiously treading on the unsteady floor above my head. They settled in, talking, laughing, and pulling metal rings off tankards of ale.

I did not wish to reveal myself, but I knew I could not allow anyone to remain in my house. They would grow comfortable and start poking around. They would see my writings. I had to drive them away once and for all.

I threw the black fabric over myself and grabbed a tarpaulin. There was a cellar door overgrown with vines that led to the rear of the house. It was off center and difficult to open because the roof and upper floor of the house sagged, but open it I did. It screeched and groaned and thumped—exactly what I wanted— and I made even more noise as I scaled the wall to the roof. I heard their excited chatter from within the house as they tried to identify the source of the noise.

I flattened myself against the roof next to the shattered remnants of the chimney and covered myself. Clouds streamed in to blot what remained of the light. Peering over the peak, I saw two boys tumble out the front door.

"Dude, it's just squirrels," someone called from inside.

"You know this place is haunted," said a female voice.

The two boys lobbed stones at the roof. They clattered back down the steep pitch and landed on the ground. One of them said, "I'll check the back."

I eased myself down to the lip of the roof where it dipped close to the ground. I tucked my arms and legs under the tarpaulin and turned to stone. Anyone who chose to do so could reach up and touch the blue material covering that section of the roof. Sure enough, the boy stared at my hiding place, squinting and turning his head this way and that. He stood on a fallen tree and reached up to feel around. The trunk rolled under his feet. He jumped down and turned his back on me, providing me the chance I needed.

I covered his face with the long bony fingers of both hands. He screamed as I lifted him off his feet and shook him. Then I threw him to the ground, quickly retreated up the roof to the derelict chimney, and flattened myself under the tarpaulin again. The boy's friends poured out the door, but when they stared at the lengthening shadows on the slate tiles, I had all but disappeared. They pointed and jabbered in terror. Then they ran for their lives. I was confident they would not return. No one would believe their wild tale if they chose to tell it.

I am pleased to write that they left their beer behind. There are two boxes of twelve casks each with only four missing. I kept the open crate for myself. The rest would be my gift to the actors. I heard them speak of a gathering—a "cast party"—following the last night of the revels on Saturday, the 30th.

I am grateful for the diversion they have provided. I will try to find more beer or spirits before the celebration commences. I will hide myself near the flickering bon fire and I will silently toast the haunters as they celebrate.

November 1, 2010

Yesterday was All Hallows' Eve, but there were no revels last night. I knew that—I had seen it so marked on the calendar, but I was not prepared for how forlorn I felt as I wandered the dark and shuttered sets of the hayride and walk-through. Demon was there, silently laughing. But while he took pleasure in my loss and sorrow, he did not seem unduly angered that I had found a few weeks' worth of distraction and solace.

Another profound disappointment: I was unable to participate in the haunters' celebration. I left the beer on one of the tables in the costuming area where it could not be missed. Justin found it and shared it later with some of his friends. But when the last revels ended and the actors removed their false faces and costumes, they filled their vehicles and traveled a short distance up the road.

I quickly scaled a tree to see where they were headed. They stopped at what appeared to be a brightly lit village. I followed the lights and found their vehicles outside a tavern with a blazing sign. The haunters were inside, feasting and drinking. I found a hiding place behind a gigantic metal container for garbage in an alley behind the kitchen.

The kitchen door was propped open, and I could hear the actors as they laughed and cheered and congratulated each other. It seemed awards were being presented for incomprehensible achievements, such as "MVP" or "Unsung Hero" or "Most Wetters in One Evening." Two haunters—Jon from the hayride and Jimmie from the walk-through, received "coffin nails" to a roar of acclaim from their colleagues. I had no idea why a coffin nail would be coveted. It did not matter. I longed so to be part of it. My heart ached almost as much as my nagging gut.

Long after the last inebriated celebrant staggered home and the tavern workers had departed, I drew my black fabric around me and wandered through the shadows of the village. It seemed to be made up of merchants, row upon row of them, many selling wares for which I could only guess the purpose. Behind the greens and the shops were taller buildings that appeared to be homes stacked one upon another. And everywhere there were flat paddocks for the metal vehicles everyone rode in wherever they went.

I came upon another large metal container spilling over not with refuse but with black bags filled with clothes. On the front of the box were the words, "Donate clothes and shoes to the needy." I was as needy as anyone, so I snatched up as many bags as I could carry and retreated to a dark alley to inspect the goods. I found two pairs of trousers and three shirts of a soft, thick fabric that would fit over my enormous belly, although they were a bit too short for my overlong limbs. I stuffed the clothing into a bag and fled to the darkness of the trees. Perhaps another time I might find a cloak or a head covering of some kind.

November 2, 2010

The sounds of construction are ringing through the woods again. They are coming from the direction of the farm. I leapt from tree to tree until I found a good vantage point. Milton, Justin, some of the actors, and farm workers were dismantling the hayride sets and carting them off to a greenhouse for storage. Some of the metal props were left where they were. This careful deconstruction can only mean that they plan to return in a year's time to stage the All Hallows Eve revels once again. So here, in my lonely, hungry hell, I can enjoy that small treasure which is hope. I would thank God if I knew where He was.

BONEBELLY

CHUPACABRA

THE KILLER WAS rarely seen. When it was spotted, it was from the corner of someone's eye, a darkly translucent and undulating mass. Perhaps eight feet long, it had grown wide as it fed, too wide for its winding trail to ever be mistaken for a snake. Floating just at the surface of the water or hidden under a pile of trash, it resembled nothing more than a contractor's trash bag. By the time its isolated victims saw it moving, it was too late.

It kept to the darkness and the damp, to the sewers and waterways. The hot southwestern sun poured right through the tough membrane of its skin, threatening to cook its gel-like insides. Keenly intelligent, it was perfectly capable of thinking its way into a new form, but it also had to avoid the notice of the Demon who was, no doubt, searching to recover his lost trophy. The escaped fiend did not want to be rushed into doing anything startling enough to bring the hell hunter down on its trail. In time, it would choose its final form and become magnificently terrifying.

At first, it did not need to feed often. After that first kill, it had watched the moon age a full cycle before it hunted again. It was content to hide in a rocky fissure and listen to the upheaval it had triggered. Even seasoned officials were deep-in-the-gut horrified by what they had seen.

This fear was the other appetite that demanded the satisfaction of a fresh kill. Yet the fiend denied itself as if keeping a holy fast. When it could wait no longer, it slowly edged away from its hiding place, sleeping during the day and slithering at night, farther and farther from the place where it had first escaped the Demon's grip.

It found its way to a river that ran beneath a bridge. Crowds of people came in the evenings to watch bats swarm from beneath the structure and wheel across the darkening sky. It ignored the spectators and waited for the still hours of the night. There were people who lived under the bridge. One man among them did not care for the companionship of the others. He always moved down the river bank to sleep behind the reeds.

The fiend chose an overcast night and waited for the camp to settle into snores and whispers. It glided below the surface of the river and eased itself onto the bank. A quick punch from its barb speared the man's heart. The venom pumped quickly through his veins. The man bolted upright, but when he tried to cry out, a clear sludge streamed from his mouth. The monster watched its victim die then sucked up the gelatinous mass at its leisure. Stubby fingers scraped the hair mat and clothing into the river before the beast floated downstream.

The creature hid among the reeds during the day, letting algae and weeds grow on its back. Within a week it resembled a mat of floating vegetation. It easily overtook the homeless or the occasional fisherman. If there was time, it liked to inject its venom where it would work slowly. It enjoyed watching its prey die in terror and confusion. Scaring people was fun.

While it journeyed through tributaries and sewers, it fed itself by taking down beasts that strayed across its path. The fiend clearly had no scent because it could easily surprise all manner of creatures—rabbits, coyotes, and armadillos. They were not as much fun to kill as humans, but the monster did enjoy the look of dumb, pained surprise as each animal collapsed into a pile of furry slime.

It found space under a pile of rocks near a great river to protect itself from the high summer sun. Daily it slept, letting a babble of voices wash over it and percolate through its dreams. Most of the voices spoke in Spanish. The fiend could understand them. It was the creature's first real memory. Somewhere, in another time and place, the creature had been well-educated. When it overheard the harmony produced by several female voices at once, something stirred inside that translucent bag of venom and hateful urges began to grow. He remembered he had once been male.

He learned from the voices that people were crossing a border between two countries. They were not supposed to be here and were fearful of being caught. The creature realized that, if any of them disappeared, they would not be missed for a long time.

The next time he heard voices in the night, he eased himself from under his shelter. As he undulated across the ground, he reasoned his movement would be easier if he had legs. But they did not automatically grow out of his desire as his other appendages had. This was disturbing, but he would have to examine this problem later. His hunger drove him forward. He eased his dusky bulk away from the water and waited. The lilt of cautious whispers floating above the river current grew closer and louder.

Ravenous as he was, he let the small group of three men pass by. One of them turned and hissed into the darkness at someone who lagged behind. A woman with a little girl scrambled breathlessly up the bank. The hissing man waited and took the child in his arms then spoke urgently to the woman. They needed to keep up with the other men. They were supposed to meet someone, and he was afraid they might lose their way in the dark. The fiend knew that if he could split the pair, he could easily take one of them down—preferably the female.

The monster needed speed. He pulled his bulk along the ground with his truncated arms while his body writhed like a frantic lizard.

Rushing to catch up to their companions, the little family heard scratching sounds behind them, like something of great size crawling on its belly through the dust and pebbles. They stopped to listen. The father gave the child to his wife, took a hunting knife from his belt, and scanned the ground with a flashlight. Some distance ahead, someone shouted at him to turn it off.

A black, scuffling shape separated husband from wife. The woman spun in a circle, breathing hard. Something punctured her calf and she cried out, dumping her daughter on the dusty ground. She reached for the girl, but a dark mass slithered between mother and child. A thin white wand flashed in the darkness.

The flashlight beam fell on the mass as it lunged for the shrieking child. The father threw itself on top of the undulating creature, stabbing frantically at what he hoped was the brain. In fact, the man was riding and stabbing the monster's posterior. A guttural, gurgling cry issued from the other end. The bulky form heaved upward and the man rolled off. The monster turned on his attacker, but the man was too agile. He leapt aside, snatched up his sobbing daughter, and lifted her off the ground—but not before the white wand speared the girl's leg.

By now, the two companions had heard the screams and raced back toward the river. "What's happening?" they cried in Spanish.

"It's a monster!" shouted the man. "It's still here. Be careful!"

His friends never had a chance to react. The malformed thing reared up in the flashlight orbs, waving its stunted arms and tiny hands. A barb flew from its mouth, connecting with the frozen men, piercing one under the rib cage, the other in the groin. Then the fiend, bleeding violet ooze from its wounds, dropped to the ground. It rolled sideways into a rocky declivity and peered over the edge with red porcine eyes.

The lone unscathed traveler clutched his girl to his chest and scanned the area with his flashlight, calling out to his companions, "Are you all right? Answer me! Someone say something." His light fell on his wife. She had dropped to her knees and stared at her husband in wide-eyed horror, hands stretched forth in supplication. Someone moaned, "It burns. My God, it burns." His wife opened her mouth to speak. All that came out was a retching sound and thick, pinkish slurry that smelled both sweet and sour. As she collapsed on her side, the man realized he could see right through her skin and watch her bones dissolve. Then his child's body sagged over his arm like a garment bag. Horrified, he dropped the child, and as she hit the ground, her fluid-filled body burst open like a water balloon.

The man was screaming now, one impossibly protracted shriek after another, but his friends had fallen silent. As his light swung back and forth, he watched each man collapse into a transparent bag of dissolving organs. Blue lights winked in a circle around him. He backed away from the ring of liquefying corpses, wailing and slashing the thick, warm air with his knife.

The man, gaping and stabbing at nothing, watched the hulking worm heave forward into the circle of the dead, to the broken bag of jellied girl-child, and noisily suck the sludge down his gullet. The beast regarded the man with small pig-like eyes. His mouth slit stretched into a smile, liquefied remains dribbling into the sand.

When the monster finished with the girl, he turned and squirmed to the flattened bag that used to be a woman. She was only half consumed when the sky lightened to rose-tinted gray. He abandoned the remaining kills and inched slowly towards the river, a thin purple trail of fluid streaming behind him. The man watched him roll over the edge of the sloping river bank and heard the generous splash as its bulk entered the water.

Two days later, a pair of border patrol agents found the man. The immigrant sat without moving under the brutal sun. He had food and water but had touched neither. To his right and left were hair mats and clothes, stiff with salts that sparkled in the sun. In front of the survivor were the outlines of two men, formed from that same chemical crust, each thick enough to fill out their clothing. Raised impressions resembled the swirls of palm and finger prints where the hands should be. Eyes, nostrils and yawning mouths stood out on flattened heads. The agents could even tell how one face differed from the other.

"What the fuck," breathed the younger man. "Is this real?"

"What happened here?" His older partner addressed the stunned survivor in Spanish. "Did you do this?"

The man stared, his lips moving soundlessly.

The agent picked his way carefully around the waxy shapes. He squatted down in front of the man and repeated, "What is this? What happened here?"

The man blinked, seeming to notice for the first time he was not alone. He gestured weakly at the remains. "Chupacabra," he whispered. "Mi nina. Mi esposa. Chupacabra."

"Look at this." The young agent pointed at the sand. There was a thick, wavy pattern in the dust.

"Is that from a snake?" asked his partner.

"It's too fat. And look there." The young man pointed to the dirt on either side of the outline. "Do you see 'em?"

The older agent inspected where his partner pointed. There were hand prints alternately placed on either side of the sinuous drag marks. It appeared they had been used to help move a huge slug-like body over the ground. A trail of deep purple dollops followed the prints. The agent stared at his younger partner and wondered again, "What the fuck happened here?"

"Chupacabra," whispered the immigrant. He fell over and began to convulse.

The Mexican died before help could be summoned. Within hours, a small army of local law enforcement, forensic, and medical specialists descended on the scene. It did not take long for them to determine that the lone survivor had not caused these deaths but had witnessed something truly gruesome. As they tried to understand what had killed the four victims, someone recalled reading about the case of a teenaged boy who had disappeared, leaving behind nothing but fouled clothing and a shock of hair.

Someone at the sheriff's office overheard a reference to the immigrant's last words, and the chupacabra story started passing from person to person. By the time the New Year arrived, the tales had surfaced in the tabloids, all with incorrect locations, imaginary witnesses, and even more fantastic descriptions.

The fiend slowly made his way along the river, stinging and gulping down anything he could find to fill his alimentary canal. As he fed, his stab wounds quickly formed scar tissue, light gray tiger stripes across his charcoal hide. Day by day he felt stronger, yet, as the summer progressed, his appetite expanded into a nearly insatiable drive. His girth ballooned accordingly.

Tangled threads of memory muddled his thoughts. He saw brief flashes that told him he had been a handsome, calculating man with lustful appetites as well as the freedom and power to indulge them. In his present form, the fiend was as far removed from that resplendent creature as a maggot from an eagle. He loved the means he had devised for killing and arousing hysterical terror in his victims. His sagging, flaccid body, however, was loathsome even to himself. It frightened him that he had wanted legs to carry him quickly away from the knife-wielding man and they had not formed. Was he to be cemented into this form forever? The fiend could not accept this.

He knew instinctively that he was better suited for colder, cloudier climes. The fiend watched the movement of the sun across the sky and began to navigate waterways that took him north. He hunted fish and mammals that abounded by the rivers, but they were not as satisfying as that sentient meat, the one that quivered in exquisite terror as it dissolved.

As he migrated, he learned that scores of people came to the great rivers to play along the banks—fishing, boating, swimming, or sometimes just lying in the grass and stroking each other. They were often nearly naked, and sight of their lithe, tanned bodies aroused a lust that could only be satisfied with cruelty.

He alternated between dark waters and patches of sunlight to dazzle and blind potential victims. When a beautiful young man or woman left their friends in the shallows and swam out to deeper waters, the creature would strike. He would grab his prey by the shoulders and pull them underwater. A quick barb in the throat incapacitated them. When he judged they were no longer able to speak, he loosened his hold slightly so their heads broke the surface of the water. As the monster towed them upstream, they could watch their friends grow smaller in the distance. His newly generated organ throbbed, and his belly growled as he watched the blue lights in the brain wink and go out. He would find some sheltered shallows where he could plunge his featureless face into the viscous guts and suck them down until he felt ready to burst. Dazed and glutted, he drowsed, lulled by the sorrowful sounds of search parties down river. It never occurred to anyone to work against the current and search up river from the supposed drowning site. When the fiend was ready to move on, he sank the clothing and hair in the swirling deeps, leaving a lovely iridescent slick on the water.

The nights grew cool, the trees changed color, and the fiend had grown fat. He kept moving but had to avoid shallow tributaries because only deep water could support his considerable bulk. On dry land, he wheezed with the effort of heaving his body about. When he slept, the great bag of guts tingled, as if hair and limbs and nails wanted to burst from beneath the sheath of his charcoal skin. It filled him with hope that the handsome man he saw in his dreams—the one with formidable cunning and a bottomless appetite for cruelty—was his true form.

Early snows fell in the forested foothills of the great mountain range that reared in the distance. He found a rocky den overlooking a river where he could surrender to his increasing lethargy and his urge to sleep through the winter. Months of gluttony had bulked him up with the raw materials necessary for shaping his true self. If he could sink into his dreams, he might emerge in the spring as the glorious monster he had glimpsed in his knotted skein of memories.

The beast labored to fetch loads of reeds to his den. When he had piled up several layers, he burrowed between them, curled tightly into a ball, and descended rapidly into a heavy slumber. Dream images rose up, and the first thing he saw was a rude dwelling with a sturdy table next to a fireplace. Two men were seated there. Everything about their clothing and furnishings suggested a different time.

One of the men was somewhat tall, but soft and round at the middle. The other was perfectly proportioned, with black hair and dark eyes. This man stared at a servant girl, who tried to keep herself at a distance. He ordered her to approach. Her eyes were filled with terror, but haltingly she obeyed. He pinched the soft flesh of her buttocks. He smiled as she gritted her teeth, refusing to cry out.

"Here, have a turn," the handsome man said, pushing the girl towards the other end of the table. She stumbled, and the pale man put a hand out to break her fall. His eyes met the handsome man's contemptuous sneer, and the hand dropped back to the table. The girl fell to the floor. Still, she did not cry out. As she pulled herself to her feet, she threw both men a glare of hatred and disdain. The heavy man responded by grabbing the flesh near her breast and pinching. The girl stifled a cry. He looked eagerly to his companion for approval. The dark-haired fiend beamed with pride.

And as the creature slept on, he acquired his true voice. He moaned a long and lustful song of satisfaction.

ALIEN ENCOUNTERS

I 'VE SEEN IT," Sean said to Amy. The cast party had ended, and they were stretched out on the furniture in Amy's living room. "I've seen Tom's yeti." Curled up on an arm chair, Amy had been drifting off to sleep. She bolted upright. "Tom's yeti? Did you really see it, or do you just think you saw it?"

Sean smiled. "I really, really saw it. It was running across the parking lot from the end of the Dungeon towards the greenhouses. It ducked behind the toilets, and it was carrying a six pack of beer."

Amy burst out laughing. "Beer? So he's the one who stole from Bill's truck?"

"I think he was paying Bill back. But he's definitely not a yeti or a Sasquatch. Actually, he looks a lot like what those lost customers described—like your drawing, too. Where are the sketches you made?"

"Somewhere in my room. Let's look at them in the morning," Amy yawned.

They slept past noon and awoke to the smells of Gloria's pancakes and coffee. They took their breakfast to the living room, where Amy spread out her sketchbooks and scraps of drawings.

"Here it is," Amy said, flipping through the pages of one of the books. "You're saying the creature looked like this?"

Sean repositioned himself next to her and studied the drawing. "Got some pencils?" He placed the picture on the coffee table, picked up an empty sketchbook and began to draw. "It's weird how close your drawing is to the real thing," he said. "You got the overall body—a skeleton covered with skin—and the teeth and claws." Sean worked quickly to copy Amy's picture then began adding features, explaining as he worked. "The head was much bigger—huge, in fact. I don't know how his little pencil neck held it up. He had long yellow hair, all tangled and stringy. He was wearing a poncho of some kind, but it was torn and up around his shoulders. I could see his whole body. And he had this."

"A belly?" Amy exclaimed. "It was that big?"

"It was enormous. I'll bet he can't see his own feet."

"And you're sure it was a he?"

"Well, yeah. There was nothing boob-like, but there was this." Almost as an afterthought, Sean sketched a stubby dog tail where the genitals would attach.

"And he was carrying beer. So why was he climbing all over Tom's house? Was he looking for human flesh or Jack Daniels?"

"Bourbon marinated man burgers." Sean shook his head. "It's so amazing. We have a creature—a real creature. I think we should go out in the woods and look for him."

"What if he *is* a man eater?" Amy wondered.

"He was bringing beer to Bill. How dangerous could he be? But we should have some kind of a plan before we go charging into the woods."

Amy leaned back, her eyes wide with amazement. "You know, whatever his story is, we should write it. This could be the graphic novel we've been wanting to do. We investigate, maybe get some pictures. We get a sense of what kind of creature it is and take it from there. And we need to give him a name." She thought a moment, and then all but shouted, "Bonebelly."

"Bonebelly," Sean repeated. "That's it. That's friggin' incredible."

They discussed how and where they should search. They considered using Google Earth to locate the swamp where the old man's remains had been found last summer. It was believed the man had died of natural causes and his remains scavenged. The creature could have been among the scavengers. However, searching the swamp felt too much like grave desecration. They decided in the end to stay close to Bone Ridge, which they knew he had visited at least twice. It suggested Bonebelly was not hunting but liked the haunt and would return if he had the chance.

"He might come back Friday night, thinking it's still open," Amy reasoned. "Then maybe hang around to watch the build-down, especially if there's beer. You're helping with that, right?"

"Yeah, if it doesn't rain. You could poke around the edges while we work and see if he shows up. Just don't go off too far by yourself."

"Maybe we should get some beer? You know, something to lure him in?"

"I can get some from my dad. He always has beer. He never remembers how much he drinks, so he won't miss it." There was more bitterness in Sean's voice than he intended.

Milton and some of the farm workers had been there throughout the week, disassembling, labeling, and storing anything that could be damaged by weather or vandals over the winter months. There was still much to do. Sean helped take down painted canvas and camouflage netting as the sun set. Makeup, masks, appliances, and latex were crated up to be stored at Milton's house. Costumes had been washed, and Amy worked alongside Meg and Jen to sort, set aside for repairs, or lay them away in labeled, plastic tubs. When they finished, she edged away from the women, pulled her hood over her hair and her flashlight from her pocket.

She first skirted the edges of the hayride, poking through the brush and peering upward through the branches of the trees. She wondered how a white, bony creature with an enormous head and belly had only been seen by Tom, Sean, and a few whacked out revelers. It had to have some kind of superb camouflage other than the pathetic black cloak Sean had seen streaming out behind the creature. She wondered if it was watching her right now. She shivered and backed up to the cornfield's trail.

Amy avoided the tunnel altogether and jogged over to the walk-through. The squeal of power drills pulling screws out of plywood reverberated through the trees. They were dismantling the maze. That placed Sean, Justin, and Jimmy near the end of the walk-through. Amy could explore the front half of the trail without drawing attention from anyone.

A six pack of cans in her backpack, she walked slowly, swinging her flashlight back and forth to illuminate the branches overhead. She spotted nothing resembling the creature Sean had seen. All she saw was a large owl, peering down at her with green eyes. She trained her light back on the path, took a few steps forward, and then stopped. *Green eyes?* She put the spotlight back where the owl had been. It was still there, watching her with cat-like emerald eyes. It had the general shape of an owl, but its wings were devoid of feathers. Its body was covered in overlapping scales. And it had teeth. Amy saw them flash as it grinned at her. She cried out and dropped her flashlight. When she raised the beam back to the branch, it was empty.

Amy backed away from the tree and ran towards the sounds of people. She reported to Sean what she had seen, and then suggested, "Maybe we should look for Bonebelly in the daytime. I mean, there's no law that says we have to search at night."

"You're right," Sean said. "That's a horror movie cliché. You want to check out that swampy area?"

"I'm thinking we should search the second cornfield—the place where those tripping idiots said they were attacked by a monster."

"We can leave the beer in the woods bordering the field. Then we'll hide in a tree and wait."

Amy shifted nervously. "Should we bring something with us, in case it's not safe? I have a big kitchen knife."

"Sure. I'll bring a bat."

There was less work available in the winter once the haunt had been taken down. There would be wreaths and Christmas trees to sell but little else until spring. Sean had fewer hours, and Amy's schedule was flexible. They set aside a Saturday afternoon in mid-November to set out their bait.

Sean borrowed his father's truck, which they parked in a field on the side road that bordered the hay ride. They entered the farm behind the greenhouses and cut across the orchard unseen. Brown and russet leaves drifted everywhere underfoot. They could not walk without making sounds like waves rolling across the shore. "This is no good," Sean said. "If he is around, he'll hear us coming a mile away."

"Let's set out the bait and get up a tree," Amy said. "Give me half the beer."

"Why? We're not separating."

"We have phones. We can take pictures and call each other if we see anything."

Sean reluctantly agreed. They headed into the trees by the cornfield. Sean helped Amy hoist herself onto a low branch of a maple tree. He took himself even deeper into the woods and found a perch as far off the ground as he could manage. His view took in the tree tops in a wide circle, the fields of Stone Ridge Farm, and the edge of the shopping center a half mile up the road.

They sat quietly except for a few text messages between them. By four o'clock the light began to fade and the shadows lengthen. That was when Sean heard the sound of someone taking long strides in the woods, cutting great swaths through drifts of crisp leaves with every step. Sean turned his head in the direction of the noise, expecting to see a hunter pass directly under him. No one was there. His attention was redirected forward by the flapping of a great pair of wings. He spied what appeared to be a giant owl skimming the air just above the ground. He knew it was no owl, and it was headed in Amy's direction. He scrambled down and ran towards his friend.

As Amy scanned the treetops and the ground below, she was startled to spy a pair of green cat's eyes staring back at her from a tree across the path. It was the strange owl-like creature she had seen in the walk-through two weeks ago. This time the creature was close enough to reveal details Amy had missed before. The sharp raptor's beak was actually a thin, hooked nose over a pair of lips and some rather threatening teeth. The overlapping scales on its chest were thick, not unlike a bronze coat of mail. It had four sets of talons gripping the branch, indicating it was some sort of squatting homunculus. Amy cried out as it spread its leathery wings and glided over to her tree, roosting on a limb just above her head. She pulled her knife out of her back pack and held it before her face.

The creature climbed down the trunk head first, pausing less than three feet away. Amy glanced down at the ground. She estimated she was about ten feet up. She could drop out of the tree and run if necessary. When she looked back, the creature's face was only inches from her own. It stared intently into her eyes and smiled. She stifled a cry and pressed back against the trunk.

Her heart pounding, Amy sized up the creature as she readied her escape. It was only three feet tall, but it looked dangerous. It watched her as if it knew her and was waiting for a reciprocal sign of recognition. "But that could be a trick," she said out loud without meaning to. The creature raised his eyebrows as if he understood what she meant.

"That could be your trick, to draw people in," Amy continued. "You act as if we should know each other. And then, what? Do you eat people? Suck out their souls?"

The creature's smile widened with delight.

"You're some kind of bad fairy," Amy guessed. "But you look more like a little demon." Amy could not conceal her fascination. "I should be afraid of you."

Demon seemed to agree. She should indeed be afraid.

"But I'm not." That was a lie. "Is that because I'm a good person? Or maybe that's part of the trick. You lull me into a sense of false security, and when my defenses are down you lunge for my soul and take it to hell." Nothing changed in Demon's nodding demeanor. Amy found it annoying. "So which is it: You can't touch me because I'm good, or you can snatch my innocent soul away to eternal darkness any time you want?"

Demon only grinned.

"That's how you do it, isn't it? You just agree with people and let them believe whatever they want. Say a child molester tells you what he does is okay because he loves little children, you agree with him. And if a president says we'll go to war because God is on our side, you agree with him. And if some preacher says, 'God is killing our soldiers because of gay marriage,' you just smile and nod. And you let them all go on hurting and hating because someday you know they will be yours." As Demon smiled back at her, she added, "And you could just be agreeing with me to trick me into doing the wrong thing."

Demon gave her a crafty sidelong glance.

Exasperated, Amy put her knife back in her pack. "Okay, here's the deal. I am a pure soul. I don't hurt people and I do a lot of good things. I know you can't touch me. So I want you to go away, leave me, my family, and my friends alone." She did not wait for an acknowledgement. She grabbed the branch on which she sat and swung herself down to the ground.

She nearly landed on top of Sean, who stood on the ground gripping his bat with both hands. His face seemed a trifle pale. "How long have you been standing there?" Amy asked.

"Long enough to hear everything," Sean replied. He peered up into the tree. "I think it's gone. Jesus, weren't you scared?"

Amy realized that her knees were indeed shaking. She nodded. Sean hugged her close as she shivered. She cast an uneasy glance around the woods. "Maybe we should get out of here."

Sean gripped his bat in one hand and put his free arm around Amy's waist. Together they moved at a steady trot through the gathering darkness until they were back at the truck. They drove to the Italian place up the road from the farm and split a pizza.

"Why do you think that thing was there?" Sean asked.

"Hunting for souls?" Amy suggested. "What does any demon want? You heard how the conversation went."

Sean nodded. "It was kind of one-sided. But I'm wondering if there's a connection to Bonebelly. Two strange, otherworldly creatures hanging around the edges of a haunt in Rhode Island? That's not a coincidence."

Amy doodled demon pictures on her napkins. "Tom says there's things in the woods. Either the demon or Bonebelly or both could have been hanging around for centuries. Maybe Bonebelly is the demon's creature. He's the instrument the devil uses to punish sinners."

"People have claimed to see the devil since Pilgrim days. No one's ever described anything like Bonebelly—until now." He thought a moment and wondered, "Why Rhode Island? Like Rhode Island's the most evil place in the entire United States?" Sean sounded offended. "I mean, it's got its weird side. We got Poe. We got H.P. Lovecraft. We got Foster. But we're small. There's got to be better places to hunt for rotten souls."

§ § §

Demon had to admit he did not know what to make of the girl in the woods. He was both amused and impressed. She'd had the audacity to look him squarely in the face and order him to go away. She was completely unaware that her boyfriend stood beneath the tree the entire time, ready to battle a denizen of hell for her sake.

It was her eyes that had drawn him into making contact. He had seen those eyes before: hazel flecked with gold, startling in their clarity, and hinting at wisdom within. She shared this time and place with the tormented hungry ghost Demon had snatched from its dark, blasphemous life. Demon had not seen this coming at all. It meant that his Boss had chosen the time and place of this particular corner of hell for the benefit of more than one soul. Demon understood the outcome his Boss anticipated, but he did not share her faith in the wretched creature he had molded. It was weak and devoid of any kind of moral compass. But he would keep his opinion to himself. Opinions had gotten him into trouble before, and she was already upset that he allowed the other monster to elude him. Demon resolved to keep quiet, find the missing fiend, and tend to his many clients according to his job description and without complaint. After all, even when he adhered to the job protocols he got to be creative. Most of the time, his job was fun.

§ § §

During the following week, it came to Gloria's attention that Sean and Jeff had no place to go for Thanksgiving. They usually had dinner with Sean's aunt in Cranston, but the family was sick with some sort of stomach bug. When Gloria heard that, her maternal instinct kicked in. She went down the hall Wednesday afternoon to convince Jeff and Sean to accompany her to her brother's house for Thanksgiving dinner. They politely declined and went out to a local restaurant. This did not deter Gloria. She bought a ham, "Just to change things up," she said, and stayed up Thursday night to make home-made pies. She succeeded in convincing father and son to come to dinner on Friday. It helped that Sean knew what a good cook Gloria was, especially when she felt inspired. But what surprised and pleased Sean was that when Gloria opened a bottle of wine, Jeff declined. Gloria nodded as if she understood and left her glass untouched.

Amy and Sean retreated to Amy's room to work on a story board for their graphic novel. They listened as their parents engaged in conversation about parenting concerns and saving money in difficult times. Jeff even committed to working for the local gift drive with Gloria. The young people smiled at each other. Gloria's simple gesture had opened some door, and after years of nodding acquaintance when she met Jeff in the hall, a friendship seemed to be developing.

Between school, the farm, and sketching, the young people had no time to resume the search for Bonebelly. Then, two days after Christmas, it snowed. They had spoken of this eventuality as their Plan B: Fresh snow meant tracks they could follow. The storm was supposed to clear out overnight, so Amy and Sean decided to go deeper into the woods the next morning to a stream where wildlife came for fresh water. They would then backtrack towards the second cornfield, hopefully without getting lost.

As they watched the drifts pile up against the building, Amy shivered and slipped an arm around Sean's waist. He hugged her to his side. If either was frightened of what they might find, they said nothing about it. They smiled at each other and the snow outside. It was fun to feel scared.

BONEBELLY

WINTERING OVER

November 6, 2010

NOW THE WOODS are quiet. There are no machines smoothing out the roads. No one is clearing out trees or building new houses. They are still bringing in apples and pumpkins at the farm, but the All Hallows revels have fallen completely silent. I have remembered my hunger or, rather, my hunger has remembered me. I was able to briefly elude it during those pageants, feeding my curiosity and my loneliness rather than my belly.

How I miss my haunters.

I thought I saw Demon in the woods today, but it turned out to be a great horned owl. He continues to watch me, but the visits have become more infrequent. I cannot be the only great sinner in this world. There must be other souls that require his peculiar care.

Without him, I fear I have no conscience. I have hurt creatures great and small and nearly killed three people in a predatory rage. It was only the prospects of even worse punishments that prevented a wholesale slaughter in my little corner of hell.

November 8, 2010

Before it is too late, I must become like the squirrels. It is getting colder and damper all the time. I must try to set aside victuals for the longest, darkest, coldest nights to come. Yesterday, I climbed to the top of the tall tree on the hill and surveyed the area farms. There must be fallen apples and root vegetables left in the fallow fields, so I decided I would forage at a different one each night, filling the bags I borrowed from the greenhouses with as much as I could find.

Last night I clothed myself in the dark trousers and shirt I had taken from the donation box. My head was so pale and enormous I needed to cover it if I wanted to be out in the open, but all I had was the black fabric I had fashioned into a hood.

The evening air was bitter. A killing frost was on its way. I found my first orchard but crushed much of the fruit underfoot. It is just past the dark of the moon and difficult to see. In the uncut grass, I probed around for apples that did not feel soft and rotten to the touch. There were not many worth retrieving, but as I lifted each prize, the scent of apples filled my nostrils. I held one that was particularly unspoiled. Its shape, its weight, its skin felt so wonderful in my hand. I carved a thin slice with one of my talons and laid it carefully on my tongue. I tasted one aching, brief flush of sweetness before the fruit turned to ashes. Sadly, I would not be vouchsafed another unspoiled taste. But I am still granted the benefice of smell. It is probably intended as a torment, but I am glad I get to keep that much.

November 15, 2010

I have visited all the local farms to glean what was unwanted by my neighbors. It was a mean harvest. I went to Stone Ridge last of all, Saturday before darkness had fallen completely, so I could forage in the makeup greenhouse for anything that might be useful. It was empty except for some chairs and the rude plank table the actors used as they adorned themselves for their dark festivities. I found more writing utensils and another box filled with paper, printed on one side with information about the revels. I wrapped it in a tunic someone left behind. I am wearing that tunic as I write. It was fashioned for a large man, so it actually covers my enormous belly. It is black and made of a thick, soft, and fleecy fabric, unlike anything I have ever seen. It is wonderfully warm.

There were also cups made of a thin, glass-like material, a rusted hammer, a box of nails, and a knife with a serrated edge I could open and close as I wished. I found a small tube-shaped torch that is wonderfully bright for its size.

Out in the field I found three squashes that had been gnawed by animals. Then I climbed to the top of one of the apple trees to search for any fruit that had been missed during the harvest. That was when I heard voices and had to make the best use I could of the meager cover the bare branches provided. I spied two youths, a male and a female, hurrying along as if they did not want to be caught by the night. My bundle of found goods lay at the base of the tree, but fortunately the pair did not notice it. I recognized them, even in the lowering darkness. They helped build the scenery for the revels and were both talented artists. They also worked at the revels but not as actors. I believe their names are Sean and Amy. They whispered nervously to each other as they ran, but I could only make out one word: demon.

I know why demon keeps watch over me. I am a sinner, and I am already condemned to my own individual hell. But why would he show himself to well-mannered young people such as these?

November 26, 2010

I climbed to the top of my favorite look-out tree yesterday morning. As I surveyed my surroundings, I saw that the local merchants seemed to be shut down and the roads were nearly free of conveyances. It appeared as though almost everyone was observing some kind of Sabbath—something I had not witnessed before, even on Sundays. I realized it would be a good day to search for something else I needed.

The near discovery of my dwelling place by those drunken louts last summer convinced me that I needed a second emergency refuge. I roamed the borders of the woodlands looking for ruined cellars or abandoned barns that might suit my need. But I was put to flight by more than one alert dog. I returned to the merchant village instead to sort through the clothing donations. I found a bowl-shaped knitted hat that I could stretch across my oversized pate. I found another pair of trousers and a warm shirt.

On my return to the root cellar, I passed along the edge of the Stone Ridge orchard. It occurred to me that the abandoned structures from the hayride or the walk-through could be put to use at least through the winter and spring. The farmer's dog was no concern. He was old, fat, and lazy. He barked at everything inconsequential and slept through disturbances that should raise alarms. No one paid attention to him.

I explored the walk-through at my leisure. A few structures and props remained in place: the mausoleum in the graveyard, the motorized hearse, the long metal structure they called a trailer, and the dungeon tunnel. I let myself into the hearse. I could sit comfortably on the cushioned seats and lie down in the back, although it was a bit cramped for my long legs and great belly. It might be useful should the area be lashed by a blizzard. Unfortunately, I discovered the mausoleum was open to the sky. The trailer was locked. The dungeon could serve but was open at both ends.

I moved to the hayride. Every structure had been removed except for the tunnel. But as I inspected it, I realized I had found exactly what I needed. It was completely enclosed. The doors at either end were not locked and easily manipulated by hand. Inside there was a stage platform and wooden panels for hiding the actors. I had concealed myself under the platform before. It was roomy enough for my gangly body. It was also closed in on three sides and thus would make a snug and cozy place to sleep.

I pulled a bright blue sheet from a nearby shed and used it to drag piles of leaves from the wooded perimeter. They were damp, but they would dry and provide comfortable bedding. I found it so satisfying that I took my rest there well into the early morning hours. As I slept, it seemed I could hear the sound of the All Hallows Eve revels once again. I could almost count myself content.

December 1, 2010

When I climb high in the trees at night, I see strange fairy lights adorning many of the homes clustered in the distance. At Stone Ridge there are signs announcing "Xmas trees and wreaths. Order your holiday pies and cakes." If I am resting in the tunnel, I hear voices singing about the birth of Jesus.

It seems that the people who live here are preparing for a month of revels, just as they did for All Hallows Eve. If every feast day is observed for an entire month, how does anyone fit them into a calendar year? How does any work get done?

No wonder their children are so lazy.

December 17, 2010

It is bitter, bitter cold. Over the past month I have carefully parceled out bits of apple and pumpkin and swallowed a ration of the ashen fruit each day. It will not last the winter. I go hunting for rabbits and chipmunks, but they are hiding in their winter dens. There are fewer squirrels out and about. I catch mice as they try to raid my winter stores, but they do not even make a mouthful. My belly is a hollow abyss and it hurts, it hurts, it hurts.

December 28, 2010

Several inches of snow fell yesterday. After a day in retreat snug in their nests, the squirrels are likely to emerge to find their hidden stores of food. Today would be a good day to hunt, so I went out and crept quietly through the woods. In the first light of dawn I found a tree and roosted, still as I could be, and waited for squirrels to stray within reach. As the light strengthened, however, I soon realized the squirrels knew I was there and were avoiding my perch.

It seems my clothing gave me away. When I am naked and still, living things usually do not notice me until I reach for them. Now, masquerading as a man in my black trousers and tunic, the forest creatures clearly see me no matter how motionless I sit. I do not understand why this should be. It almost seems my grotesque face and form are so beyond belief they confound the senses of the living.

The squirrels were chattering warnings to each other, so I knew I would have to reposition myself. Suddenly, I heard human voices calling out, "Look! What's that in the tree?"

I immediately clawed my way up the tree and leapt from crown to crown until I had put considerable distance between myself and the intruders. But they continued to shout to each other, and the increasing volume of their cries indicated they were in pursuit. I dropped to the ground, peeled off my clothing, and stuffed it under a log. Then I ducked behind a tangle of bare grape vines and held my breath. I was shivering badly, and it was difficult to stay still. Even so, my pursuers walked right by me. They stopped, turned in a circle and scanned the tree tops.

I recognized them. I had seen them several weeks before, passing through the orchard, speaking of the demon they had encountered in the woods.

"It was big and black," the boy said to the girl. "It might have been a bear."

"They can't leap from tree to tree like that, can they?" she said. "Anyway, bears should be hibernating. I think it's our yeti. He's wearing clothes. It's cold, after all."

They sat down on the log where I had hidden my garments. I was right in front of them, but they did not see me even as I cautiously raised my head to get a better look at them. It was indeed Amy and Sean. They held small, flat rectangles in their hands and whispered to each other. I strained to listen to them. They discussed how they wished to make a likeness of the creature the young man had seen carrying beer at the haunt and how they even hoped to engage it in conversation. They were talking about me!

They remained there a long time, hugging each other for warmth and sharing a hot drink. Crouching naked in the snow was becoming painful, but I did not dare move. Finally, Sean said, "If it was him, I think we scared him off. Let's look for some footprints." Amy nodded and they plodded through the snow in the direction of Stone Ridge Farm.

I was freezing. I wanted to retreat to my cellar to dry my clothes and get out of the cold, but my curiosity was overpowering. I let the pair get ahead of me then crept after them. As they neared the back corn field, I climbed a tree so I could continue watching them. I lost my footing on an icy branch. My claws raked the bark as I scrambled for a new hold. They heard the noise and turned to look. I flattened myself against the trunk and went still. The girl lifted her face, and I looked into her eyes. Her brow furrowed as if she was trying to distinguish my form from the snow cloaking the tree. She motioned for Sean to follow her, and soon they both stood at the foot of my tree, looking straight up.

Her eyes were a clear, bright hazel, possessed of an understanding beyond her years. Something stirred inside me, and I thought I had seen those eyes before. And suddenly, I felt overwhelmed with shame, as if I had somehow wronged the girl. I carefully lowered my eyes so our gazes could not connect. She stared at me several moments longer without perceiving me. Then she shook her head and said, "I thought I saw something. Nothing's there. Let's go." She crossed from woods to field. Sean followed, but not before casting one last look around. He scowled with a fiercely protective look, as if there was nothing he would not do to shield Amy from harm. It seemed to me I had seen that look before, too.

December 31, 2010

It is snowing again today, the last day of the year. It is windy as well and bitingly cold. I have spent the daylight hours stripping lichens and twigs from the trees, like deer in the winter. I would call it a dry and flavorless fare, but in truth it is indistinguishable from the bitter ashes I taste when I bite into a beautiful gold and red apple. Hunting remains difficult in this weather. I have searched the roads at night for animals killed by vehicles, but there are few to find.

Tonight, the old year will end and a new one will begin. Nothing will change for me. The pain in my belly is made worse by the way my bones ache in the cold, my feet and hands in particular. I have not yet found shoes or gloves that will fit my oversized extremities. Some animals sleep through the winter. I found myself wondering if I could do the same. My den under the tunnel stage is a comforting place to me. It is risky to be so close to people for great lengths of time, especially if I should enjoy the sweet oblivion of a lengthy slumber. But I must try it. I do not know how I shall make it through a cold and prolonged period of starvation without losing whatever sanity I have left in this mad existence.

January 3, 2011

I cannot go to the merchant village ever again. It is too risky. I went because there are public houses there such as the one the haunters used to hold their "cast party." Great amounts of food are thrown away in huge refuse barrels every night. It is so wasteful. Does no one keep pigs around here? Since no one else seemed to want it, I decided to help myself to the leavings. In the cold weather, it does not spoil—not that it matters.

I learned last night the village has a watchman. I was behind a victualer who baked "donuts" and brewed coffee. Scattered on the ground were pamphlets that I realized were calendars for 2011. I picked one up and turned through the leaves. Each month had a picture of donuts or other baked goods, all of which looked foreign to me.

Suddenly, a bright light shone in my face. I looked up to see a young man in uniform. I was clothed, but his mouth gaped when he saw my face and claws. He backed away from me, pulling from his pocket one of those small boxes I have seen so many people speaking into or tapping with their fingers. He pushed it in my face. I was not sure what he was doing, but it flashed in my eyes and that infuriated me. I bared my teeth at him and lunged. He dropped the box and ran.

When I retrieved the object, I was both amazed and horrified by what I saw. It had made a miniature portrait of me. I heard the banshee wail in the night air that told me the sheriff was on his way, so I took my calendar and my portrait and ran through back alleys to the woods.

The undulating howl quickly died away, but I do not think I will leave my cellar for several days.

January 4, 2011

I explored the little box until it sputtered and died. There are small, numbered discs on it. I spent hours tapping them in different sequences to see how they responded. They produced a series of odd sounds, mostly bells and gongs. I even heard muffled, disembodied voices that spoke to me but, dissatisfied by my silence, called me names and went away. I found a portfolio of other miniatures, including nude poses by one particular young woman. There were also pictures of some of the actors at Bone Ridge. That means the young watchman either visited the haunt or was one of the actors. There are written messages stored under a title called "text." I read them, but they revealed little of the watchman or his activities. Some words and symbols made no sense. The rest were of little interest. Finally, the little box chirped and turned black and would give me neither word nor sound nor image.

I mourned, as if I had somehow killed it. Once again, I felt so alone. I wished I had such a box of my own, to show me the outside world and speak to me, only to me. I wished I knew how to work such a marvel and understood how to keep it alive.

January 11, 2011

I made my first attempt at hibernating my way through the winter. I wrapped myself in my warmest clothing and crept to the farm on a dark night thick with clouds. I slipped inside the tunnel, shut the door, and burrowed into my leafy den under the stage. The wind blew through the cracks, but I felt warm and dry. I fell asleep quickly and slept deeply—how long I do not know. I dreamed so many dreams. I am trying to separate and remember them all so I can record them. I think what I dreamed will tell me something about how I came to be in this hell. But right now, I will confine myself to describing my attempts at hibernation.

As I have already stated, I slept deeply, but it was not unbroken sleep. I opened my eyes often to hear the sounds of birds in the morning or the call of owls in the night. I watched bars of light illuminate the cracks in the wood and angle across the ground with the movement of the sun. The pain in my stomach periodically troubled me and woke me. I found I could stretch, reposition myself, and go back to sleep.

Twice in as many days I was awakened by the farmer's fat old dog. During the All Hallows revels, he did not seem to notice me at all. Perhaps I was just one more distraction when all the actors were swarming across the farm. But now he seems fascinated by my faint scent and has started scratching at the earth on the other side of the wall next to my bed. Once, he barked an alarm, but no one was working the fields so he was ignored.

Four, perhaps five days passed. I woke with pain in my joints and a sense of cold creeping in. I could not go back to sleep. I had to get up, stretch, and move. The pain in my stomach stabbed like a knife and would not be ignored. So ended my first experiment with hibernation. I returned to my cellar. It seems that I might be able to take occasional periods of extended rest at my beloved haunt, but will never be able to shut out my hell entirely or drink the wine of sweet oblivion.

Some good news: I did find a dead opossum on the side of the road.

January 13, 2011: My Dreams

There were two types of dream. I wrote the fleeting images on small scraps of paper I brought with me to the tunnel. I will now assemble them into a single narration.

One series of dreams was about Bone Ridge. In the first of these, I sat in the greenhouse before a mirror. I placed a wig on my head and daubed creamy face paint on my skin, blending it to make myself look like a human being again. I pulled on tall boots and long leather gloves to hide my clawed hands and feet. When I looked in the mirror again, I realized I had made myself into Bill, one of the haunt overseers. Suddenly, actors burst through the door and began assembling their costumes and props. They plied me with questions: Where am I working tonight, Bill? Do we get paid tonight? Anybody want to order pizza?

I backed away from them because I realized I did not have the answers. Then I woke up. In the second dream, I was outside the greenhouse watching the actors get themselves ready. Jon, the gregarious trickster, spied me and pulled me by the hand into the greenhouse, which bustled with activity. The clowns gathered around me, and all the actors smiled at me. They all knew me and welcomed me as one of their own. They told me how terrifying I was and congratulated me on my haunting triumphs. I felt as though I had found a home.

There was a third dream, but the images remain scattered. I saw actors at their scenes along the hay ride. Clowns, zombies, and ghouls lay strewn about the ground. I knew they were corpses, but they appeared more like life-sized poppets, bleeding and oozing loathsome fluids. Then I found myself at the walk-through. It was nearly deserted except for a handful of actors hiding behind the seats of the hearse or in the blackness of the maze. I saw a trio of actors running, veering away from the trails to hide in the woods. I felt a presence behind me and turned around. I could only make out a fog and a pair of black, burning eyes. And even though I was a monster to be feared, this other being terrified me to my very core.

The second set of dreams took me to another time and place. I had seen these images before: Two men in sober dress from another time were seated at opposite ends of a table. A girl, who might have been beautiful if she was not cowering, limped as she served food to the men. She winced as she moved, and I knew they had beaten her. One man was handsome with black hair and black eyes that gleamed with cruelty. The other was pale with a soft round face and belly. His feet were big and his hands were long. He had the look of someone who lived a life of incurious indolence. He certainly loved his food and drink. As he watched the girl, I could feel his lust rising to match the ravenous light in the handsome one's eyes.

Then I saw the two men in a rough-hewn church. The handsome one was shouting from the pulpit, berating his congregation on the depths of their sinful natures and the torments that awaited each of them. The portly man watched the sermon and the effect it had on the congregation. His pale face and eyes were alight with fascination and admiration. I had the sense that this young man was a deacon, who was absorbing everything he could from his mentor, the minister.

There was another fragmented dream where the minister had hold of the girl. She was terrified and struggled to get away. He was fully aroused and eager to use her, but he restrained himself. Instead, he pointed to the corpulent young man and, without uttering a word, seemed to command him to take the defenseless maid. I can remember, as I dreamed this, being filled with a sense of horror and revulsion. At the same time, I felt my truncated member stirring with a lust that matched that of the man in the dream. The young deacon seemed to have no will of his own. He abused the girl as the minister covered her mouth with one hand and gripped her wrists with the other. I can remember how I awoke from that dream with an overwhelming sense of shame and despair.

I now recall how, when I first found myself in this cold and hungry hell, I had silently begged Demon to tell me what I had done to deserve such pain. I remember what he did to me. There is now no doubt in my mind that he showed me exactly the depravity of which I was capable.

February 5, 2011

This winter has turned milder, but that has not prevented it from being extremely unpleasant. Day after day passes with neither sun nor stars. The precipitation is mostly frigid rain and sleet. Both my cellar and my leafy den in the tunnel are constantly damp. The only good that comes from this weather is that more rats and mice take refuge in the dilapidated house, so it easier to ease my hunger—one rodent per day, two if they are very small.

Outside of hunting for food and writing, there is little with which to occupy myself. I have learned which days my neighbors put out refuse to be collected. There are stacks and stacks of broadsides with news of the town and the great world beyond. It is risky, but I have crept out in the dead of night to avail myself of this discarded library. I have learned that many people in Rhode Island and beyond are suffering from want and woe, struggling for honest work, food, and shelter. I have also learned that this is a place of great hedonism and licentiousness. If I had the courage, I would ask Demon when I next see him why I am being so savagely punished when so many other sinners are going about their wicked business with impunity.

February 14, 2011

Something is wrong. If I wander the woods at night and come near one of the clusters of homes that dot the area, I hear the sound of women and children weeping. It wakes the dogs in the area. Once, deep into the night hours, I heard the banshee wail that signaled the coming of the sheriff. I saw Demon crouching in a tree last night. He seemed to have no interest in me or what I was doing. He sat with his head cocked to one side, listening. He grinned at what he heard.

So I am not the only sinner he is watching. I am curious. I will risk Demon's displeasure and try to learn what has fascinated him so.

February 18, 2011

I did not see Demon again, but I heard new sounds of weeping and terror on the night air. I followed it even though I felt uneasy, as if Demon knew exactly what I was doing and would somehow be angry for involving myself in things that were not my affair.

Following the shouts and cries to the edge of the woods, I came upon a home where a dog was tied outside in the cold. At first he barked, but when I offered him the comfort of some shared warmth he calmed himself.

I approached one of the windows and used my claws to lift myself up on the sill. I saw a thin, bloodied, and frantic woman putting herself between a man and a small boy. The boy cowered in a corner as the woman—no doubt, his mother— covered him with her body. She took blow after blow. Then the banshee cried out its warning. The man slumped to the ground as if exhausted by his own brutality.

I clambered up to the roof and hung myself upside down in black shadows so I could watch what happened when the sheriff and his men arrived. The woman was so terrified she did not want to tell the sheriff anything. She did not need to. They could see plainly enough for themselves that mother and child were in danger. The men forced the brute's hands behind his back and placed them in restraints. One of the men gently guided the woman and child to a box-like conveyance outside. He explained something called a "restraining order" to her and said something about getting "checked out at the hospital." Later, someone came by to take the dog away. The house was dark, deserted and quiet.

March 1, 2011

The woman, the child, and the dog are all back at the house. The dog was not chained outside anymore. I noticed a black cat sleeping in a sunny window. The man was not there. As I watched mother and child play together, I felt a surge of rage. Someone intervened to help these two powerless beings, but it was not me. They took the brute away and no doubt threw him in the stocks, but I pictured all manner of punishments that better suited a man like that. And I regretted that I had not had the opportunity to inflict them on him.

March 11, 2011

The man still has not returned to the house. Perhaps the sheriff took him to the edge of town, telling him to leave and to never come back.

There were a few days of thaw this week, but the cold came back today. It snowed for the first time in a month. A thick, soft, and gently drifting snow began to fall in the early morning hours and continued through the day. It was not terribly cold, so I went out naked to hunt. The snow fell thicker and faster, sending the small game running for cover. I crept through tree and brush back to my cellar. Miles away from home, I found myself slowing my pace as the snow drifted. A deep and peaceful silence fell over the land. I stopped and beheld all that lay around me. The ground, the air itself was immaculate and white, and the hush in the air was like that of a cathedral. I felt an overpowering and abiding joy in my solitude and situation. In the midst of my hell, I found beauty and solace.

And as I filled the emptiness of my defiled soul, I realized I was not alone. A few feet away on a low branch crouched Demon, shrunk to the size of a large owl. His green eyes were half closed as he gazed outward over the scene. Once again, he seemed uninterested in me. He was completely entranced by the wonder of his surroundings.

It seemed to me that if there was a God, he lived in this stillness. And in that stillness, even a demon could find peace.

March 19, 2011

I have ruined myself again. I am beyond redemption. If there ever was the slightest chance I could be freed from this hell, I have utterly destroyed it.

Two days ago, I attempted some night hunting. I heard a great howling from both man and beast. There was the loud report of a musket being fired. I followed the din to the home where the woman and child had been terrorized weeks earlier. I crouched in the deep shadows between the trees and surveyed the scene.

The woman's stricken face appeared in the window. The dog lay dead on the ground. The man had the black cat by the scruff of the neck. He swayed back and forth, clearly intoxicated. He brought a knife up to the cat's belly, but the beast clawed the hand that gripped him. The man dropped the cat and it streaked past me into the woods. He followed it to the edge of trees and stopped as if wondering what to do. He gazed at the knife in his hand then lurched unsteadily towards the house.

And then I became possessed by a towering rage. Before he could take one more step, I grabbed his collar and jerked him backwards into the shadows. He sprawled face up on the ground, but it was not until he struggled to his feet that he really saw me. I was dressed in black, but my face and clawed hands were starkly, deathly white. He opened his mouth to cry out, but I did not give him the chance. My long, thin fingers arched over his face. The nails on my index and middle fingers dug into the back of his scalp and right into his skull while the long nail of my thumb pierced the skin under his chin, penetrating right through his tongue and into the roof of his mouth. He struggled to scream but gurgled instead on the blood pouring down his throat.

I heard the banshee cry again, so I swiftly clawed my way up a sturdy tree, dragging the bloody, flailing soul after me. When I knew I was safely out of sight, I laid my victim across a branch. He twitched and gasped as I released his face and closed one hand around his throat. I smelled his sweat and his fear and drooled as I anticipated the sweetness of his flesh on my tongue. He seemed to understand what was to be his fate, for his eyes widened with horror. Then the light in his gaze dimmed.

Suddenly, I heard a limb over my head creak and groan under a great weight. There, crouching above me, was Demon at his full, terrible height and breadth, leering at me—or so I thought. But he was not interested in my sin. He reached down with his immense hand and closed it over mine. He removed it from the man's throat. Then the hand closed around his waist and raised him right up to Demon's face. Demon grinned at the dying man, and suddenly there was a shapeless, gray mass where a body had once been. It resembled a jelly-like substance that should have easily slipped through the devil's fingers. Demon had no problem maintaining his grasp. He stared into my eyes, his stare knowing and malevolent. He was letting me know that he had seized me the same way. He had watched me commit this new crime, and understood what I wished to do with my kill. Now he was appropriating it before I could take any enjoyment, however small, from this mound of flesh.

The branch groaned again and threatened to break as Demon sprang into the blackness and disappeared. Another evil soul was about to meet its own private hell. Was it possible that this man had done even worse things than those

I had witnessed? Was Demon returning when he was through with this soul to mete out an even more dreadful punishment for what I had done? Or was I now condemned to be his dog, hunting and taking down souls even more depraved than I?

March 23, 2011

I seem to have acquired a cat. She does not remain with me always, but she is a frequent visitor. The dusky creature that saved herself from her abuser seems to think I had some part in it. A black cat is supposed to be evil, the devil's familiar. She might be Demon's spy, but I cannot escape the suspicion she sees me as a benefactor. The first time she appeared, I shared a mouse I had just caught. I could certainly slay and eat her as well, but I find I am pleased by her visits. I have no voice, so she cannot know I have named her for the shades of despair through which I flail and blunder. In my mind, I call her Darkness.

I have hidden out in my cellar for countless days, listening for the sounds of a search party seeking the man I attacked. I have heard nothing. They must think he is far away from these woods and indeed, he is. I remain in hiding, nonetheless.

I fear Demon's wrath. There is no place I can hide if he comes looking for me. He caught me committing one abomination and preparing to indulge in another. As I cringe in this cellar, translating my terror into words on paper, I am unable to conceive what further torments Demon could rain down around me. I cannot bring myself to stir beyond these sunken walls until I know.

AN EDUCATION IN THE STREETS

I T WAS A Sunday in early April, and Demon was enjoying some first-rate entertainment. He crouched in the dusty corner of a dingy store-front church. The self-appointed minister was urging his tiny flock to burn Korans in a park the next Sunday. Demon always found it diverting to observe the variety of ways people used the Boss to justify their hatred for each other. Demon did not plan on making an appearance to this so-called holy man as he had with Reverend Phelan. This man was already too far gone. Demon would be unable to claim a shred of credit for corrupting this soul.

He listened to the hysterical man and his small but frenzied congregation for an hour. He desperately needed this break. Hundreds of new souls had been added to his case load, and he was still intent on searching for his lost fiend. He was worn out from the hunt, not to mention the Boss's displeasure.

The escapee had Demon completely confounded. A bad soul was usually much easier to locate. All he had to do was follow the stench of the soul's corruptions. But this one was cleverer than most at hiding his tracks.

Many months ago, late in the fall, Demon thought he had fixed where the monster had landed. He enjoyed reading the tabloids and came across an article regarding a horrifying mass murder in the southwest United States. The writer placed the blame on the mythical chupacabra. An unidentified source said the remains of four people had been found—if they could be called remains. There was an obviously faked photo of four sets of clothes forming the outlines of four bodies. They had distorted, balloon-like heads protruding from the collars. The article described the silhouettes in the dust as saturated with fat and salts. A lone survivor croaked the name of the monster then collapsed from dehydration and died. This was exactly the type of horror a self-made monster in the process of becoming could generate.

Demon scoured the western and southwestern states and even Mexico. Too much time had passed. The fiend's scent had evaporated and the trail had gone cold. There were plenty of disappearances and suspicious deaths, but few bore the earmarks of this particular soul. Demon could search the entire western hemisphere—perhaps even the entire planet—or wait for news of fresh atrocities.

§ § §

When the fiend awoke from his long winter's sleep, his stomach cramped with hunger. He folded his arms over his middle and paced back and forth in the cold, damp cave. A moan escaped his lips, and he stopped in mid-step.

He was pacing. He had legs with which to pace. He had a stomach and other fully formed organs. He had a voice and lips and teeth with which to form words.

And he had a name: Martin Godfrey.

He crawled on his hands and knees to the mouth of his winter den. Now that he could stand up straight on two long legs and take in his surroundings with sharp color vision, he could see that he was in beautiful country in the foot hills of a spectacular mountain range. The land showed signs of spring. The ice was nearly gone from the river below him. New green plants poked their shoots out of the few remaining patches of snow. Martin felt the cold, bracing air of a spring morning sweep over him and realized he was naked. It was good to have a body again, but it suffered all the frailties of the human form.

He took himself down to the icy waters and found a deep pool still enough to show his reflection. Martin was profoundly disappointed by what he saw. He remembered the man he saw in his dreams: tall, well-proportioned and handsome, with black hair and flashing, dark eyes. The body he saw was bony and malnourished with skin as pale as milk. In place of the black hair that once flowed from his crown to his shoulders was short, pale fuzz that covered his head, his face, and even his body. It looked like the silken down of a milk weed. Only his dark, hypnotic eyes remained. Martin was repulsive.

He ran his tongue along the roof of his mouth and was disheartened to feel a hollow tube running the length of the hard palate. He opened his mouth and shot a bony barb, not unlike a stingray's tail, at the air, confirming his worst fears. The old means of hunting had not been dreamed away. He was more monster than man.

He was filthy, too. Martin waded out into the river and ducked down in the bone-numbing water several times, scrubbing himself down with his bare hands. Then he found some rocks on the shore warmed by the strengthening sun. He lay across them and basked like a reptile. He felt much better, but he knew he would need to find food and clothing before dark if he was to survive his first night as a man.

It was no longer possible to hug the ground and undulate unseen. He blundered noisily through brush that whipped and cut his bare skin. Any beasts he might hunt had already picked up his human scent and disappeared. Despite his clumsy humanity, however, he did come across an unsuspecting rabbit. Crouching close to the ground, Martin sent the thin white barb almost clear through the rabbit's body. The animal succumbed quickly, but the liquefied remains were meager and made for a scanty meal when Martin scraped away the fur.

As the sun set, Martin shivered from both fear and the cold until he saw the gleam of fire through the trees. He tempered his desperation and called on all his cunning and stealth as he approached the campsite. Within the circumference of the fire light, he could see a canoe pulled onto the sandy bank of the river. Seated in front of a tent near the fire were a young man and woman, talking and laughing. Martin was able to pad across a carpet of soft pine needles until he stood right behind the couple. He delivered a quick barb to each, through the back and into the heart. He stepped into the fire light to watch the uncomprehending horror on his victims' faces as they collapsed into masses of jelly. Then he ripped open their clothing, buried his face in the sludge, and feasted.

When Martin finished feeding, he washed in the river and helped himself to the man's clothing. He found pants, a sturdy plaid shirt, a quilted vest, and a jacket. The pants were a bit long and too large in the waist. The shirt and jacket hung on Martin's thin frame.

At dawn, he rolled up a sleeping bag and stuffed a backpack with useful items he found about the camp site: money, plates, cups, and a serrated knife. He loaded these things in the canoe and taught himself how to maneuver the craft. Then he let the current take the canoe wherever it wanted.

As he traveled and hunted, Martin learned from his victims. A young college dropout crossing the country taught Martin how to hitchhike and find soup kitchens. He devoured the youth and took his wallet. He learned that it was important to have a "photo ID," but it was impossible to get one without a birth certificate. A fellow traveler showed him how to do that, too. Martin killed that tutor, drank his liquefied tissue, and took a large amount of cash from him as well.

Within a month, he found himself in a large city nestled in the mountains. The noise, the color, and the throngs of riotous people confused him. He kept to himself, sleeping in dark corners off the streets, trying to understand the world he was in. His reflection in the many windows—so many windows!—offended him. The looks he got from others told him they found him repulsive, too. Was this the best he could expect from his new life?

Martin's past had come back to him in the dreams that filled his mind as he hibernated. There were tantalizing images of simple people who worshipped his beauty, his intelligence, and his gift for preaching holy words to further his own ends. He could talk them into believing anything. His beauty had been part of that domination. Martin did not know if he would have another chance to remake himself, but he was determined to proceed as if the power of becoming was still his. He would feed his body well during the warm months and nourish his pitiless will as well. To that end, he would sow impotent terror wherever he went.

He learned there was a place in the city for the homeless. The first time there was a summer thunderstorm, Martin took himself there. He could bathe, dress in clean clothes, and eat a hot meal. He had forgotten there were foods he enjoyed. They could not compare to the savory complexity of his prey, nor were they as nourishing, but neither did his body reject them.

The people who ran the shelter seemed worried about him. With his pale skin, his spare frame, and thin, downy hair, they thought he was ill. The next morning, a young man took the Minister into his office and asked if he was undergoing chemotherapy. Martin did not understand.

The social worker, who introduced himself as David, seemed uncertain and stammered, "Do you, do you have cancer?"

"Cancer," Martin repeated.

"I'm, I'm sorry. We thought you were ill. We thought you might need a hospital."

"I am not ill." Martin was enjoying the man's discomfort. He gave David a rueful smile. "In me you see the effects of a luxurious, wanton life. I was a man of God who fell from grace. I am certain it shows I have fallen a long way."

There was something in Martin's dark, penetrating eyes that fascinated David. Weak and ill as he seemed, the man's face and demeanor hinted at a charismatic power. David wanted to get this newcomer back on his feet again.

On the streets, Martin put on a different face. He let his features go slack and widened his eyes with witless wonder. He gave his name as Simon Hogg—the dullard deacon from Martin's old life—and affected his protégé's over-eager smile. It was a face that invited the street people to share their stories and their knowledge of the streets. It also invited those who preyed on the weak to approach him.

The Minister quickly learned to recognize the city's parasites. He let it be known he had money or that he wanted to buy drugs. He allowed himself to be lured to isolated spots where Martin turned on his would-be assailants. Since his victims were always engaged in some sort of illicit commerce, they often had money on them—sometimes a lot of money. So he feasted, night after night, and took anything of value that remained. He took to carrying black trash bags in his stolen back pack. He filled them with the oily clothing and hair of his victims then threw the bags into the closest dumpster.

The homeless were also vanishing. Some transience was to be expected, so only their street friends and a handful of street workers felt anything resembling alarm. That was how Martin met Alayna and brought Demon down on his trail.

Another stormy summer afternoon came, and Martin availed himself of the hospitality of the shelter. David confided his worries to the Minister.

"Simon, I've noticed that a lot of our usual guests haven't shown up for several weeks," David said. "Their friends are asking me if I know anything. Case workers at the women's shelters are missing clients, too."

"I have noticed that. And a number of prostitutes have stopped working their usual places." Martin suppressed a smile as he recalled how he had recently rediscovered his lust. He had money, so the four women he murdered willingly followed him to any deserted spot he chose. He satisfied himself then gave each one a last kiss, pushing his poisoned barb down their throats. He smiled as he watched them drown on their own liquefying tissues.

"You have a way of getting people to trust you," David continued. "I've noticed what a wonderful listener you are. Maybe you could ask around and find out who saw these people last or if they said they were going somewhere." Martin promised to help, and David handed him a sheet of paper. "Wonderful. Here's a list of names and a description of the men. My girlfriend's coming by with some information about the missing women. She's a social worker, too."

When Martin met Alayna, he was immediately captivated. She was lovely—golden haired and delicate, with a compassionate soul that shone through her eyes. She reminded him of the handsome and pious young women he'd known in his congregation. Seducing them had been supremely pleasurable because he desecrated their souls as well, leaving them lost in a valley of despair. He would do the same to Alayna.

The social worker handed her information to Martin after David introduced them. "You've really impressed David," she said. "Have you thought of becoming a street worker yourself?"

The Minister cast his eyes down like a bashful maiden and pretended to be humbled by her notice.

"We could help you get started. The jobs don't pay well, but if you have a calling for the work…" Alayna shrugged and smiled.

Martin raised his eyes to hers, holding her in his gaze. "I would very much like to talk to you about it."

They made an appointment to meet at Alayna's agency. She would introduce him to her contacts at shelters and food pantries throughout the city. Martin smiled as he watched David circle Alayna's waist with his arm, hugging her to his side as they walked away.

Martin wanted this girl beyond any obsession he could remember—except perhaps his unreasoning lust for the obstinate servant girl who had been his downfall. If he was still handsome, he had no doubt he could snare Alayna. But his face had all the appeal of a fat white grub. He had his dark, flashing eyes, however, and he already had Alayna's trust.

He had no intention of even pretending to look for the disappeared. Fewer mouths looking for meals, he thought, and fewer homeless looking for beds. *They should thank me*, he thought. He waited for his chance with Alayna and enjoyed the delicious thrumming of his hunger. It kept him awake that night. No other prey would do.

Martin met Alayna the following afternoon. He followed her to youth centers, food pantries, and soup kitchens well into the evening. She asked him what kind of work he preferred, if anything "resonated" with him. Martin feigned interest then skillfully turned the conversation so the young woman began talking about herself. They sat together on a park bench until she received a call from David. She apologized and went to meet her boyfriend.

Over the following week, Martin avoided contact with David. The Minister hid himself each morning in an alley opposite Alayna's office and followed her wherever she walked in the city. He learned her schedule and knew where she lived. Finally, eight days after he met her, Martin found his opportunity.

Alayna walked from work to a restaurant where she met two women friends for dinner. When she left several hours later, she retraced her steps back to a parking garage. Martin followed. Just as Alayna reached her car, he grabbed her by the arm. As he pulled the young women towards himself, she cried out and dosed him with pepper spray. It was a glancing shot, but Martin roared in pain.

Alayna broke free and ran for the stair well. Martin's eyes stung, but he was not incapacitated. He caught up with her and tackled her as she tried to sprint up the stairs. Her weapon flew from her grasp as she shrieked for help. Martin clapped one hand over her mouth and shot his venomous barb into her thigh. She bit his hand and kicked hard with the other leg. She struggled free and tried to run again but stumbled as a burning pain spread up to her abdomen. The poison would travel swiftly in her blood as her heart rate accelerated. Martin would have to pin her quickly if he was to enter her before she dissolved.

He lunged at her knees as she clung to the banister, her muscles trembling. With the last of her strength she kicked and connected with Martin's nose. As blood spurted from his nostrils, she tried again to escape. Then her bones turned to gelatin and she collapsed. The fight had cost Martin his chance to play with his prey before consuming it.

Then he even lost the opportunity to devour his kill. He was interrupted by cries of alarm on the stairs below. He turned to see several young men watching him. Each had one of those palm-sized phones in his hand. One was taking his picture. One was recording the scene. Another was speaking to the police. They were all cautiously approaching.

Martin cursed himself for allowing his appetites rather than his intelligence to rule his actions. He knew he could kill the three men in front of him before they even realized what kind of threat they faced. But could he do the same with the police who were already on their way? He had money and knew how to become invisible. Martin turned and ran.

The next day and 500 miles to the west, Demon shrank down and perched in a tree arching over an outdoor café. Below him sat a man of no particular interest. The photo the man was watching on his laptop, however, was riveting. It had been taken by a witness on a stairwell where a man had murdered a young woman. The story that accompanied the picture questioned the claims made by the witnesses: The woman collapsed and dissolved into a gelatinous mound. The police could not say whether they had a murder or a strange disease on their hands. The attacker, who looked straight into the camera, had a peculiar appearance:

pale, covered with down rather than hair, somewhat heavy, and shapeless. He had the larval look of an unfinished human being. Demon knew this was the soul he had been seeking.

Demon took himself quickly and silently to the scene of the murder. It had happened barely twenty hours earlier so he could smell it well before he could see it. It was sweet and pungent, a mixture of the dead woman's remains and the scent of her killer. At last Demon had what he needed: the signature scent of the escaped fiend. He could now track the soul with each killing and, hopefully, there would not be many more of those.

§ § §

Martin realized he still had much to learn about the technological wonders of this new world. Too late he understood it was possible for his image to show up anywhere and everywhere moments after it had been captured. He left the city for a smaller community where he bought a black wig and a broad-brimmed hat to cover his head and clothes two sizes too large to camouflage his ballooning waistline. Those who knew him remembered him as a sickly homeless man. No one expected him to have the money to travel by bus or train. Several weeks later he changed his look yet again to a longer, light brown hair piece and neat, casual clothes. He tinted his skin with a liquid foundation. He paid a handsome amount of money for a new identity and disposed of the procurer.

With the constant movement, he started to lose weight. Delicious as it was, the Minister derived little benefit from normal food. Autumn had arrived, and Martin felt driven to gorge and find a den for the winter. He needed to hunt again and to replenish his funds. He moved south, killed, moved east, killed again, then moved north and killed again. He learned to vary the populations from which he chose his victims, sampling a little bit of everything: the homeless, the transient adventurers, unsupervised teenagers, the isolated elderly, solitary bird watchers, and early morning runners. He got better at locating surveillance cameras and made sure his victims did not have time to pull out a device that could take his likeness. He did nothing that would establish a pattern. He found dens everywhere, especially in the crowded urban centers. Boarded up houses were abundant, each with a notice of foreclosure nailed to the front. Martin could often find a way in and just as frequently found squatters or addicts on which he could feed.

By November's end, he was so thoroughly glutted his torso resembled the great undulating slug he had been a year ago. He was growing lethargic, almost apathetic about finding a place to den for the winter. He didn't even want his last victim. He was hitchhiking through the Poconos and killed a young man driving home for the Thanksgiving holiday. He propped his victim in the passenger seat and watched him dissolve into gel that sparkled with blue stars. He sampled the remains and buried the rest. Then he abandoned the car and hiked into the woods to a remote summer cabin he had scouted weeks earlier.

§ § §

Even in the cold, the peculiar odor of the young man's liquefied remains put Demon on Martin's trail. Martin had just forced open a window on the cabin when Demon seized him by the throat and lifted him off the ground. The Minister's eyes bulged with terror. The barb behind his teeth flailed wildly, but could not puncture Demon's leathery skin. Demon grinned and raised his free hand to work the change he'd been denied eighteen months earlier. He allowed Martin a glimpse of the personal hell Demon envisioned for him. The Minister contorted like an impaled serpent.

Suddenly, Demon felt an insistent tug at his elbow. A deep purple shadow clutched at his arm. Soft blue eyes within the violet mist admonished him. The green feline eyes flashed with rage. The misty creature regarded him with sorrow, but stood firm in its directive. In despair, Demon dropped his gaze to the ground and relaxed his grip on the errant soul. Martin crouched against the cabin wall, frozen with fear, but the devil no longer seemed interested in him. Demon was facing the misty shadow, his posture one of utter defeat.

The amethyst vapor had a message from their Boss. The fiend and his trail of murders had been Demon's doing, however inadvertent. But something had changed in Rhode Island, and the resolution to this matter would lie there, in the hands of a soul who might yet redeem himself by acting as he should have centuries before. It was up to the hell hunter to keep up with his caseload and prevent as much of the terror as he could on his own time. The winter would provide a respite, a chance to come up with a plan to limit the carnage. The mist evaporated. Demon staggered as if bent under a terrible weight.

It slowly dawned on the Minister that he had been reprieved. He laughed in Demon's face and slunk away into his den. He padded a dark closet with bedding and went to sleep. This winter, he would dream himself handsome, lean, and strong. Come spring, no one would refuse him anything.

Demon crouched in a tree among the crows and the owls. An early snow was blowing through the mountains. He tried to fathom how many innocents would be slaughtered before this blunder played itself out. Then he dropped his head into his clawed hands and wept.

MONSTER VS. MONSTER

B Y JULY, AMY and Sean had rough sketches and a draft of the story for their graphic novel. They incorporated the demon they had seen in the woods into the plot. Bonebelly was a hell hound of sorts, kept on a chain and used to hunt down souls who had bargained with the devil and lost. The hero was a high school loser who needed help from other losers to outwit the devil and save his soul.

They had no sooner finished it than Amy declared, "It's all wrong."

Sean agreed. "Horror movie clichés, nerd clichés, and not enough Bonebelly. We have to get his backstory right."

They turned their attention to the 2011 edition of Bone Ridge Farm. This year's theme was New England Horrors, which meant everyone was reading a lot of H.P. Lovecraft and familiarizing themselves with all things Cthulhu. In addition, the hayride would have sites dedicated to Mercy Brown, the Exeter vampire, the Salem witch trials, the haunted Ramtail Factory in Foster, and the walled-up Lieutenant Drane at Fort Independence in Boston—said to have inspired Poe's "The Cask of Amontillado."

In addition to building and painting scenes, Sean and Amy learned the fundamentals of airbrushing and making prosthetics from Ron and Cheryl. The young people demonstrated an aptitude for the craft and were hired to help with makeup during the haunt season. They were still not allowed to act—neither would turn eighteen until 2012—but this summer was the best of their lives.

When they were not working, Amy and Sean were often seated at a picnic table in front of the farm store, reworking the back story for their graphic novel. The latest attempt involved a race of beings that had lived for millennia in underground caverns. Bonebelly was the last of his kind. He had ventured east as he hunted for food and for a mate. He had survived for generations before showing up in South County and had been the inspiration for Big Foot sightings across the country.

"I like the way the underground world looks," Amy commented over their rough sketches. "It'll look fantastic when we add color to the stalagmites and stalactites."

"But he's too much like a wild animal," Sean said. "We know for a fact he likes beer."

"A sure sign of intelligence," Bill said as he paused behind the pair and looked over their shoulders. "Is this the famous graphic novel?"

"Not yet," Sean said. "We tossed our first idea."

"I'd like to see if you could turn your idea into some kind of makeup." Bill picked up the Bonebelly sketches and examined them. "You know, we had customers who said they saw something like this last fall."

"That's where we got the idea," Amy lied.

Someone else was interested in their art work. Tom had hired a new landscape worker, a pleasant young man who had recently moved to South County. Cam was something of an amateur artist himself. He frequently asked to see their drawings, although the pair often declined. Like many fledgling writers and artists, they were afraid of having their ideas stolen, and there was too much of Bonebelly's story that remained to be fleshed out. Sean also suspected that Cam wanted an excuse to flirt with Amy, although he kept that suspicion to himself.

Early one July evening, Amy had just finished her shift at the farm store and was waiting for Sean, who was helping Milton build the new sets on the walk-through. Cam sat down next to her on the back steps of the farm store and offered her a soda. Amy edged away from him but politely sipped from the cold drink.

"Did you hear the story about Tom?" Cam asked.

"People tell lots of stories about Tom," Amy said somewhat peevishly. Tom was a character, but the stories about him were told with great affection by those who knew him. Amy did not really want to hear what amounted to gossip from Cam.

"Jack told me that Tom thought he saw some sort of yeti climbing up the wall of his house. He shot at it, and his wife got pissed at him."

"That's not funny. Jack shouldn't have told you that."

"Then there's the customers who got lost…"

"Got high and got lost." Amy was annoyed now and began pacing at the foot of the stairs.

"All right, got high and got lost," Cam said. "But they said they were attacked by some big white thing." He paused dramatically before adding, "What if I told you I've seen that thing, too? Not here on the farm—farther out in the woods, way off the side road. I could show you and Sean."

When Amy told Sean of Cam's boast, Sean was skeptical. "I think he just wants your attention."

"Something about him weirds me out, but maybe we should check it out."

They agreed the following morning to accompany Cam after work. By 5:30 that afternoon, Amy had ridden her bike to a spot Cam had designated off a winding road bordered by woods and wetlands. There was a private road that led to a long deserted farm, but it was now narrow and overgrown. Amy knew it from the granite boundary marker she had passed hundreds of times as she traveled to and from the farm. She was surprised to find herself alone. She thought Sean and Cam were following her within minutes. She waited in the lengthening afternoon shadows, sipping a few mouthfuls of flavored water from her sports bottle.

Long minutes passed and Sean still had not arrived. Amy was suddenly overwhelmed with the need to sit. She sank down on an overgrown stone wall. Her knees shook, and black spots swam before her eyes. She watched with detached curiosity as Cam came out of the woods and hid her bicycle behind a clump of trees. Then he slipped an arm around her waist and lifted her to her feet. He alternately guided and dragged her up the overgrown road and into the trees. Amy could hear herself asking what had happened to Sean, but Cam said nothing. She tried repeating the question, but her tongue was clumsy and would not form the words.

She could not remember exactly how they arrived there or how long it took, but she found herself lying on the ground at the base of a large, drooping white cedar. She thought she saw a wall with a tilted window growing right out of the cedar. *That can't be right*, she thought. She tried to make out the corners of the structure, hidden by weeds and vines, but Cam shoved her down every time she tried to sit up.

He was trying to pull Amy's shirt over her head. Amy knew she should be pushing Cam away. All she could do was weakly flail her arms in his face. She knew she should be calling for Sean, even screaming, but found she was fighting to stay awake. Then something else caught her attention. A bone-white creature with gangly limbs, an enormous skull crowned with stringy yellow hair, and a huge belly crawled down the trunk of the cedar. Its head was cocked to one side, watching as Cam worked at Amy's clothes.

She wondered why Cam seemed so unconcerned with the phantasm looming behind him. Amy watched with increasing horror as the skeletal face hovered just above them, as it creased with fury, and the amber eyes blazed like flames. Tapered claws extended from the drooping greenery and grabbed her assailant by the hair. The creature jerked Cam's head back. Two long, thin fingernails from the other yellowed hand forced their way up his nostrils while the monster's thumb stabbed the roof of his mouth. Cam gave a strangled cry as the thing lifted him by his face right off the ground. Blood dripped down the cedar's trunk. The man disappeared amid the branches. Just before the monster retreated from sight it turned its head and stared at Amy, almost as if it recognized her. Amy thought it was about to speak to her, but it made not a single sound.

She knew this creature, even though she had never laid eyes on it before. "Bonebelly?" she said.

The creature's jaw dropped, as if stunned. It started down the trunk towards Amy, but then seemed to think better of it and backed away again. It turned to the quarry stowed high in the branches and clambered out of sight. Amy heard a long burbling groan. A dollop of blood dropped out of the greenery and landed on the leg of her jeans. She stared at it—for hours it seemed. Then she stopped fighting and allowed her eyes to close.

DAMNATION HAS A NAME

July 6, 2011

MY HAUNTERS ARE back! Even now Milton and Justin, the farm workers, and a few of the actors are toiling in the woods. They are clearing new paths for the walk-through and reusing last year's materials for new sets. I hear a name repeated over and over again: Lovecraft. I do not know who he is, but the haunters seem to anticipate and celebrate his eventual arrival with both joy and dread. This Lovecraft must be an extraordinary man.

July 9, 2011

Apparently, Lovecraft has been dead for over 70 years. He wrote tales of demons and monsters and madness. My haunters are completely enamored with his stories. Justin carries around a copy of the author's writings, something called the Necronomicon. If he leaves it behind in the greenhouse, I will borrow it.

The farmer's wife brought sweets she had baked to the greenhouse yesterday evening. She called them "Cthulhu cookies," which provoked great hilarity among the haunters. She explained that she used a snowman-shaped cutter and made the top portion appear like a monstrous gourd-like head. The bottom half was all green tentacles. The plan is to sell them along with other victuals during the haunt season.

After everyone went out to work, I sampled a cookie that had fallen to the ground. It was amusing but much too sweet for my taste. It quickly turned to ashes anyway.

July 11, 2011

It has been so hot and sultry that I have refrained from wearing clothing. Yet I am not an animal, and it does bother me to go out into the woods with my shameful form on display, even if it is only to the beasts and the birds. Once again, I returned to Stone Ridge Farm to scavenge. I found some light colored rags from which I fashioned a sort of loin cloth. Perhaps it is silliness on my part, but it makes me feel less like a beast and more like the man I once was.

July 16, 2011

It has happened again. Oh, I am truly damned for all eternity.

It was late yesterday afternoon when I heard a commotion outside my dilapidated dwelling. Someone was thrashing about on the overgrown path. I crawled stealthily out of the rear cellar door, up the back wall, and across the roof to the white cedar that drooped over the shingles. I positioned myself high in the thickly needled branches and watched the path.

I saw a young man half-walking, half-dragging a girl towards my shelter. I recognized her. Her hair was black, her eyes were painted, and her clothes had the tattered look of a pauper's, although I knew she wore these by choice. It was Amy.

It was clear the man intended to have his way with her. She could barely stand. She seemed intoxicated but, as I saw her weakly trying to push the man away, I could not believe she had chosen to become so. He had clearly slipped her some sort of draught. He pushed her down on her back on the cedar needles covering the ground. Then he set about trying to remove the girl's clothes. First, he tried to pull her blouse over her head, but she kept flailing her arms in his face. He then tried to remove her trousers.

As I watched him work so relentlessly to overcome the child's feeble efforts at self-defense, I felt a violent rage growing in my belly, even greater than that provoked by last winter's wife beater. That he should violate this innocent! I would not allow it. Without another thought, I scrambled down the trunk and grabbed him by the hair, forcing his head back. Clinging to the bark with my sharpened toe nails, I drove the claws of my free hand into the roof of his mouth and up his nostrils. I pulled the flailing sinner away from the girl and up into the branches. I pinned the man against the trunk.

I was about to climb well up and away from her when I looked down at her face one more time. I found myself stopped in my tracks. Even in her inebriated state she gazed at me with her wise, luminous eyes. Then she did something amazing. She acted as though she recognized me. She sat up and addressed me by a name: Bonebelly.

I turned and climbed away as quickly as I could. I did not want her to see what I did next. The criminal was squealing—the only sound he could make—and struggling to pull my claws away from his face. My fury flared anew and I clenched my fist, crushing the bones of his face. He released his dying breath in a horrendous moan as blood sprayed my face, my chest, and the green fronds of the cedar.

I looked back at the ground. Amy lay there with her eyes closed. I prayed she was unhurt, but I dared not approach her. Somehow she knew me. For some unfathomable reason, she had named me—and aptly, too. That she recognized me even as the evidence of my crime hung limply from my bloody fist suddenly filled me with unbearable consternation. I had to flee.

I climbed high and leaped with the criminal's carcass to a neighboring tree. Concealed by the leaves, I laid the corpse across a stout limb and waited for Demon to appear. I had no doubt that this was a soul he would wish to have. But an hour passed and he did not come.

The stirring of a warm summer breeze wafted the sweet smell of human flesh to my nostrils. I tried to resist the growling of my gigantic belly but it was no use. My mouth watered with the aroma, and finally gave way to uncontrollable drooling. Still Demon did not show himself. If this was a test, I was about to fail it miserably. At last, I could stand it no longer. I tore open the man's shirt and sliced a few strips of flesh from his chest. I savored the sorry repast with boundless joy.

Even as I relished these morsels, I had the sense I was being watched. I panicked but quickly realized it was not Demon who saw me. Perched on a branch below me was Darkness. Her green eyes regarded me fearfully. She had seen violence before. I reached out to her with my bloody fingers, hoping to reassure her, but she backed away from my touch. She streaked down the tree and disappeared into the woods.

I looked at the corpse again with its lacerated chest and stove-in face and saw—really saw—what I had done. I felt a crushing despair. I cradled the body and soundlessly howled. Then I climbed down the trunk, dragging my victim into the evening shadows of the woods. I slung the bleeding corpse over my shoulder and carried it to the swamp. It was mostly dry, but there was enough soft, moist peat to dig a shallow grave. I wept as I buried my victim. Thick black tears spilled down my face and made stinking puddles on the ground that quickly teemed with flies. I covered the corpse with mud and peat and dragged stones and rotten logs to the spot.

I found the stream I use for washing and scrubbed away the blood. Then I remembered Amy and hurried back to my dwelling to see if she was in need of assistance. But she was gone. I sat on the roof until dark then slunk back into my fruit cellar. I stayed awake all night, in case she alerted anyone of the murder. No one came.

Now, in the light of dawn, I recount and record all my offenses. I have desecrated the corpse of an elderly man. I have savagely murdered two men. They were evil men, to be sure, but it was not my place to judge. Demon did not even want this last soul. And I do not know if Amy even made it safely out of the woods.

By now, my sins have grown too numerous and grievous to ever be forgiven. I shall turn my attention to making my hell as comfortable as possible. I will be dwelling here a long time.

July 18, 2011

I have often seen Amy working at the bakery with her mother on the Sabbath.

She was not there yesterday, nor did she come to the farm today. Now I wonder if perhaps she suffered serious physical harm. Words cannot express the depths of my self-loathing. I was too absorbed in my own hunger, and subsequent guilt and self-pity to give the girl assistance.

The sheriff's men were coming and going at the farm all day. I kept my distance, watching from the top of a tall oak as they talked to the farmer and all those working in the woods. I surmised they were trying to piece together what happened to the girl and where her attacker might be.

It is raining softly as I write these words. It is a tranquil sound, but it does not bring me contentment. When the woods are peaceful as they are tonight, I sometimes hear a voice inside myself I did not know I possessed. I firmly believe for the first time in my existence that I am listening to my own conscience. It whispers to me of my sins—the terrible things I have done and the things I have failed to do. I know I will not sleep tonight.

July 22, 2011

Amy came back to the farm today. She worked in the shop in the morning, shared a noonday meal with Sean, and then accompanied him to the greenhouse. I had to go deep into the woods then backtrack around the fields and orchard so I could approach the greenhouse unseen from the rear. Turning still as stone in the bushes, I peered through a hole at what was happening inside.

Ron and Cheryl, the makeup artists, were showing the two young people the technique they referred to as air brushing. I have observed them before with their noisy little machines, but today was the first time I had a good view of how they actually worked. They started with grumbles and growls that forced air into narrow tubes. It exited at the other end in a hissing rush. The air, in turn, picked up paint from a tiny cup and sprayed it on the intended canvas—in this case, someone's face. Amy and Sean practiced designs on each other. I recognized the masks as belonging to the resurrected dead, or zombies, so beloved by the haunters. Both young people possess a good deal of artistic ability. They could make it appear as though there were gashes and blood and mold where none actually existed. Ron and Cheryl congratulated them on their progress.

When Amy and Sean finished their air brushing, they washed off their faces and left the greenhouse. They whispered something to each other, and Sean embraced the young woman. She leaned her head against his shoulder, seeming to draw strength from him. Then they returned to the bakery.

July 30, 2011

It has been so sweltering hot the last two days that I have kept to my root cellar by day, pressed against the cool damp earth, and hunting only at night. Many animals are active then, and I can usually smell if an opossum or a raccoon has been killed by a speeding vehicle. It is much easier than waiting for game to approach me. Unfortunately, I have no means for preserving the bounty around me. Animal flesh putrefies quickly in this heat. Fresh or decayed, everything tastes equally foul. But I do not like bringing the odor of rot into my humble cellar.

Last night, I returned from my hunt to the sounds of intrusion within my tottering sanctuary. I managed to convince all would-be ghost hunters that this place was treacherous and could not be purified by fire, prayer, or incantation. So I did not expect to find more than a curious raccoon when I crept down the rear stairs to my cellar. As I lifted myself through the hole in the parlor floor a red light fell on my face.

I lunged forward and knocked the light to the ground. Then I grabbed the glowing tube and raised it to identify the trespasser. It was Amy.

I was both enraged and terrified. I could not fathom why she had come, but I knew nothing good could come of it. I lacked the voice to howl at her. Instead, I thrust my face into hers, baring all my terrible teeth and raking the air with my claws. She cried out and fell backwards. I sprang again, and she scrambled to her feet, retrieved the light I had dropped, and bolted for the front door.

She stopped and faced me. "You saved me," she cried. "I just wanted to thank you." Then she was out the door and flying through the grass towards the road.

I sat on the rotting floor and wept. I longed so to hear more of her voice, to understand how she came to name me or know anything about me. Her voice, her childlike gratitude, opened another great hollow inside me—this time in my heart. I am lonely. I want a friend. This hell spawn with no parents longs for a child of his own

But that can never be. My hunger is too implacable to ever allow for any genuine intimacy. This is my hell, and there are no friends here.

THE NATURE OF THE BEAST

THE AFTERNOON OF Amy's disappearance, Cam found Sean in the walk-through and told him they would have to postpone their monster hunt. "I got to help a friend move," Cam said. "I'll show you the place later next week."

"I'll tell Amy," Sean said.

"I already told her. I think she's gone home already."

Sean watched Cam walk away and muttered under his breath, "I knew it. He's full of shit."

When Sean went home, he saw Gloria in the hall outside her apartment. "Where's Amy?" she asked. "Is she still at the farm?"

"I thought she went home over an hour ago," Sean replied. "Maybe she went to the greenhouse instead. I think Meg's working on new costumes."

Gloria was clearly troubled. "I'll try calling her." She let herself into her apartment. Sean stood in the hall. The prodding in his gut told him something was not right. He borrowed Gloria's car and drove back to the farm.

§ § §

When Amy opened her eyes again, the sky was still light, but the shadows in the woods were deep and dark. She thought she had been dreaming. Then she sat up and saw the blood on her jeans. She vaguely remembered watching it as it fell from the tree above her, feeling the wet warmth soaking through the denim. Now it was drying.

"Bonebelly," she said. She had seen Bonebelly. The creature had done something beyond belief, something horrifying. She shook with fear yet had the sense she had come through this afternoon unharmed.

Amy knew she should leave this place. At first, she could only move forward on her hands and knees. When she came to a fallen tree alongside the path, she was able to pull herself to her feet and walk.

§ § §

Jeff Michelson was driving home from work and passed the granite marker

107

just as Amy staggered out of the trees. He pulled his truck across both lanes to the weed-choked shoulder. He spotted the blood on her clothing and bolted out of the cab.

Amy tried to call out to Jeff, but her tongue still would not work properly. As he tried to get the girl to sit on the ground, she mumbled, "I'm not doing that again." *I sound drunk*, she said to herself.

Sean spied his father's truck and pulled in behind it. "What happened?" he cried. He ran to Amy's side.

"I just found her wandering," Jeff replied. He handed his phone to Sean to call for help. He saw the blood and tried to inspect the girl for wounds. "Are you hurt, Amy?"

"Cam," Amy said.

Sean swore. "Cam? Did he hurt you? Where did that blood come from?"

Amy stared at the blood on her clothes. "It's Cam's. It's his face—his nose. Blood was coming from his face."

"Is she on something?" Jeff asked.

"It's Cam," Sean said. "I'll bet he gave her something. I don't know how he got her here, but he did this to her."

The first responders arrived. Before they could bundle her onto a stretcher, Amy grabbed Sean's hand and whispered, "Bonebelly. Bonebelly has him."

Rohypnol had been slipped into Amy's water bottle. She had only drunk a little, which is why she probably had the strength and muscle control to break Cam's nose—the probable source of the blood on her clothes, according to the police. Amy was unmolested and unhurt, and she was released from the hospital the next morning. It appeared Cam was on the run.

"I'm not even sure if what I saw was real," Amy said as she sat with Sean on her sofa that evening. "I saw Bonebelly crawling down the trunk of this tree. He had claws on his fingers, and he dug these claws into Cam's face. He pulled him right up into the tree. Cam was...I think he was hanging from Bonebelly's fist—just hanging in the air. And Bonebelly looked right at me—like he knew me. I actually thought he was going to say something. I think I called him Bonebelly. I couldn't see Cam anymore. I had the feeling he didn't want me to see what he did to him. Then there was blood. It just...just fell out of the tree." She was quiet for a moment. "Should I be feeling more traumatized than I do?"

Sean shrugged. "Maybe you will later. Right now, it probably feels surreal. You're sure that bastard didn't get a chance to do anything to you?"

"I'm positive. He must be dead now. Jesus." She shivered.

Sean did not answer. Instead, he booted up his lap top and typed into the browser: "Missing persons in South County, RI."

"What are you looking for?"

"I'm wondering what we're actually dealing with. We've been treating Tom's yeti like it's something cool. He drinks beer, and he likes the haunt. But what if he's a predator, pure and simple?"

"But then why didn't he come back for me?"

"I don't know. Maybe he was full."

They spent an hour online scouring local newspapers for disappearances over the previous decade, a timeline they chose based on the assumption that Bonebelly was a relative newcomer to the area.

"No missing children," observed Amy, clearly relieved.

Sean scrolled down the page. "We have a few people running from arrest warrants. Two teenage runaways. There's the old man who went missing the winter before last. They don't think he was murdered. But there is this."

He handed the laptop to Amy and she began to read. It was a news story about a local man who was arrested for beating his wife. He violated a restraining order and returned to the home with a gun. His wife had changed the locks so he could not get in, but he shot and killed the family dog in the back yard. Then, somewhere between the death of the dog and the arrival of the police, the man disappeared. His car remained parked on the street. He left a few possessions at a local motel room but had taken his wallet with him. Eight months later, he had not yet been found.

"So Bonebelly was seen at the haunt but never threatened anyone there," Sean said. "He didn't threaten Tom. He just peeked through the window."

"You're forgetting about the group that got lost in the woods," Amy corrected him. "They said they were attacked by one of the actors, but they described a big white thing that sounds like Bonebelly. One of them said it lifted him right off his feet. They were so wasted no one paid any attention to anything they said."

"There's another story. I don't know if you heard this one. You know my friend, Finn? He was out in the woods last summer. They were all drinking. Finn steps into some bushes to take a leak. He's leaning against a tree. He swears something licked his arm. He starts screaming and everyone starts laughing at him. Then one of the neighbors called the police so they all scattered."

"Where in the woods did this happen?"

"I think it was behind that new subdivision. If that's an actual sighting, then throw in the haunt and the place Cam took you, it seems like he wanders over a really big area."

Amy frowned. "It sounds like he killed two abusers. If you include me, he's had three, maybe even four, opportunities where he could have killed and chose not to. What does it mean?"

"I don't know. But I think we should stop trying to find him."

"Agreed," Amy said.

§ § §

She did not like the way everyone tiptoed around her as if they expected her to shatter into pieces at any moment. After all, Cam had not really harmed her. What had been terrifying was the sight of Cam being lifted by his torn face until he vanished into the green canopy and that single splotch of blood dripping onto her clothes. She replayed the scene over and over in her head, wondering if what she saw was real, but she had not had a single nightmare or panic attack as she'd been told she might.

Amy had no intention of halting her hunt for Bonebelly. She would carry out a plan she had been mulling over for days, a plan that would confirm that what she had witnessed was not a drug-induced hallucination. She would find the decaying house in the woods, look Bonebelly in the face, and thank him for saving her from harm. Unwilling to risk anyone else's safety, she would go alone.

That Saturday, she claimed she did not feel well and went to bed early. She set her alarm for one a.m. and silently slipped out of the apartment. She debated taking her mother's car but was afraid of attracting attention if she left it on the side of the road. She rode her bike to the granite marker and used a red LED flashlight to help her find her way.

The path to the ruined farmhouse was overgrown but not difficult to follow. It ran uphill perhaps a quarter mile and had probably once commanded a 360-degree view of fields and stone walls. Amy forced herself to walk it without once looking over her shoulder.

She found the cedar that grew next to the south wall of an old house. She used a fallen limb to prod her way through the tangled vines that ran over the structure. From what she could see it seemed that the house stood two stories high, although part of the second floor had collapsed towards the rear, giving the roof a peculiar, bowl-shaped slope. The back door, if it still existed, was completely overgrown. She worked her way back to the front and saw that the sagging weight of the upper floor had forced the door out of alignment. It leaned away from the house at an angle, permanently ajar. The narrow aperture would not budge when Amy tugged on it but was wide enough to squeeze through.

The floor of the front room groaned alarmingly underfoot. Amy carefully felt her way across the floor with her stick. She turned slowly in a circle, scanning for hazards and signs of habitation. Then she stopped. Someone had written on the walls.

The script, a long and sloping cursive, filled up parts of the ceiling and three of the four walls from the top to within a few inches of the bottom. The letters were thick, black, and shiny, almost as if they were written in tar. It was difficult to follow, but a few words leapt out at Amy: demon, corpse, hunger, hell, and damned.

Under the glare of the flashlight, the words seemed to pulse and shimmer.

Amy drew closer to examine the medium that formed the letters. As the intense red light homed in on a single sentence, dozens of tiny black beetles swarmed and scattered in all directions. They had been feeding on the ink. Amy stifled a cry and dropped her flashlight. She pounced on it and dimmed the light. She crouched fearfully in the darkness, shivering and panting. The house creaked but was otherwise silent. Amy drew a deep breath and got to her feet. She trained her light on the words again and waited for the beetle hordes to disperse. The letters beneath were still black but not as shiny. The ink, whatever it was, smelled faintly of skunk cabbage and swamp. Amy did not want to speculate how it had been made. As she inspected the wall, lines separated from the tangled script and coherent sentences emerged: "Here follows a true account of my first thirty days in hell."

"Oh, my God," Amy whispered. "He's being punished."

A board off to her right cracked. Startled, she swung her light around. It fell full on Bonebelly's face. A long thin arm with skeletal fingers shot forward and knocked the flashlight out of her hand. Amy screamed and fell backwards.

The creature lunged forward, shining the light down on his head as if he wanted Amy to see him in all his repulsive horror. He flexed his phalanges in her face, displaying his terrible claws. He put his face right up to hers. She could see the yellowed skin stretched taut over an oversized skull, the rope-like muscles of the skinny neck, and the mouthful of savage teeth. His breath reeked of earthworms and damp soil. Although his mouth gaped as if to howl, not a sound issued from his throat. Then Bonebelly stamped a clawed foot against the floor and lunged at her face again. Amy shrieked and scrambled to her feet. Somehow she retrieved her flashlight and found her way to the door.

"You saved me. I just wanted to thank you!" she cried over her shoulder. She flew up the path, never daring to look back. She shook with sobs as she pedaled her way home.

It was still dark when she let herself into the apartment, but birds were rousing themselves and calling to each other. She took a warm shower and calmed herself with a cup of tea. She woke Gloria to tell her she felt sick and could not go into work with her that morning. Then she tried to sleep.

Amy could not relax. The night's events—the swarming beetles, the spidery script, the tortured words, Bonebelly reaching for her—played repeatedly in her head. Suddenly, she sat up in bed. "He never touched me," she said out loud. Bonebelly had put on an extravagant display but never laid as much as a claw on her. He wanted to frighten her away.

Amy leapt out of bed and pulled lined paper and a sketch pad from her desk. First, she wrote down the few sentences of Bonebelly's written confession she'd had a chance to read. Then she recorded all her recollections of the house, the layout and condition of the rooms, and everything Bonebelly did. When she finished the written record, she began to sketch. She drew the exterior of the building and the one room she had examined from every angle she could recall. And she drew Bonebelly: first as she saw him crawling down the trunk of the cedar, then as he grimaced inches from her face. Finally, she feverishly sketched the creature as he came up behind Cam, grabbed him by the hair and pulled him by his face up a tree.

With the last drawing, Amy began to weep the way everyone had been telling her she would. When she finally cried herself out, she tossed the sketchbook and legal pad under her bed and slept without dreaming until Gloria woke her well after dark with a bowl of chicken soup. It had been made from scratch, and Gloria had truly outdone herself. When Amy was finished, Gloria cradled her daughter's head on her shoulder and let the girl cry herself back to sleep.

BLESSED OCTOBER

September 2, 2011

I N MY DREAMS I saw those eyes again—the same clear, bright hazel, the same open, knowing gaze. They were watching the minister, the deacon, and the abused serving girl. She had been dragged back to the minister after running away from him. He was calling her a liar in front of the congregation and charging her to repent. She bowed her head before the pulpit and wept quietly but would not own to any sin. An old woman in the congregation offered to take the girl in and try to correct her waywardness, but the minister stated the girl's soul must be cleansed and humbled before he could allow her into someone else's home. The old woman gave the minister a disapproving stare. So did her aged husband, who stood at her side. His blue eyes were intense with threat and fury. I could not place where I had seen those eyes before.

The dream shifted to the minister's quarters. He was goading the deacon, making sport of his soft, lumpish body, of his courage, and even his manhood. He pushed the deacon towards the girl cowering on the floor. When the deacon hesitated, the minister pinched his soft flesh, whispering filth and insults into the young man's ear. Finally, driven by rage and lust, the deacon took the girl, hurting her in his turn, covering her mouth to muffle her cries. The minister watched them with barely suppressed excitement. Peering from a dark corner, devoid of form, were those radiant hazel eyes, brimming with bewilderment and pain.

When I awoke I found myself cringing with mortification and covering my nakedness with my bony hands. If these dreams tell the story of my sins, then my disgrace is deep indeed.

September 4, 2011

It is yet another interminably long holiday weekend. This one celebrates "labor," even though there is little work going on. One exception is at the farm, where they are rushing to finish Bone Ridge for what the haunters refer to as "Septober."

It appears that Sean has purchased his own motorized conveyance. That means he is frequently driving off to pick up something Justin or Milton have run out of. Many of these errands are for things I do not recognize such as "duct tape" or "PVC." And even though they have boxes and boxes of nails and screws, they sometimes decide none of them are right and send Sean on yet another errand. He never complains. He is a most congenial and obliging youth.

September 10, 2011

Milton and the managers held a rehearsal for the haunters on the walk-through. I saw the event written on a large calendar posted in the greenhouse. They assembled in the second vehicle paddock right outside the exit of the long, dark tunnel everyone refers to as the Dungeon. It has a false wall that made a hiding place for the last haunter on the tour. Unwilling to miss any part of the haunt season, I secreted myself in this closet as the actors gathered beneath the setting sun. I found it hard to remain still, however. The jocularity among the returning actors was just too infectious. The hiding place was open to the outdoors, so I crept into the woods and hid behind a gigantic pile of finely chopped timber.

Some of last year's haunters were missing, but I recognized many returning faces. Milton gave out costume and character descriptions and a "script" which told the actors what they were supposed to do. Then he introduced Meg, who everyone referred to as the "costume notsee." I must confess I have no idea what a notsee is. Perhaps it is a native word. She railed and threatened as she told everyone how to find their costumes and what punishments she would inflict if they did not take care of them properly. They all sounded painful, and some of them might have been impossible for anyone other than Demon to inflict.

Finally, Bill stepped forward to warn the haunters against any rowdy behavior. He used particularly foul language as he railed against drinking while on the job, especially among those haunters who were less than 21 years of age. "It's a fun job, but it is a job. You don't party at your day job if you expect to keep it, and you don't party here. The bon fire after we close is 21-plus. And Rhode Island's finest are just waiting for you assholes to peel out of here at the end of the night so they can pull you over. Tom and Jen have to pay a fine if anyone underage is drinking on their property. They could also lose their insurance, which means Bone Ridge closes down."

"They give us a great horror playground and then they pay us to play here," Justin said. "If you want to be a dick and exploit it, we don't need you. We have a waiting list of people who want to work here, and they'll show up at a moment's notice."

Once again, I planned to help myself to any beer and spirits stashed behind the scenes at the haunt. It was my duty to take it. I silently pledged to patrol the scenes diligently every night for the duration of the All Hallows revels.

I did not follow the group as they headed into the woods to rehearse the scenes. It was still light and there were too many people on the trail. I would wait for the season to begin and watch a few scenes at a time as I had last year.

I cannot wait for opening night to arrive. I am almost mad with anticipation.

September 13, 2011

I am so overjoyed with the approaching haunt season that I have caught myself looking over my shoulder for Demon more than once. He would most likely be enraged if he knew I was feeling so much pleasure despite the torments he devised just for me. When I catch myself bounding happily through the woods, I stop and take pains to look depressed and to move in an attitude of prayerful penitence.

The truth is, I have not seen Demon for months. He did not even show himself as I slew and desecrated Amy's attacker. Surely, this crime is not hidden from my jailer. I know I must pay for it at some unanticipated time and placed.

September 18, 2011

Last night was the rehearsal for the hay ride actors. However, I did not come to Stone Ridge for that. Instead, I watched Justin enter the greenhouse with his copy of Lovecraft's works and then walk out of the structure without it. I knew this was my chance to lay my hands on the book and escape with it into the woods. I would read as much as I could and sneak it back to the greenhouse the following week.

I read several stories by the light of a small torch until I fell asleep. I awoke just before dawn and recorded my impressions.

The stories seem the products of a fevered imagination. Even Dante's "Inferno" did not describe horrors like these. "Under the Pyramids" made my poor tortured stomach lurch as I pictured the parade of decayed, animal-headed bodies worshiping the monster of the Sphinx. Lovecraft seemed, however, to take particular pleasure in describing slimy creatures from watery depths. I wonder what he would make of a rather dry and desiccated monster like me.

My favorite story was "The Outsider," even though the tale broke my heart. A man, devoid of memories just like me, lives his lonely life in a dark and rotting castle. One day, he climbs the highest pinnacle of his fortress to push his way into a world he has never seen. When men and women flee from him in terror he learns his true and repulsive nature as a phantasm from beyond the grave. I grieve for this outsider because he is so much like me. But I do not weep. The outsider in the story is an innocent while I am a criminal. It is true, I have wept copious amounts of tears since Demon brought me here, but a sinner like me has no right to any.

Self-pity has forced me to set the book aside for now, but I must read "The Call of Cthulhu" tomorrow. The haunters are so excited by this story.

September 21, 2011

The harvest is coming in, and I am trying to plan ahead for the bleak famine of the dark winter months. I do not wish to compound my sins by thieving, so I have devised what I think is a brilliant plan to provide myself with the meager nourishment I am allowed. If I am able to confiscate enough contraband beer, I could leave it as trade for the apples and pumpkins and squash available at the local farms. They will keep well in my root cellar and, I pray, will ward off the terrible pangs I suffer for the Great Abomination. They might also lure mice and squirrels, making winter hunting somewhat easier. Of course, I will have to fill my cellar now and pay my debts later. I hope there will be enough libations to enjoy myself and perhaps to share with Bill for the bonfires.

Bone Ridge Farm is opening earlier this year, on "Septober" 23. Only two more days until I can watch my beloved haunters at work!

September 26, 2011

I watched the first nights of the walk-through. There are twelve scenes this year. Over the course of four hours I was able to spend twenty minutes at each. There is a grave yard with the hearse and a large vault similar to the scene from last year, ruins with ghouls and shambling corpses, and a new maze. There were nine new scenes: One that Milton referred to as "zombillies" where recently deceased mountain folk had victims tied across the front of an old truck; a conveyance Milton called a school bus—an unnatural yellow thing meant to take children to school—filled with grotesque, life-sized poppets and two live haunters. The guests were forced to traverse the narrow aisle in the dark, never knowing which monstrosity would reach out for them until it was too late. There was a hospital where the sick were tormented and dismembered, a Greek temple haunted by harpies, a hall with multiple doors where guests had to choose which way to go or fall victim to the clowns (and there was a clown behind each and every one), a garden inhabited by lizard men, a victualer referred to as "Bubba's Bone Pit" where human carcasses were roasted in a hot sauce, and two moveable spots where the customers would be chased by fiends in leather masks and aprons wielding chain saws. The last scene in the Dungeon was modeled after "Under the Pyramid," with the beautiful Synova as a dead Egyptian queen attended by animal-headed monsters.

I find it disconcerting that so many people enjoy this form of entertainment. They complain and demand their money back if they are not scared badly enough. Sometimes the adults are the most frightened, and their children laugh and jeer at their discomfort. I noticed also that many a stout young man pushes the female he is courting into the midst of the haunters, especially the ones with chain saws. The experienced haunters do not like this and talk among themselves about how cowardly it is. "It's the easy scare," they say. Whenever they are able, they remain hidden and attack the males, exposing them for the craven cads that they are.

As much as the haunters love what they do, they have numerous complaints. They dislike the drunken revelers who show up at the end of the night. I myself saw them this weekend try to rip sets apart or hit the haunters. Bill, Susan, or large men wearing shirts with "SECURITY" emblazoned across the back followed them through the sets. I heard the zombillies gossiping that some of the drunks had attempted to set Cthulhu on fire on the hay ride. They were quickly escorted to the constables, who took them away. They shared this information as they snuck sips of beer between their scares. That was Friday night. I started confiscating beer on Saturday.

Haunters feel most impatient with eleven-year-old boys who try to cover their fear with false bravado. They engage in behavior that they seem to find amusing but actually makes them look ridiculous. For example, when a haunter surprises them, they scream back at the actor and shout, "I scared you!" Usually, the haunter will refuse to respond, will "stay in character," and silently follow him until the boy runs. From my hiding place in a muddy drainage ditch, I watched one boy run at full speed through the school bus to draw out Travis and Joe, the two haunters. Then he ran back through the bus to join his friends. I assumed he planned to give away the scare and impress his friends. The two haunters exchanged looks of disgust and immediately changed position. Joe moved the "driver" and took its place while Travis climbed on top of the bus and laid flat. The boy led his friends to the aisle of the bus and jumped in front of the seat where he thought Travis would be. "He's right here!" the fool shouted triumphantly. The "driver" came up behind the boy and tapped him on the shoulder. He was first to vault for the emergency door where Travis swung down to greet him.

"What a dumb little ass wipe," Joe said to Travis as the boy ran screaming for his life.

"Newbies" who could not learn how to act were another problem. There was a lovely young woman named Therese who seemed disappointed that she had been transformed into a grossly disfigured nurse in the death hospital. She complained to Alex, the equally monstrous physician at the scene, how she had once worked as a pirate princess at another All Hallows celebration and had wished to do the same at Bone Ridge.

"A pirate princess?" Alex exclaimed. "That's little kid stuff. That's not scary."

"I didn't really want to be scary," Therese confessed.

And scary she was not. She began to sing to the patrons as soon as they entered the scene. She was so distracting that it was difficult for Alex to frighten anyone.

"Show tunes? Why?" cried Alex after the customers had gone.

"I'm making it more of a theatrical experience," she explained.

"Scaring isn't theatrical enough? This isn't Disneyworld!"

The girl looked as if she might weep. I do not know if she actually scared any-one that night, but I did not hear her sing again.

Another newbie was Aaron, the eighteen-year-old son of one of the farmer's business colleagues. He was one of the roaming corpses in the ruins, the first to lurch out at the patrons when they entered the scene. Aaron was not especially good. He broke character to chat with the customers and went for the easiest scares, usually nervous young women. When he succeeded in making one of them scream he would chase her through the remainder of the scene, actively interfering with the other actors. He was clumsy, so he posed the only actual threat to life and limb at Bone Ridge. The experienced actors took him aside and patiently explained that it was wrong to "hog" the scares or to leave his spot empty as new patrons were entering the scene. It did not help.

By Saturday night, Aaron was chasing patrons up the path and through other scenes. He ran into Melanie at the harpy scene, knocking her flat on her back. He finally stopped running, which allowed Melanie to pin him against a tree and unleash a torrent of threats and curses, most addressed at his manhood. Later that night, I saw Bill take the young man aside at his scene for a lengthy discussion. Aaron appeared crestfallen. I overheard Bill telling the harpies that Aaron would be directing traffic next weekend.

On Saturday, I confiscated more beer than I could carry. I removed one box from the ruins before the evening even got underway. While they were smoking tobacco at the entrance to the scene, I was able to lift it high in the branches of the tree where I was hiding. The zombillies kept theirs under the seat of their dilap-idated truck. The lizard men hid theirs on a stump behind a bush. I took them all, drank one, and saved a few more for myself.

I was dressed all in black so I could blend into the shadows. I slipped through the tree cover that separated the walk-through from the hay ride, laden down with libations. The greenhouse was empty, so I moved into the clearing to Bill's truck and left a gift in the cargo hold. I took the rest to trade for food at Stone Ridge and other nearby farms.

October 3, 2011

Friday night, I was able to see every part of the hay ride except the tunnel where I attempted hibernation last winter. One scene resembled an ancient city overgrown with green slime and filled with emerald, fish-like creatures. There was a mortuary where the dead were reanimated. I noticed that Therese had been

118

reassigned as one of the Salem witches. She was beautiful and vengeful and theatrical. It suited her. She was, however, saddened that she could not wear green makeup or sing something she referred to as "wicked." Crystal, who had been born missing part of one arm, took Therese's place as the disfigured nurse. She wore a bloodied false limb which she pulled off and waved at the guests. I did not see the much heralded Cthulhu. I realized he must be in the tunnel.

Saturday afternoon, I crept into the tunnel before anyone else arrived. The same stage I had nested under was there, draped with black cloth. I secreted myself underneath and waited for the performance to begin.

The tunnel was kept in complete darkness until the first wagon rolled in. Then the doors swung shut and a pulsing "strobe" light revealed the horror that was Cthulhu. If I craned my head just a little, I could see him emerge and menace the right side of the wagons.

Cthulhu was actually Justin in a green and gray creation Meg the notsee had put together. It had bloody tentacles hanging from Justin's face, and he waved monstrous claws. Two grotesque acolytes of Cthulhu jumped about the guests on the wagon, crying, "Obey Cthulhu!" and "Cthulhu lives!" In the flickering light, everything had the look of a hellish nightmare. It was quite an effective end to the hayride.

But I think I know a way to improve it.

AN UNINVITED GUEST

WHO NEEDS WHITE?" shouted Sean over the din in the greenhouse. "Green base coat over here," Amy called out. There was a lot of green on the hayride this year.

When no one responded, Susan shouted, "Hayride! Get your asses in a chair. We open in 60 minutes. You can visit when your makeup's done."

Amy and Sean smiled at each other from their separate stations. They didn't always have a chance to get as creative as Ron and Cheryl, but they were ecstatic to be part of it all.

Jeff was part of Bone Ridge this year, too. Gloria convinced him to sign on as a tractor driver, for which Sean was grateful. When Jeff worked, Jeff did not drink.

"Did you just get here, Travis?" demanded Bill as the haunter tried to slip into the makeup queue without being seen. It was the second weekend of operation and the fourth time Travis had been an hour late. The young man sheepishly ducked his head.

"Make him pretty, Cheryl," Bill told the makeup artist. "You're wearing a dress tonight, Travis. Next time you're late you get fired."

From the back of the greenhouse, Travis's friends offered to help him with his boobs. "Why do men find men with breasts so fascinating?" Meg said.

By the time the first weekend ended, it was clear that Bone Ridge Farm was going to be much bigger than it had been last year. Melissa and Jon were shifted to crowd control, largely to help scare and entertain patrons as they waited in line. Melissa spent most of the night on stilts. She was able to run people down as they broke from line and fled, screaming. Jon alternately dressed as a toothsome jester or a saggy-breasted hag who kept up a stream of jokes as she did flips and hand stands with her walker.

That second Saturday, as Sean and Amy applied base coats to haunters' faces, they eavesdropped on Bill, Susan, and Milton huddling over their waiting list of actors. Two of the newbies had not shown up. They had demoted Aaron to parking lot attendant before he ran down and killed one of the other haunters. They were missing the theatre major who thought haunting would be a fun and interesting bit of performance art to add to his resume. He quit at the end of the first night, exhausted from jumping on and off the hay wagons with no time to deliver his soliloquies. One of Cthulhu's acolytes ignored the warning signal and jumped from a moving wagon, breaking his ankle.

When the hay ride actors were off waiting for the first wagon and the walk-through actors went to their sets, Milton approached Sean and Amy.

"How old are you?" he asked Sean.

"Eighteen in November," Sean lied.

Milton pondered a moment. "Ok, you're a Cthulhu acolyte tonight. I'll get a third actor as soon as I can. Don't be stupid around the wagons." He turned to Amy. "What about you?"

"Eighteen in March," Amy said.

"Don't make me sorry. You're a harpy tonight. Get a robe, get some snakes and ugly yourself up. Do whatever Carrie and Mallison say."

The first wagon was already out when Sean arrived at the tunnel. He got a few tips from Justin on where to stand and how to work the groups on the wagons. Until they got more actors, the action would be frantic.

Milton texted the women at the Grecian ruins. "We have a harpy baby." Allison greeted Amy.

"A harpy baby," cooed Melanie and Carrie.

They showed her the shadowy places where their dark gray makeup and costumes all but disappeared and places where the lighting blinded the patrons until they were right in front of the actor. They pointed out a perch where, in the dim lights, she could pass for a gargoyle until she chose to spring to the ground.

Carrie gave Amy a final piece of advice. "Stay in character unless someone tries to assault you. Never, ever say, 'Boo.' Don't hog the scares and…"

"No show tunes?" Amy finished.

By nine o'clock, the lines were growing and the actors were in nearly constant motion. Amy and Sean were happily exhausted, sending pictures to each other when they could take a break.

Sean felt somewhat disoriented by the frequent bursts of strobe light. As he stood on the stage, he thought he saw a long, skeletal arm snaking out from underneath. There was something oddly familiar about it, but when he peeked under the black draping at the end of the night there was nothing there. He kept it to himself. He was afraid he would get pulled from the scene if anyone thought the strobe was making him hallucinate.

As the night wound down to a close, Bill went back to the greenhouse to check on the video camera mounted on the roof of his truck. Friday night, he briefly returned to the greenhouse. As he came around the corner, he saw a tall, oddly proportioned figure reaching into the bed of his truck. A black stocking cap was stretched over a bulging skull. The man wore black pants and a shirt but had long, white, horny-looking feet. The fingers were also unusually long, thin, and white. He appeared to place something in the truck bed. When the visitor turned away, Bill clapped his hand over his mouth. He saw a huge stomach and a gaunt face with teeth, protruding and ferocious. Then the creature—for it clearly was not a man—ran into the darkness on its long, thin legs, cradling a box under one arm. Bill inspected his truck and found a six pack of beer that had not been there before.

"Tom's yeti? And leaving gifts?" Bill laughed. "Yeti Claus. I'll be damned."

He set up a camera the next day, but when he inspected the footage he saw nothing but a few actors taking a smoke break.

Justin and Sean were alone in the tunnel again on Sunday night. It was a slower night, mostly families, but it was still strenuous work keeping everyone entertained. Sean almost failed to notice the new animated figure in the corner.

It wore a long robe and had a sophisticated range of gestures. Its long skeletal arms all but brushed the faces of the startled patrons in the wagon. The mouth rapidly opened and closed, flashing a fierce row of fangs. It appeared to be sound-lessly laughing. Then the strobe light went out, the tunnel turned black and the tractor moved on.

"When did we get an animatronic for this scene?" Sean asked Justin.

"There's nothing in here but us," Justin said.

"Then what was in the corner?" Sean trained a flashlight beam on the far end of the tunnel. It was empty.

Two wagons later, he saw it again. It was Bonebelly, crouching on the stage, stretching his long arms for the terrified customers in the wagon. Justin had his back to the figure but turned and spied the creature just as the wagon pulled away. The actors extinguished the strobe and searched with flashlights. No one else was there. Justin inspected the corner where Sean first glimpsed the appa-rition. There was a double panel of landscaping fabric hanging from the roof to provide a hiding place. He pulled the fabric aside. The nook was empty.

Sean's eyes strayed to the black skirting around the stage where he had seen the skeletal arm last night. He wanted to look but knew he would not. He felt like a little boy again, afraid of monsters under his bed.

Another wagon was approaching, and they put their lights out. Sean and Justin positioned themselves opposite the stage. When Justin turned on the strobe again, the creature was in the corner again, gyrating grotesquely. The wagon moved on but Justin did not turn off the strobe. The creature appeared to make a slight bow in the hallucinatory light then deftly vanished from their sight.

"What the fuck," Justin whispered. The next few wagons came through, and Justin left the strobe light flashing. The figure did not reappear.

Justin plunged the tunnel back into darkness. When the next wagon entered, the strobe flickered again but they saw nothing. Then, as Sean turned to jump off the wagon, he saw patrons in the middle of the wagon squealing and looking sky-ward. Bonebelly had ditched his robe and clung to the ceiling, waving his claws. Justin was working the rear of the wagon and did not turn in time to catch a glimpse.

"Did you see anything that time?" Justin asked as the wagon pulled away.

"Nothing," Sean lied as he shut off the lights. "Think we're seeing things?"

"I don't know. It's either Tom's yeti or an actor having some fun with us. He was good, whoever he was."

Sean agreed and excused himself to take a break. He crept outside the tunnel where the stage would be, crouched close to the ground, and said, "If you want to scare, that's okay. But I assume you don't want to be discovered. So unless you plan on filling out an application, you should stick to the shadows. Pop out of the trees just before the wagons return to the parking lot. Hide between the scenes on the walk-through. They'd be great scares. Did you hear all that?"

Three sharp raps sounded on the plywood wall of the tunnel. Sean shivered. He wanted to ask for assurances that Bonebelly simply wanted to play with the haunters. But he couldn't be seen talking to the tunnel wall so all he said was, "I'm going back inside now."

The night was almost over. A few more wagons came and went. Bonebelly did not make another appearance. By the time the haunters returned to the greenhouse, Justin had decided their guest haunter had to be an unknown actor playing a prank. He planned to record this actor if he showed next weekend and suggested they keep it to themselves until then. Sean agreed.

Of course, he shared everything with Amy. "Bonebelly was in the tunnel tonight, haunting with us. It was just a few times. The strobe lights went on and he lunged at people in the wagons. Then we didn't see him again."

"We?" Amy exclaimed.

"I saw him three times. Justin saw him twice, I think."

"What did he think it was?"

"He made a joke about Tom's yeti, but he seemed to think it was an actor."

"And was Bonebelly haunting? Or was he hunting?"

"He looked like he was enjoying himself. I gave him some suggestions. I said if he wanted to haunt, he should find a spot with more cover. If he wanted to be discovered, he should fill out an application in the greenhouse."

Amy pondered a moment. "There were no reports of any attacks. Do you think it's safe to have him hanging around?"

"You'd know that better than me. But he is one hell of a haunter."

There was no bonfire that night, but Bill strolled along the dark edges of the parking lot after closing, searching for something pale and misshapen. He noticed Justin scanning the perimeter as well before giving up and going home.

Later that week, Bill reviewed his video footage one more time then erased it. He reset his camera and parked away from the lights of the greenhouse the following Friday. He was rewarded when he inspected the footage Saturday morning. There was the same figure reaching into his truck bed, but this time he was nearly naked. He left a twelve pack of beer behind and loped away into the darkness with another pack tucked under his arm.

"Yeti Claus returns," Bill marveled as he reviewed the footage, "and he's wearing tighty whities. Just what the hell is this thing?"

The third Saturday was a good one for the harpies. The baby harpy scored her first major scare. A group of preteen boys reached the scene. Carrie and Mallison hit different parts of the line, evoking jumps and squeals from all but one of the boys. He backed away from his friends, laughing at their distress but complaining, "I went all the way through the hayride and halfway through this trail and I haven't been scared once."

Then Amy flew from her perch on the wall and landed right in front of the boy. He threw his arms up and fell backwards, screaming, into the dirt. "Thank you," he said fervently as he got up and dusted off his back side. Then he went down on one knee and implored, "Will you marry me?" Amy shrieked and chased him up the trail. "I love you," he called over his shoulder. The older women whistled and cheered her triumph.

"You don't think that was too over the top?" Amy asked.

"At a haunt? There's no such thing," Allison said. "This isn't community theater."

"Sure it is," Carrie said. "It's *demented* community theater—for those of us who don't want to do 'Steel Magnolias.'"

The crowds grew heavier and there were no more breaks. The customers were in good humor and eager to be frightened until around 9:00 when the harpies could hear the wailing of a small child. "Stupid parents," sighed Melanie.

A woman carrying her little girl stepped into view. Allison intercepted the other people in the group back on the trail and broke character to ask them to wait a few minutes. "I'm sorry," the woman said. "We thought she could do this. She's terrified. Is there another way out of here?"

"There are only five more scenes," Carrie said. "You're almost through."

"She can't take any more," the mother implored.

Carrie sighed. "I'll take you to the parking lot."

There were several trails that cut behind various scenes and back to the entrance. Carrie took the little girl by the hand and explained how a haunt works and the kind of people who worked at Bone Ridge. "We have teachers and nurses and some EMTs. We even have an officer from the naval station. Someday you'll come back and scare people, too." She brought mother and child to the parking lot and wished them a happy Halloween. Then she visited one of the port-a-johns, scared a group of teenaged girls as she burst out the door and, snickering, took the back trails to her scene.

She visited Biggie and Mike at the maze and ducked through the woods to approach the Greek ruins from the rear when she saw an oddly shaped figure crouched behind the trunk of a thick old hickory. She did not recognize him. He was stripped down to his underwear, and his skin was the color of weathered bone. The limbs and digits were skeletal and much too long. The head was huge—too large to be supported by its thin neck. It did not move, and Carrie thought it must be a sculpted figure, although it was placed where few would see it.

She crept forward for a better look. The figure suddenly came to life and whirled around to face her. She cried out and fell hard against the base of a tree. The scattered clouds parted, and the waning moon filtered light through the branches onto the scowling white face and the bloated belly. Carrie blinked several times as her heart calmed and her fear settled. "Oh my God," she cried. "I can't believe it."

The scowl was replaced by a quizzical look. The creature cocked its head and listened.

Carrie took a deep breath and said, "I know what you are."

THE NATURE OF THE BEAST

I DID IT. I took a foolish chance, but it was wonderful. When I reached my cellar last night, I was exhausted but ecstatic. I slept a contented, restful, and dreamless sleep.

I joined my haunters last night. I did not do as much as I would have liked, but I had to minimize the risk of exposure. They were missing actors in the black tunnel, so I decided to help. In the strange flutter of the strobe light, I looked even more unreal than I do in the light of day. The guests reacted with outright terror. It was intoxicating.

I did not fool the haunters, however. They played with the light and darkness in an attempt to expose me, but I would not be caught. Then, to my great surprise, Sean spoke to me, almost as if he knew me. Perhaps Amy told him about our encounter. He seemed to appreciate my efforts and suggested a better, safer way to scare. I took his advice, moving away from the tunnel and into the trees. It *was* a better scare. The guests assumed they were safe and that the show was over when they could see the lights of the parking lot. How wrong they were. I only attacked the rear where the drivers were not likely to see me.

But even as I relive my triumph, I am nagged by fears. Will I be allowed to keep this diversion, or will Demon take it away from me? I delighted in the screams and laughter I provoked, but I could also smell the fear and excitement. My monstrous stomach groaned and rumbled with want. Can I continue to haunt, or will I forget myself and drag some poor guest into the trees? I could do it. The patrons would assume it was part of the show until the guest was silenced and I was well away.

No. I must not think like this.

October 5, 2011

When the night was well underway and the world was slowing down and going to sleep, I visited two of the local farms. At the first, I left six beers at a cider house and filled a bag with apples. At the second, I exchanged beer for four pumpkins. I hope that is a fair trade. I will continue this secret barter for as long as I have goods to trade.

October 8, 2011

There is a name for what I am.

She called me a hungry ghost.

First, I must admit I took chances I never should have. My first misstep was the Pucker.

I was checking for contraband on the walk-through. My search of the zombilly site turned up a bottle of spirits. It was bright green, and the label read "sour apple schnapps." I took this curious liquor to the top of a fir tree to examine it. Neither the color nor the scent was like anything nature intended, but there was something intriguing and irresistible about it. I took several long pulls from the bottle. It was a mistake. My stomach was emptier than usual because, in a flood of happy anticipation, I neglected to eat so much as a single mouthful before going to Bone Ridge. The spirits raced through my sluggish blood, and in short order I was lightheaded. I nearly fell out of the tree.

Foolishly, I decided I would have some fun. I found a spot on the walk-through that was thickly wooded and away from the back trails. I could remain completely hidden then lunge through the murky briars as guests passed between the harpy scene and the maze. It was amazingly effective. I think I made a grown man piss himself.

The trail grew frenetically busy, and I feared I would be exposed, so I withdrew behind a tree until the crowds thinned out.

She came up behind me almost without a sound. I expect she thought I was a fellow actor, and she wanted to greet me or trade stories. I whirled around at the snap of a twig, my heart pounding, and recognized the intruder as Carrie, the oldest matron at the haunt. She cried out and fell to the ground. Then she calmed herself, peered closely at my hideous visage, and said, "I know what you are. You're a hungry ghost."

I was so stunned to hear a name applied to my unearthly figure that I sat down and made myself as small and unimposing as I could. I motioned to her to continue.

She regarded me curiously. "You understand me?" she asked.

I nodded.

"Can you tell me how you got here?"

I shook my head and gestured at my throat to indicate I had no voice.

"Do you know what a hungry ghost is? It's someone who was a slave to his appetites and desires, ignoring the needs of others. His punishment is to inhabit hell with his huge stomach and tiny throat. All but the smallest morsels of food cause pain."

I nodded vigorously. How did she know this?

"You suffer terrible hunger in this hell of yours, but if you find anything small enough to swallow, it turns to ashes in your mouth."

This statement was not entirely true. I slowly shook my head.

"There is something that actually tastes good to you? What is that?"

I nodded and smiled, my terrible teeth flashing in the moonlight. Carrie took a step back and seemed to debate whether or not to bolt. If I wanted answers to my questions, I would have to be honest without sending her screaming into the woods. I rose to my feet but took a step back so as not to intimidate her. I reached out for her hand and brought it close to my face, smelled it, and licked it. And then my stomach betrayed me. It cried out, and I felt the icy stab of ruthless craving at the core of my gut. I know it showed in my eyes, because she snatched her hand away and bolted behind the tree. Her breath was rapid, panicked. "Oh shit, oh shit, oh shit," she cursed breathlessly. She was tensed and poised to flee. I returned to a seated position and tried to make myself appear small and humble, like a child awaiting his lessons.

Carrie did not run. She kept her distance and slowly regained her composure. At last, she asked, "Is that what condemned you?" she asked.

I answered in the negative.

"So this hunger is punishment for some other type of sin. Have you ever…" Carrie could not finish her question, but I knew what she meant. I hung my head in shame. I held up one finger to represent the one time I had committed the two Abominations together. It was not the truth entire—Demon had taken away my first victim before he surely would have died—but it was true enough.

Her breath caught and shuddered in her throat. In a quavering voice, she said, "You are more monster than ghost. Did you actually, physically die?"

I really did not know the answer to that question. I could remember being snatched up by Demon and regaining sentience in a new and terrible form. Through my dreams, I pieced together some idea of who I once was and what I had done. But I do not remember ever drawing my last breath. So I looked at the woman, raised my hands helplessly, and shrugged.

"I don't understand this hell," she continued. "You're the one who's supposed to suffer. But you're a threat to innocent people. We have children who come through here."

I shook my head frantically. I had been tempted, but I had never taken an innocent life.

"You just said you killed and, and ate…" She faltered, and then demanded, "Who exactly did you kill?"

In reply I broke through the thin, desiccated skin of my arm and carved out the name "CAM."

She trained her torch on my skin and whispered, "Oh my God." She paced back and forth in agitation. "You saw what he tried to do. You saved the girl. But then you judged and executed him. You had no right to do that." She gazed at the ground, pondering. "You mustn't ever do anything like that again, not if you want to change your karma. I have to think about this. I have to decide if I should even try to help you or if I should turn you in—if I can make anyone believe me. Did Amy see you?"

I indicated that she had.

"She was drugged. I don't think she remembers."

There was no way I could tell her I knew otherwise.

"Come to the Greek ruins tomorrow night before we open. My name is Carrie. I'll try and figure out if there's anything I can do to help you and keep everyone safe." She backed away then turned and ran through the trees like Demon himself was after her.

I have no notion of what karma might be. But if it is something I can change, I am in favor of it.

October 9, 2011

Yesterday evening, I crouched in the woods behind the Greek ruins before the sun set. Night was lowering, and blue lights came on as Carrie arrived. She had a large pack slung across her shoulders which she dropped to the ground behind the ruins. She looked around nervously. I was in the thick undergrowth, unclothed and still, so she could not see me. She took something out of her pack and whispered, "Are you there?"

I rattled the brush and then made my appearance. Carrie turned around to face me with a curved blade in her hand, the kind the farm workers used to clear brush.

In a low voice she said, "I was awake all night. I kept thinking about what you are and what you've done. I debated whether I should tell someone that Cam isn't on the run, that he's dead. But I don't know if anyone would believe me."

I had not threatened her in any way. I was offended that she was now brandishing a weapon at me. Nonetheless, I reined in my anger and held out my hands in silent supplication. Carrie turned her weapon over in her hands. "I know what you did. How do I know you won't turn on me? To be honest, just the look of you terrifies me."

I stared in disbelief. I knew this woman refrained from eating meat and treated everyone with maternal kindness, then transformed herself into a disfigured monster with snakes twisted into her wild and matted hair. Her aspect was truly horrible as she stood there in the eerie blue light with her long knife, hurling insults. The effect was supremely comic. I could not help myself. I laughed—shuddering spasms of silent mirth that sounded like I was gasping for air. Carrie regarded me as if I was mad. I made a sweeping gesture with my hand to indicate she should look at herself before she insulted others.

130

She understood. She gave a short laugh and tried to suppress a smile. She relaxed and dropped her weapon to the ground. As she looked into my eyes, I thought I could see compassion behind her mask of horror. She said, "I get it. All of us here—zombies, lizard men, Cthulhu—we're pretending to be you. We want to look like you. The people who come here want us to act like you. But everyone knows they will walk out of these woods in one piece. If someone walks into your territory, will they be able to do the same?"

I realized it was imperative that I pledge to disavow all violence in front of this living witness. I looked into Carrie's eyes and solemnly nodded.

A brisk wind kicked up and whistled through the hole the farmer's gun had made through my heart. A light flickered in Carrie's eyes. She was calculating the chances that I could be killed if she had to defend herself. Then, without taking her eyes off me, she picked up the blade and returned it to her pack. She pulled out a small metal cask and handed it to me. "Try this," she said.

I pulled the ring off the top and sniffed. It was not ale. I let a small trickle wend its way down my throat. It had a milky consistency and was pleasantly but not overly sweet. More important, it did no hurt going down and turned only mildly bitter. I looked at the woman and smiled.

She smiled back. "I suspect acts of compassion are always allowed, even in hell. Let me know if it helps."

I nodded and backed away into the brush and briars. She went about the business of haunting with her friends. I remained at a safe distance, finishing off the liquid in the cask as I listened and watched. It was oddly amusing: These women and their "newbie" shrieked and feigned threats and abuse for the delighted horror of each paying customer. Then they would lapse into conversations about their husbands, children, or sporting games with "the pats." It comforted me to hear people talking of their lives, their loves, their triumphs, and their worries. But I also knew that, if I was to keep the vow I had sworn, I could never share in these lives. I could only befriend my haunters at a distance.

October 10, 2011

I found several more little casks labeled "protein shakes" behind the Greek ruins on Sunday night. There was a note that read, "How many per day?" I used the pencil she left to write, "one," and explained why. Happily, the liquid did calm the raging pains in my stomach even if I was not allowed to enjoy a full belly.

I received another gift of sorts on the Sabbath night. I have listened to the haunters extol the virtues of Pumpkinhead Ale since last year. Apparently, it was available only in the autumn and was brewed in limited supply. They boasted to each other of the number of cases they bought or how they got the last of the ale at a particular merchant. So I was immensely gratified when I found some of this fabled brew hidden at Bubba's Bone Pit by one of the recently hired actors. I took it all and carried it back to my root cellar. I could taste the pumpkin, and it paired surprisingly well with the ale—or it did until it all turned foul.

I also found the bottles appealing. They bore labels depicting a mounted ghoul. His large head was a glowing, carved pumpkin. His toothy grin reminded me of myself. I will save most of these bottles for myself, but I think I will try to trade some of them for some candles. I could fashion some cheerful lamps for myself against the cold and dark of winter.

October 15, 2011

I hid outside the greenhouse while the actors readied themselves, watching from the hole I made near the makeup tables. A student from a local school wanted to take likenesses of the haunters and write a story about their work. Milton came in to prepare the haunters and request they behave. He was right to admonish them. The haunters are usually quite rowdy.

"So I shouldn't do this?" Synova asked, as she lifted her blouse and exposed her bosom. She was a lusty and forward young woman who seemed to enjoy shocking others. I was about to avert my eyes, but the young woman quickly covered herself again. Biggie boasted, "This is what everyone wants to see." He lifted his blouse and made his ample stomach ripple and dance to the great amusement of all.

When the young woman entered the greenhouse, all the haunters had tamed their behavior and language. They were models of decorum.

Once it was dark, I returned to the hayride circuit. I found a tree close to the Exeter vampire set. Most of the haunters were dedicated to their craft. But the hayride actors had to be especially so. Once they inflicted the initial shock on their guests they had to continue confronting and intimidating for several minutes while the wagons were stopped.

There was light rain falling, so the crowds were momentarily thin. I listened as they spoke of visiting other hayrides nearby. *There are other All Hallows revels?* They were critical: Too many props, relying too much on "hydraulics," not enough actors.

"Props don't scare people. Actors scare people," said one of the haunters.

So do real monsters, I thought.

October 17, 2011

The crowds were heavy throughout the weekend. Susan was in costume helping Jon and Melissa keep the throngs of people entertained while they waited for the next wagon. I wished I could have joined them, but it was too much in the open. The constables and security staff were everywhere, and it seemed as though everyone had one of those devices for speaking and making images. I did not want anyone to take my likeness.

There were more protein shakes waiting for me behind the Greek ruins. There was also another note which read, "I can leave more once Bone Ridge closes for the season. Wait until they take down the sets then look in the Dungeon at the end of the walk-through. Namaste." There was a printed page describing karma and the hell realms. They appear to be dogmas of some kind of Eastern pagan religion. The broadside of the hell realm had a drawing of a hungry ghost of the Far East that resembled me somewhat. However, he did not have my claws or teeth.

There was actually no beer this past weekend. Either the reprobate haunters got tired of having it taken, or they found better places to hide it.

I spent much of Saturday night at the Greek ruins. I hoped to learn more about my benefactress. I was not disappointed. It seems Carrie and her husband own a small farm where they raise herbs and make salves and tinctures. She also has a friend and partner with whom she teaches classes in herbal medicine and an Oriental practice called yoga. She credits this practice for her stamina and flexibility. She often bakes things for her fellow haunters. Some of the younger haunters come to her for motherly advice. Biggie always refers to her as "Moms." It is amusing to watch this kindly woman turn so ferociously on hapless guests blundering into her lair.

October 19, 2011

I visited some of the local farms where I left beer in exchange for more apples and pumpkins. I found candles in a storage shed at one of the farms, and I left beer for those as well. I also collected small flaming torches that were abandoned on the walk-through by customers who ran for their lives. Now all I need to do is find reading material. There are places where people leave books just as they leave clothing they no longer want.

I have learned since last winter that these places often have devices that secretly take one's likeness. The constable I surprised at the merchant's village last winter was indeed a haunter. I heard him talk about strange things he had seen on "surveillance cameras." He went on to describe a deformed man who purloined his phone device after he had taken the intruder's likeness. He referred to me as a man, so I know my disguise is successful. I wish I had a broad-brimmed hat to pull over my face. I have only found knitted caps that sit on top of my bulging skull.

October 20, 2011

I returned from a fruitless hunt to find Demon in my cellar. He held one of my tube lights in his hand and was reading my journal. When I entered, he shone the beam on my face then resumed reading. My knees went weak with fear. I had not seen Demon for months. Did he know what I had done? Foolish question! I scolded myself. Of course, he knew.

He tossed the journal aside and scanned the shelves of the fruit cellar. He seemed amused by my meager stores. He picked up a protein shake in one hand and a Pumpkinhead Ale in the other. He drank the ale, watching me the entire time. He grabbed an apple and crushed it. The juice dripped through his fingers. Then, without warning, he lunged and grabbed me by the throat. He lifted me off my feet and shook me as if I were no more than a rag in his fist. He threw me to the earthen floor and pinned me with a great clawed foot on my face. It occurred to me to clasp my hands in supplication and beg to be left in peace. But I could not bring myself to do it. I held his gaze as best I could and awaited my punishment. Demon grinned and picked up two of the smaller pumpkins. He held one in each of his open palms and seemed to be weighing them as he mentally measured my deeds to determine if I was worthy of these sorry gleanings and small gifts from a distant friend.

It seemed nearly an eternity, but he finally put the pumpkins back on the shelf, released me, and left. I rose, my knees shaking with relief. Then Demon burst through the door again. If I had a voice I would have shrieked, and Demon knew it. Grinning, he helped himself to a protein shake and, finally, left me alone.

October 22, 2011

Watching the actors transform themselves for the night's revels is almost as entertaining as watching them scare. Yesterday evening, Justin, who publicizes the haunt, related a "post" on the Bone Ridge "page." I think he is referring to a news broadside. A woman complained that she wanted her money refunded because the show was too terrifying. The farmer refused to give it back.

"Let me get this straight," Jon said. "She goes all the way through the hayride and the walk-through with her kids and then wants a refund?"

"She said we gave her nightmares. I'm leaving that post on the page. We couldn't get a better recommendation."

"That's great. We don't just scare 'em, we fuck 'em up for life," Jimmie said.

The haunters roared with laughter, and then Big Ed led them in a raucous cheer. "We don't just scare 'em," he shouted.

"We fuck 'em up for life," the company shouted back. They took up the cry again and again as they marched to their scenes.

I spent much of the night at Lovecraft's doomed city of Sarnath, covered with green slime and crawling with water lizards. Some of Bone Ridge's finest performers, including Brian and Ellis, slither around the wagons at this scene. I heard something curious as one of the wagons pulled away. A newbie turned to his fellows and said, "My friend came through last week. He was scared shitless by this white monster hiding in the trees just after the Cthulhu scene. He said it was the most awesome makeup he ever saw. Do you guys know who he is?"

Of course, his companions had no idea, but I knew he was talking about me. It was a wonderful feeling. As I crouched in my tree, I pictured myself celebrated as a famous thespian, bowing before an exhilarated audience, acknowledging their accolades. Then I felt a crushing weight on my heart as I realized I had to stop interjecting myself into the scenes. Too many people knew about me. They were growing curious and might soon come looking for me.

October 24, 2011

Bone Ridge was closed Saturday due to heavy rain. Sunday was intermittently misting so it was a slow night. I spent much of it with the clowns. I have no idea what their real names are. Even their closest friends refer to them as Tik-Tok, Punch, Sylence and Gastro. During the long stretches between guests, Punch was receiving comfort from his compatriots. He had visited a "page" where clowns shared news about their work as jesters. He introduced himself to clowns who performed for children and the like and told them what he did. Many of them admonished him as terrible and wicked. Poor Punch was inconsolable. He was, after all, well liked and as kindly a man as any on this good earth.

"What about them? They scare children," TikTok said. "They don't mean to, but they do. If we see little kids coming, at least we stay out of their way."

A new group of paying victims strayed into the hall and the clowns descended on them. Punch got one of them to wet himself.

"Feel better now?" asked TikTok. Punch had to admit that he did.

October 27, 2011

There are only three more nights before Bone Ridge closes down and the haunters return to their everyday lives. I am already filled with sorrow and loneliness. So are some of the performers. As they got ready, several of them spoke about why they haunted and their reasons went beyond the fun of scaring. Some of them, such as Crystal, Synova, and Gastro, had grown up with stern and cruel parents. They faced their unhappy memories when they haunted. A few, like Alex and Brian, were of a melancholic nature. Acting out their dark personas gave voice to their despair. Several of the younger haunters were worried about their futures. Times were hard in Rhode Island. Long-term work was scarce.

Still others, like Carrie and Jon, had lost people close to them. Haunting was a way of laughing in Death's face. I even overheard Amy talking with Mallison about her near violation. She told the harpy women, "I don't know why, but haunting makes me feel safer. It's like I control the evil—and when I control it, no one gets hurt." I thought her words were wise beyond her years.

I wished I could speak to my beloved haunters. I would tell them there are hells worse than theirs, but even in those terrible depths, there are kindnesses that can assuage suffering if one can but recognize them.

October 31, 2011

It is early morning on All Hallows' Eve. Bone Ridge has closed down until next year. The haunters celebrated their successful season with feasting and drinking and laughter. For some, the festivities continued back at the greenhouse. Bill and the farmer built a bonfire, and they all celebrated well into the early morning hours. There was a large boulder surrounded by tall grass at the edge of the lot where many haunters parked their vehicles. From this spot I could watch and listen to the merriment.

At last, the fire died and it was time for the revelers to depart. The farmer looked at Jimmy and said, "How about it? One more time before we call it a night?"

Jimmy grinned and said, "Why not? On three."

He counted down, and the haunters roared at the top of their lungs, "WE DON'T JUST SCARE 'EM. WE FUCK 'EM UP FOR LIFE!"

"We'll probably have to clean that up a bit for next year," Farmer Tom said. And then the actors all went their separate ways.

Bill and Tom tarried to put out the fire. Then Bill did something extraordinary. He got into his truck, reached across the seat, and produced a large box with twenty-four bottles of Pumpkinhead Ale. He leaned out the door and placed it on the ground. He looked around the edges of the lot and announced, "Thanks for the brews, man." Then he closed the door and drove away.

I had been as stealthy as I knew how when I brought beer to Bill's truck. He could not possibly have seen me. Yet somehow, he knew the beer had been left as a gift from a stranger who loved this macabre theater.

I shouldered the crate and made my way back to my ruined shelter. I am drinking an ale as I finish this entry. It is filling me with pleasant warmth, no doubt because it is beer but also because compassion is always allowed, even in hell.

November 3, 2011

I knew Meg, the costume notsee, would be organizing and storing costumes today with Amy and Jen, the farmer's wife. I waited, still as stone, in the tall grass until they finished their work and left. It was almost dark. I knew I could easily slip into the greenhouse unseen to search among the haunters' leavings for useful objects. I found writing instruments, lined paper, and leaflets I could use for my journal. There were also discarded articles of clothing. I found a short coat made for someone with an enormous girth. It had a hood I could pull over my head. It also had one of those interesting closures known as a zipper. There was a long black robe that was torn and was no longer useable as a costume. Black garments were helpful when I needed to move about in the open. I found several small flaming torches. I filled a large black bag with my plunder and was about to leave when I noticed Justin's book of Lovecraft stories on one of the tables. I had returned it, but it seemed he no longer wanted it. There was another book underneath the first: TALES OF POE. It was intimidating in its length, which is exactly what I need. I placed both books in my bag.

I could not find out if Carrie placed anything for me in the Dungeon. The work to disassemble the sets was still going on. I will come back for the rest of this week to witness the sad work of closing down Bone Ridge Farm. I will watch it from a high tree and at a distance. When it is finished at last, I know I will be tempted to go back to my hovel and down all my ale at once. I swear, if I could become that thoroughly intoxicated, I would.

FRIENDS OF BONEBELLY

THEY HAD ALL been watching each other for weeks. It started when Carrie, who loved to cook, began stopping by the farm store once a week to buy bread or muffins. Amy was well aware that Carrie did not need to buy baked goods from anyone. She made a point of commenting on it.

"I've just been too busy to do much baking lately," Carrie said. "And I like supporting local businesses."

"Yeah, lots of people are hurting now," Amy agreed. She noticed as Carrie left that the woman had parked at the far end of the parking lot and that she did not immediately drive away.

Bill had noticed Carrie's activities, too. He drove past the farm after business hours a week before Thanksgiving and spotted Carrie parking on the side of the road. She left her car and ducked through the trees. He turned around and came up behind Carrie's car. He parked and watched. She carried something and kept to the shadows until she emerged at the farthest end of the back lot by the Dungeon. She went inside, and when she reemerged she was empty-handed.

Bill returned to his truck and pulled into the lot of a package store. When he saw Carrie drive past, he backtracked to the farm and retraced Carrie's path to the Dungeon. He searched the tunnel and found a plastic shopping bag with twelve protein shakes. It made no sense unless Carrie had seen what he had filmed. "What are the odds?" he wondered. He decided to find out.

Thanksgiving morning, Bill's wife sent him out for a last minute run to the local convenience store. Bill took a detour to the farm, parked on the side road, and cut behind the greenhouses to the walk-through. When he inspected the Dungeon, he found the shopping bag was gone. He left a twelve pack of Pumpkinhead in the same corner with a card that read, "Happy Thanksgiving, Bro."

A week later, the beer was gone. Tom could have found it, but Bill thought it unlikely.

Amy continued to watch Carrie's comings and goings and kept Sean informed. He was selling Christmas trees and poinsettias, so he always had eyes on the parking lot. Ten days into December, Sean noticed Bill crossing behind one of the green-houses, a box tucked under his arm.

"That's it. We have to follow them," Sean said to Amy that evening.

"You think they've seen what we've seen?" Amy asked.

"Bonebelly was at the haunt. Tom saw him. Justin won't admit it, but he saw him. It's safe to say we're not the only ones who know there really is something in the woods."

The young people bided their time. The next time Sean spotted Carrie moving through the shadows, it was nearly closing time. Amy had just closed up the store when Sean called her. Carrie had not yet reemerged when Amy found Sean. Tom had gone back to the farmhouse. Sean promised to close the gate then ran with Amy across the back lot.

"I think we should check the Dungeon," Sean said. Amy nodded.

When they surprised Carrie in the tunnel, they discovered she was not alone. She was watching a video with Bill on his laptop. They both cried out when Amy and Sean burst in on them. Sean felt flustered, not certain what they had walked in on, but Amy did not wait for explanations.

"Tom's yeti. We've seen him, too," she said.

The adults were silent a moment, and then Carrie admitted, "I knew you had seen him, Amy. I didn't know if you remembered."

"I saw him at the haunt a couple of times," Sean said.

All four of them sat on the Dungeon's earthen floor as they watched the footage of Bonebelly dropping beer into Bill's truck.

"Why does he share beer with you?" Carrie asked.

"I think he stole beer from your truck last year," Sean explained. "He took it from the newbies, and now he's paying you back."

"You two have been drawing pictures of this thing since the haunt started," Bill observed.

"Yes, and we gave him a name," Sean said. "We call him Bonebelly."

"Good name. So he's been hanging around since the haunt opened, watching and listening. He heard us talking about not drinking at scenes, and he knew about the bonfires. He confiscated the contraband and shared his booty with us. But I can't even imagine what he is or where he came from."

"He pulled Cam off me." Amy's voice caught in her throat. "He dragged Cam up a tree, and I don't know what happened after that."

"He killed Cam." Carrie stared at the ground.

"Jesus," Bill said. "So he's dangerous?"

Carrie related her one-sided conversations with Bonebelly and explained what it meant to be a hungry ghost. "But he's not actually a ghost. He can't speak with that tiny throat of his, but it seems he was put here by a demon as punishment for a terrible sin."

Amy and Sean exchanged glances. Bill and Carrie noticed.

"So we have a devil running around here, too?" Bill exclaimed.

Carrie continued, "I think he was yanked out of whatever life he had before and dropped here. So this Bonebelly is always hungry, and he is always suffering. Everything he eats hurts his throat and turns to ashes."

"So that's why you bring protein shakes," Bill said.

"That's part of it. He can only drink one a day without his stomach cramping up. There's something else: There is one food that doesn't get spoiled for him."

"Beer?" Sean asked.

"Human flesh. He knows it's wrong and he works to avoid it. He failed—once he says."

Amy shuddered. "Cam. That's why the police can't find him. He's been eaten."

"Not entirely. Remember, Bonebelly can only consume a few morsels at a time. More than that and he doubles over with pain."

"Okay, so he's cursed with this bottomless hunger and this terrible desire that he knows is wrong," Sean said. "If he gives in to this desire, he only gets a few scraps, and then he's condemned to even greater damnation. That's kind of a dick move."

"He's no innocent. He did something to deserve this," Carrie reminded him.

Amy remembered the frightening aggression Bonebelly displayed when she tried to thank him. He had been trying to drive her away. "He can't be close to anyone because the temptation might be too great for him to resist."

Carrie nodded. "So he's not only starving but lonely, too."

"And hell is in South County, Rhode Island's ocean playground," Bill said. They all laughed. "So the haunt breaks up the loneliness and keeps his mind off his stomach. What do we do about this?"

"I told him he can't hurt anyone ever again if he wants help. But if someone else goes missing, I'm not sure what we can do. We don't know where he hides," Carrie said.

Amy stared at the ground.

"Do we know if he's killed anyone else?" Bill asked.

Sean explained the research he and Amy had done. Bonebelly could have been responsible for as many as three disappearances, but possibly only the single death the creature had claimed.

"We have to agree on how we want to handle this," Carrie said. "Does anyone think we should go to the police?"

"What would we tell them?" Bill asked. "I could show them my videos, but would they buy it? People fake videos all the time."

"They'd think we were promoting Bone Ridge," Sean said.

"I have a friend in the state police. I'll show it to him with no explanation and see what he says. Otherwise, we keep it to ourselves. If this gets out, we'll have people tramping all over the place hunting for the monster."

Everyone agreed that would be a disaster for the locals. In the end, they decided to watch for any signs that indicated the creature was a threat. Amy offered to leave gifts in the tunnel because she was often at the farm early on the weekends or closed up for Jen several week nights.

"We belong to a club," Sean said as he drove them home. "Friends of Bonebelly. We should design tee shirts." He thought a moment. "You know what? He's probably literate. We have some of his back story. We could leave a letter in the Dungeon and ask him for the rest."

Amy shook her head. She knew he kept a journal but had seen a side of Bonebelly Sean had not. "I think Carrie's right. We can't push a friendship. We need to keep our distance for his sake as well as ours. I saw what happened to Cam." She was angry at herself for letting her eyes tear up. "I haven't thought about it for a long time. Then, talking about Bonebelly tonight, I saw it in my head again." She rubbed away the tears that spilled down her face. "On the other hand, he could have killed me. He didn't."

"He could have killed any of us a dozen times over. If we had to find him, do you have any idea where he, um, lives?"

"I'm not even sure I could find the tree where it happened. I couldn't show the police any more than the general area." It was true enough that Amy had initially been confused and her descriptions had even led tracking dogs astray. Although she now knew exactly where to go, she was not about to let anyone, especially Sean, risk confronting the creature.

They dropped things off in the Dungeon for Carrie but put off plans to contact Bonebelly. They focused on their futures, revising the graphic novel and practicing air brush and makeup techniques. Sean was accepted at the New England Institute of Technology, where he planned to complete a program in graphic arts. Amy earned a scholarship to the Rhode Island School of Design.

They tried again to flesh out Bonebelly's back story. They depicted him as a Victorian gentleman who played at being a vampire. He killed and cannibalized innocent victims in Providence until he was condemned to his private hell. Then they began working in earnest on the first of their graphic novels. Their story began with a grotesque creature waking up in the Rhode Island woods with no memory, cursed with endless hunger and a taste for forbidden meat. They alternated his discoveries of the new and wondrous age in which he found himself with his attempts to ease his suffering. They imagined his blunders and new sins, such as dining on the corpse of a deceased homeless man who camped in the woods. The first volume concluded with his discovery of the haunt. But it still did not feel authentic to them. The real Bonebelly remained just beyond their reach.

Bill did not ask Sean or Amy to place beer in the Dungeon. He insisted on doing it himself. He half-hoped he might encounter the creature and have a face-to-face conversation.

Two days before Christmas, Bill found himself feeling sad and sentimental, remembering his father and friends who were no longer with him. He imagined how lonely it was to be cursed and starving, haunting the woods in the cold and dark of winter. In a fit of generosity, he bought a bottle of expensive scotch and left it in the Dungeon with a Christmas card. "Enjoy the spirit(s) of the season," he wrote and signed it. As he turned to leave, it occurred to him that a shit-faced Bonebelly could be a catastrophe, so he picked up the card and added, "Please drink responsibly. You know why."

KARMA

CARRIE WAS TRUE to her word and left a box with a dozen protein shakes in different flavors. At least, that was what the label stated. They all tasted the same to me, but none were revolting, so I remain grateful. She also left more things for me to read about suffering, enlightenment, and karma. They are tenets of the heathen religion she practices, yet they seem to apply to my case. If they are true, it confirms my hope that hell is not some never-ending universe of suffering. I may yet become worthy of release, even with new crimes added to my list.

Last night was overcast and dark, so I began a search of nearby farms for anything left in the fallow fields. It was slow work. I toiled for hours at one farm and came away with some squash and a few potatoes. The dark of the moon is two weeks away. I will search orchards then for more fallen fruit.

There are more voices around the perimeter of the woods. When I climbed high in the bare trees, I could count more finished houses than I saw a year ago. After the stillness of winter settles in, I must again search in earnest for a second dwelling.

Hunting season has begun. Two days ago, I was returning to my cellar when I nearly crossed paths with Farmer Tom. He was hunting for game birds with a companion. I was clothed in black, so he easily spied me climbing a tree to avoid him. "Is that a bear?" I heard him ask his friend. They crashed through the trees to my hiding place and trained their muskets on the high branches. I jumped to the crown of the neighboring tree. When I looked back, Tom was lowering his barrel and shaking his head. I think he realized I was not a bear. His friend asked, "Is that your yeti?"

Tom swore at his friend as they moved away.

November 15, 2011

I think I have nearly perfected my disguise with the addition of a few new garments. I filled a bag with fallen fruit at one of the local orchards. The night was impenetrably dark except for the street lanterns, and I could have easily remained hidden. It was well after midnight, but I decided to test my costume by walking on the side of the open road. My head was hooded and my face shadowed by a partial hat called a visor. I wore long black trousers and the short, zippered coat. Two conveyances approached me on the road and continued on without slowing. I did not merit a second glance.

It was exhilarating to play the part of an ordinary man. I will have to try it again soon.

November 21, 2011

Demon has returned, but it seems he has not returned for me. I spied him sitting on my roof this morning. His gaze was fixed on his feet. He did not seem at all aware of my presence. I left my cellar just after dark, and Demon was still in the same place and in the same attitude. I brought back bags stuffed with dried leaves so I could manufacture a featherbed of sorts. A half-moon was rising; the night was clear and full of stars. Demon roosted in the same spot as before and paid absolutely no heed to my comings and goings. I do not understand why he is here.

November 22, 2011

Demon was still on the roof this morning, completely unaware of my presence or movements. I did not wish to draw attention to myself, yet I could not escape the feeling there was something so out of place that everyone and everything was somehow endangered. I had a few bottles of ale left, so I took two of them and climbed the white cedar until I was within arm's length of the demon.

I tapped my claws against the roof tiles to get Demon's attention. He raised his green eyes to me where I could read a look of utter weariness and defeat. Something in that look suggested that Demon had lost control of the hell he ruled. I did not see this as a reason to exult. I shook with an unnamable fear.

I pulled the metal cap off one of the bottles and pushed it towards Demon. He gazed at me as if seeing me for the first time. He leapt off the roof to the back of the ruin. I followed him, libations in hand. I found him in my cellar, stooped because the ceiling could not accommodate his full height. He was inspecting the additions I had made to my stores and the small comforts I had found—candles, a coat, small torches. He nodded as he often had but without his mocking grin. He downed his ale, looked around and nodded again. Then he vaulted through the hole in the floor and was gone.

When Demon visited me last month, he beat me and mocked me. Now he seems somehow reassured by my modest larder and the human touches I have added to make my poor root cellar snug and secure.

He was saddened and fearful and that diminished him. I think anything that can diminish a Demon is something to dread.

As I write this, I find myself wondering about the nature of hell. I know I am not the only sinner. Where do these other sinners go? How are they punished? And if it is possible to change, how does Demon know? Can he scrutinize thousands of souls at one time? After all, he is neither God nor angel. When I found him squatting on my roof, he seemed as one who was utterly vanquished. It occurs to me that, if some souls can be redeemed, there must also be souls who sink beyond redemption. I worry that Demon has been bested by just such a soul, and he does not know what to do about it.

November 24, 2011

It is yet another multi-day holiday. It is the time for giving thanks in quiet prayer and reflection, but there is still activity on the roads and little of it in the direction of the local churches. I climbed to the top of the highest tree on the highest hill to survey the area. I thought I spied Bill near the farm, striding behind the greenhouses with something under his arm. I lost him in the heavy tree cover, but I saw him emerge near the parking lot and cross in the direction of the Dungeon. Then he went back the way he came.

Bill had clearly left something in the Dungeon. With almost childlike anticipation, I leapt from tree to tree until I reached the walk-through. I hurried to the tunnel and found twelve bottles of ale waiting for me. On top of the box was a small, colorful likeness of a harvest scene printed on heavy paper. On the back of this Bill had written, "Happy Thanksgiving, Bro." I could not contain my delight. I could feel a wide smile stretch across my skull-like face.

I cradled my gift in my arms as I ambled at a leisurely pace through the walk-through, reliving some of my favorite moments from the past season. It was a long walk through the woods to my shelter. I watched deer and grouse and turkeys search for food. I managed to snare a grouse for myself. It was an overcast day, but as the sun set, breaks in the clouds revealed streaks of gold through the trees.

I truly did feel grateful for the small pleasures of this day. I always assumed that my prayers would be ignored, so I never offered any. But this evening I expressed my heartfelt gratitude to any beneficent being who might hear my thoughts.

November 26, 2011

From my forested crow's nest I could watch streams of conveyances clogging the major thoroughfares. They were not giving thanks. They were all visiting merchants in droves—and at an ungodly early hour. That meant that there were likely to be fewer people around the perimeter of the woods. It meant I could work in peace.

I found what I believe could become an ideal second dwelling should my hovel be discovered or collapse into a complete ruin. I discovered it at the back of the orchard at Stone Ridge Farm. There is an old stone wall that runs along the rear boundary. Behind the wall is a mound of debris: warped planks of wood, trimmed tree limbs and brush, and old fencing. There is also a large old oak that died and fell over, pulling up a huge ball of soil with its massive roots. When I probed the depression below the arching roots I found the soil was soft and easily moved.

So today, I began digging with my claws, reinforcing the cave that was forming with the wood and fencing debris. I worked at this until sunset. I covered my new shelter with fallen branches. It will need to be substantially enlarged so that I can stand and sit in it with some measure of comfort, and I will need to complete my labors before the ground freezes.

I find it agreeable to have so much purposeful work ahead of me. I will return to it tomorrow after sundown.

December 5, 2011

I borrowed a heavy pick, a shovel, and several tall buckets from the farmer that I found in an unlocked shed. I spent the past week crawling into the opening I had made, removing earth and rocks, filling buckets, and dumping the earth at the base of the fallen tree. In time, I will use it to hide the opening.

I finally dug so deep that I needed to work with some daylight, so I could see what I was doing. I did not want to waste my torches. The apples had all been harvested a month ago, so I knew there was no need for anyone to visit the orchard. I began my labors just before dawn and kept at it until I could hear sounds of activity coming from the farm.

I had to dislodge some scattered boulders about the size of my belly. It was exhausting work, but I have now dug out a room that is perhaps two feet wider, longer, and higher than I am tall. I could stand, turn, sit, or recline comfortably. My next task is to further reinforce the roof and walls and find a way to keep it from filling with precipitation.

All this heavy labor has my cavernous stomach howling, complaining, and cramping with pain because it wants even more sustenance than usual. But I am not allowed to increase the amount of victuals I devour each day. Should I ingest more than a few morsels of vegetables or more than one protein cask each day, I will feel the vicious twisting in my intestines, even as my stomach cries, "Famine!"

December 14, 2011

There was freezing rain last week which made the interior of my cave muddy. I set about making it somewhat water tight. I spent the past week lining the room with discarded lumber and tree limbs. I borrowed more of those waterproof sheets from the farm. One was sufficient to line the floor. A second one was stretched across a roof that covered about two-thirds of the opening, and a separate sheet of discarded wood that would act as a door. The tarpaulin was secured in place with rocks and boulders. Then I fashioned an arch over all by interlacing limbs with bundles of grape vine and thorny brush. I climbed to the top of one of the apple trees and was satisfied that my second home appeared to be no more than a heap of vegetation.

Today, I moved in a few articles of comfort: a mattress of dry leaves stuffed in a large black bag, two of the small lights I found on the walk-through, and a few casks of protein shakes. I sealed a supply of blank paper and pencils in a transparent bag and left it on top of the mattress. Then I spent the night to test it for comfort. I found it quite snug and cozy.

December 18, 2011

A driving blizzard has trapped me in my cellar. No protein shakes were left in the Dungeon this week, and I have none left. I am parceling out my scant stores of apples, squash, and potatoes.

I distracted myself from my nagging belly by reading. I began with the fantastic stories of Edgar Allen Poe. As much as I enjoyed the writings of Lovecraft, I find the dark ravings in Poe's works much more akin to my inner voice—not to mention that Lovecraft's "The Call of Cthulhu" describes a world even more horrifying and devoid of hope than the one I inhabit. I feel that I, too, have teetered on the edge of black madness as described by both authors, particularly during my first months in hell. But the sins of Poe's characters seem to parallel my own, particularly in "The Tell-Tale Heart" and "The Black Cat."

December 23, 2011

Today I went to the Dungeon. Along the way, my empty stomach roiled with pangs and complaints. I was angry, my rage increasing with every step. It had, after all, been nearly two weeks since anything had been left for me. As I stumbled through the deep drifts of snow along the trails of the walk-through, I imagined what I would do if I found Carrie there. I pictured myself grabbing her by the throat and baring my fangs in her face to let her know that she dared not fail me again. I exulted as I envisioned her fear and her powerlessness. Then I came close enough to the farm to see the colored lights strung across the parking areas. I heard the sounds of music and the laughter of people who had come for Christmas garlands and pastries. I saw Amy cross the lot to greet Sean with a kiss and a warm drink. They were the very image of mutual regard.

I crept to the Dungeon and sat there on the cold earthen floor with my head cradled in my hands, regretting all the violent phantasms I had allowed to fill my mind. No one was obligated to help me. Given my crimes of the past twenty months heaped atop the transgressions that put me in this place, I certainly did not deserve anyone's sympathy or succor. I sighed and silently begged Carrie's forgiveness, even though she had not been there to feel threatened.

After berating myself for a while, I beamed my little torch across the ground, praying I would not be denied a second time. What I found made me cringe with mortification. There were two sacks filled with metal casks and a short letter from Carrie, apologizing for the delay: "I am so sorry. Some of the people who work with me have been ill. I've had to work longer hours and have been unable to do much else. I'm leaving enough cans to see you through if I am delayed again. Merry Christmas and Happy New Year."

Bill had left a bottle of spirits and a printed likeness of a tree adorned with lights. On the card he wrote, "Enjoy the spirit(s) of the season, bro. Please drink responsibly. You know why." I understood exactly what he meant. I was to enjoy the warmth and cheer without becoming heedless. I had already made that mistake with the spirits I confiscated last October. I could have done much worse than risk exposure.

There were two other gifts with a letter from Sean and Amy, wondering if I might wish to share correspondences. They left a blanket with the feel of fur, although it was clearly made of fibers dyed dark blue. It was large enough to completely wrap my bulky form. The second gift was a large black blouse with the half sleeves that everyone seems to wear. It had the words "Bone Ridge Farm Staff" written on the front. The back displayed a picture of Cthulhu as the stone idol worshipped by the monster's followers.

I left the Dungeon overwhelmed with emotion. As I write these words, I am thankful no one was there to feel the brunt of my childish rage.

December 25, 2011

It is late on Christmas Day. In my time here, I have noticed that the feast of Christ's birth is one of the few days that merchants close up their shops for the entire day. I pulled the long black robe over black trousers and covered my head with the hood. I wrapped dark rags around my feet and put on my short coat. Then, many hours after sunset, I took myself to the merchant village up the road from Stone Ridge Farm. Off to one side of the lot that lay alongside the tavern was the huge metal strongbox where people left garments for the poor. I had to angle my long, bony arm through the opening and pull up a bag without knowing what was in it, peruse the contents for anything useable, then return the remainder to the box. I only found two blouses that would fit me.

Near another merchant there was a box for donating books. I pulled out several volumes until I found some that interested me. I found a book of poetry by various authors and a history of Rhode Island. Then I spotted the lanterns of an approaching vehicle. I stuffed a handful of random volumes in my bag and galloped into the shadows and back to the woods. When I reached the root cellar, I lit a candle and inspected my literary plunder: NIGHT, written by a man with a foreign, perhaps German name, a book on cooking vegetables, and LITTLE WOMEN. The winter days and nights are long. All will be read before spring comes.

January 1, 2012

The candles have been used sparingly but will soon be gone. There are perhaps a half dozen small lanterns left, and they are brighter than candle light. But I must hold the short tube between my teeth if I am to read or write by it. It causes much drooling. Candles are not things one finds discarded in the snow. I could go back to the barns and sheds and search for more, but I have nothing to trade for them. My new friends would probably bring some to the Dungeon, but I found myself loathe to ask. It is not advisable to do anything that encourages closer contact.

I have reflected several times on the rage I recently felt and the terrible ways in which I wished to express it. It was as great as what I felt against the man I killed, who was a violator of women. And it was all because Carrie had been late in bringing me something that was a gift, not an obligation. As I pondered, I began to understand that the kindness of my long distance friends had assuaged much of the pain I had experienced. Yes, I was always hungry, but I did not feel the terrible, hollow agonies that were my constant companion during the dark, starving season of the previous winter. Now I was free to feel other things: pleasure, loneliness, and anger. I am stuffed full with fury and it wants out. But what is its source? I am starting to remember some of my crimes, and I believe there is worse yet to be recovered. But the memories do not explain why I should be angry with anyone but myself. I do not understand it and it worries me.

A new year is upon us all. It seems important at this time to settle one's obligations, so the next time I go to the Dungeon, I will leave a note of thanks to my benefactors. I would do more, but I do not know what I could possibly give them.

January 12, 2012

I spent much of the daylight hours reading LITTLE WOMEN. It tells the story of four sisters during the time of a civil conflagration somewhere in the past. I will have to peruse my Rhode Island history to get a sense of the historical period. It is not a thrilling tale, but it is pleasant and heartwarming.

I went to the Dungeon at sunset. I had just left my note when I spotted Amy carrying a bag as she hurried across the empty lot. Ducking into one of the actors' hiding places I watched her leave some casks on the ground. She spied my note. I had written it on the back of a Bone Ridge flyer, sealed it shut with wax, and written, "To my friends" on it. Amy broke the seal and read it. I had signed it "Bonebelly," the name she had called me when I rescued her last summer. She whispered the name several times then pulled out one of those small speaking devices.

"Sean?" she spoke into the device. "He left a note. Bonebelly left a note thanking us. Can you meet me at Eli's? He asked for candles. Can you bring some?"

She took the note and left. I did not know if it was worthwhile, but decided to wait and see what she might do next. Perhaps two hours later she returned with Sean. They left two white boxes along with sheaves of yellow paper and writing utensils. Amy placed a folded sheet of paper on top of the bag. Without a word, they left.

The boxes contained two dozen candles as well as boxes of matches. I lit one so I could read the note. It was signed by both of them. It read: "We understand that it is not wise for us to meet, but we are your friends. We are the grateful ones because you saved Amy. Be well and keep writing. Amy and Sean"

January 21, 2012

My cellar is filling up with bottles and casks. There is printing on them that reads, "Please recycle." I often see barrels outside homes that are labeled with the same words and symbols. I cannot carry all of this refuse at once, even with the black bags I have taken from the farm, but I can leave it, a little at a time, in these barrels. It seems they are hauled away every two weeks. I can now keep the refuse from taking over my living quarters.

After disposing of my trash, I went by the Dungeon. Bill had left more beer. I still had plenty of spirits left, but I had drunk all the ale a week ago. There was another note as well. It was in a different hand but was signed "Amy and Sean" as before.

"Bill and Carrie said hello," it read. "We were wondering if you like to write. We thought you must enjoy it, especially in the winter with so much time on your hands. If you would like to write down your story and share it with us, we would be happy to read it. We would not relate anything you did not want us to share. In the meantime, don't be afraid to let us know if you need anything."

I went to my shelter behind the orchard and drafted a short note which I immediately placed in the Dungeon: "I am atoning for my sins, which are grievous and many. It is best to leave me to myself. Thank you again for your kindness."

As soon as I finished the note, I realized how true it was. I am living as a hermit in forced contemplation. It is not an easy life, but there is a spare sort of contentment within my reach. I may yet become the man I never was in my previous life.

February 9, 2012

Beth has died.

Gentle Beth, the kindest and most beloved of the March sisters, fell victim to her weak heart. I know Mistress Alcott is merely using a device to provoke sorrow and pity in the reader. But Beth is dead and I am quite devastated.

February 18, 2012

Demon was back in my woods today. I heard something scrabbling across my roof. It was much heavier than a squirrel, so I crept up the back of my ruins to take a look. There he was, hunched over and brooding, oblivious to the freezing rain pelting his leathery hide. I climbed up and sat next to him. I do not know why I did this. He would not speak and I could not. There was no way of knowing if he would choose to inflict some new abuse on my poor hide.

When my clothes were soaked through, he turned to look at me. He looked exhausted and haggard. There was no doubt that something was not right in hell. I felt terrified—not of Demon, but of anything that could make him appear so defeated. He looked at me and nodded as if to say I had surmised correctly. Then he brought his finger close to my face. He touched my forehead. I was immediately filled with a terrible knowledge.

Images of thousands of hells cascaded before my eyes. I saw sinners transformed into the lowest of creatures: worms, flies, and slugs, trod underfoot and devoured by birds and toads. But they were sentient. They knew they were prey, and they suffered in silent terror. They were reborn over and over into the same situation to be everlastingly hunted. I had devoured some of these unfortunate souls myself. I saw that a blessed few somehow earned the right to become creatures higher in the predator-prey hierarchy. How one accomplishes this as a humble worm is beyond my ken.

Then I saw hells similar to my own. Men and women were transformed into creatures both fantastic and grotesque. Many of them spent ages in their private hells and became the stuff of local legends and ghost tales. They, too, had difficult choices to make as they hid within the world of men. They could hunt or be hunted. They could isolate themselves or become a boon to the narrow world they occupied. Sometimes they earned the right to die.

There was something even worse. I saw a vision of a hell for the truly un-redeemable. These souls had to be quarantined from all living things and even sequestered from each other. Their punishments, suffered in suffocating isolation, were hideous and unrelenting—so much so that I cannot bear to describe them. Then I was made to understand these evil ones sometimes attempted an escape. It could happen when a devil has seized them and placed them in a state of un-becoming. If they are in this clay-like form but get free of the demon's grasp, they can remake themselves into whatever they wish. Since they are robbed of their memories of past crimes—part of their punishment is to be denied the pleasure of reliving them—they do not know what to do with this power of transformation. They make themselves over into hapless, malformed creatures that can barely function and are easily recovered.

Demon then showed me a select minority among the evil souls. They pos-sessed the intelligence, the hatred, and the rebellious will to take full advantage of the unbecoming. When they escaped, they were able to feed their cruel desires and elude capture. I saw one such creature inflicting terror and painfully protracted death on victim after victim, although the means of delivering their destruction was not clear. He had no pity towards women, children, or defenseless beasts. The greater the cruelty, the stronger he grew. He had learned how to further his trans-formation and make himself into a man. And when I saw the man he had become, I was stunned. He was the image of the minister I had seen in my dreams.

I stared at Demon. I do not know how I dared, but I formed a wordless ques-tion in my mind: If you know who he is and where he is hiding, why have you not taken him?

Demon smiled that old wicked smile. He lifted his hand, and I thought I was about to be struck down for my insolence. Instead, he brought a finger to my chest. His tapering claw probed the bullet hole until he touched my shriveled heart. I immediately understood, and I began to weep black, putrid tears. The task of ending this evil had been allotted to me.

For my sin was the greatest of all possible sins. Long ago in another lifetime, I could have intervened before this horror began. Instead, I chose to do nothing.

NONCOMPLIANCE

W HEN MARCH BROUGHT the first thaw of winter, Demon returned to the cabin in the mountains of Pennsylvania. Instead of resting on the Sabbath and enjoying the bleat and bray of holy hypocrites, he now spent Sundays watching and waiting for the Minister to awaken. His employer had staid Demon's hand and allowed the fiend to escape. There was nothing to be done about that. That would not prevent Demon from trying to keep the body count among the innocents as low as possible. Of course, he was expected to keep up with his case load. But whenever possible, Demon would stalk the Minister and drive the creature to the northeast.

Losing rebellious souls was something that happened to other caseworkers. Until now, Demon's record had been unblemished. But the Minister was not just another rotten soul. Even in that confused state of unbecoming, he had glimpsed the possibilities of his formless state. He had been robbed of his memories but not his terrible drives. With lust and imagination alone he had devised a means to hunt and kill unlike anything Demon had ever seen.

The problem for the Minister was that he did not know how to work the sequence from unbecoming to becoming the way an experienced demon could. Once he turned thought into form, he could not undo it. He could add, but he could never subtract. To remake himself into the man he had once been, he had to fuel the process, fattening himself up and then dreaming his way to the next transformation. Now he was stuck with his venomous barb, his hunger, and the need to hibernate.

When Demon visited Martin's den, he was forced to witness a nauseating metamorphosis: The grub-white skin softened and enveloped the Minister like a caul. Bones, teeth, and organs collapsed into a mass of sticky cartilage, slowly reforming to match the dream form. By February, it was all there—the hypnotic black eyes, the flashing teeth, the flowing black hair, and the beautifully proportioned body.

However, the Minister would not be pleased to learn that he would still need to lose three months each year to hibernation or that he would be driven to gorge relentlessly to maintain his form, bloating unnaturally in the process.

Demon's surveillance had not been without cost. He had not checked in on many of his clients over the summer. Now he was in trouble over the incident in Rhode Island. The Deacon he had placed there had been passive to the point of amorality, content to follow and never exert his own will. Even cursed with that savage, gnawing hunger, Demon had assumed the Deacon would lack the ambition to do more than scrounge for insects and lichens. Instead, the Deacon had exhibited both curiosity and enterprise in the most unsettling ways. The murders and the subsequent desecrations, of course, were the worse. If Demon had been following his client the way he should, this never would have happened. It didn't matter that both victims were serial offenders who richly deserved their doom.

The world of free men was meant to torment the damned as the unobtainable reminder of what they had squandered. Instead, the Deacon was filling his lonely hovel with homey comforts. He made friends who pitied him and left him gifts of food. Demon had been moved to brutally remind the Deacon he was meant to earn his way out of hell, but he was not supposed to enjoy himself as he did so. The Deacon even fancied himself a thespian!

But all this happened before Demon cornered the Minister and was forced to grant a reprieve. Now Demon needed the Deacon to find a fortitude he had lacked over three hundred years earlier. He had saved the girl Amy. He sensed the connection with her soul. It was a start.

Demon watched and waited on the roof of the cabin until Monday dawned. Then he was forced to begin his supervisory rounds anew.

§ § §

Martin Godfrey smiled in the twilight sleep of his hibernation. His dreams were pleasing and full of promise. The lengthening light and birds of spring roused him from the cabin's closet. Martin woke to find his clothes hung upon his frame. He needed food, but first, he needed to look upon what his dreams had wrought. He found a mirror in the cabin and inspected his face. He was beautiful again. Then he ran his tongue along the roof of his mouth and scowled at his reflection. The tube located along his pallet was still there. He opened his mouth and the thin bony barb thrust forward, flicked the mirror, and left a smear of venom. Not all his dreams had come true.

The Minister inspected the canned food left in the cabin. The sight of it turned his stomach. He followed the sounds of a rushing stream where he gulped down the icy water. Then he quickly dispatched a fox and a turkey. Next, an inventory of his possessions revealed several changes of clothes, almost $500.00 in cash, and a handful of credit cards. He had learned a lot from his victims over the past year. Now he needed to get new identification cards graced with his handsome face.

When darkness gathered, Martin stuffed his belongings into his back pack and hiked to the closest road. He affected a halting, shambling gait that told the world he was waiting to be victimized. In the early morning hours, his patience was rewarded. A car approached, passed him slowly, and pulled over. The middle-aged driver offered a ride and lost no time engaging Martin in conversation. When the driver was satisfied that Martin was homeless and in need of a job, he offered him a place to spend the night and a job on his construction crew. Martin was effusively grateful.

It was still dark when they reached the businessman's suburban home. As soon as Martin walked through the door, he could smell that this had been a house of death. He stepped confidently into the shadowy room and waited—an open and easy target. The burly man came up behind him and whispered filthy suggestions in Martin's ear. Martin betrayed nothing.

"I knew you wanted this," his host said as he slipped a knotted rope around Martin's neck. The Minister smiled even as the garrote tightened and his throat constricted. He immediately dropped to the floor, a dead weight that threw his overweight assailant off balance. The knot's pressure eased just enough to allow the victim to turn his head and deliver the barb into the man's thigh.

The venom burned, the man gasped, and he released Martin. The Minister found a small lamp on a desk and switched it on. It was dim but furnished enough light to allow him to watch his assailant as he dissolved. "How many drifters have you buried here?" he asked.

The man was fumbling with the phone he pulled from his pocket. His arms and legs were turning rubbery. He dropped the phone and stared at Martin with a look of stupefied panic. The muscles in his face were going slack, too.

"Where are they?" the Minister asked. "In the basement? That's probably where I'll put you—what's left of you, anyway. There won't be much but your clothes."

The man was on his knees now. He struggled to work some sound out of his throat, but all he could produce was a gelatinous vomit.

"People would thank me for this if they knew," Martin said. "But they never will."

The man collapsed into a bag of goo. The Minister watched the terror in the man's eyes freeze while the blue lights winked out. *Scaring people is fun*, he thought, and then he feasted.

There was a crawl space in the basement where indeed several bodies moldered in shallow graves. Martin retrieved the man's wallet and keys and tied everything else up in a plastic bag. He tossed the bag in with the bodies then set to inspecting the dead man's home.

It was a modest dwelling set back from the road and hidden by trees. It seemed clear that no one else lived there. Martin closed the blinds and searched the man's desk. He found and unlocked a strongbox that contained passwords to a computer, cards for two different bank accounts, and cash. There was also an assortment of key chains, rings, and other mementos that most likely belonged to the man's victims.

He was able to log onto the computer, search his victim's bank accounts, and locate branches across the state. By the time the Minister left the area, he would have a license and most of the man's money in his pocket.

Admiring his own face in the bathroom mirror, Martin once again flicked his barb at the glass. It was, he decided, an elegant oddity. Light and strong, thin and flexible, it had a sheen not unlike mother of pearl. He showered and shaved and again inspected his face and nude body with delight.

Martin was wholly satiated, but he surveyed his victim's pantry and freezer with fascination. He opened cans, broiled steaks, and roasted chickens, sampling and savoring a few bites of each before tossing all of it in the back yard. He did it because he could. Every pleasure in life was his to enjoy. In his previous life, he had specialized in seduction that compromised the women of his congregation and left them unable to speak against him. He had killed only once and had done so out of necessity. Now he killed for its exquisite pleasure, leaving nothing that could be used to incriminate him. And both God and the Devil were unwilling or unable to stop him.

Identity theft was easier than he thought it would be. Martin let his beard grow, padded his victim's clothing, and used his talent for mesmerizing others to clean out the man's bank accounts. He continued to prey on drug dealers, con artists, and prostitutes, taking any valuables they left behind. They all saw him as an easy mark, they all knew to avoid security cameras, and they were always astounded when the tables were turned. It was easy to stuff the meager evidence down a storm drain.

It occurred to the Minister that, if he was careful not to tarry too long in one place, he might travel the world in comfort. Perhaps he could even find some remote corner with no cameras where he could rule men and beasts as a demon prince.

But as the Minister drove the mid-Atlantic highways, killing was simply becoming too easy. He needed a bigger challenge. He wanted a piteous, more excruciating type of fear.

On a warm day during the spring school vacation, Martin found himself at a park in a rural town. It was a day of family celebration. There was a barbeque, games, a children's concert, and no security cameras. As he hugged the shadows, he located a child—a highly distractible boy, perhaps four years of age—who had already eluded his parents twice that afternoon. Without getting close enough to draw unwanted attention, Martin kept the child in his line of sight. When the afternoon shadows began to lengthen, he had his chance. No one was looking when he reached out from behind a bush and took the child's hand. Martin tugged at the boy and drew him into the brush. When he smiled, the boy smiled back.

Before Martin could engage the boy in conversation and lure him even further away, the child stared at something behind the Minister's shoulder and gave an ear-splitting shriek. The boy stumbled onto the grassy field, sobbing incomprehensible syllables. Martin turned to run and plowed right into Demon's massive chest. Demon gripped him by the arm and lifted him high into a tree as adults swarmed the area.

"You're not allowed to touch me," Martin said in a contemptuous, measured tone. Demon kept his hold on the Minister's arm and dangled him over open ground, threatening to drop him among the throng of adults gathering at the base of the tree. Martin frantically shook his head. Demon brought him back to the limb and set him down.

Opening his other fist, Demon produced a phone. He opened it to reveal several photos of Martin. The last one showed the Minister kneeling in the dirt, gripping the boy by his hand. The devil let the device fall from his hand. It was quickly discovered and turned over to the police.

Martin fumed silently while Demon grinned. Then Demon was gone, leaving the handsome monster to figure out for himself how to get out of the tree. The Minister waited for the night then awkwardly clambered down. He kept to the shadows and away from the roads as he slipped out of the area.

The message was clear. Demon could not claim his escaped quarry, but he would interfere with the Minister's pleasures as often as he wished. Martin avoided the beloved innocents. He returned to the fringes of society where men and women could vanish and it either went unmarked or was assumed the disappeared had somehow courted disaster.

Demon, however, kept a careful tally as he deftly pulled the Minister's strings. He crafted his interference with meticulous care, foiling the killings just often enough to deflect the direction of Martin's path. He succeeded in convincing the monster that it was his own decision entirely to move in a northeasterly direction until he reached South County, Rhode Island.

HELL, RHODE ISLAND

H ELL, RHODE ISLAND—THAT'S the hayride theme for 2012," Bill said. He made the announcement at an informal meeting of The Friends of Bonebelly at a tavern near the farm. It was April, and the Friends wanted to discuss the Bonebelly situation as the summer approached.

"How did you manage that?" Carrie asked.

"I ran into Milton just after the holidays. We held a planning meeting with Justin, Susan, and Tom, and I threw the idea in there. I described it as a place where the condemned actually live and walk among us, and they liked the idea. Got some weird looks from Justin."

"I'll bet you did," Sean said.

Bill continued, "I showed my video to Francis, my friend with the state police. He assumed it was fake. Then I asked him what he would do if he thought it was real and this creature was responsible for the disappearance of a sexual predator. He said, 'If that's the case, I'd like to shake his hand.' So there you are. I've gone to the police. They won't take us seriously."

"Next order of business: we have a letter," Amy said. She produced a paper from her pocket. "My dear friends, I thank you again for your generosity. However, it is easier to scavenge for food as the weather warms. You do not need to leave anything for me, although I will continue to receive your gifts with gratitude. I have kept my promise. I have harmed no one. When the summer comes, I know work will begin on new sets. You risk discovery if you continue to leave items in the Dungeon. There is a pile of debris behind the orchard wall. If you leave letters and such in there, I will find them."

Carrie took the letter and examined it. "He signed it Bonebelly."

"He knows we gave him that name. We used it when we left notes," Sean said.

"Who is this guy?" Bill wondered as he examined the spidery, flowing script.

"That's why we kept writing to him. We want to find out."

"For your graphic novel?" Carrie asked.

"That was the idea originally," Sean said, "but now we just want to know. What did he do to earn hell? Has he reformed himself?"

They agreed they would continue to provide basic sustenance. Since Sean was working on landscaping and farming tasks, he would move goods and messages back and forth.

"The next time I leave stuff, I want to hide in a tree and wait for him," Sean confessed as he and Amy left work one evening. "If it seems safe, I might try to talk to him."

"Not sure I like that," Amy said, "but if that's your plan, I guess I'll have to go with you."

They had been making deliveries every two weeks on Saturday afternoons, just before closing. When the next delivery date arrived, Sean dropped off the goods while Amy moved his car to the side road and waited. They went to the pizza shop and then returned to the side road after dark. They cut through the hayride corn field to the orchard.

The young people spent hours with hoods pulled over their heads in the branches of an apple tree close to the stone wall. It was close to midnight when Bonebelly appeared. He was dressed in black, but there was no mistaking the long, white hands and feet or the bulging gut. He found the bag they left for him and set it on a level section of the tumbled down wall. Before they could speak to him, he dropped to all fours and disappeared under the debris.

Amy and Sean waited in silence. About fifteen minutes later, Bonebelly emerged and hurried away before they could call out to him. They lowered themselves from the tree and crept to the wall. Sean crouched and probed the debris with his flashlight. "There's plywood here," he whispered. He handed Amy the flashlight and pushed the plywood aside, revealing an opening. Amy trained the flashlight beam down the hole.

"Oh, my God, do you think he dug this out?" she asked. She shivered as she scanned the darkness around them. "Maybe you should leave it alone."

It was too late. Sean moved a couple of tree limbs aside and discovered that the opening was larger than it initially appeared. The tarp-covered plywood had been positioned over the hole to form a roof, all artfully disguised with brush and dead leaves. Before Amy could protest a second time, he easily slid feet first through the opening. His flashlight beamed up into Amy's face. "You need to see this."

Amy was more curious than reluctant, so she followed Sean into the hole. With two flashlights they could almost fully illuminate the hand-dug cave. It was an eight-foot cube, reinforced with lumber and open at the top. Although the air was damp, the plywood roof had kept out the elements. There was a tarp on the ground and a blue blanket rolled up neatly in a corner. Two milk crates and a plank served as a table which held two small LED flashlights and a Pumpkinhead candle holder. An alcove dug in the wall held three protein shakes and two Sam Adams.

"I would have loved a place like this when I was a kid," Sean said. "This must be where he lives."

"He took the bag when he left," Amy said. "I think he must have more than one hiding place. That's why so few people have seen him." She was still determined to conceal what she knew.

They took a last admiring look and pulled themselves out of the hole.

Work started in July on the new scenes for the hayride. The sets would alternate between sinners transformed into fantastic but unhappy gargoyles and demons trying to entice questionable souls into hell. There would be actors on each wagon who would get dragged, kicking and screaming, to a world of eternal torment. At one of the scenes, Milton fleshed out a suggestion from Bill based on Sean's and Amy's drawings for their graphic novel. The actors would wear costumes and makeup that would appear skeletal with long, clawed fingers and large bellies, all in shades of yellow, ivory, and gray. Finally, the tunnel would house Satan's throne room.

The walk-through would have a tomb full of zombie clowns—clownbies—an ice-coated scene for a pair of yetis, a diner serving man-burgers, a haunted curio shop, undead soldiers in a post-apocalyptic war zone, a traveling medicine show with malformed entertainers, evil children at a playground, castle ruins haunted by Nosferatu-style vampires, a prison transport bus leading to an execution scene, and Hell's torture chamber in the Dungeon. The graveyard and the maze were reconfigured and repositioned. Finally, there would be random lumberjack ghouls with chain saws roaming through the woods.

In August, Bone Ridge Farm set up a booth at the county fair. It was supplied with mock contracts so fair goers could sell their souls in exchange for a job at the haunt. Susan, Justin, and veteran actors took turns throughout the week manning the booth, dressed as demons or roaming the fair as zombies, handing out discount coupons. One Thursday evening, Mallison worked the booth while Amy and Sean shambled through the fairgrounds.

Several actors came by, some with boyfriends or girlfriends, spouses, and children. Biggie and Mike brought two friends to the booth for job applications. Scott was someone they had known for years. He had been their roommate until he lost yet another job and could not pay his rent. He spent the last decade going to school so he could learn to program games, leaving job after job because they did not feed his soul, and periodically moving back in with his mother. She was about to throw Scott out again when he met a new friend at the neighborhood pub.

The friend was introduced as Martin Godfrey. He claimed to be in his thirties but was so self-assured he seemed older. His perfect features, dark hair, and eyes got a second look from men and women alike. He spoke in a crisp, clipped accent, not quite British, not exactly American. Everything he said sounded intelligent, cultivated, and more interesting than what anyone else had to say. He regaled his new acquaintances with stories of his travels across the country. Scott in particular was enamored with Martin's talent for making things happen for himself.

"I work long enough to replenish my funds, then I go visit somewhere else," Martin said. "Right now, I'm working on a construction crew for a couple of months.

The contractor has a trailer parked on some property where he's building a house for his daughter. He's letting me stay there to keep an eye on things until his daughter moves in. When it gets cold, I'll probably go north for the ski season."

Martin offered to house Scott while he looked for more permanent employment. Scott had convinced his new roommate to apply at Bone Ridge Farm. As Martin stood at the booth, charming his listeners, Sean and Amy shuffled up behind the group and moaned. They actually scared the newcomer, who whirled around with a cry. The haunters laughed, but Martin's eyes blazed with anger. The zombie couple took a step backward. Then Martin's gaze—no longer irate but clearly fascinated—fixed on Amy. It remained on her for so long that she finally said, "Did you want something?"

"I'm sorry. Your eyes remind me of someone I knew years ago," he said. "I didn't mean to make you feel uncomfortable."

Sean and Amy resupplied themselves with coupons and lurched away. "Perv," Amy murmured to Sean. Glancing over their shoulders, they both laughed as they were swallowed by the crowd.

Martin forced himself to smile as he turned to face the haunters, but he was furious. He did not like the forceful way young women comported themselves these days. He had, however, learned how he needed to behave if he wanted to remain above suspicion. Be friendly, he told himself at the dawn of every new day. Be helpful. Feign care and concern. Exude trust and even tenderness.

He liked what he heard about the haunt. Whenever he made friends, feeding in his accustomed way became riskier. He had to find excuses to be alone to scout isolated places where a victim could be killed and eaten without being recorded. He owned a vehicle, but it did not give him perfect autonomy. After all, it was a means by which he could be identified.

Working an outdoor haunt, however, might provide opportunities for feeding. To hear Mike and Biggie tell it, there were always stumbling drunks who got separated from their friends. Off trail areas were heavy with foliage and often foggy. He could find a place in the woods to hide his kill and then feed at his leisure after the farm closed for the night. When the haunt season ended, he would assume another of his false identities and quickly move on. Martin Godfrey would disappear again.

In the meantime, the Minister returned to the places where the homeless slept, preying on those who isolated themselves and would not be missed for days or even longer. He also went to the watery playgrounds of South County and resumed the method that had been so effective when he was a bloated bag of monster. He would wait at one of the many area beaches for an isolated swimmer to appear, usually in the early morning or after sunset. He could strike underwater, drag his stricken victim down, and then tow him to secluded shallows to enjoy his meal. There was little clothing to dispose of. Anything that remained went out with the tide.

Throughout August, Martin joined Scott at the farm to help finish work on the sets. He spoke to Milton about the roles still available to play. He liked the idea of the wandering lumberjacks. He could be anywhere at any time and would not have to constantly answer for his whereabouts.

"We already have Jimmy and Big Ed slated for those spots. They kind of own those characters," Milton explained. "What I need is a fire-and-brimstone minister for the entrance to the hayride. You would shout warnings to the sinners about to enter hell while devils with pitchforks run around the wagons."

"I was hoping to work at the walk-through," Martin said.

"Well, I think you'd be good as the proprietor of the curio shop. You'd wear a suit and carry around a mysterious box. When you press a trigger on the box, it bursts open to release a wriggling, nasty creature. There'd be two other actors hiding behind drop down paintings." Milton took Martin to the set and demonstrated how the drop downs worked.

Martin agreed to work the curio shop. It was the fourth stop on the walk-through—far from perfect, but it would allow a small measure of freedom to move about.

As work continued to finish the sets ahead of the September rehearsal, Martin tried to get closer to the women on the staff. Amy especially fascinated him. But whenever he tried to walk behind her, she seemed to sense he was there. She would turn quickly, as if to confront him, but Martin would already be retreating. It was clear she didn't like him. He overheard the girl complain to Meg one afternoon, "Is there something wrong with me? Why am I attracting these creeps?"

"You're not the only female he's weirding out," Meg replied. "Synova hates him. If he crosses the line, let us know. Tom will dump him."

Martin fumed over this fragment of conversation all afternoon. Amy had called him a "creep" and a "perv." Apparently, several other women shared her opinion. He knew what the words meant. The insults would be addressed.

On Friday nights, the haunters resumed the traditional bonfire outside the greenhouse after work finished for the night. Martin joined them but always left after an hour or two. He pulled his car around the corner, parked in a field, then crept back on the grounds. He would commence a sectional search of Stone Ridge for a place to lure or drag his victims once the haunt season was underway.

One of the first likely spots he discovered was beneath a footbridge situated between the yetis and the clownbies. It spanned a wide runoff pipe between two swampy areas. The space was prone to flooding even with moderate rainfall and was usually boggy. Martin rehearsed in his mind the way it would work: He would separate out inebriated customers, promise to help them find their friends, and guide them to the bridge. A quick barb in the throat would silence them. He would pull them down to the rushes and the mud and, as their muscles turned rubbery, he would stuff them in the pipe until he could come back to feed.

On the following Friday, Martin discovered the orchard. The area was too open to be of much use. Crimes would be exposed in the light of day. He probed the decrepit stone wall that ran behind the orchard. As soon as he swung his leg over the tumbled stones, he spied the tangle of branches and construction debris. It looked promising. He pulled branches away to inspect the pile's underside. His flashlight beam was swallowed by a hole. Martin slid inside and scanned the interior with his light.

The Minister could not believe his luck. Clearly, a homeless person had made a shelter here, but Martin was not worried about any potential inhabitants. They could be easily dispatched. It was an ideal spot for seduction and murder. After dark, no one would see him come and go. He could dispose of hair, clothing and personal articles at his leisure.

Martin truly did plan to go north after the haunt closed for the season. He refused to give in to the instinct to fatten up and hibernate as he had the previous two winters. Hibernation made him a slave to his physical needs. Yet despite his powerful will, he could feel an irresistible drowsiness stealing over him as he sat in the cool and damp earthen hideaway.

He climbed out of the hole. He needed to get some sleep so he could go out for an early morning swim. As he moved the branches back in place, he heard the scratching of nails on bark in the tree above him. Startled, Martin peered through the branches to find something the size of a man crouching on a limb over his head. The figure was pale as bone and oddly shaped. Its long white fingers, toes, and teeth gave it a threatening look, but its huge gut was ridiculous. In the moonlight, amber eyes glowed in their shadowy sockets.

The creature hissed at Martin. The Minister cried out and fell over the stone wall onto his back. It occurred to him that he might be the butt of a haunter's joke and he ground his teeth with fury. "If I discover who you are, you'll be sorry," he called as he struggled to his feet and sprinted across the orchard. The thing stood on the wall, misshapen and menacing, watching as Martin retreated.

As he ran, the Minister made a vow. Once he learned who or what had scared him off, there would be hell to pay.

THE CURSE OF MEMORY

August 18, 2012

A STRANGER APPEARED LAST night at my hideout behind the orchard wall. I had spent the evening watching the construction work on the hayride sets. After they started their Friday bonfire, I took a leisurely stroll through the sets. The theme this year is "Hell, Rhode Island."

I find it amusing and cannot help but think the theme came about as an expression of a private joke among my friends. Most likely, this was Bill's influence. He is a jovial man with a wicked sense of humor.

A crescent moon had risen high when I decided to leave Bone Ridge. For someone who had not lifted a hammer, I felt somewhat fatigued. I thought I might take a rest in my shelter by the orchard wall. Before I could slip into the hole, however, I heard a commotion in the orchard. It was so noisy it could only have been a human being thrashing through the tall grass. I scrabbled up the trunk of the adjacent oak to wait for the intruder to leave.

Well-hidden and still as stone, I watched a man step over the wall and cross from moonlight into deep shadow. With great purpose he began to probe the pile of debris as if searching for something. Then he disappeared down the hole I had labored to excavate. I was filled with panic as I waited for him to reemerge.

It seemed forever, but at last he climbed out and laughed. There was something in that sound I recognized. It was foolhardy, but I wanted to get a better look at his face. I climbed down the trunk even though I knew I risked being discovered. He turned at the sound I made.

The sight of my bizarre form terrified him. But I was no less frightened when I realized I knew that face. I had seen it in the dreams that revisited my crimes. This was the soul Demon was looking for. The stranger cried out and fell backwards over the wall. Then he picked himself up and ran like Demon himself was on his heels.

Now I am back in my root cellar wondering what I should do. It was clear this man did not recognize me. But he could not fail to know that I inhabited the underground dwelling. If he returned, he was certain to discover that I had benefactors who brought food and messages of cheer. I do not want this man near my friends. I cannot trust him to do no harm. I will visit this site whenever I anticipate another drop off. I will try to communicate my fears with whoever comes.

August 23, 2012

It is worse than I feared. I have seen this man at the haunt. He is working on the sets, laughing and easily making friends with the haunters. I overheard him discussing his role with Susan and Justin. He is to be the proprietor of the curio shop on the walk-through.

It bothers me that my dreams have deserted me. I know we did evil things together, but I have a woefully incomplete picture of our crimes. Demon has made me to understand the Minister escaped punishment and that I must assume the responsibility of bringing this man to his well-deserved doom. But I am hesitant to act. I do not know enough, and he has committed no new crimes as far as I know. The last time I chose to intervene in a crime, it resulted in murder—by my hands.

I do not understand why, but I am truly and deeply afraid.

August 26, 2012

I watched from the oak tree behind the orchard wall last night in anticipation of a visit from one of my friends. A few hours after sundown, I spied Sean walking through the orchard with a sack of goods. I climbed part way down the trunk to claim his attention when I spied another dark shape moving among the apple trees. Sean was about to hide the donations under the debris so I moved quickly. Clinging to the trunk with my toes, I covered his mouth with one of my huge hands and grabbed him by the arm. Sean was a strapping young man, and he struggled desperately, but my long arms gave me superb leverage. I dragged him to a high branch where we would both be concealed.

When I released Sean, he backed away and flattened himself against the trunk of the tree. He flinched as I placed my bony finger on his lips and pointed to the ground below. He saw the figure approach the tree, move the plywood, and disappear underground. He was startled but remained silent. He looked at me and nodded.

Together we watched and waited for the Minister to leave. When he climbed out of my shelter and crossed the orchard, Sean whispered. "That's Martin Godfrey. He just joined the haunt."

I nodded. Of course, I could not tell him where I had seen this man before. I beckoned him to follow me down the tree. We slid inside my cave and I handed Sean a torch. Together, we scanned the interior. In one corner, we found a box labeled "Contractor Trash Bags." There were several packages of moistened cleaning cloths the haunters used to remove their makeup, and a bundle of those flexible restraints I had seen the sheriff's men use on the wife beater.

"It looks like he wants to move in. Or hide evidence of a crime. Do you know what he wants with this place?" Sean whispered.

I shook my head. I had my suspicions—perhaps this was to be a place to carry out seductions—but I could not be sure.

"You have to take everything that's yours out of here right now—especially journals and letters. And we have to find a different way to communicate. A phone, the greenhouse or…" Sean paused to think. "I know where. Have you been inside the greenhouse?"

I nodded.

"There's a black cabinet where we keep the makeup. The ground's not level there. You can slip a note underneath late at night and we'll find it the next day. We'll do the same. I'll tell the others what we saw, and we'll all keep our eyes on him. OK?"

I agreed and tied my belongings up in the blanket. I was uneasy enough to follow Sean back to his vehicle. I stayed and watched until I saw him drive safely away.

September 2, 2012

As far as I know, Martin Godfrey has not been back to the orchard.

I have tried to track my quarry without being discovered. It has not been easy. I am glad that both Sean and Amy now own enclosed vehicles to provide safe transport to and from the farm. No doubt, my young friends have conveyed their concerns to Carrie and Bill, but I am writing my own letter to place in Bill's truck as soon as I have a chance. I do not know what this man wants, but I feel it is important to warn my friends he is not to be trusted.

September 8, 20012

Yesterday evening was the rehearsal for the walk-through. The actors found their places at their stations and, without benefit of costume or makeup, tried to frighten each other on the strength of their characterizations alone. I saw the Minister among the others, sharing their cheer and companionship. He seemed a man like any other. He appeared to bear no ill intention towards anyone, so I allowed myself to relax and enjoy this reunion with the old haunt companions and to become acquainted with the new. But I thought it wise to follow the actors to see what Martin might do.

I noticed that Therese, who last year wanted to sing at her scenes and give away the scares, had returned. I saw Carrie exchange looks with Melanie and Allison, especially when they learned she would play one of the ghosts in the curio shop.

"That ought to work," Allison said. "She can sing, shriek, whatever she wants, as long as she does it on cue."

I rather liked her singing. She is a charming, if somewhat silly girl.

As the evening progressed, Therese's attention became increasingly focused on handsome Martin. He returned her flirtations. When they approached the ruined castle set, they lagged behind the group. The other actors rounded a bend in the trail. Martin pulled the girl behind a door in the castle wall. Crouched in the thick bushes behind the set, I watched as he kissed her quickly on her throat then planted his open mouth over hers. He probed under her blouse with his hands. He whispered something in her ear then ran up the path after the other haunters. She quickly followed.

After rehearsal ended and the other haunters left, Martin returned to the castle ruins with the girl in hand. I had no intention of watching him seduce her, so I climbed high in the tree overlooking the scene. I suddenly heard a cry of pain that brought my attention back to the couple.

She yielded herself to him willingly enough, but that was not enough for the Minister. He was pinching her and otherwise inflicting pain and seemed to be deriving great pleasure from it. I am burning with shame as I write these words, but once I turned my gaze back on the scene, I could not look away. And as my eyes remained riveted on his perversions, my mind was overwhelmed with memory after memory of the disgraceful past we had shared. Even my truncated manhood remembered and stirred with a feeble sort of lust.

He finished with her and helped Therese to her feet. She took to the path, but the Minister paused, raised his eyes to the sky, and smiled at the waning moon. I recognized the look of sated appetite and loveless triumph in his face. I pushed my head through the screen of leaves so he spied me. Martin hissed, "Who are you?" His face registered both impotent rage and fear. Then Therese called to him and he followed her up the path.

September 16, 2012

My name is Simon Hogg.

In another time, in another life, I was a deacon in a new land. I have learned enough local history to believe I lived some 330 years ago. The image I have of my former self is not a flattering one. I was above average height but shaped something like a nine pin. I had lanky yellow hair, pale gray eyes, soft muscles, and soft hands completely unaccustomed to honest labor. My memories present a picture of an educated young man who found a life in the clergy as a means to avoid serious toil. I took the easy side in every conflict. Usually, I took no side at all. I owned no ideas, no passions, no morals I could truly call mine. I could not quote the Bible nor was I even sure God existed. I have since formed a firmer opinion on the matter.

The Minister, however, had very definite ideas, deviant passions, and a total lack of morals. A younger son, he had been pushed by his father into the religious life. He took the opportunity to shepherd an isolated congregation in New England because he would have little oversight. I think I came to the colony as a boy. I had already fallen short at other apprenticeships and occupations. It seems I severed my family connections with an abundance of bitterness and shared recriminations. So, with no ties of love or blood, and having failed all other endeavors, I went to learn the ways of God from Martin Godfrey.

From the start, he ridiculed me for being soft and fat, for loving books, and for never having known a woman. He made fun of my name and made pig noises at me when we should have been asking God's blessing over the evening meal.

It was not long before I did lie with a woman. Once Martin established his authority over his small congregation, he began to seduce the female congregants. When their husbands were away, he found excuses to visit their homes, offering prayer and spiritual support. He goaded me into joining him so I would be as compromised as his conquests. I quickly learned to silence the feeble protests of my lax conscience. I even looked forward to our trysts. And as Martin continued to ridicule and abuse me, sometimes in front of our victims, I felt compelled to perform for his amusement and approval as well as for my own pleasure. I cannot recall feeling happy with this life, but I do not believe I had actually ever been happy. I lacked any strength or ambition to change my condition.

Then the girl came into our lives. Catherine was indentured but proved to be an unruly servant. She was no more than sixteen and without family or friends. She had been sent to the Minister to learn obedience. He began his lessons the very first night.

The first hour she was under our roof, he beat her so viciously she could barely stand. He threatened to beat her again if she did not complete her chores the next day. She learned quickly to do as she was told.

I believe the women of the congregation suspected what abuse Catherine endured, but they were in no position to speak. They were more concerned about protecting their daughters from Martin and me. They need not have feared. For the moment, Martin was more interested in his new plaything. Many an evening, after she cleared away the evening meal, we took turns using her. If she protested, she was beaten again. I did not wish to hurt her, but Martin belittled my manhood and goaded me into it. He seemed to enjoy watching me use her more than when he did it himself.

Catherine's suffering eventually roused my feeble conscience, although I did nothing about it. When she stole food and ran away the first time, I was secretly glad. She was gone for a week before she was found and brought back. The girl was forced to stand in the meeting house in front of the congregation and was told to proclaim her sins. All the women of the congregation stared at the floor except for one old woman and her husband whose eyes burned with wrath. They took care of our animals and garden and kept the meeting house in repair. More than once, the old man had hidden Catherine in the barn when the Minister threatened a new beating.

I watched Catherine grit her teeth, refusing to speak. I knew she wanted to expose us for the degenerates we were. As Martin thundered and screamed at her from his pulpit, something hardened in her young face. Finally, she declared her guilt and promised to do penance.

What we did not know was that while Catherine was gone, she encountered some native women who took pity on her. They had shown her where she could disappear and how to find food. I believe it occurred to her that, if she could live off the land, she could remain safely hidden. So she played the part of the humble and obedient servant. Martin was convinced he had made her over into the most obliging slave he could ever desire. But she was merely waiting for her opportunity.

One spring day, the Minister rode to some of the more distant farms in our congregation. We had new members. The Minister wanted to introduce himself and investigate any new dalliances that might present themselves. I spent the morning reading. When no noontime meal materialized, I realized Catherine was missing. I searched our dwelling, our meeting house, the garden, barn, and grounds. The old man glared at me with burning blue eyes, daring me to question him. I suspected he and his wife were hiding the girl. I turned away and felt a surge of hope that Catherine might escape her torment.

Martin took his walking stick to me when he learned Catherine was missing. Enraged, I grabbed it, raised it over my head, and threatened to beat him. He laughed and dared me to do it. At that moment, I realized how much I hated the man and wanted to strike him dead. But I hated myself and my cowardice even more. The minister stepped forward until he was within inches of my face, still taunting, still daring. I lowered the rod and placed it against the wall by the fire, but stared at him until he sneered and looked away. I took some small satisfaction from that. I sat up by the fire most of the night, reflecting on all I had done, pondering if I should leave as well. But I did not know what I would do next. There was nowhere else to go.

Weeks passed with no sign of the girl. Even the poorest in our congregation did not wish to send their sons or daughters to work for us. Only the old man and his wife helped us, their eyes blazing with contempt whenever my gaze met theirs. The Minister would not confront them. He punished the rest of the congregation with dark and threatening sermons.

I find myself compelled at this point to break off this narration. There are worse deeds to confess, but right now I am too exhausted in mind and spirit to continue.

September 19, 2012

It has taken me days to stoke my courage, especially now that I have been forced to acknowledge that I had once lived as the most dissolute of men. As cruel as Martin Godfrey was, I am truly the greater sinner. Had I refused to participate in that first molestation, had I exposed him to the congregation, none of the later atrocities would have occurred. I feared that if he stood accused, he would charm the congregants and no one would believe me. But what punishment would I have faced? I would have been cast out and forced to find honest work to support myself. That is all. I would have been forced to become a man. For the first time, I understand why my personal hell has taken the form it has. My physical shape and my cravings are no more than logical manifestations of the monster I became 330 years ago.

Catherine disappeared in the early spring and was missing for months. Martin seemed to think she was beyond his reach. I avoided him, taking my meals alone, reading for hours in the small alcove where I slept, and attending to my paltry duties. Sometimes he mocked me, but since I had threatened him, he largely ignored me.

One of our congregants visited his brother who lived some distance to the south. They went hunting for geese and ducks in a vast marsh dotted with tussocks of land. Some of these were large enough to remain as islands at high tide. They noted that one such island was occupied. They saw the smoke of cooking fires rise above the tall reeds and glimpsed a hut built of bent limbs and bark. It resembled a native dwelling, so they paid it no mind until they heard the crying of a babe and spied a thin pale girl at the water's edge. The congregant found it curious enough to mention it to his wife. The Minister overheard her gossiping about it to the other women in town. She speculated it might be Catherine, but had no intention of telling her chief tormentor.

I did not want to accompany Martin to the marsh, but he threatened to expose me as the sole despoiler of the townswomen. "The men will credit me and the women will keep silent. No one will listen to you," he sneered. I believed him.

We left before sunrise on a cold December morning. We rode most of the day and took lodging for the night. We reached the marsh the next day. It was low tide, so our horses easily waded out to the island. We surprised the girl as she was nursing a babe that could not have been older than a few months. Martin tore the child from Catherine's arms and threatened to drown it if she did not come with him immediately. Needless to say, she obeyed.

She confessed all as Martin held her child. Catherine ran to the native women who had aided her after her previous escape. They taught her how to build a shelter and find food, which they supplemented when it was time for her to deliver. She even hoped to take one of the men as her husband. She wore a heathen talisman around her neck, meant to protect her from evil. Martin tore it off and threw it in the marsh.

I cradled the babe as we rode. It was a girl with yellow hair and clear hazel eyes. She looked at me as if she could see my very soul. She seemed a marvel of understanding for one so new to this world. I was ashamed to meet her gaze.

Martin laughed. "That little bastard must be yours. She's ugly and has the look of a simpleton. There is none of me in her."

I ignored him. I thought the child was beautiful.

He rode with Catherine in front of him and whispered threats in her ear all the way back. I did not like the look of the day. There was a yellow cast to the sky one might see when a colossal storm threatens in the summer. A cold sleet fell as we rode, yet sometimes, when the wind changed direction, it smelled foul and felt unnaturally warm on our faces, like the breath of Hell itself.

The Minister refused to stop. It was close to midnight the following day when we reached our village. The wind howled and thunder rumbled even as sleet pelted us. All the townsfolk were sensibly shut up in their homes. Martin did not want to warm himself by a fire, however. He covered the girl's mouth as he dragged her to the door of the meeting house. A bolt of lightning flashed above our heads while thunder cracked the sky. Our horses trumpeted and bolted for the safety of our barn.

Martin threw Catherine to the floor. I followed him, still carrying the babe, and shut the door behind us. The minister lit a single candle. Its guttering light was all but swallowed by the unnatural blackness of that night. He tore the girl's dress down the back and used a strip of cloth to bind her hands. He stuffed another piece of cloth in her mouth. She did not resist. She only kept her eyes on her child. The Minister forced her to her knees and commanded, "Take her."

I stammered something about the holy ground on which we stood. "We should take her to the house," I said.

Martin walked up to me as I clutched the babe and slapped me across the face. "This ground is mine," he said. "If God had strength or concern, do you not think he would have stopped us by now?" He pointed to the girl and repeated, "Take her. She needs to be punished." He hit me again.

I placed the child on the floor. I could feel both anger and lust rising in me. I wanted to punish someone. It was easier to punish her. She cried out in pain as I grabbed her by the shoulders. But before I could begin my depredations, I felt eyes on me—someone other than the Minister, watching me, judging me. I scanned the candle-lit room to find the child's bright eyes fixed on me. They were grave and sorrowful, as if she could see deep into my debased soul. But there was someone else. On the high pulpit I saw a creature roosting there. I might have taken it for an owl, except that it had green cat-like eyes. Another stroke of lightning illuminated the room, and it grinned at me. It was there to take stock of our souls. Drained of all sensations save terror, I cried out and backed away from Catherine.

The Minister seemed unable to see it. He snarled, "You are more maid than man." He grasped Catherine by her arms and roughly pulled her to her feet. He made ready to abuse her, but Catherine had worked her hands free. She raked Martin's face with her nails and pulled the gag from her mouth. She started shrieking, less like a woman than a wild beast defending her young. Enraged, Martin evaded her blows and backhanded her across the face. He wrapped his hands around her throat and began to squeeze. She struggled desperately to break free but quickly went limp. Lightning hit the roof of the meeting house in a mighty explosion as she died.

There were flames above our heads as the Minister scooped up the child from the floor. He handed it to me and said, "This is your bastard. You have to do it."

I could not comprehend what he asked of me.

"We cannot be caught this way," Martin explained. "We shall both hang. The child must die, and we must let the fire consume both of them. Or would you rather let the bastard burn alive?"

I wept, but I realized he was right. It was so easy. I simply placed my hand over the babe's face and pressed down. Her eyes watched me, calmly and without blinking, until they glazed over.

My daughter was dead. I raised my eyes so I would not see her lifeless gaze and glimpsed yet another pair of eyes at the window. They were icy blue with contemptuous fury. It was the old man. He turned away to raise the alarm with the congregation.

The fire raged above our heads. Voices shouted outside, and we knew we had to flee. But the meeting house door would not open. The old man had probably barricaded it from without. Martin pointed to the smaller rear door behind the pulpit, but when we turned we found ourselves confronted by a monstrously huge demon. He had calmly roosted on the pulpit and watched us commit murder and infanticide, all on consecrated ground. Now he grinned gleefully, grabbed both of us blasphemers by the hair, and lifted us up into the violent night sky.

I always wondered why Demon threw me into this time and place of all the other possibilities open to him. I now understand that I am here to set something right. I can do nothing for Catherine. I pray she is blessed with everlasting rest. But I do believe I was placed here to meet Amy, with her bright and knowing hazel eyes. I am here to somehow earn her forgiveness and love and to protect her from all harm.

STALKING MONSTERS

WHEN THERESE FAILED to show up for opening night, Martin could feel Scott's eyes on him. Milton and Bill called her several times before going to the backup list. She did not show up Saturday evening, either. Scott made the mistake of saying to Martin, in front of everyone in the makeup queue, "She stayed with you Thursday night, didn't she? I had to sleep in my car 'cause you had the sign on the door."

"Yes," Martin said. "If you recall, her car was there when you came home and gone in the morning. So clearly, she went home."

Therese's friends picked up on the conversation. "I got a text from her roommate. Her car is in the parking lot, but no one has seen her since Thursday afternoon," Crystal said.

Later that evening, with the scares well underway, a police officer showed up to interview anyone who knew Therese. Her parents had reported her missing. No one had anything particularly helpful to say. Scott corroborated Martin's assertion that he never left the mobile home until he went to work after sunrise.

There was video footage from the apartment complex. It showed Therese parking in a shadowy lot, getting out of the car alone and walking away. There was nothing to indicate she had been followed.

Dark and tree-shaded areas around the perimeter of the lot were searched. There was a greasy slick crusted with salts behind the dumpster, but it seemed to be no more than kitchen waste.

After they made love Thursday night, Martin feigned sleep as Therese dressed and used the bathroom. While the bathroom door was closed, Martin donned a hooded black robe and crept out of the trailer. He eased himself onto the floor in the back of Therese's car. Minutes later, the young woman slipped into the driver's seat without a single glance behind her. Scott snored in his own vehicle, oblivious to everything.

Therese walked through the deep shadows of the apartment parking lot. The Minister crept up behind her and stabbed his barb between her shoulder blades. He covered her mouth and dragged her behind the dumpster to watch her melt. When he was finished with her, he stuffed the robe, her clothes, and her oily hair into a back pack. It was an easy, three-mile jog back to the trailer. He would dump the pack behind the orchard wall at his convenience. Scott was still asleep in his car when Martin got back.

Scott would not shut up about the disappearance. "Here's the thing," he said Sunday night as they shared a six pack. "I was asleep outside the trailer. You were asleep inside the trailer. You woke me up as you were going to work. You could have gone somewhere and I wouldn't have seen it. I could have gone somewhere…"

"And I wouldn't have seen it," Martin finished. "What's your point?"

"They'll come back to talk to us sooner or later. They might try to pin something on one of us. I just don't want to end up as 'a person of interest.' You know what I mean?"

Martin wondered how difficult it would be to convince the police that Scott should be their person of interest. Scott was annoyingly verbose, a trait that grated against Martin's patience as his urge to feed grew more urgent. It would be so easy to silence Scott by making a meal of him. But Scott was not a safe choice. He would have to remain untouched until the Minister was ready to move on.

By summer's end, he found he needed to hunt several times a week. His plan to master his cravings was not working out. He was going further and further afield to find prey no one would miss. He was eager to start hunting at the haunt. If he did it right, he could eat his way through the clientele until the season ended.

On the first Saturday in October, as he stood in the makeup queue, Biggie's arm came from behind and poked Martin's belly. "Packing on a few pounds?" he said. "Pretty soon you'll be able to make it dance like I do." Biggie lifted his shirt and demonstrated, rolls of flesh undulating to some inner beat. The haunters cheered.

Martin swallowed his fury and forced a laugh as he replied, "I still have a long way to go to match you." He caught his profile in one of the full-length mirrors and scowled. He was accumulating fat around his waist line. *I will not hibernate*, he told himself. His stomach growled in protest. Biggie laughed and patted the Minister's soft belly, "Easy, big guy."

First to go, Martin swore to himself.

Martin was one actor away from being seated at Amy's makeup station when Sean called out, "Martin, Biggie, over here. I can take you."

Biggie switched lines compliantly. The Minister ignored Sean until Amy said, "Over there, Martin. Sean will do your makeup." She inclined her head toward Sean's chair, her hazel eyes glaring with disdain. Then she called one of the hayride demons to her chair.

Martin took his place behind Biggie. He kept his face still to hide his rage as Amy and Sean exchanged knowing glances. He did not like being ordered around by young women. He also did not like the nagging suspicion that Sean and Amy knew more than they should.

Big Ed led the haunters in their new, PG-13 cheer. "We don't just scare 'em; we mess 'em up for life." Then demons and sinners headed for the hayride. Punch, TikTok, Sylence, and Gastro led a parade of walk-through actors to their scenes.

Travis wore a black strapless evening gown studded with sequins that suited his lithe figure remarkably well. He spent so much time in a dress the previous season he was the obvious choice to be the bearded lady in the medicine show, along with Synova as a snake woman and Justin as a charlatan healer, peddling bottles filled with body parts.

Amy was with Mallison at the playground scene, which was painted fluorescent colors and bathed in black light. Mallison wore matching pinafores, but the scene needed a ghostly little boy. Amy tucked her hair up under a baseball cap and wore a Little League uniform. Mike and Biggie worked the maze again while Carrie, Brian, and Ellis donned bald caps and Victorian funeral garb for the Nosferatu scene. Rob and Sean were criminal and guard at the execution scene.

The Minister walked from scene to scene, greeting and joking with his new friends: the yetis, the prisoners on the bus, the cook and waitresses at the manburger diner, the lumberjacks, and the devils of Hell's torture chamber. Martin found the mood among the haunters celebratory and electric. He could not help being infected by it. He grew lighthearted as he took his place at the curio shop with Scott and Therese's replacement, a newbie named Jenna. He enthusiastically played his part and enjoyed himself, all the while watching for a likely victim.

His chance came as the last customers straggled through. A group of inebriated young adults entered his set. The actors scared two in the group. The others were busy trying to pull apart pieces of the set to take as souvenirs. The actors broke character to chase them off the scene. "I'm going to follow them," Martin said. "You should call Bill."

When the errant group noticed that Martin was close on their heels, they laughed and broke into a run—except one young woman who stumbled and fell to her knees. When the Minister offered her his hand, she seemed confused. "Didn't I just see you back there?" she asked.

"I could tell you needed help," Martin said as he lifted her to her feet. "I'll show you a short cut back to your friends." He guided her past the yeti set, sharing a laugh with the actors as he disappeared around a sharp bend in the trail. Then he quickly pulled the woman through a thick hedge that concealed the drainage ditch.

"This doesn't look like a path," she said. She giggled as Martin kissed her neck. "I think we should go the other way."

Martin kissed her mouth, grabbing her chin when she tried to pull away. She tasted of vomit, but he was too hungry to care. He kissed her open mouth again and delivered the barb to the back of her throat. She squealed with pain as he held her. When her legs went soft, he let her drop to the bottom of the muddy ditch and returned to his scene.

After closing, Martin got out of his costume quickly and bid his fellow haunters good night. He hid his car along the side street and jogged back to the ditch. Bill and

Justin had already done a final inspection so the walk-through was dark and silent. The lights in the girl's brain had gone out and her dermis had thinned to something resembling tissue paper, but the essentials were there for him to enjoy. He admired his kill under the beam of a small flashlight then fell to his knees to feed.

As he shoveled the gel into his mouth, Martin felt his scalp prickle. Someone was watching him. He leapt to his feet in alarm and scanned the area with his light. He caught a flash of white in the tree over his head. It was the same creature he had seen before. It climbed down the trunk head first, bared its teeth at him and glared.

"What do you want?" Martin hissed. The creature held his gaze. Its eyes hinted at some kind of intelligence, but it seemed unable to speak. "You want some of this?" he called, scooping up a handful of jelly and hurling it at the tree.

The creature sniffed at the gel and gave Martin a look of open-mouthed horror. "Go to hell," hissed the Minister. He finished feeding, keeping one eye on the bony monster with the swollen belly. He stuffed the slimy hair mat and clothes in a trash bag and hurried to his hiding place behind the orchard.

The next evening, a message in long, flowing script was written in black makeup crayon on one of the greenhouse mirrors. It read, "I know who you are and I know what you did." It was signed "Simon."

Martin and several other actors read the message before Susan erased it. "If there's a joke here, I'm not getting it," she said. "Stop the high school drama bullshit if you want to keep working here."

Martin knew the name, and he recognized the penmanship. He found it difficult to hide his alarm. Where was that pig, Simon, and how did he know what had happened? He vaguely remembered the demon grabbing both of them by the hair and turning them into some sort of malleable plasma. Once Martin had escaped the demon, he had not given Simon another thought. Clearly, that dolt was here, in this time and place. He seemed to know the haunt, but the Minister could not recall seeing his watery gray eyes, gourd-shaped body, or limp yellow hair anywhere on the farm.

He pictured the creature atop the stone wall in the orchard, shaking his fist at Martin. It had the same ridiculous silhouette, the same limp yellow hair. The Minister choked back his alarm. That creature was Simon—the man who never took a stand or spoke for anyone, least of all himself. *He would have gone meekly into whatever hell Demon created for him*, the Minister thought contemptuously. Well, the Deacon could leave all the messages he wanted. There was no trace of the killing and nothing to tie Martin to the young woman.

He took himself out to the smoking area where he could laugh and joke and settle his composure. As he exited the makeup area, he noticed Sean and Amy sharing two separate notes. A quick glance over their shoulders revealed the same spidery script on the slips of paper, and he felt agitated all over again. When the

Minister had calmed himself and returned, he saw Sean and Amy showing their notes to Bill and Carrie. They appeared as alarmed as Martin felt. When they saw Martin get into one of the makeup lines, they broke apart.

Martin knew he needed to exercise the greatest caution if Simon was somehow communicating with any of the haunters. But his hunger drove him to scout possible victims through the night.

"I'm taking a quick break," he called out to Scott and Jenna. A teenager scrolling through his messages had become separated from his friends. He stood in a patch of deep shadows, entranced by the glowing screen. Martin slipped behind a tree and waited for his opportunity to send his barb into an arm or a thigh.

Something thrashed in the grapevines behind the Minister. The commotion startled the boy. "Hey, guys?" he called as he hurried up the path. He ran into Big Ed revving up his chainsaw and took off screaming.

Martin turned to see what had made the racket. The huge skull face of the creature peered from behind the grapevines. "You don't scare me, Simon," the Minister whispered.

The monster bared his teeth at him.

"You went into your hell without a word of protest," Martin jeered, "exactly where you were told, too spineless to fight back. I took my fate into my own hands. And now you think you can scare me away?" If the creature heard, he made no sign. He had already disappeared from sight.

Throughout the night, Martin searched the area above his head to find Simon staring back at him. When he tried to move closer, the face seemed to dissolve away. He tried to find out if his coworkers had seen anything.

"There's something thrashing around out there, but I don't know what it is," Jenna said. "It's probably an opossum."

Martin went to bed hungry that night.

The police made an appearance at Bone Ridge as the Sunday performance drew to a close. Tom and Milton assembled the actors in the greenhouse as the inquiring officers described the disappearance of a college junior either late Saturday night or early Sunday morning. "She was with a large group of students that came in three different cars," one officer said as they passed around a photo. "One of them said she went home in his car, but he was kind of fuzzy about where she got out. Her roommates said she didn't sleep in her room that night, but they thought she went home with one of the boys."

Martin could not believe his good luck. He cheerfully volunteered, "I remember her. That entire group was drunk."

"They were trying to pull the sets apart," Scott said. "Martin followed them 'cause they were a bunch of assholes."

"The woman you're looking for actually fell down," Martin said. "I had to help her stay on her feet and find her group. I took her around the maze because I was afraid she'd pass out in there. I left her when she saw her friends just a few feet ahead."

Except for the yetis, no one else could remember seeing the young woman but thought nothing of it. It had been a large group, and the haunters were focused on protecting sets and props.

Martin noticed Sean, Amy, Carrie, and Bill exchanging looks. Bill leaned over and whispered something to Justin, who reacted in disbelief. The police speculated that the missing woman had wandered off somewhere and got injured after she left the haunt or had fallen in the river that ran next to her apartment.

Martin needed to feed again. Providence had become over-hunted. He called in sick to his day job for the next few days. He decided to familiarize himself with New Haven and prowl among its invisible people.

He also needed time to make meticulous plans. Somehow, he had to draw Simon into a trap. After Martin killed the creature, he would go after anyone who had exhibited even a shadow of suspicion. More than anything, he wanted to corner the young woman who seemed to despise him so. She always looked straight through him and deep into his poisoned soul, and he hated her for it. He wanted to deliver his venom right into her heart, hold her close, and laugh as he watched the lights go out of her eyes.

THE FRIENDS DEVISE A PLAN

CARRIE WAS RANTING. "So now we have two monsters. It's like the universe is this social service bureaucracy. The case workers keep losing track of their clients, and the people in charge have their heads up their asses."

"Be careful what you say," Sean said. "You might piss somebody off."

"And you're already in Rhode Island," Bill added. "I hear it's a quick trip to hell from here."

The Friends of Bonebelly were holding an emergency meeting in an out-of-the-way diner a few days after the second woman disappeared. Amy and Sean had found a total of three notes from Bonebelly. The Friends now came together to analyze them and plot a course of action.

"And why is that?" Carrie said. "Don't we have enough problems without being hell on top of it?"

"I don't think it's just us," Amy answered. "Think of all those Big Foot sightings around the country. I bet they're all condemned souls." She spread out three sheets of yellow lined paper on the table. The first two smaller leaves had been rolled up and tucked into the tool box where she stored her makeup. One had appeared at the end of that first Saturday night. She read, "If harm has come to Therese, it was not me. It could be Martin."

The second one was waiting for her when she arrived the following Saturday to set up her station. "Dear child, please keep your distance from Martin. He kills with a kiss."

There was also the message scrawled in black crayon on the mirror. Most of the haunters thought it was a joke. The Friends now knew better.

"What does it mean to kill with a kiss?" Carrie asked.

"We didn't get it either until we found the letter under the makeup cabinet," Sean said. The letter had been the impetus for the emergency meeting.

Amy unfolded the letter and read aloud, "My dear friends, I thank you for the likenesses you gave me of the haunters dressed to look like me. It is a shame that only we five can appreciate the joke." He was referring to photos Sean had taken of hayride actors in Bonebelly costume and makeup.

Amy continued, "I know what I am about to tell you will seem like madness, but you must believe me. I have known Martin Godfrey before. He was a blaspheming man of God who should be suffering in his own hell. He escaped his fate and created himself a monster. Now he lives among the innocent, committing even greater atrocities. I will not tell the shameful story of our past sins. I have remembered all and recorded our history together. When I have done what I should have long ago and this sad story is finished, Amy will know where to look."

Amy lowered the letter to find her friends watching her expectantly. "I know where he lives. Cam said he knew where to find Tom's yeti. That's how he got me to meet him. When the drug kicked in, he dragged me into the woods." She took a deep breath before continuing. "We were near the ruins of an old farmhouse. I was on the ground and looked up through the trees. That's when I saw him. He grabbed Cam by the face and hauled him up into a tree. Then I couldn't see either of them anymore. Somehow I knew Bonebelly wanted to help me. I swear he looked at me like he knew me. A week later, I had this idea. I wanted to thank him. I guess I thought it would be therapeutic. I went out in the middle of the night and found the house."

"Why alone?" Sean sputtered. "It could have been dangerous."

Amy shrugged "I wanted to protect you." Sean was not mollified. "There was writing all over the parlor walls and ceiling. It was Bonebelly's record of his first 30 days in hell. I didn't get to read much of it. He snuck up behind me. Then he got in my face and scared the shit out of me."

"He couldn't let you be his friend," Carrie said. "He wanted you to keep your distance."

Amy nodded and resumed reading. "Even with all that has happened to me, I scarcely know how to relate the evil I just witnessed. I am a creature to be feared, yet I am deathly afraid. Your sheriff was inquiring about a woman who went missing Saturday night. Her drunken companions are mistaken. She did not go home with them. I saw Martin kill her. She was intoxicated and could barely walk. Martin promised to help her, and then he led her to a drainage ditch. He kissed her and she cried out in pain. As he held her, her legs collapsed beneath her. He left her there and I went to her. I took her hand. She was afraid of me and tried to cry out, but some unctuous liquid filled her mouth. As she wept, her tears burned her face. All her bones went soft, and her hand felt like a bag of jelly. I saw blue lights flashing under her skin. When they went dark, I knew she was dead. I do not know exactly how, but I am convinced he delivered some sort of poison to that poor woman when he kissed her. Whatever fell substance he gave her had all but dissolved her from the inside.

"He returned after the haunt closed for the night. He fed on her softened remains until there was nothing left but her clothes and hair. He put these in a bag and headed towards the orchard. Most likely, he hid them behind the orchard wall in an underground shelter I built for myself. I suspect he killed Therese in the same manner. I will put this monster back in hell if I can. In the meantime, everyone must be warned. No one must allow him to get close. Even the sheriffs and the farmer with his musket must be wary."

The friends stared at the table in silent horror. "What do we do with this?" Carrie asked at last. "If we show this to the police, they won't believe us. They'll think it's a marketing ploy."

"If he's hiding evidence in Bonebelly's hideout, maybe we should take a look," Bill said.

"What if he's in there?" Sean asked.

Bill pondered a moment. "We could leave an anonymous tip. Then we find a reason to fire him and keep him away from the haunt."

"Sexual harassment," Amy suggested. "I know a few women like him, but he creeps out the rest of us. He's always bothering Synova."

Bill nodded. "That'll work. This is seasonal employment—no time for re-training. Tom will just cut him loose."

It was agreed that Bill would talk to Tom and Jen. Martin would be banned from the farm, and all employees would be warned to avoid him. Later that evening, Bill stopped by the farmhouse to do just that. He told the farmers he had received numerous complaints from female haunters and that Martin needed to be fired. Tom and Jen agreed. Bill promised to give Martin the news. Before he drove away, Bill slipped a letter under the door of the bakery. It was printed in block letters on a dirty, creased sheet of paper. The author claimed to be in the woods the night the coed disappeared. He went on to describe how someone fitting Martin's description disposed of something suspicious behind the orchard wall.

Gloria found the note the next morning and turned it over to Jen, who called the police.

"Do you have any idea who might have left this?" Officer Gilchrist asked.

"We've had homeless people camp behind our property before," Tom said. "I haven't seen anyone back there recently, but who knows?"

The farmer and his wife took the police to the orchard. It did not take them long to find the hole in the ground.

"I had no idea that was there," Tom said.

"Someone made himself a shelter," said Officer Monroe. "Looks like an underground room."

"I can't believe no one ever saw anyone digging back there," Tom marveled.

"I told you to clean up that rat's nest ages ago," Jen grumbled.

The policemen crawled into the hole. The space was almost bare. They inspected what was there with a sickening and growing sense of dread: a box of trash bags, disinfecting wipes, zip ties and two bags of strange-smelling refuse.

"Jesus, what is this?" Monroe asked as he beamed his flashlight inside one of the bags. "It looks like clothes, a wig, and what the fuck is that smell?"

It was not exactly an odor of decay. It was foul but also sharply sweet and acidic. The interior of the trash bag was slick with some kind of oily substance.

Gilchrist found something similar in the second bag. The only difference was the color of the garments and the shocks of hair: one of them was blonde, while the other belonged to a redhead.

"These aren't wigs," observed Officer Monroe.

"Oh, fuck," whispered Gilchrist. His legs gave out under him. His partner had to help him out of the hole.

The farm was now a potential crime scene. Tom contacted Milton and the managers to let them know the haunt might have to close for the rest of the season. Fortunately, the police finished their search by Friday. The orchard and the abutting area were cordoned off, but Bone Ridge was only closed for one night.

The police checked the homeless shelters for someone fitting the description in the note. A half dozen men who worked at the farm and haunt shared similar features. Of the six, only Martin had been with Therese, who had disappeared after staying with him into the early morning hours two weeks ago. The police questioned Martin at his day job but had no evidence to connect him to the missing women. They were weeks away from identifying the remains or determining a possible cause of death.

After the police left, the Minister's boss informed him that he would have to vacate the trailer. There was no more work for him, either. He was paid and expected to leave.

Days earlier, Scott had already packed up his clothes and thrown himself on his mother's mercy. Martin checked messages on the contractor's phone and found he no longer had a job at Bone Ridge, either. This had to be Simon's doing. He had gained the trust of a handful of the haunters and was exchanging messages with them. The Minister understood he should disappear right away, but he also needed to remove anyone who knew too much. How could he do that without access to the haunt? How could he remove them quickly yet ensure the deaths were sufficiently and exquisitely painful?

He'd been told by the police to remain in the area while they investigated. He would oblige them—at least until he could devise and carry out a plan. He checked into a cheap motel and waited. While it wasn't continuous, Martin knew he was being watched. He let himself be seen going out for food or to the movies. A few times he went shopping for large, loose sweatshirts to camouflage his rapidly expanding waistline. He could no longer placate his cravings with ordinary food, however delectable it might be. His hunger was now so enormous the Minister needed to hunt nightly. When he could not, he raged about his dreary room, pounding the floor with his fists. He was, however, able to slip out a rear window several nights that week, jog to a second car concealed behind an abandoned garage, and drive to the smaller cities in Connecticut and Massachusetts to hunt. The kills were quick, furtive— hardly the panoply of pleasures he had dreamt for himself.

Bone Ridge was set to reopen on October 6. Most of the haunters came in early to discuss what had happened. Support and security staff all crowded into the greenhouse along with the actors. The police had shared little with the public except that they had recovered items possibly linked to two of the missing women. At Tom's request, they made it clear that the items had not been found on the farm itself. They did not claim to have found any human remains, partly to protect their investigation and partly because they could not yet say exactly what they had in those trash bags.

Many of the haunters had already heard from Scott about what happened to Martin. He had posted it, along with his speculations, on Facebook. This created both hysteria and gossip, and Scott had been fired as a result. "Keep your private dramas out of here," Milton scolded the employees. "Starting rumor campaigns will get you fired."

Milton then told the haunters what was actually known. "Apparently, there was an anonymous tip that a seriously shit-faced young woman who went missing might have been abducted from here last Saturday night," he said. "Her equally shit-faced friends insist she got into a car with them. So no one can say exactly what happened to her. The police did find some things that might have belonged to her off the property. Based on a description, they questioned Martin Godfrey. Even before that happened, Bill received complaints that Martin was sexually harassing some of the female employees. Martin was fired because of the complaints and for no other reason."

Tom addressed the assembly. "We've been getting calls and emails all week. A lot of you want to know if it's safe to be here. We have no reason to think there's a problem, but we've hired extra security just to be cautious. We'll have police directing traffic like always, but there will be one cruiser parked on the side road to make sure no one sneaks on to the property."

What the farmer left unsaid was his concern about whether Bone Ridge would be open past this weekend. He did not need to say anything. Everyone whispered among themselves, wondering if paying customers would even show up. The online gossip about Bone Ridge was even worse than the truth. Who wanted to risk a walk along a wooded trail when people were being murdered as if it was part of the entertainment? With the extra people Tom and Jen hired, they might not sell enough tickets to cover payroll that weekend.

As it turned out, their worries were unfounded. Traffic on the main road was backed up over a mile, with carloads of fans who wanted to get scared near the site of a possible murder. The security staff was kept busy preventing revelers from going off trail to hunt for the serial killers of their inebriated imaginations. All night long, the haunters listened to bad jokes about the missing women. If a customer ran into a haunter, the actor was accused of trying to hurt the customer.

The ticket booth closed at ten o'clock, but the last group straggled through the walk-through well past midnight.

"We just survived Night of the Living Assholes," Justin said as the weary haunters trudged back to the greenhouse.

There was a murmur of agreement from the actors as Big Ed said, "And they say haunters are weird."

THE DEACON AND THE MINISTER

September 24, 2012

WHILE I LOOKED forward to this haunt season with happy anticipation, my pleasure has been vastly tempered by the appearance of Martin Godfrey. I have not seen him do anything threatening towards anyone else, but he does often follow the women haunters around. Some, like Therese, enjoy his attentions. But some call him a "creep" behind his back. I feel obligated to watch his movements while he is at the farm. The man I knew in my other life was incapable of kindness. The man I knew enjoyed inflicting pain. When I saw him charming and seducing Therese, I knew he would find no lack of trusting, easily manipulated girls to hurt. And now Therese has failed to show up to work. Five days have passed, and she is still missing.

The opening weekend at the haunt has always been unusually festive, but I found myself feeling distracted and subdued. I stayed near the walk-through so I could keep watch on Martin's movements. A few times I saw him make some excuse and follow this straggler or that up the trail, but he always came back to his set. He seemed to enjoy performing. His jokes were good and his timing was superb. While I am loath to admit it, Martin is an excellent haunter.

By Saturday night, I felt I could relax my vigilance and went on beer patrol. Last year's newbies, who did not get fired because I consistently relieved them of their contraband, understood at last that it was not wise to bring alcohol to their scenes. Thus, I could only harvest among the current newbies, and the yield was meager. It was cheap and watery stuff, too. "Lite" beer is a true abomination.

I did enjoy many of the changes in the haunt. The maze was modified so that part of it had low ceilings, forcing the patrons to stoop as they went through. They also built a scaffold over the top which allowed Biggie and Mike to take turns reaching down from above to grab hats and hair. Sometimes they would listen to the chatter below and learn someone's name. They would shine lights on their faces and call out the names. To hear them boast, more than one customer soiled himself after a trip through their set.

Sean worked a prison execution scene. The patrons stood on a platform while Sean seemingly directed a form of lightning into the condemned. Rob, the hulking prisoner, writhed and screamed amidst smoke and flashing lights but would not die. Sean then asked the witnesses if he should try one more time. He encouraged them to cheer him on. When he threw the lever a second time, the entire platform vibrated and hummed under the customers' feet. It was hilarious watching them jump and scream.

When there was a lull in the flow of customers, however, Sean would take a path through the woods that brought him up behind Amy's scene at the playground. I knew he wanted to be sure Martin was not bothering her. Sometimes he watched her for a moment or two. She was slight of build and tucked her hair up under a cap to play a ghoulish male child. The effect was actually charming. There was a wonderful innocence in her feigned malevolence that made her seem younger than her years. I swore I would not allow that blaspheming preacher to lay a single molesting finger on her.

On Sunday night I allowed myself to relax enough to take in the hay ride from a high leafy perch that overlooked everything but the tunnel. As the actors took their places chanting, "We don't just scare 'em, we mess 'em up for life," I could scarcely contain myself. After all, I was a partial inspiration for the theme. The first wagon rolled through and I forgot my hunger, my fears, and the unbearable uncertainty of what was to come. I watched my beloved haunters mock death, suffering, and all the terrors of hell, and I felt a surge of joy.

During the lulls, I heard the haunters talk about Therese. The sheriff's men had questioned all the haunters about her whereabouts that very evening, which in turn led them to focus their attention on Martin and Scott. The haunters speculated wildly about Therese's fate. They even tried to connect her disappearance to Cam's. No one seemed to find the Minister particularly suspicious, but I know better.

October 1, 2012

I left warnings for Amy and a detailed letter about what I saw Martin do Saturday night. And using my Christian name, I publicly accused Martin in a message written on a mirror in the greenhouse. I know him better than anyone, and I will not let him hide behind his smiles and his charms. But I cannot bear to relive the horror again on these pages. Yes, I am a killer, but what I saw the Minister do is beyond comprehension. God help us all.

October 3, 2012

I have kept close watch on the farm since I left the letter relating the horrible murder I witnessed. Today, from a high tree that overlooks both the entrance to the hay ride and the walk-through, I saw two constables arrive, then several more. They were mostly in the orchard and behind the wall where I dug my shelter.

The uniformed men pulled black bags from beneath the ground. Even from my perch I could pick up their peculiar, pungent smell on the wind. It was not unlike meat that has been pickled after it has already gone bad. One of the sheriff's men ducked behind a tree and retched.

October 4, 2012

The officials are still all over the farm. I heard the farmer talking to them. There might be no haunting this weekend. Bone Ridge will certainly be closed Friday night at least.

October 8, 2012

Bone Ridge reopened for Saturday and Sunday nights. I found hiding places overlooking the parking lots and listened to the gossip the customers shared with each other. Most of them came to the haunt because they had already planned the outing and declared that fear would not turn them away. But a few had heard lurid stories worse than the probable murder of a missing girl and came hoping to witness something truly gruesome. The world was full of terrible people when I last lived as a man. I was one of them. It is discouraging to realize that, with all its wonders and miracles, it has not gotten any better.

A note from Sean and Amy was left for me under the black cabinet. They explained that Martin had been fired and was forbidden to set foot on the farm. I felt greatly relieved, but had no intention of relaxing my vigilance.

October 10, 2012

A sense of restless unease has plagued me since I witnessed the murder, and I find it difficult to rest. For several nights, I found myself wandering with no particular aim well into the early morning hours. I always ended up in the orchard. After inspecting the underground shelter, now closed off with a yellow garland, I patrolled the walk-through, the hayride, and the greenhouse. The farmer owns nothing that will take my likeness, so I can move about freely if I keep to the shadows.

Last night, I saw something other than the random skunk or raccoon. I overheard that Martin was in a rented room, his movements watched by the sheriff's men. Somehow, he eluded their surveillance and was strolling through the hayride sets. I silently crept up a tree and watched him carefully inspect the details of each structure, then the wooded and brush-filled areas behind each set the way a military scout might survey the ground before a campaign. He took his time, smiling now and then as if filled with a wicked inspiration. Then he moved on to the walk-through. It was difficult to follow him because he kept crisscrossing the hidden paths that threaded through the trees. If he did not find a path to his liking, if the way he wanted to go was choked with thorns, he pulled out a machete and hacked a trail for himself. He lingered longest at the playground set. "Little bitch," he swore under his breath. "Little whore." My gut went cold, for I knew he was directing his curses at Amy.

He did not seem to possess any understanding of the connection between the two of them. He hated her without really knowing why. He used the tip of his knife to scratch profanities into the bark of a tree where the girl often hid. This man of God was much at ease with the vulgarities of this age.

With all the stealth I could manage, I lowered myself to the ground. If I could grab the Minister from behind, I could drag him deep into the woods and hold him for Demon. But he took to the path again and was quickly beyond my reach. He followed a shortcut to the execution scene. There, on the wall of the set, he gouged out a lewd depiction involving a man and his private parts. The man bore a passing resemblance to Sean. I was astounded. It seemed as though he hated Sean even more than he hated Amy. Was it because the young man stood between the Minister and something he wanted? Or was it the disturbingly familiar glare in the boy's blue eyes when he spied Martin staring at his beloved?

I crept out of the trees and was about to throw an arm around his neck when the Minister dropped to all fours and turned. Something hissed past my ear and struck the bark of the tree behind me. Martin cried out in pain. I could not see how he had been injured. I crouched low and lunged for him, but he sprang to his feet and bolted up the path. He disappeared into the darkness.

I should have followed him but found my gaze drawn to the tree. There was a faint phosphorescence on the bark that quickly faded. The wood smoked slightly. When I touched the spot, my fingertips tingled with a burning sensation. As I rubbed my fingers the sting diminished with no apparent harm to either skin or bone. This new piece of information seemed more important than taking up the hunt again.

I had left a note stating he had murdered that poor girl with his kiss. No doubt, they would assume they were safe if they kept their distance from Martin. None of us could imagine any situation where the Minister could plant an uninvited kiss on anyone. But it now appears I was wrong. He could spit his venom from a distance of a few feet. Even worse, he nursed an almost lunatic hatred toward Sean and Amy without even comprehending why. I do not believe he knows what I know. He had not looked deeply into the infant's eyes as I had. Nor had he seen the blue eyes at the meeting house window, raging with righteous condemnation. But he has sensed the connection, and it was driving him mad.

I will pen a new warning to my friends and take it to the greenhouse. Then

I will maintain a vigil around the farm. It is left to me to protect the farcical monsters from the genuine fiend.

October 12, 2012

It is Friday morning. Bone Ridge will open in less than twelve hours. I have prayed to see Demon before I again go hunting for the Minister. I implore either angel or devil, I care not which, to guide me in my endeavors.

Yesterday, I waited for sunset and took a new letter to the greenhouse. I tucked it under the makeup cabinet. I heard someone approach the door, so I ducked behind the cabinet. But the intruder had seen something. She crept closer until she could peer around the side of the cabinet. I smelled her sweat and her fear. My stomach whined and, God help me, my mouth watered. And, suddenly, there was Amy, bearing an armload of costumes, staring at me in revulsion as I drooled. She quickly backed up to the door while I cringed and covered my face in mortification. I turned to bolt out the other door but realized she was still there, her hand on the door, costumes littering the floor. I could not look her in the eye, but I retrieved the letter I had hidden, placed the note on the table, and pushed it towards her.

After an eternity, Amy took a deep breath and said, "Okay. We're okay." She took the paper and began to read.

The note warned my friends that Martin was able to spit venom a distance of two or three feet. My observations indicated that it was caustic. It seemed minimally dangerous in the open air but lethal if somehow swallowed or absorbed into the body.

A spasm of panic shivered across Amy's face as she read. "He spits venom?" she exclaimed as she slipped the note into her pocket.

I nodded.

She shook her head slowly, struggling to comprehend the unfathomable. "I'll tell Jen I saw Martin near the greenhouse when I go back to the store. He's not supposed to come on the property. She'll call the police. Maybe they'll lock him up. Why was he walking the haunt?"

I took one of the leaflets out of a box and gestured for a pencil. I wrote, "He suspects some of you know things about him. He is making plans to remove witnesses." I could not bear to tell her about his unreasoning vitriol towards her.

"He saw us reading the letter you left for us the first week of the haunt. We showed it to Bill and Carrie. Martin gave us this look like he knew it was all about him. If looks could kill…" Her voice trailed away, and she looked frightened. Then, with all the hope of a true innocent, she smiled and said, "But you'll keep watch, won't you?"

I was touched that she trusted me. But it broke my heart that she needed a hell dweller to protect her. I cursed myself for letting the Minister run away while I satisfied my curiosity.

Amy said, "Carrie says you have to earn your way out of hell. I think you're getting there." She turned and hurried back to the store. I hid in the shadows and watched her until she was safely inside. Minutes later, she was on her way home with her mother. I pray the sheriff will have Martin in custody before Bone Ridge opens again.

October 13, 2012

I patrolled Bone Ridge last night and will do so again tonight. I kept myself at a greater distance than usual. I am still distressed by the way I reacted to Amy. I realize now that I have been so fretful and nervous that I have not been eating for days on end. My belly was more deprived than usual. It becomes an unreasoning brute when aroused by the perfume of human flesh. This mistake cannot be repeated.

Martin did not appear at the haunt last night. Much of my time was divided between the playground set and the execution scene. A normal night with happy patrons and only a few of what Bill calls "garden variety assholes."

October 15, 2012

Last night, I dreamed again that I feasted, filling my belly until I wept with joy. My usual phantom fare is roasted joints of beef and golden-brown fowl with potatoes, onions, and carrots, all washed down with tankards of ale and wine. Last night was different. The Minister laid dead before me, terror frozen in his eyes. I tore off his limbs and swallowed great mouthfuls of flesh. It was savory beyond anything I had ever tasted before. As I gorged myself, I replayed his pleas for mercy in my mind.

Now that I am awake, I cannot rid myself of those images—or the desire. My rage against this man who repeatedly humiliated me demands revenge. I want him to die slowly, bound and debased and fully aware of the desecration I will visit on his corpse. It is an overwhelming lust, but to yield is to seal my damnation. Where is Demon? Why is there no one who will tell me what I must do?

SHADOWS AND SOCK PUPPETS

THE POLICE WENT to Martin's hotel room to question him. He was able to produce receipts from a supermarket that proved he was at the store at the same time he was supposedly trespassing on the farm. When the police went away he pounded his fist against the wall until he put a hole in the cheap wood paneling. He covered the hole with an ugly framed print.

He wanted to go to the farm immediately and hurt someone. The Minister prided himself on his intelligence, and going to the farm was not intelligent. Instead, he poured whiskey into a glass and downed it. In his new incarnation, alcohol had a strange effect on him. Drink gave him visions. Drink gave him ideas.

§ § §

The lurid graffiti the Minister had left at the execution scene was painted over before Bone Ridge opened that weekend. The haunters were asked to be particularly mindful of any patrons straying off trail. They gave a chain saw to one of the security staffers and added him to the roving lumberjack crew. Friday night turned out to be relatively quiet.

There was a short burst of rain Saturday night. It cleared away quickly but delayed the crowds the haunters were expecting. It was nearly eight thirty before the actors on the walk-through heard the first screams drifting through the woods.

The clownbies positioned themselves for the first scares of the night. Sylence and Punch used the decrepit hearse as a clown car, bursting from both front and rear. TikTok hid behind a monument to dead clowns before lunging into the center of the groups. The trio chased the customers up the path where Gastro loomed in the shadows.

They had terrorized four groups when the clowns heard something creeping though the brush behind TikTok's monument. TikTok shared a look of disgust with his compatriots. No doubt, it was another customer sneaking behind the scene so he could jump out and try to spook his friends. He would not be scary and would accomplish nothing but a collision with an actor and ejection from the haunt.

TikTok put his finger to his lips and borrowed Sylence's puppet, which was fashioned from a long tube sock. He stuffed a rubber ball in the puppet's head. Edging closer to the bushes, he swung the sock with all his strength and connected with the intruder's head. The stranger made a satisfying grunt as he crashed into the woods. Punch texted Bill about the trespasser.

Martin, the intruder, found himself up to his ankles in muddy water. "Fucking clowns," he swore. The clownbies heard him but did not recognize his voice. They shouted insults at the stranger, howled with laughter, and focused on their next group of victims.

Despite the rain, Bone Ridge set a new attendance record that night. The usual group gathered around the bonfire to celebrate, tired and gratified. Tom's fat old dog was unusually active that night. He poked and snuffled around the edges of the parking area, woofing at each stirring of the wind.

Bill watched the normally slothful dog with interest. After the haunters departed and Tom shoveled dirt over the last of the embers, Bill strolled to his truck and found the baseball bat he now kept in the back. He poked around in the tall grass where the dog had lingered longest. Nothing stirred there, but he thought he saw a shadow move off just beyond the greenhouse. Bill shivered. Something wasn't right. If the shadow was Bonebelly, he probably would have signaled a greeting. Bill hastily scrawled his concerns on a flyer, tucked it into a box of Pumpkinhead, and left it in the tall grass for Bonebelly to find.

PRIDE AND THE FALL

October 22, 2012

WHAT HAVE I done?
No time for regrets. I must write.
Martin was at the haunt Saturday night. All the haunt managers, the security staff, and the parking lot attendants were watching for him. A law officer waited on the side road to make sure Martin did not approach the farm from the rear. It did not matter. He was there.

He initially escaped my notice as well. A light rain restricted the number of early visitors. I heard the clownbies discussing an intruder, but I dismissed it as a typical "asshole." I quickly toured the perimeter of the hayride. Then I went to the walk-through where I visited Carrie, Sean, and Amy and inspected the darkest spots along the trail. As the night wore on, I saw several inebriated groups with disoriented members who lagged behind. They were easy prey, but the Minister did not appear.

Near the end of the night, Bill walked through the scenes to let the actors know the last group was about to come through. At a bend in the trail where the wood-cutter ghouls hid with their chain saws, the Minister finally made his appearance. Bill sent the lumberjacks ahead to the Dungeon. He paused to speak into the device he constantly carried. I hid in the brush on one side of the path. I spied Martin's face in the shadows on the opposite side. Bill resumed his patrol. Just as he disappeared around a bend, Martin stepped silently on the trail to take up his stealthy pursuit.

He did not get far. I threw myself at Martin, seized him by the collar, and flung him face first to the ground. I knew I should not let him spit at me, so I grabbed him by his long hair and lifted him to his feet. I locked my free arm around his neck and propelled him forward into the woods. "Simon, you ridiculous pig," he gasped as I throttled him. "You can't face me?" But he could not goad me into a face-to-face confrontation. I wished I could have laughed out loud. Martin hissed all the vile names he had ever called me, and some of the new ones he had learned, as I forced him past thorns, brambles, and whip-like twigs.

We reached the bare cornfield behind the haunt when I paused with my prisoner. I waited for Demon to appear and take the Minister to that terrible place for irredeemable souls he had shown me months earlier. But it became clear, as Martin struggled and flailed, that Demon was not about to show himself.

197

"You're not man enough to do it," Martin taunted me in a wheezing, strangled voice. I realized then that even my enemy understood the terrible task I was expected to carry out: I was meant to execute this monster. I did not want this burden. What if my hunger got the best of me? A wave of fatigue washed over me. Martin could sense it and renewed his furious thrashing.

He kicked violently as an angry mule. Then he dropped his weight to the ground, trying to wrench himself from my grasp. He jabbed my stomach with his elbows, brought his fingers up behind his head, and tried to gouge my eyes out. He even groped below my belly in an attempt to find my male organ. He rent great holes in my trousers as he ridiculed my stunted manhood. Then he fell silent except for a strange rhythmic gasping sound, as if repeatedly thrusting his tongue in and out of his mouth. With all my weight behind him, I forced the Minister to his knees then prostrate on the ground. I pinned his arms with my knees and sat on him. I was winded and panting, but Martin was also exhausted. He ceased struggling. As he wheezed, a low inhuman growl issued from his throat.

I did not relax my hold as I deliberated how best to kill the Minister. The intensity of our physical struggle did much to temper my rage. It seemed best to do it quickly. I decided I would simply grab his head with both hands and break his neck. Martin's head was turned to the left, his right ear pressed against the soil. I slid one hand under his head and placed the other across his face. "No, no, no," he rasped and he shuddered with sobs.

A sharp pain burned the palm of my left hand. I saw what looked like a thin, jointed bone with a delicate spear point poking right through the back of my hand. I snatched my hand away and saw the barb issued from Martin's mouth, and slapped repeatedly against the ground. This flailing organ is what had produced the peculiar, breathy sounds I heard. It was a repulsive sight.

My hand burned, and the pain swiftly spread to the tips of my thin, clawed fingers. In the waxing moonlight I could see a circle of black radiating out from the puncture. As the sting became more intense, Martin sensed his chance and wriggled out from under me. But instead of running, he stood just beyond my grasp and laughed.

"Is that not an ingenious weapon?" he gloated. "While you submitted to your doom, I bested Lucifer and made myself over anew. Simon, am I not a marvel? This poison is born of my malice, my will. It will spread and it will melt you from the inside."

I held up my hand. The pain stopped, and the black rot in my flesh halted, contained within a circle the size of an acorn. It was not spreading, and I was not melting. Martin realized it, too. As I rose to my feet, his mocking smile froze into an open-mouthed gape of disbelief. Then he turned and ran.

He sprinted for the woods on the opposite end of the rear cornfield. I followed with long, easy strides. Just before he reached the trees, I put on a burst of speed. I swiftly overcame him and threw him to the ground.

I quickly clapped my hand to Martin's face. I dug my claws into the top of his skull and punctured the soft skin under his chin with my thumb. I did not thrust the claw into his mouth in case there was some kind of venom sac concealed within. With his jaw clamped shut and his poisoned barb incapacitated, I began dragging him into the deepest part of the woods. His screams were muffled, and he flopped about like a speared fish. He was clearly in excruciating pain. I smiled.

I hauled him for miles, stopping only to catch my breath. A renewed fury and hatred surged through me. I intentionally heaved the Minister over roots and through thorns. He was thrown against every stump and boulder and dragged through every stinking bog. By the time I reached the great swamp, the Minister shook from his wounds and the cold and sobbed like a child. Blood dripped from his nose and sealed mouth. I held his head so he could see his final resting place. Martin understood this was where I would kill him and where I would hide his body until Demon wished to retrieve it. As I pinned my broken enemy to the spongy ground, I was so intoxicated with hatred that I felt it only right to reward myself with a modest feast from his remains before I buried him.

I pulled my claws away from Martin's skull and released my hold. He was clearly too injured to run. He groaned and curled into a ball on the ground. "You will kill me now?" he whispered hoarsely. I crouched down on one knee and nodded. Martin weakly pulled himself up to his knees and stared at me dully. He was bruised and bleeding. He supported his left arm with his right. We both panted with exhaustion. In the moonlight, I saw something like respect in his gaze. His head dropped to his chest, as if surrendering to his doom.

The wind rose and moaned through the trees. A flurry of dead leaves beat against us, and the gust whistled through the flap of torn skin in my bare chest. Martin stopped shaking. He raised his head. His gaze hardened and fixed on the black hole in my white breast. Before I could react, the pearly barb flew from behind his teeth and pierced my shriveled heart to the core. He held it there as venom pumped into that poor shrunken muscle. I sprang to my feet, but it was too late. My chest burned as the poison made its sluggish way through the heart and into my withered veins.

Martin grinned and said, "If you don't mind, I'll just sit here and wait for the inevitable."

I looked down and saw the skin over my heart blacken, the rot spreading outward along with the burning pain. I could scarcely breathe. Martin watched me expectantly. But his grin faded when my legs did not give out and I did not collapse into a jellied mass. I was wounded grievously, but I was not about to die any time soon.

The Minister staggered to his feet and ran, although his pain slowed him considerably. I chased him, but the fire in my chest all but paralyzed my lungs. I closed the distance between us and reached out to grab his collar. Martin dodged between the trees and disappeared into the shadows. I fell to my knees, hugging my burning chest and cursing myself. Had I not gloated over my prey, the Minister would already be dead.

I stumbled back to my root cellar and collapsed. Deep shadows clouded my senses. Light brought new pain. Blackness came again, then light.

I believe two days have passed. The skin across my abdomen and shoulders has turned black. It brings searing pain. Based on the agony I feel, my neck and much of my back has turned black as well. I once feared I could not die, but it seems I was wrong. The Minister's venom will be the end of me. Because of the peculiar composition of my body—muscles stringy as salted meat, fibrous organs and veins clogged with black, sluggish blood—I think it does not affect me as it does innocent men and beasts. I am not dissolving; I am decaying.

Nearly three years ago, I prayed for death. Now, as it seems imminent, I am filled with regret. So many of my days in this personal hell have been filled with sorrow, but I have experienced greater happiness here than I ever did in my previous sinful life. I love my strange, riotous, bawdy haunters. I love my friends, especially Amy and her beloved Sean. I have failed them all. While I can still flex my fingers, I will write a warning and try to deliver it before the last weekend of the revels. There is nothing more I can do to protect them.

October ?

Awoke to green eyes staring. Not Demon. Black cat. Have not seen her for over a year. Darkness left two mice in outstretched hand. Hand is now black. Darkness watches. I am to eat the mice. Grind them with my teeth and force them down my throat. They are delicious. Compassion, even from a cat, is allowed in hell. Reach out to stroke Darkness but she slinks away. Afraid to get close. Another friend at a distance.

October ?

Occurs to me now I could have bound Martin and kept him in cellar until Demon came. Foolish rage, foolish creature.

Did not see Darkness today. She left two more mice. Legs and feet turned black. Devour mice. Food revives but movement is hard to control. Writing almost illegible. Wrote warning but it is gibberish. Hands are useless. I am useless.

October

HUNTING SEASON

THE MINISTER SAT in his motel room and wrapped his left arm in a sling. He could move his forearm, but there was throbbing pain in his dislocated shoulder. His body was covered with cuts and bruises, and there were puncture wounds under his jaw and in his scalp. He needed medical attention but was reluctant to seek it. He did not want to attract any more attention from the local police.

Martin fought to quiet the rage rising in his throat. Someone in that accursed Simon Hogg support quartet had lied to get him locked up. Simon had somehow gained their pity. It would not have been difficult to do. Simon *was* pitiful. Martin did not know what his deacon had said about him, but whatever his four friends knew, it was too much.

The Minister had been feeding heavily and planning his escape since he'd been fired. The trunk of his second car, hidden among the abandoned vehicles at a closed down garage, was packed with camping gear, winter clothing, tools, and non-perishable food for his trip north. He would find a remote cabin, hunt the nearest towns, and then disappear back into the wilderness.

He vowed he would not be a slave to his circadian rhythms. But he had been sleeping later and later each morning. If he did not have his rage, he would be unable to motivate himself to do anything.

Now, with his battered body, Martin worried he would never settle his scores against his enemies. He did not know if Simon was dead or merely injured. He did not want to leave with that loose end unbound.

After he bathed and inspected his oozing wounds, Martin decided he had no choice but to seek help. He took one of his stolen IDs and credit cards, called a cab, and went to the nearest emergency room. He concocted a story about a bar fight he could barely remember. The puncture wound under his chin required a few stitches. They treated his shoulder and bandaged his cracked ribs. They gave him pain medication and antibiotics and scheduled a follow-up appointment Martin had no intention of keeping.

Martin's wounded body demanded rest. He was hungry, too. He had not hunted since the previous Thursday. He was eating enormous amounts of ribs, rotisserie chickens, and meaty sandwiches, but they could not replace the strangely sweet and sour electric soup his victims provided. Everything—his wounds, his rage, his enormous hunger—exhausted him. As much as he longed for vengeance, the cost at the present time was just too high. It made more sense to run away, recuperate at his leisure, and retaliate next fall.

He had all but decided to do exactly that when the pain killers took hold. They opened his mind to startling visions. He saw everyone who threatened him— the police, all those defiant young women, Simon, and his friends—bound and helpless in the greenhouse, whimpering as he strolled among them to choose his next victim. He paused in front of Amy. She begged for mercy, and it was now Martin's turn to laugh. He was aroused by her terror and her helplessness. Then the visions faded and he slept for eighteen hours.

When Martin awoke, he had a plan in mind. All he had to do was refine the logistics. First, he needed to find out if Simon still presented a problem. It was risky, but the Minister would have to prowl the shadows of Bone Ridge after dark to see if the Deacon was standing guard.

The roads were deserted as he slipped out late Tuesday night and drove to the empty field near the farm. When he hiked in from the rear of the property, he saw the yellow police tape fluttering around the perimeter of the underground shelter. He winced as he carefully lowered himself into the hole. Everything he had secreted there had been removed. He smiled. It appeared no one was watching this spot. He could hide here undetected and wait for the proper moment to hunt down his prey.

He took a slow tour of the walk-through and found no hint of Simon's presence. He mentally mapped out the best paths to herd and trap his quarry. Nothing would be left to chance. How convenient it was that the troublesome quartet all worked the same side of the haunt.

Martin skirted the parking lot and farmhouse and approached the greenhouse from the rear. He explored the makeup area in the dark, trying to remember exactly where Sean and Amy worked. Although he did not know their prearranged drop spot, he hoped to locate any notes Simon might have left the pair. His search was thorough but fruitless.

On his way back to his car, Martin delivered a barb to an opossum and a fat raccoon. Neither was as satisfying as a panicked human being, but once he devoured them, he felt better than he had in days.

He was back in his motel room while it was still dark. He had one more task to complete before he rested. He was well acquainted with Simon's long flowing hand. He found a writing pad and practiced until he could produce script that resembled that of his former deacon. Then he wrote a message in Simon's voice to his haunter friends.

He held the letter out in front of his face and stared at it, as if close inspection would help him balance the need to punish his enemies against the wisdom of fleeing to the north. Finally, he crumpled the yellow paper in his fist and tossed it in the trash. He forced some soup down his throat, took an extra dose of pain medication, and waited for a new vision to guide him.

THE LAST BEST SCARE

CARRIE HAD PLACED protein shakes behind her hiding place in the Nosferatu scene Saturday night. They were still there Sunday. Carrie left them there only to find them waiting for her when she came to work on the final Friday. She jogged over to the playground scene and whispered to Amy, "Have you seen Bonebelly this week?"

"I haven't seen him since last Saturday," Amy replied.

"He never took the shakes I left for him. Any notes since the last one?"

"No, but he promised to keep watch in case Martin came around. Bonebelly seemed scared of what that creep could do."

Carrie regarded Amy's fear-filled eyes and said, "Martin isn't allowed on the property. Everyone's been warned he's dangerous. Our security is watching for him. So are the police. We're safer here than anywhere else."

"What if Martin got to him?" Amy said.

"We know what Bonebelly's capable of. I don't think Martin could even get close." Carrie said. But as the night wore on and Bonebelly failed to make an appearance, she texted the other Friends, "I'm beginning to think our boy isn't going to show."

Later that night, when Bill was following a group of belligerent 20-somethings, he paused long enough to inform Amy, Carrie, and Sean what the detail cop had told Tom. "He said Godfrey packed up and left his motel in the middle of the night without paying. That was last Wednesday. They think he's probably out of state by now."

The Friends of Bonebelly met for breakfast the following morning to discuss the situation.

"Godfrey's a person of interest in the disappearance of two women," Bill said. "I don't think he'd dare show up at Bone Ridge."

Sean agreed. "No one trusts him. The smart thing to do is to disappear." They all stared silently at their plates. "He's gone. He won't show up," Sean repeated.

"Then why are we still worried?" Bill asked.

"Because Bonebelly's disappeared, too." Carrie said.

Amy pushed eggs around her plate. "He loves the haunt. He'd never miss the final weekend. We could check his main hiding place."

"We're friends at a distance for a reason," Carrie reminded her. The memory of Bonebelly licking her hand to illustrate a point still made her shudder.

205

Bill said, "Let's be alert, but let's kick ass our last weekend. If we don't see him by closing time tomorrow, we'll look for him Monday morning. Does everyone have something to keep Martin from getting close, just in case? I have a couple of baseball bats."

"I have a walking stick," Carrie said.

"We have a bat and a closet pole," Sean said. "Should we put nails on the end?"

That afternoon, Sean and Amy joined Ron and Cheryl at their makeup stations and began putting faces on the last horrors of the season. The mood was festive and nostalgically weird. The haunters relived their favorite pissers. Big Ed and Jimmy tested their chain saws and argued over which of them actually scored a puker, which was rare in the haunt world.

Joe, however, who ruled over the hayride as Lucifer on his throne, had been complaining to Susan since Friday night that the tunnel smelled. "I'm telling you, something crawled in there and died," he said. "And you know I don't piss and moan about stuff."

Susan handed him three packages of Little Trees.

"What am I supposed to do with these?" Joe asked.

Susan shrugged. "Hang 'em in the tunnel. Wear 'em around your neck. You want some Febreeze, too?"

As Amy and Sean turned to their own costumes and makeup, Amy found a crumpled piece of yellow paper on the ground where she hung her little league uniform. She signaled Sean who stood next to her as she read the sprawling, nearly illegible message: "I am poisoned dart inside mouth if he opens mouth run."

"What the hell," Sean said. "We've got to find Bill and Carrie."

They took their clubs and went to their scenes, Sean watching their backs while Amy scanned the trail ahead. They cut across the side trails and came out behind the execution scene. Sean spied a folded piece of paper tucked behind the switch that operated the vibrating platform.

"You got fan mail?" Rob asked as he was lounging in the electric chair, an iced coffee in his huge fist.

"It's an arrest warrant," Sean joked. "We have to see Carrie. Be right back."

He sent a text to Bill, who joined them at the Nosferatu scene. The light was failing. Sean read the note by flashlight: "My dear friends, I've been grievously wounded by our common enemy. I don't know if I'll survive without your help. You'll find me hiding in the dugout behind the orchard." The note was neither signed nor dated.

The four Friends puzzled over both notes. "He writes like a cross between Edgar Allen Poe and Louisa May Alcott," Carrie said. "Sean's note sounds like Bonebelly."

Amy gestured with her torn, dirty scrap of paper and said, "But if Bonebelly truly is hurt, he might scrawl a message like this. It's a warning. 'Dart inside mouth.' Who could make that up?"

"He could have written both, maybe days apart," Bill said. He glanced at a text that warned the first wagon was nearly through the hayride. "We've got to haunt. We can't do anything right now. We'll figure this out after we close. Stay alert."

The actors turned to go to their respective scenes. Amy halted and blurted out, "Contractions."

Bill and Carrie stared at her. But Sean exclaimed, "Bonebelly never uses contractions. The note I found isn't his."

"So it's Godfrey, hiding in the orchard, hoping we'll show up," Bill said.

"It's a crime scene. Why would he go back there?" Carrie asked.

"He can come at us from below," Sean said. "Like haunters crawling on the ground. Scared people are watching their backs. They're not looking at their feet. It gets them every time."

Bill decided to tell the detail cop that someone thought they saw Martin heading to the orchard. The actors turned to their performances. Amy stuck to the open path as she hurried to the playground scene. Mallison had been trying something new with their evil twins. They velcroed themselves together and blocked the path as the customers approached. Then they tore themselves apart, oozing blood, and ran screaming at their intended victims. While everyone focused on the twins, Amy snuck into the midst of the group from the side to complete the scare. It was not easy to reset but it was a good effect.

Visitors were in high spirits that night. Milton came through to tell the actors that Bone Ridge was set to break another attendance record. Tom called in extra drivers to keep the lines moving.

An early check of the area around the orchard wall had yielded nothing. Around ten o'clock a patrol car noticed a car parked in a field on the side street bordering the farm. It was registered to Martin Godfrey. The two officers exchanged glances.

"He takes off, he's missing for four days, and then he shows up here?" exclaimed Officer Gilchrist. "What's wrong with this bastard?"

They crossed the field behind the hayride and explored the perimeter, interviewing actors as they went. Susan alerted the other managers. Gilchrist and Monroe explored the orchard and the surrounding woods. Finally, they found themselves at the stone wall.

Monroe threw his leg over the wall and ducked under the yellow tape that marked the hole in the ground, followed by his partner. They stood at the lip of the dugout and scanned the pile of debris with their flashlights. Suddenly, one after the other felt a stabbing pain in his ankle. Both policemen gasped as the burn spread up their calves.

"What the hell just happened?" Gilchrist asked. He stumbled to the stone wall and sat down, rubbing his leg.

Monroe fell to his knees as a dark figure vaulted out of the hole and stabbed him in the eye. The officer screamed as the burn spread to his brain.

Gilchrist lurched to his feet and trained his flashlight beam on Martin Godfrey. His thin, elegant barb glowed in the light, lustrous as a pearl. The Minister quickly plunged it into Gilchrist's throat and heart.

Martin sat on the wall and waited for the feast that would sustain him through the tasks of this night. He was in no hurry. The men dissolved and the blue lights faded. Then the Minister gorged himself, greedily funneling handfuls of gel down his throat. When there was nothing left but hair and uniforms, Martin checked his watch, took four pain killers, and reviewed his plans for the night. He was still hungry.

§ § §

By eleven thirty, the last two wagons were moving through the hayride. Within thirty minutes, the final groups of the night would descend on the walk-through. Amy felt her phone vibrate in her pocket. It was a text from Sean which read, "Didn't think of this before. Might know where Bbelly is. Meet me at hayride entrance ASAP."

Amy was about to respond but was distracted by a large owl sitting on the slide. She crept from her hiding place to take a picture then froze. The owl had green cat's eyes. "You," she whispered. "Why are you here?"

Demon grinned.

"I'm not afraid of you." She climbed two steps up the ladder until she could look Demon right in his eyes. "You messed up, didn't you? None of this was supposed to happen."

If Demon was angry at her impertinence, he did not show it. He brought a clawed hand from underneath one of his leathery wings and touched a finger to Amy's forehead. Her eyes widened as lightning filled her brain. She fell backward into the tall weeds, unable to move. Her body vibrated as images crowded her mind. She instantly knew everything: the connection between Bonebelly and Martin, their many sins together, and their final blasphemies. She knew that she had been there, too, wide-eyed and innocent, watching as her mother was murdered, watching as her final breaths were stifled. Then her mind went black.

When Amy's senses returned, she was still flat on her back in the thick grass. She remained there, trying to make sense of the horrible things she had seen. There was movement in the trees, and she thought Sean was coming to take her to Bonebelly. Then she saw someone dressed in black standing next to her. It was Martin Godfrey. She held her breath, wondering if he would open his mouth and bring death down on her. He did not see her and moved away. She squeezed her eyes shut and opened them again. She saw Sean, staring down at her, alarm etched on his face.

"Amy?" he cried, dropping to his knees next to her. "What happened?"

"I thought I saw Martin," she replied, getting to her feet, "but then he turned into you. I saw that little demon again. He showed me…everything—the past, the present, everything. But I can't tell you now."

"You think you saw Martin?" Sean was looking at Amy strangely.

"I'm not sure. I saw a lot of weird stuff. We should tell Bill just to be safe."

They sent warning texts to Bill and Carrie. Sean already had one of the lumberjacks covering for him. Amy told Mallison she needed a break. They cut through the wooded barrier to the hayride where the actors had finished and were returning to the greenhouse.

As they waited out of sight, Sean explained, "We know Bonebelly's poisoned, and he's so sick he can barely write. It might have taken everything he had to get to the greenhouse. If he needed a place to hide—maybe even a place to die—where would he go?"

"Joe's dead mouse smell. The tunnel on the hayride," Amy said. "He's under the stage where he hid last year."

They sprinted to the tunnel and crouched behind the tree cover as Susan and Milton walked through the sets, turning off lights and sound. Once everything was dark and silent, Amy and Sean crept into the tunnel and knelt before the stage. They lifted the skirting but saw no bone-white limbs, no belly, and no skull-like head. But there was the musty odor of decay. Two amber eyes opened and squinted in the flashlight beam.

Amy and Sean pulled the gangly creature free of his hiding place. His skin was black, mottled with splotches of purple and green—the colors of putrescence. Bonebelly was barely breathing, but his two friends managed to get him on his feet, out of the tunnel and into the trees.

Amy's eyes filled with tears as she inspected the damage to the monstrous body. Sean found her hand and squeezed it. Bonebelly looked as though he was rotting, but he emitted the dry, fusty odor of something long mummified. His muscles were limp and trembling. He gazed at his friends blankly.

"We got your note. Don't worry. We'll know what to do if we see the bastard," Sean said.

Amy took the creature's hand. Bonebelly smiled, displaying his fearsome teeth. "I know what happened," she said. "The demon showed me. I know everything. You're forgiven. Do you understand? You're forgiven."

Bonebelly turned his eyes to hers. They closed, and a small plaintive moan escaped his throat. It was the only sound he'd ever made. Then the creature was still.

"He's dead," she whispered. Sean put his arms around her, and they held each other in silence. They felt more frightened than they ever had.

§ § §

Because it was the end of the haunt season, the haunters turned to scaring each other. It was considered a coup to make a fellow haunter jump, the management in particular. Susan had been endlessly assailed throughout the night along the hayride. At the walk-through, many of the haunters went straight to the greenhouse to warm themselves. But several hung around their sets and repositioned themselves to scare Bill and Justin as they did a final inspection.

Travis left the medicine show to meet a girl. Synova tired of waiting for her chance to go after Justin and decided to return to the greenhouse. She smoked a cigarette then paused on the bridge long enough to take a final haul and stub out the butt. She felt a burning stab through her shoulder. She whirled around to see Martin standing inches away. "You're not supposed to be here," she cried as she backed away from him. Martin leered at her and shot his barb into Synova's throat.

§ § §

Justin swung his flashlight back and forth across the trail, looking for lost phones, keys, and wallets. The lumberjacks tried to sneak up behind him without success. All three Nosferatus came out of the trees at him. "Not bad," he called as he turned towards the maze.

Mike lay flat across the cat walk above the maze, ready to record the scare he and Biggy had planned for Justin. Biggy was positioned next to him. The cat walk trembled alarmingly under their combined weight, but the risk would be worth it if this prank paid off. Justin was afraid of spiders, so Biggy captured a giant in a jar and tied a clothesline around the top. When Justin rounded the corner below the haunters and triggered the strobe lights, Biggie would drop the spider in front of Justin's face.

Mike began to record the moment Justin stepped into the pulsing light. Biggie wrapped the clothesline around his fist, ready to lower away. Before he could move, a figure dressed in black stepped behind Justin. Someone was about to steal their scare. The two friends sighed. The approach was too predictable. It was bound to fail and it would spoil their fright as well.

The man in black turned his face into the strobe light. The haunters recognized Martin. Something resembling a thin white blade shot out of Martin's mouth, stabbing Justin in the back. Biggie clapped a hand over Mike's mouth. Mike shuddered violently but kept recording.

Justin braced an arm against the plywood wall then turned slowly. The haunters above could hear him panting heavily. The spear shot again from Martin's mouth and straight through Justin's heart. Justin sank to his knees then flopped to the ground like a scarecrow. Martin gazed at his victim and said, "We don't just scare 'em. We fuck 'em up for life." He stepped over Justin and exited the maze. Mike kept recording as a clear gel flooded from Justin's mouth and his skin turned transparent.

"Send it. Send that video to everyone," Biggie whispered hoarsely. "Then we got to find anyone who's still here and warn them." He climbed down from the catwalk and wrested a stud free from one of the walls. "I'll go towards the front," he called. "You go the other way." Biggie ducked into the brush and crept towards the Nosferatu scene.

Mike's hands shook as he sent the video to every haunter's number he had, including Bill's and Milton's. He sent it to his mother and siblings as well so they would know what happened if he did not make it home that night. Then he ran toward the Dungeon.

§ § §

Carrie's companions had departed. She was packing up her belongings when she spied a dark figure emerge from the woods behind the set. The stranger broke into a jog. She did not wait to see who it was. She threw her pack across her shoulder and ran, peeling the pale bald cap from her head and flinging it into the woods. She looked over her shoulder as she sped through the deserted diner toward the clownbie scene. The stranger was running, too.

She would never outrun him. She would need to hide. At the bridge, she leapt into the mud and crawled through an inch of frigid water to the cover of the rushes. She rubbed mud on her face and hands, praying, "Please, no leeches. Please, no leeches." She crouched and flattened herself against the bridge supports where the shadows were deepest.

She watched Martin stride across the bridge. He stopped to scan the area, knelt, and peeked over the edge. He peered to his right and then to his left.

He stared right at Carrie, but the light at the end of the bridge was in his eyes. She held her breath and froze, ready to drop flat in an instant if he tried to fling poison in her face. Martin was more interested in the wide drainage pipe just inches from her face. He felt around inside, located what he wanted, and patted it as if it was a pet. A dazzling smile lit up his face as he straightened up and continued up the path.

Carrie sucked in a lungful of air. Her phone was vibrating. She ignored it and crept to the culvert that Martin found so fascinating. As she peered inside, her hand strayed into a pool of warm jelly. She jerked her hand back and held it up to the light. The substance was clear and burned ever so slightly. She rubbed her hand with mud until the tingling stopped.

She pulled a flashlight from her pack and beamed it into the culvert. She saw what appeared to be a transparent doll, its clothing shredded. Long blonde hair lay in a tangled matt beneath the bag-like head. Carrie could make out the distorted, tissue paper face. Metal rings flashed in the light where a nipple and the navel would be. "Synova," she whispered. "Poor, freaky little girl." She sat down in the mud and wept.

Biggie moved slowly along the path, stud in hand, doing his best to watch all directions at once. He was halfway across the bridge when a light flashed in his face. Biggie cried out and slammed the stud against the bridge, just missing Carrie's free hand.

"God damn it, it's me," she cried.

"Moms?" Biggie said.

Carrie put her finger to her lips and pointed to the drainage pipe. Biggie climbed down and inspected the interior. "Oh shit," he whispered. "Is that Synova?"

Carrie nodded. "Don't touch it. It burns."

Carrie held a flashlight on the woman's remains while Biggie took several photographs and sent them to Bill and Milton. Armed with clubs, they returned to the greenhouse together.

They arrived to find the place crowded with nearly all the employees on the farm: actors, drivers, parking attendants, and security. There were police outside the greenhouse and a sergeant was addressing the crowd inside. Biggie showed his pictures to the sergeant while Carrie related her run-in with Martin. The police had already seen Mike's video.

Carrie spied Jeff and Gloria and pushed through the crowd to join them. "Have you heard from Amy or Sean?" she asked.

"We've both tried calling them. They aren't answering," Gloria said.

Jeff said, "The police won't say exactly what's happened, but we heard they checked on the patrol car next to the farm and think Godfrey killed the two cops inside. He could be hiding somewhere on the farm. No one can leave until they're sure it's safe."

"Did you see either of them?" Gloria asked.

Carrie shook her head. "Not for hours. They weren't at their scenes." She pulled out her phone and texted her three friends: Where the hell are you?

§ § §

Bill watched Mike's video as he made his way to the maze. He knew the police were looking for Martin. He was not about to return to the greenhouse until he had accounted for any stragglers along the walk-through. He came across Justin's remains and knelt to inspect them. They were a macabre effigy, features painted on a bloated cellophane bag. He texted Tom to send the police to the maze and continued on his way to the prison bus. He gripped his bat and prayed he would have the chance to beat the shit out of Martin Godfrey before he was arrested.

Bill checked under the bus seats as he made his way down the narrow aisle. It was not until he reached the emergency door that he noticed it was closed. He turned the handle but the door would not open. He propped his bat against a seat and rammed his weight against the door. It wouldn't move. He turned to exit through the front and found Martin blocking the aisle.

Martin grinned and stepped forward. Bill quickly scanned the seats for his bat, but Martin lunged. A long thin barb resembling a ray's tail thrust between his teeth. It flailed back and forth like a sightless worm probing for a place to attach. Bill cried out and backed up against the emergency exit. His only safe means of defense was his steel-toed boots, so he braced himself, brought one foot up, and slammed it under Martin's chin with a satisfying crack. Martin staggered backward, spitting blood.

The Minister charged again, but Bill kicked at his chest and knocked him down. The barb flew out of the monster's mouth towards Bill's calf. Bill dodged it and slammed against the emergency door. This time it flew open, and he tumbled down the ramp. He landed on his back and stared up into the face of the bearded lady.

"Someone jammed a landscaping timber against the door," Travis said. "You all right?"

Bill scrambled to his feet and peered inside the bus. Martin was gone. "That freak, Godfrey, is running around killing people. What are you doing here? You need to get back to the greenhouse," Bill scolded.

"I stayed back to meet up with a girl. She said she liked my dress," Travis replied. "I didn't know there was shit going on. I think I've been stood up."

"For her sake, I hope so. Hike up your skirts and run, Travis," Bill said, retrieving his bat from the bus. "We need to clear everyone out of here. All hell's breaking loose."

§ § §

Seething fury drove the Minister through the woods. His mouth bled where he'd lost a tooth, but his barb was safe. So far, the night had been an abysmal fiasco. He failed to kill Carrie or Bill and had no idea where to find Sean and Amy. Blue and red lights flashed through the trees. The police would have found their fallen brothers in the orchard by now. Martin had no choice but to run, but getting to his car was nearly impossible. If he could create a distraction, he might still reach the abandoned garage and escape.

He crept to the edge of the back parking lot where he saw his chance. Jon, dressed as the old lady, was smoking with Punch, Sylence and TikTok.

Moments earlier, Mike had shown the haunters his video. While Mike went ahead to the greenhouse, his friends remained to clear stragglers out of the parking lot. As they were about to disperse, Martin strode boldly into the light and marched straight for TikTok. Jon saw the Minister and moved to intercept him. The barb flew into Jon's chest. Smoke rose from the puncture site, but nothing else happened. Jon picked up his walker and rammed it into Martin's face. Then the haunters bolted for the Dungeon and pulled themselves up on its roof.

Martin disappeared into the shadows again. Jon inspected his costume. There was a quarter-sized hole burned all the way through his overstuffed brassiere. "What the hell," he said.

"Don't take this the wrong way, but I love your boobs," Punch said.

"Me too," Jon said.

Bill and Travis emerged from the Dungeon to find three clowns and an old lady peering down from the roof. "Godfrey was just here," he said into his phone. "He attacked some haunters right in the parking lot. Get the cops over here."

§ § §

As they crouched in the trees next to Bonebelly's body, Amy and Sean's phones vibrated with one message after another. They did not dare read any of them. While the police rushed to the Dungeon, they watched Martin pass through the tunnel and disappear behind the adjoining set. He seemed to be trying to sneak around the edge of the hay ride and deeper into the woods.

Sean tapped Amy on the shoulder and gestured at a depression amid the trees behind them. They crawled on their bellies through the frosted leaves and slid into the declivity. From their hiding place they watched Mike's video for the first time and read messages from their parents, Bill, and Carrie. Sean texted a report of their whereabouts and where they had sighted Martin.

"We should get back to the greenhouse," Sean whispered.

"It doesn't feel right to leave him," Amy said, gazing mournfully at the spot where Bonebelly lay.

"He's dead. We can't do anything for him. Let's leave while we have the chance." Sean pushed himself to his knees and crept up the incline. Before he could rise, a foot slammed down on his neck and pushed his face in the dirt.

Amy leapt forward and swung her pole against the back of Martin's knees. As he stumbled and fell, she hit him across his shoulders and drove her baseball cleats into his kidneys. Sean scrambled to his feet and grabbed Amy by the hand. The barb flew out of Martin's mouth. It flashed past Amy's leg but missed.

Shouts came from the road leading to the hayride. The farmers, Gloria, Jeff, Carrie, Bill, and two state police—one of them Bill's friend, Francis—were charging

214

towards the tunnel. Amy and Sean had nearly cleared the trees when the Minister tackled the girl. He pinned her shoulders with his knees and pushed her head into the dead leaves and dirt. Amy cried out, anticipating a puncture to the back of her skull, but nothing happened.

Sean lifted his bat over his head as the others ran up behind him. The police had their guns drawn.

Martin wanted to bargain. "Let me leave and you'll never see me again. Try to take me, and this is going right into the back of her head." He opened his mouth and flailed the barb back and forth, grinning at the horror on their faces. He retracted the spike and leered at his enemies, but they were no longer paying any attention to him. They were focused on something behind him. A huge, black hand loomed over the Minister's head and quickly covered his face. Something grabbed his collar and jerked him away from Amy. He shrieked as he was thrown against a tree.

Martin saw nothing but black. As his vision cleared, he could make out glowing amber eyes and a mouth full of sharpened teeth. The Deacon leaned heavily against the Minister and pinned him to the trunk. The amber eyes glittered with hatred. The creature's legs trembled, threatening to fold right under him.

"You're in pain, aren't you? Let me help you, Simon," Martin said, and he drove his barb straight through Bonebelly's narrow throat.

His friends cried out, but Bonebelly bared his canines in Martin's face. The Minister wondered vaguely why the creature did not clamp his jaw shut. Bonebelly grinned as Martin again buried the barb in his heart.

He shook with pain but held the Minister's gaze. "Move! Move away," Amy cried. He ignored her. Martin dropped his jaw and let the barb fly once again. This time a black-clawed hand blocked it and grabbed the hideous appendage. Martin screamed as Bonebelly wrapped the white, segmented tube around his fingers and wrenched it out at the root. The Minister's mouth filled with venom. Bonebelly pushed the heel of his hand under Martin's chin and dug his claws into the Minister's scalp, locking his mouth shut. Poison poured down his throat. Martin thrashed and made a gurgling squeal. Spellbound, the witnesses stared as Martin's thrashing slowly took on a fluid, undulating quality. He went limp as his bones softened and he collapsed in a softly shivering mass on the ground. His skin turned transparent and blue lights coursed through his body. Then, one by one, they pulsed out.

The officers remained motionless, their weapons still in their hands. The black creature looked into the faces of his friends. He took one step forward then sank to his knees. His eyes closed and his head fell forward on his breast. When Amy ran forward and placed her ear near his cavernous mouth, she could hear no breath.

TRIBUTE

THE OFFICERS MOVED forward to inspect what was left of Martin Godfrey. Francis nudged the body with his boot. It tore a hole in the tissue-thin skin, and what had once been the Minister oozed out onto the ground. Francis swore as he jumped aside. He looked to his partner for some explanation, but everyone else stared at something beyond the fallen monsters.

An immense black shadow emerged from the trees. It bent over Martin and inspected the jellied remains. A dim thread of light throbbed under the transparent skin. A huge black hand hovered over the body, all but covered it, and squeezed. Everything collapsed into a dense gray mass. The Minister was unbecoming.

Demon gathered up the squirming charcoal blob and stuffed it into a black bag. It quivered as Demon bound it with silver chains thin as spider silk. He hung the bag from his massive neck and turned to Bonebelly.

Bonebelly opened his eyes and gazed up at Demon. He nodded slowly as if acquiescing to whatever was in store for him. Demon placed his hands on either side of Bonebelly's head. He squeezed until he had another handful of dense gray matter. It did not writhe the way Martin's had. It was complacent putty in Demon's hands. Demon weighed it as if trying to decide what to do with it. Then he closed his fingers around the mass.

"Wait!" Amy cried.

Demon looked at her with an air of detached amusement.

"I know what he did to earn hell. And yes, he killed again. But they were bad men, and what he did tonight…hasn't he earned another chance?" Amy begged.

Demon pointed at Amy and smiled.

"Sure, why not? A do-over. We could give him that."

"Amy, maybe you should be quiet," Sean suggested. "Look over there." He pointed at the trees.

A violet shadow emerged from the darkness into the moonlight. It was blue-eyed but otherwise faceless. Its vague form suggested a tall and lithe human being. It took silken strides until it stood in front of Demon. It took the dark putty from Demon's hands. The mass turned misty and gave off a feeble light. The violet shadow turned to Amy, extending an arm until it rested on her lower abdomen.

"Not now!" Amy exclaimed. "Sean and I have to finish school. We need to

217

make a good living and a good home. Bonebelly can rest for a while, can't he? He saved us. He's earned a rest."

The shadow took a step back, as if taken by surprise. Then it nodded, turned, and walked into the trees, its misty jewel still cupped in its hands. Demon surveyed the group assembled before him: the befuddled policemen, the parents, and Bonebelly's friends. He held up the black bag before him and beamed a smile of intense satisfaction. Then he and his prize were gone.

"You knew that creature? You were friends with...that?" Gloria asked her daughter.

"We all were," Amy said.

Sean nodded. "He was a great haunter." His friends murmured in agreement.

"Did I hear you propose to my son?" Jeff asked Amy.

Sean shrugged. "We were going to do it sooner or later. But did you just offer us as parents to..."

Amy folded her arms across her chest. "When the time is right and not before."

"None of this thy-will-be-done stuff for you," Bill said.

Bone Ridge Farm closed that night. Instead of a cast party, the employees held a memorial the following night. A few people posted accusations on the Bone Ridge social media page. They claimed the haunt was the kind of entertainment that attracted evil people and encouraged violence. Bone Ridge had also accumulated a large group of fans who defended them, but the conflict deflected focus away from the victims. Milton removed the site.

Weeks later, the police held a press conference to share what they had learned. They believed Martin Godfrey overpowered his victims and injected them with a potent venom. When he was finally cornered, he committed suicide by drinking the poison himself.

Mike had shared his video to warn his fellow haunters, but someone posted it online. Soon, it was being compared to a similar but much shorter video from Colorado that showed the murder of a young social worker in a parking garage. The killings were similar in execution, although the Colorado assailant had a peculiar grub-like appearance. Over the ensuing months, a pattern of strange deaths and disappearances emerged that stretched back nearly three years and covered territory from the southwest, through the heart land, and up the east coast. No one believed Martin Godfrey was the monster's real name, but neither could anyone identify who he was or where he came from. The Minister quickly became the stuff of urban legend.

Through it all, less than ten people had any idea who Bonebelly was or what he had done. Jen realized that Tom's yeti had actually existed. Gloria and Jeff learned that Amy had a benefactor that summer day in the woods, and that Cam would never be seen again. Francis, who had seen the images of Bonebelly and declared them a fraud, sought out Bill and asked him to explain just what they had seen at the haunt that night.

Summer came. Tom and Jen invited all the haunters to a barbecue at the farm and told them Bone Ridge would not open that fall. It was disrespectful to run a Halloween carnival where at least five people had been murdered. However, Tom was in discussions with a friend who owned a nearby farm about partnering on a new haunt in 2014.

A short time later, the four friends, along with Francis, visited the house in the woods where Amy first encountered Bonebelly. Development was encroaching on all sides of the woods. Sooner or later, the ruins would be bulldozed to make way for another subdivision. Amy wanted to photograph every inch of the place, especially the writing Bonebelly left on the walls before complete destruction—whether natural or man-made—visited the wreck. She planned to recreate a scaled down version of the parlor as part of a student art show, complete with a fabricated Bonebelly figure posed in the act of recording his fantastic story. Simultaneously, Sean and Amy hoped to have the first volume of their graphic series in print. It would tell a fictionalized story of a haunt visited by a fearsome hungry ghost who grew to love the theatre of the place and the haunters themselves. Subsequent volumes would relate the creature's backstory, the battle between good and evil that played out at the haunt, and the redemption of the hero. The series would be a labor of love and their tribute to Bonebelly.

Francis asked to accompany Bill to satisfy his curiosity about the creature and to reassure himself that Bonebelly was not responsible for any other deaths. After a fruitless search for the tell-tale crust of fats and salts, he felt satisfied there was nothing to find. He joined Amy and Carrie. They collated plastic bags filled with loosely bound journal sheets as Bill and Sean handed them through the hole in the floor. Sean photographed the fruit cellar and retrieved relics of the creature's sad and lonely life: Pumpkinhead Ale candle holders, several books, including a vegetarian cookbook, and drawings and printed flyers for Bone Ridge Farm tacked to the wall.

When the words were put in order, the group decided to read it all. They sat inside while they still had light. Then Amy claimed the heat was making her nauseous and they moved outside. Her friends regarded her curiously, and she said, with some irritation, "Nothing's happened. We're using birth control."

"Are you worried at all about what you may end up with when the time comes?" Bill asked.

"Like some kind of devil child?" Sean said. "This is real life, not some sucky horror movie sequel."

"We know how this works," Amy explained. "He learned how to love. We'll have a clean slate to work with."

When the light began to fail, they built a fire. Bill and Francis went to get food. They returned an hour later, dragging a giant cooler over the rough path. It was filled with hot dogs, real and vegetarian, junk food, beer, and bourbon.

"Expecting company?" Carrie asked.

Bill shrugged and said, "Bonebelly could never feast like this. Hell, he couldn't even join us at the bonfire for a brew. So tonight, we'll indulge for him."

They ate and drank and rebuilt the fire as they took turns reading the monster's words. They retold their favorite stories of Bonebelly and of the haunters of Bone Ridge into the early dawn. They poured the last of the beer and spirits on the foundation of Bonebelly's cellar. Carrie lit incense and placed it at the four corners of the dwelling. "Namaste. Find peace, old friend," she whispered.

"Time to go home, old man," Amy said, wrapping her arms around Sean's chest. Sean scowled. "You don't like it? It means we've always loved each other in one form or another."

"I'm still not sure what to believe," Francis said as the group trudged out of the woods.

"I lived it, and I still don't know what I believe," Bill said. "But I plan on being really, really good from here on in."

ACKNOWLEDGEMENTS

I would like to name every actor I've haunted with since 1999, but the list is enormous and I am certain to inadvertently leave someone out. Suffice it to say that if you acted with me at Spooky World in Foxborough or Boston, at Evilville in Carver, Massachusetts, or Trails to Terror in Wakefield, Rhode Island, you were part of the inspiration for the actors of Bone Ridge Farm.

The characters in BONEBELLY are, of course, fictional, but I believe that haunters everywhere will recognize actors and situations depicted in the story. Many of the themes and scenes are common to haunted attractions. However, several are based on the creations of "Scary" Larry Wilhelm, who was the brains and creative drive behind Trails to Terror since 1996.

The haunters' cheer from Bone Ridge's second and third seasons was developed by John Burton and Ed Gannon.

I also wish to recognize Jack Sumner and Martha Bradley, the owners of Highland Farm in Wakefield. They've provided a home and playground to many dedicated haunters for nearly two decades. Stone Ridge Farm and the layout of Bone Ridge are loosely based on the topography of Highland Farm.

Season of Mists
by Jennifer Corkill

Justine Holloway prepares for her début into Society, compliments of her godparents, while the under-world of London groans with unfettered abhorrence. When a deadly vampire makes his devious intentions known, her survival might depend on a mysterious Egyptian. Unfortunately, he can't figure out why he's so drawn to her, and whether he must kill her to save humanity.

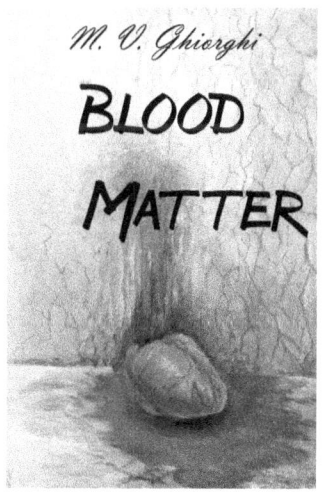

Blood Matters
by M.V. Ghiorghi

A broken-hearted FBI Agent on the run from his demons…a sadistic genius with a penchant for vengeance…a beautiful forensic psychiatrist with a monstrous past…A doomed love triangle born of crime. Can Agent Vasquez survive the *Blood Matter?*